"I enjoyed reading this novel. I li
gave the book, and I like their writing. They have a warm and
engaging style. What a special opportunity that they were given to
write this book as part of their family history. The tale of the co-
author finding those treasures in a box in her garage is fascinating.
I also like the spiritual side of their book, as it brings a deeper
dimension to their tale."

Kimberly Yoghourtjian,
author of the children's book,
Emily Explores the ABCs of Salvation.

"Great book!! It only took me two nights to read it! I am distantly
related to the authors and appreciate their hard work of putting it
together and getting it published. I will be buying the sequel when it
comes out too!!!"

Thomas Walden

"I found this book to be very interesting, I read it all in two days.
To tell you the truth, I have had this book over a year on my Nook.
I have known Cora for a long time. I was afraid that I might not like
the book and I would not be able to make eye contact with her at
church! It turns out there was no reason to worry, it is a good story
and I am glad I finally read it."

Lea Anne Nuez

"I eagerly bought this book from the co-author after hearing her
read her favorite passage aloud. I loved it so much that I didn't want
it to end, so I paced myself- reading no more than six pages per day.
I can hardly wait to read the sequel to find out how the rest of Mary
Alice's life plays out!"

Teri Kimberling

"A copy of this book was given to me by my mother as a gift. I didn't
read it right away because it isn't the genre of literature that I usually
read. But once I got started, it drew me in! I was surprised at how
much I enjoyed it. I'm looking forward to the sequel, which I hear
will be out very soon."

Carissa Gilliam

MARY ALICE

Gypsy Nurse

Author: Ilda Weatherford
Co-Author: Cora Brantner

authorHOUSE®

AuthorHouse™
1663 Liberty Drive
Bloomington, IN 47403
www.authorhouse.com
Phone: 1 (800) 839-8640

Published by AuthorHouse 01/29/2016

ISBN: 978-1-4772-7843-7 (sc)
ISBN: 978-1-4772-7841-3 (hc)
ISBN: 978-1-4772-7842-0 (e)

Library of Congress Control Number: 2012918864

Print information available on the last page.

Any people depicted in stock imagery provided by Thinkstock are models,
and such images are being used for illustrative purposes only.
Certain stock imagery © Thinkstock.

This book is printed on acid-free paper.

Because of the dynamic nature of the Internet, any web addresses or links contained in
this book may have changed since publication and may no longer be valid. The views
expressed in this work are solely those of the author and do not necessarily reflect the
views of the publisher, and the publisher hereby disclaims any responsibility for them.

Foreword

from the co-author

I took possession of my mother's box of writings when my father died, but it sat in my garage unopened for years. During a time of injury recovery a couple of years after mom's death, I started sifting through the box. I found the Mary Alice manuscript and read it. I loved it and knew right away that I had to do something with it – but how? I had done a little writing of my own, but nothing so large and involved as this! I knew nothing about computers or self publishing. I didn't even remember how to type.

And so the journey began – a bumpy one that lasted about seven years. In the midst of a particularly rough patch, I finally broke down and prayed to God, "Father, I need your help. I can't do this by myself!"

His reply was, "If I help you, will you honor me with it?" At once I knew what to do and began editing out anything questionable and adding new passages of Scripture and other Christian themes.

Like many people, I battle with pride sometimes. After submitting the manuscript and checking for mistakes in the galley proofs. I realized that I had jumped the gun and was not as ready as I had thought. I had eaten crow before, but not like this! I had to do some studying on English grammar, as I could not afford to have it edited professionally, and go through the whole book again, for the umpteenth time.

After the book's release, I found more, glaring errors and made the decision to fix it, once and for all and resubmit it for a second edition.

Many of my friends, after reading the book, pleaded with me for a sequel. They wanted the rest of the Mary Alice story. That book is in the works as I write this. My goal is to release it for sale in the summer of 2016.

Acknowledgments

from the co-author

I want to thank:

My Great grandmother, (Mary) Alice Walden, for being such an inspirational character.

My Mother, Ilda (Bauer)Weatherford, who's talent birthed this work.

My daughter, Carissa, and her husband, Leland, for their technical help.

My friend, Scott Bovard, for technical help, and painting the cover portrait.

My wonderful husband, Dan, for his understanding and patience; as I sometimes got so involved in this work that my household chores didn't get done!

Amy Stewart, my church's secretary, for the suggestions she gave me, which helped make this work as understandable and enjoyable as (I hope you will think) it is.

All my pastors and Bible study teachers through the years, who's teachings and examples have impacted my life.

And last, but not least:

Christ, my Savior, without who's leading this book might never have been completed; and certainly not in it's present form.

Characters

Helen	Alice's friend and neighbor
Peter Arnborg	Frank's 2nd supervisor
Mr. Henner	Bridal Veil Mayor
Grace #2	Alice's friend and helper
Thomas Williams	Alice's co-worker and doctor
Katie Williams	Dr. William's wife and nurse
Henry (Tucker)	Alice's second son
Ka-teen-ha	Alice's Indian patient
Ka teen-ha's grandmother	
Ka-soo-nee	Ka-teen-ha's sister
Ka-ma-tahn	Ka-teen-ha's brother
Stephen Thatcher	Walden's Pastor
Bettina Thatcher	Stephen's wife
Becky Ingeborg	Alice's neighbor and friend
Jim Ingeborg	Becky's husband/logger
Mattie	Abused waif
Andy	Junkyard owner
Carol Engen	Alice's friend and neighbor
Dr. Gunderson	Tucker's doctor
Sister Superior	Portland hospital's head Nun
Frank Junior	Alice's third son
Ernest (Lafe)	Alice's forth son
Dolores (Doley)	Alice's third daughter

Timeline

1865	(spring) Ernest and Ercyline meet, (autumn) marry.
1866	(Feb.) Mary Alice born, (late spring) move from soddy shack
1866	(spring) Ercyline meets Hilda, gets saved
1867	(Jan.) Ercyline and Mary Alice move in with Mrs. Forrester
1868	(June) Mrs. Forrester dies, (Aug.) Ernest gets sick
1868	(autumn) move to Illinois
1869	(spring) Carson #1 born, move to cottage
1878	(Feb/Mar) Mary Alice moves back to mansion
1884	(Sept.) Mary Alice goes to finishing school, (Dec.) meets Frank
1885	(spring) Mary Alice and Frank go to Oregon, wed
1886	(Feb.) Carson #2 born
1887	(Feb.) flu epidemic, (July) M.A's parents visit, (Sept.) Minot dies, (Nov.) Ilda born
1888	(Feb.) Carson shot
1889	(May) Grace born, (Dec.) train wreck
1890	(Mar.) Beebe mansion burns, (Aug.) parents move to Oregon, (Oct.)Tucker born
1891	(spring) Ka-teen-ha comes for help
1892	(fall) Indian funeral (Dec.) Frank's injury
1893	(June) move to West Lynn
1896	(summer) Tucker gets sick, (Sept.) Oregon City, help Mattie
1897	(Aug.) Frank gets sick
1897	(Oct.) little Frank born
1898	(May) move to Blue Mt. cabin
1899	(Aug.) Carsie gets sick, (Sept.) Lafe born
1900	(Sept.) Grace and Tucker find whiskey
1901	(Oct.) Dolores born, (Nov.) forest fire

Chapter One

THE GYPSY AND THE SCALLAWAG

Under the overhang of a low bluff, at the edge of a sloping April-green meadow, huddled four Gypsy wagons. There were four crude shacks built against the rock. The Gypsies all moved about in the lethargic shamble of the half-starved. Most of them had sallow skin, black, greasy hair, and lanky frames.

This was the last day of winter quarters. The four Gypsy men were readying the wagons for their annual trek north from this warm south-central Mississippi region alongside the great river. Several young children scampered about, getting underfoot and causing a commotion.

The Gypsies were transferring personal effects from the makeshift shacks into the wagons. An old woman sat sewing up bedding sacks stuffed with soft new balsam twigs.

There was a campfire burning nearby with the carcass of a skinny deer and a soup kettle roasting over it.

In late afternoon, the oldest of the men bellowed, "Everbody gather 'round! Winter's over! Time t' party! Tomorra we hit the road agin!"

Everyone converged on the still, built cunningly into the largest wagon. Cups and pitchers were filled at the spigot. Though only half a barrel of weavily flour and a few shriveled root vegetables were left, and the area hunted out, the men had appropriated the last of the corn for the still in preparation for this day.

After dinner, one man started playing a fiddle. Some of them started to dance to the music. The old woman sent two boys to the river to fetch some water for washing purposes. The children returned running, excited, wet and panting. "Pa! Pa!" the oldest boy yelled, "We found a man floatin' in the river. We think 'e's dead! We pulled 'im ontuh the rocks, but 'e's too heavy for us to tote, Pa!"

The men and boys ran off to the river's edge. Here they found the man, half-drowned and unconscious. His body bore the marks of a severe beating. Sticks, feathers and tar were matted in his shirt and golden locks, and his face and arms were bruised and cut. He was a tall young man; well built, with chiseled features. The strength of all four men was needed to carry him back to camp.

The newcomer was bedded down in one of the wagons and nursed by the old woman and Ercyline, a plain girl of 14.

"He sure is a mess. What do yuh s'pose happened to 'im, Granny? You think e'll live?"

"I imagine 'e'll come 'round eventully. 'E was strong and healthy afore this happent to 'im. But if you ask me, he's trouble."

"I dunno. I think e's nice. Just got in the wrong place at the wrong time. Besides, I think e'll turn out t' be really handsome once his wounds heal."

The old woman just grunted and went on caring for the man.

The next morning, the caravan departed, its teams of mangy mules balking at every step after their winter's ease. The injured man groaned at every bump and jar along the trail.

As he returned to health, Ernest Beebe was entertained by this nomadic tribe and found himself to be entertaining to all of the children, but of special interest to Ercyline. Never did they refer to his condition when he arrived in their camp, nor did they question him in any way.

Riding on the rickety wagon seat with the women, and later walking with the men, Ernest exercised his innate charm. In a short time he had even the most taciturn of them conversing freely.

"Granny," he commented one day, "your people must have an interesting history. You don't look quite the same as the others, and two of the children are fairer."

The old woman puffed on her corncob pipe for a minute, then she told him, "My ma was a Cree Injun woman. As fer the yunguns: their ma was a girl whut run off and joined us 'cause 'er pa beat 'er alla time. She died birthin' small 'un."

Little by little, Ernest tactfully drew out the stories of their lives. Few formal names were used among the Gypsies. "Boots" was a cobbler and an expert in curing and tooling leather. "Caesar" was a maker and seller of snake oil, the oldest man, and therefore the leader. "Jem" was the woman who made and sold jewelry. "Granny" was the oldest of the tribe and the fortune-teller. "Hoss" tended to the mules and wagons and "Luna" intoxicated the men of the towns with her dancing. She had trained Ercyline to fill in for her during her pregnancy. "Stitch" was a maker of garments and "Wolf" was the woodsman/hunter. Ercyline's parents had died of a mysterious ailment several years before, along with three others.

The Civil War, just ending, had not touched the Gypsies. They traveled far enough west to avoid it, or when necessary, disappeared into the forest out of danger. Able-bodied men were off to war and, cashing in on their absences, the Gypsies plied their trades profitably in the towns they camped near.

Northward in spring and summer, south in late summer and early fall, their travels ended each autumn in semi-permanent camps near the juncture of the Mississippi and Arkansas rivers.

In this year of 1865, Ernest traveled with them but disappeared to hunt in the forests as they neared the towns. He reappeared a few miles beyond when the Gypsy troupe moved on. At first he thought it wiser to avoid any chance encounter associated with his recent misadventure. As the northward journey came into his home territory in Southern Illinois, he thought it better not to risk accidental meetings with acquaintances while in the company of the Gypsies.

Caesar passed off any curiosity by remarking, "Ernest's is a handy back t' have when a weel breaks. No need fer a pry when 'e can heft axle 'n all 'til we get a prop under it. Right smart pervider, too - good eye and steady wit a rifle."

Ernest developed a growing romance with Ercyline - not that he found her attractive, but because she was so innocent and flirtatious. She followed him everywhere and fawned over him. They often went for walks in the woods to gather herbs and firewood. He yielded to temptation because he was after all, a virile young man and an opportunist. This was the reason for his condition when they found him. He had incurred a large gambling debt and seduced several young women in a town upriver from their winter camp, resulting in at least two pregnancies and a big uproar among the townspeople.

Along the way, Ernest captivated his hosts with his skill at story-telling around the campfire after the evening meals. He also began to teach the children the rudiments of reading, writing and figuring. Ercyline was not included in this, as she was old enough to be occupied with adult tasks.

One evening in early September, Caesar found Ernest tending to one of the horses. Slapping him on the back, he said, "Ernest, if you're done here, come join us. We'd love t' hear another of your tall tales."

As they approached the camp, Ernest noticed that the whole troupe was standing all huddled together. In their midst was a stranger with a black hat. As they arrived, the group parted to reveal a blushing, slightly bulging-bellied Ercyline holding a small bunch of flowers. Ernest thought to run, but the men had their rifles at the ready. The stranger was a circuit preacher. So Ernest and Ercyline were wed.

Soon the caravan crossed the upper reaches of the Mississippi River at the southern border of Wisconsin, into Iowa, and headed southwest. Where their track turned south across the Missouri River near a town, Ernest and Ercyline left the troupe and camped on the shore a short distance from the outskirts of the town.

In a couple of days of scouting, they found an abandoned sod dwelling dug into the riverbank above the flood line. A minimum of repair was needed to make it habitable. Ernest installed Ercyline and her meager dowry of household goods, a supply of firewood and a brace of rabbits he'd shot nearby. Explaining that he would be away for a few days and not to worry, he went on into town.

A few hours of judicious shuffling of cards in a saloon garnered enough in funds to purchase respectable clothing and a hot bath for the first time in months. Casual talk in the saloon gave him directions to the home of a cousin whom Ernest had met many years before when he was still a lad. Ernest's family had been host to this man on a journey to the East.

His self-esteem bolstered in his cleanliness, Ernest presented himself at the door of a prosperous looking house.

"Good day, Madam." He proffered his deepest bow and sweetest smile to the middle-aged housekeeper who answered his knock. "Would you kindly tell Mr. Smitherton that his cousin, Ernest Beebe wishes a word with him?"

The woman ushered him into a dark hallway. In a moment a sturdy man of about forty greeted Ernest. The man tried nonchalantly to cover the fact that he had no memory of this handsome well-dressed young man. Over a glass of port Mr. Smitherton probed for verification of the relationship.

"And have you news of Minot Beebe in Linton?" asked the host, using a twist of the town's name as a trap, should the younger man be an impostor.

"Uncle Minot's plantation prospers, now that Linnville has grown a good deal," answered Ernest, discreetly correcting the name of the Beebe's home town. "Aunt Caroline passed away two years ago, poor soul. Uncle does well with the three girls, however. The housekeeper cum governess is quite amply suited to the task. Cousin Carson went off to the war in sixty three. He hasn't been heard from since. It was a blow to Uncle, the boy being his only son."

The talk continued half an hour in this vein before cousin Smitherton was quite convinced of Ernest's authenticity, and relaxed his wary appraisal of his kinsman. The younger man's wit and cultivated conversation captivated Smitherton's plump pretty wife. Over dinner cousin Elmira insisted that Ernest be their guest for his stay in town. In a few days the young man had met and become a part of the society of the river town.

On the third day, riding a borrowed horse, Ernest rode into the dooryard of the soddy. Ercyline came running, throwing aside the length of canvas that served as a door.

They went inside where he spread before her calico, ribbons, needles and thread, even a bright shawl. From his pocket he produced a child's primer, filched from the bookshelves of his host. There were also foods such as Ercyline had never imagined.

Ercyline had never seen such bounty. She hid her face with joy. "I thought you'd fergot about me, stuck way out here off'n th' road by myself."

Ernest spent the night in the soddy, then rode back to town. Cousin Smitherton greeted him heartily. "Don't know where you've been off to overnight, my boy," he said with a wink, "but you've returned just in time. Some of the gentlemen of the town would like a word with you at the preacher's house at four o'clock. They've a notion you might take on a tutor school for some of their boys. The schoolmarm here is only seventeen, and hardly suited to prepare their sons for further schooling in the East. Would you think on it and give them your decision?"

Ernest had some trouble restraining his enthusiasm that afternoon. A small show of reluctance might coax up the fees a bit. He was a natural teacher and enjoyed watching young minds open to learning. At the meeting the committee and the new teacher came to an amicable agreement on salary. A small apartment attached to the parsonage was to be his living quarters and classroom.

And so it became a routine; Ernest lived in town, but visited the soddy one afternoon a week and over Friday night. Ercyline never questioned this, neither did she ask why she was not permitted to move into town. She seemed to be content with the provisions and pretty things he brought her. She spent the time daydreaming and sewing garments for her coming *"beautiful daughter"*. She studied the simple books her husband brought her and searched for firewood and wild berries and herbs to supplement her diet.

Ernest was relieved at the lack of questioning. It would never do for his marriage to be known, especially to this homely, ignorant girl. The daughters of the town were fascinated with his conversation, dancing, flattery and gallantry. The young men of the town were naive enough to serve as the source of ready money at the card table. He could not risk his standing in the eyes of the town's gentry.

Chapter Two

A TRUE FRIEND

When Ercyline had approached the old Gypsy woman with her question, "Granny, whut do it mean when you miss your bleedin' time?" the old woman cackled and winked an eye. "I seen you both comin' back lookin' like the cat afta cream. You've been doin' some funnin'."

"But 'e weren't the first one. Never did miss a bleedin' before. How's it different with the teacher?"

"Well, might be cuz our young fellas ain't been eatin' too well over winter camp. Seems t' me, most our babes get a start after we's on the road and eatin' better. The big 'un was well fleshed out and come t'us just when we's startin' out again. I'd say you might be droppin' a babe come last part o' winter."

From that moment on, Ercyline dreamed of Mary Alice. Her baby would be a girl, robust and beautiful. Like her father, she would have golden curls, rosy cheeks, bright, blue eyes and softly rounded limbs.

Winter in the soddy passed slowly. Characteristic of her people, Ercyline accepted her lot. She was glad for Ernest's short visits, but resented his insistence that she use the washtub he'd brought her every week and keep the soddy neat and tidy.

Ercyline yearned for the pretty words spoken to her last spring. She was accustomed to being sewn into her clothes every autumn. Her people didn't bathe until the streams ran warm again in the spring. They had marveled that Ernest had bathed in every pool they camped near. The younger children speculated that the reason his skin and hair were so light was that he washed all the color away. In late February, Mary Alice was born; a long, thin baby with a full head of black hair and a sallow complexion, just like Ercyline's.

Like her half Indian grandmother before her, Ercyline birthed the baby alone. She tied the umbilical cord with string and cut it with an unwashed knife.

Ernest arrived a few days later to find his new daughter being held with distaste at her mother's breast. A noisy, greedy suckling, she was not a pretty baby. Seeing Ercyline's attitude, Ernest praised her for her bravery. He admired the baby's strength and her large, intelligent eyes. Watching the tiny, slender fingers, he prophesied that one day she would be an artist or perhaps a musician.

None of this comforted Ercyline in the least. Her dreams were shattered. She resented the "changeling" child. What care the baby got was more for fear of Ernest's scolding than from duty, and none for love.

Had Mary Alice been capable of learning words through infancy, she would have developed a rich vocabulary of curses: her reward for draining her mother's breasts until they ached, and waking her at night.

Other than crying for food, Mary Alice was a quiet baby. She gazed out of her dark eyes at her small world, constantly turning her head at the least movement or sound. Her long hands were always moving, fingers open and grasping. She was most content lying on a quilt outside. The trees, clouds, insects, grasses and wildflowers received her cooing admiration for hours at a time.

By late spring, Ernest's gambling losses to the older men of the town exceeded his winnings from their sons, and the suspicions by the fathers of a few young ladies became more pressing. It became advisable for him to leave the area quietly. So he packed up his wife, daughter and their few possessions. A freight wagoner, conveniently passing through, was grateful to earn a few extra dollars on his way back home.

Near another, slightly smaller town two days journey away, the Beebe family camped. A few days later mother and child were moved into a small house that Ernest had found to rent. It had one large room and a sleeping loft. The weathered gray clapboards of the exterior were only slightly rougher than the planks which covered the inside. It was lighter than the soddy, though. There were two oil-skin-glazed windows in the main room and one at the back of the loft. It was quite some distance from town and far from any neighbor dwellings.

Ernest left for the town when he had settled them in. He supplied them with a minimum of food and firewood, as before, and established himself in the good graces of the leading citizens. This time, though, he had no kin in town. The name of Beebe was known only slightly. It happened that the young woman teacher of the town had recently accepted a proposal of marriage. Since marriage in this day for any teacher was unthinkable, Ernest kept his marriage secret and was installed without ceremony. Living quarters were found for him in a respectable boarding house.

He explained to Ercyline that he was a teacher in the town and that teachers could not be married and keep their jobs. Since their house was not as isolated as the soddy had been, he feared that his situation might be discovered. He instructed Ercyline in the role she must play if it became necessary to associate with other people. She must not use the Beebe name nor hint at any connection with it. They planned a plausible story and rehearsed it well.

Life for the Beebe family went on as before. Two short visits each week kept the wood and food supply ample and satisfied Ercyline's loneliness. The yard of the house was large enough for a good-sized garden. Ernest found a farmer far on the other side of town who rented him a small plow. A borrowed saddle horse snorted in indignation at his role as temporary plow horse. With seeds brought from town, Ercyline soon had a garden started. It was a completely new experience for this child of nomads.

"Halloo, what a treat! A neighbor!" Ercyline heard the clatter of hooves and wheels as a small cart came to a stop at her doorstep. An attractively plump woman of thirty or so jumped down quickly. She ran to Ercyline and grasped both of her hands: "I've had no neighbors for over a year!" she exclaimed, "A body gets lonely for the company of another woman. No other neighbors for over four miles, then here you are!"

The woman chattered on for several minutes, cooing over Mary Alice, admiring the neat rows of the garden, commenting on the weather, on and on.

Finally, she stopped for breath and flushed with embarrassment. "Forgive my rattling on. It's so good to have someone to talk to. I'm Hilda Briarson. My place is just down the road about a mile. I was out for a drive after church. It's such a lovely day. I think we'll have a good season for crops this year." She paused, "There I go again! *Do* tell me your name!"

Ercyline sat back on her heels, nonplussed at this effusive greeting. She'd never heard a woman of her family say more than one or two curt sentences, especially to strangers. Her people didn't touch others needlessly either.

Mindful of Ernest's coaching, her reply was slow and studied. "Pleased t' meet yuh, I'm shore. I'm Ercyline Biggs and this's my baby, Mary Alice."

Hilda stooped down and picked up Mary Alice and cooed at her. Mary Alice smiled and cooed back. "I think she likes me. Is your husband nearby?"

"No Ma'am. I'm a widder, I think. My man went off t' the last o' the war and I ain't heard nothin' from 'im. Don't know if e's alive or not. His brother's takin' care of us. He found this place an e's in town doin' what work 'e can find."

"You poor soul," Hilda consoled, patting Ercyline's shoulder. "I'm alone, too: My husband went off to the war two years ago and his letters just stopped. I've no idea, either, whether I'm a widow or not. It's been so lonely out here since my boy died of the fever last fall. I must hold onto the land for Jeremy if he comes back. We must have faith, my dear. We must have faith."

Hilda sat on a clump of grass and chattered on. She grew impatient at Ercyline's hesitant answers, but was kind enough not to show it. "You must come down to visit me," she said heartily. "I've a deal of handiwork I've been dying to show off. There's no pleasure in making pretty things if no one's there to see them. Please come over soon."

On his next visit, Ernest pondered as his wife told him of her pleasant visitor. He put on the crude deer-skin suit made for him by the Gypsies, then rode to the widow Briarson's house for a brief visit. Knocking on the door of the neat cabin, he was impressed with the orderliness of the yard and the colorful curtains at the windows. Hilda was surprised to find this big, blond, handsome man on her doorstep.

Tempering his language and manners suitably to the brother-in-law Hilda might expect, he said. "G'day Ma'am. Are you Miz Briarson?" He doffed his cap, holding it in front of him in the unsure posture to be expected of lower-class countrymen.

"Why yes, I am. May I help you?"

"Thankee, Ma'am. I'm brother-in-law to Miz Biggs down the road. She told me about your visit and your invite to your home."

"Oh, yes. It was so nice to find another woman so near. I do hope you approve of her making a visit here. It'll be good for her to get out, too, I expect. It's hard to be a woman alone."

"Ma'am I'm mighty beholden to you for befriending the girl," he told her. "I'd take it kindly if you'd take her under your wing. Your place is mighty homey. The girl needs to see more of such. Don't know where my brother found her, but she ain't much on housekeeping.

"It's a chore to be saddled with such a responsibility, but I figure it's my duty to look after them 'till my brother comes back."

"Of course! I enjoyed visiting with her and that bright little baby. I'd love having them over. I'm so glad you approve. Do tell her to come soon!"

Ernest encouraged Ercyline to associate with their neighbor. He also warned her to watch her tongue. "Remember," he told her, "any word that I'm married and my teaching position is gone. I'm no farmer or laborer. This is the only way I can support us. The woman will be good company for you, and you can learn a lot from her." After giving this advice, he rode back to town.

Shortly thereafter, on a warm morning, Ercyline fashioned a makeshift sling in which to carry Mary Alice on her back, and set out for Hilda's house. She was pleasantly surprised with her neighbor's neat home and colorful flower garden.

Hilda came running around the corner of the house to greet her new friend. "How nice of you to come. Aren't you warm from your walk? Come along to the back. I keep a pitcher of lemonade in the well house where it stays cool. It'll be a treat for both of us. I'm warm from working in the garden and you are a welcome excuse to stop for a rest. You *will* stay for lunch, won't you?"

Ercyline's natural shyness melted under Hilda's hospitality. She found herself exclaiming over the neat kitchen and the colorful pottery tableware. The cold luncheon salad was something new to her. It was attractively arranged on the plates. Fresh, yeasty biscuits and cooked dry peaches completed the meal.

"But Hilda" Ercyline asked, "How do ya keep peaches over the winter? The only fruit I ever had was fresh off'n the tree in summer."

Hilda promised to show her friend how to do these simple things when the time came.

Another wonder to Ercyline was the spider-web-fine doilies and tatted lace-trimmed cloths on the tables and chests throughout the house. The fine stitching and ruffled trim of the curtains were astonishing to her.

The afternoon turned unseasonably hot, so Hilda insisted on harnessing the cart to drive Ercyline and Mary Alice home. She brought along seeds and slips from her flowers and showed Ercyline how to plant and care for them before she left in the early evening.

The two women became fast friends. Hilda was glad for the companionship and she opened a new world for Ercyline, not the least of which was the spiritual world.

There was something unique and attractive about Hilda that Ercyline couldn't understand. She was always praising God and said a prayer before eating every meal. When Ercyline asked her about it, Hilda started reading the New Testament to her.

Ercyline had never been exposed to the Gospel before and had many questions. She was intrigued about the stories of Christmas and Easter. When they came to John, chapter 1, and Hilda explained how Jesus is God and that He was the Creator of all things, it was like a light bulb came on in Ercyline. When Hilda saw the Spirit working in her, she turned to John, 3:16 and read:

"For God so loved the world (meaning all people) that He gave His only begotten Son, that whosoever believeth in Him should not perish but have everlasting life."

Ercyline was amazed and delighted! With tears in her eyes, she said, "God loves me? Nobody ever said they loved me b'fore." Then she looked puzzled and said, "But how can anybody live forever?"

Hilda explained that we all have eternal spirits that live forever in either heaven or hell. "It's not our bodies that live on but the essence of who we are inside." Then she read the passage in John, 3:3, where Nicodemus came to Jesus and asked this very question. This led to Romans, 3:10-12, where it explains that we are all sinners.

"What does that mean, '*sinner*'?" Ercyline asked.

So Hilda turned to Exodus, chapter 20 and read to her the Ten Commandments given by God to the Nation of Israel. "Breaking any of these commandments is a sin," she explained.

"How can anybody do all that?" Ercyline asked. "That's too hard."

Hilda explained that only Jesus kept *all* the Commandments his entire life, but that God gave us these rules to show us that we can't live perfect lives or get to heaven all by ourselves. "We need someone, namely Jesus, to pay for our sins."

"And He did that by dying on the cross?" Ercyline asked.

Hilda gave her a big hug as tears welled in her own eyes. "That's right. See here in Romans, 6:23 'For the wages of sin is death, but the gift of God is eternal life through Jesus Christ our Lord'.

"You see? It's a gift. But it's not automatic. We have to ask for it, by faith."

Ercyline wanted to know what faith was, so Hilda turned to Hebrews, 11:1 to explain that faith is believing what we cannot see with our eyes. "It's like this:" she said; "You have faith that a chair will support you without testing it first, that the seeds you plant will grow, that the sun will rise tomorrow and so forth. Faith in God is just like that. You just have to trust that it's true."

When they finished reading these verses, Ercyline was eager to give her heart to Jesus, so Hilda led her in the "Sinner's Prayer":

"Dear Jesus, I am a sinner. I believe you are God and that you came to earth in human flesh to die on the cross to pay for my sin. I now ask for your forgiveness and accept your free gift of salvation. I want to live for you. Please come into my heart today and make me everything you want me to be. Amen."

Ercyline started reading a children's bible that Hilda gave her and attending church with her faithfully. Ernest was against this, as he had blamed God for taking his parents away from him when he felt he needed them most.

Ercyline tended her garden and came to love it more and more. It grew abundantly with Hilda's help. This was a heady experience, and Ercyline blossomed along with her garden. She sewed bright curtains like Hilda's for the oil-skin windows. She made fir-needle-filled cushions to pad the crude benches in the house. Flowers in makeshift vases adorned the tables and mantelpiece. One Friday afternoon, mother and daughter greeted Ernest in bright new dresses and sunbonnets, hoping for a buggy ride in the country.

As Ercyline harvested her garden, Hilda showed her how to dry some and pickle and preserve others in the earthenware crocks and jars that Ernest brought from town. She learned to make them airtight by tying stout fabric over the tops and sealing them with wax. Root vegetables, pumpkins and squash lay in burlap sacks under straw in a lean-to shed.

Though there was plenty of food, Ercyline remained gaunt and bony. Mary Alice grew rapidly in length but seemed to inherit her mother's physique. At seven months, she was starting to imitate the noises of birds and insects and the occasional coyote she heard at night. Wide-eyed, she sat on her father's lap while he read to Ercyline from children's books. His voice fascinated her. He spoke to her more in the few hours he was at home than her mother did in all the days between his visits.

Ernest's evenings in the town were busy. If he was not winning at cards with the young men, he was gambling with their elders. Both circles welcomed his cheerful company and ready wit. While the younger ones were no match for his skill at cards, some of their fathers were. Often he was hard put to keep even, much less ahead of his losses.

He also danced and acted the gallant with the ladies, playing no favorites. One young lady, however, accustomed to favoritism by her beauty and her father's status in town affairs, began to claim more than her share of his time. She gave herself to him eagerly and arranged for secret rendezvous. By December, she was growing possessive and petulant, hinting at marriage.

"It would be a real advantage to become a member of our family. My father has but to snap his fingers and any ambitious young man could have his pick of well-paid positions in this town. Father owns the bank here and a goodly share of the stock in a St. Louis firm. Why, one could travel downriver and have a gay time with all the distractions of the city."

She was beginning to try his skill. Too many other young ladies had set their caps and traps for him in the past. He was an expert at slipping out of their clutches. Though sometimes it meant slipping out of town as well.

On a lightly snowing January evening in 1867, Ernest drove up to Ercyline's door in a small wagon. The rig had been rented from the same distant farmer who had lent him the plow. Skirting the town, Ernest had left a half day ahead of an appointment with the angry father of the insistent beauty. He suspected that the appointment had to do with the frequent dalliances he and the young lady had shared over a period of months. Since he was already married and would have to reveal it, angering the man even more, it was more prudent to withdraw from the scene completely.

Ercyline objected strongly to the idea of leaving the first real home she'd ever lived in. The prospect of parting from her friend Hilda was equally as sad. "We're all settled here. It's our home. Why do we hafta leave? I got a garden now and a real good friend. I don't wanna go away!"

"Girl, tie yours and the baby's things up in bundles. It's not safe for me to stay around here anymore. If we don't get out, I'll be in serious trouble. Then you'll *really* be on your own. I'll get the food-stuffs packed into the boxes I brought along and help you pack the household things. Now get to packing; we've no time to waste!"

Cowed by his outburst and accustomed to obeying the orders of men, Ercyline packed. She bundled herself and Mary Alice in the new quilts Hilda had helped her to make. She rode resentfully through the night, not speaking to her husband.

Ernest was fairly certain that the whereabouts and even the existence of his family were unknown to the townspeople. For two nights they traveled, sleeping in the barns of hospitable farmers, stopping only after dark.

Ernest had chosen a much larger town on the banks of the Missouri River for their new residence. Going ahead into town, while his family lodged on a farm, Ernest sampled the gossip at the taverns and made inquiries at the courthouse.

Approaching the old house he had heard about, he knocked firmly on the door. After a long pause, a crippled old woman answered.

"Good day, Ma'am. My name is Ernest Beebe. I understand that you may have a room for rent?"

"Don't know, young man. I might. I hadn't thought to rent it to a young man, though."

"Oh no, Ma'am," Ernest pretended shock. "Not for myself! My brother's young widow and her baby have need of shelter. Perhaps she might be able to assist you in your daily chores. I will be nearby for heavier duties, also."

The tiny woman moved back from the doorway, inviting Ernest to enter. Over a cup of warming chicory drink, they rocked and talked. Ernest discovered that Mrs. Forrester was a frightened old woman. Widowed and childless, she was fast becoming unable to fend for herself. Her neighbors were kind enough, but she was no longer able to care for her own needs. Ernest persuaded her to take on Ercyline as companion and housekeeper.

Driving back from the farmhouse where his family had stayed for two days, Ernest coached Ercyline again in her role. He warned her that Mrs. Forrester was very alert. He warned her about cleanliness and care in her personal habits. This time he explained that she was to be Mrs. Beebe, but still the widowed sister-in-law.

"I don't like lyin', Ernest. It's wrong. And besides, if I live with the old lady, how're we gonna be t'gether without 'er knowin'?"

He smiled and patted her hand. "I'm sorry, but it's necessary if I get a teaching position. The other thing will work out alright. The old lady dozes off now and again, so it's a sure sign that she goes to bed early. We'll have evenings together, and sometimes we can go to your room after she's asleep. You'll see - it'll work out. You won't be lonesome this time. You can even go into town occasionally."

"I don't wanna call you Uncle Ernest anymore t' Mary Alice. That's a lie, too."

"Alright," he said, "I'll come up with an excuse for the practice of referring to me as her father. I don't mind lying."

Returning the light wagon to its owner was a simple matter. Ernest drove it on Saturday to a town well off the route they had traveled. He turned it in to a livery stable, explaining that he had found the driverless rig and horse in an abandoned farmyard along the way. The owner's name and address were found, conveniently, on an empty envelope under the seat, he said. Ernest quickly hopped aboard a stagecoach headed back to his family. It hadn't been necessary to give his name or any further particulars.

Ernest found out that the town's school was in need of an additional teacher for the older children. He lost no time obtaining the position. To this he added three evenings each week and some Saturdays as a clerk in the local men's clothing store on the main street. He found a vacancy in a rooming house. Ercyline persuaded Mrs. Forrester that it would be proper for him to take his evening meals with them.

Mrs. Forrester fell in love with Mary Alice. It had been so long since she had held a baby. None of her three children had survived to adulthood. "It will brighten the house," the old lady crooned, "to have a little one playing here again." She brushed away a tear and picked up the little girl. "We must fatten her up a bit, poor baby."

Mary Alice thrived as Mrs. Forrester lavished attention on the lonely little girl. Though she filled out but a little, she grew and matured rapidly. Within a month, she was taking three or four hesitant steps and speaking in short baby sentences.

Chapter Three

THE ILLNESS

Under the influence of Mrs. Forrester's and Ernest's conversation, Ercyline's speech patterns improved rapidly. Though she had lacked encouragement and education in her early life, she was intelligent and learned eagerly and easily.

Mrs. Forrester's eyesight was failing and she could no longer read. At dinner, early in their stay, Mrs. Forrester brought up the subject of books and reading. She asked, "Would one or both of you read to me now and again? I do miss stories and newspapers. My husband and I were both great ones to take turns reading to each other in the evenings."

Ercyline perked up, "Oh, Mrs. Forrester, I'd be glad to, if you don't mind easy books. Ernest's been bringin' some for me. I like to read, and maybe you could help me get better at it."

Ernest applauded Ercyline's offer. "Yes, and in the evenings I can read to both of you sometimes after dinner. Mrs. Forrester, would you help Ercyline further, by letting her write your grocery lists and other notes and correspondences? I'm going to bring her a book to write in - Sort of a journal of her thoughts and such. I think it's important that she get more practice. She'd be more marriageable or employable, if the need ever arises."

To Mrs. Forrester's delight, reading aloud became an important part of life in her household and in Ercyline's intellectual development. The time they spent together reading helped to forge a strong bond of affection among the members of the household.

Her new-found faith, and Ernest's and Mrs. Forrester's loving influence did soften Ercyline's resentment of Mary Alice, but she wouldn't come to really love her daughter until many years later.

Mrs. Forrester took over nearly all care of Mary Alice. The two became almost inseparable. The little girl thrived on the loving attentions of her *"Gamma"*. It was the love she craved from her mother, but never got.

Ercyline soon found out that Mrs. Forrester shared her faith in God, but had fallen out of the habit of attending services when her husband died five years earlier. When an old friend from her church visited and asked her to return, Ercyline asked to come along, too, and they convinced Ernest to take them to church regularly. After a while, he started going in with them from time to time.

Ercyline worked diligently at whatever household chores needed to be done. She even had time to resurrect the flower beds that had fallen into neglect. While Mary Alice and Mrs. Forrester napped, Ercyline had opportunity to stroll through the town. It was some weeks before she gained the courage to enter the stores. Her favorite one was the milliner's. The perky little hats with their cherries, flowers, feathers and bows fascinated her. When she finally entered the shop, she found the proprietress to be a cordial woman.

Shyly, Ercyline asked, "Does it take a long time t' make these hats? Where do you get all the pretties to put on em?"

The young woman suppressed a smile. "Once one knows the basic construction, it doesn't take long at all. If you're handy with a needle, it's easy to learn. We order the trimmings from St. Louis and they are sent to us by post. Would you like to look at the hats more closely; perhaps try some on? You have such lovely dark hair. I'm sure you would be able to wear almost any of them."

Ercyline almost stammered, "No Ma'am, I don't have money to buy any of them and I don't want to spoil any of the pretty things."

Seeing that Ercyline was genuinely distressed, the proprietress hurried to reassure her, "Nonsense, they aren't that fragile. Here, do sit down before this mirror. Do you mind if I pin your hair up a bit?"

Ercyline nodded shyly and sat nervously on the chair as the young woman pinned her hair up.

"Oh, you have such a lovely, graceful neck. I have just the hat for you." She perched a saucy, narrow-brimmed hat a little off-center of Ercyline's new coiffure. "Now, see? The yellow pheasant feathers sweep back in smart contrast to your raven hair."

Ercyline agreed with her but gingerly took the hat off again. "I'd be obliged if you could show me how t' make one of these fancy ones. A friend showed me how to do a simple one and I really liked doing it."

Ercyline's naive eagerness appealed to the older, more sophisticated woman. "Why, yes, I could. As a matter of fact, my assistant is ill and I just can't get caught up. Do you have an hour now, so that I might judge your ability with fine needlework?"

Ercyline was surprised. "Yes I do - just about that, before I need to get back home to my baby."

At the end of the hour the two were on a first-name basis. Ercyline's skill, taught her by Hilda, proved satisfactory, and Jeanette gave her some simple work to take home. Nearly every day, while Mary Alice slept and Mrs. Forrester dozed in her rocking chair, Ercyline worked and reveled amid the bolts of fabric, spools of ribbon and bins of feathers, wax fruits and artificial flowers in Jeanette's workroom.

Ernest was pleased at this new facet of his young wife's development. He encouraged her to continue, but warned her to be careful not to reveal their secret.

Come spring, Ernest built a picket fence around Mrs. Forrester's property, "So Mary Alice can play outdoors safely while Mrs. Forrester sits out in the sunlight," he said.

"Warms these old bones," she told Ercyline later. "You can spend more time in that hat shop. I know how much you love it."

Ernest had little time for gambling and the society of the town, though he was much in demand. He seemed to be content to spend his free time reading to his womenfolk and teaching Ercyline. He continued to spend his nights in the boarding house. Only occasionally did he accept invitations to social events on Saturday evenings or Sunday afternoons.

For a little over a year, this way of life continued for the little family and their hostess. In mid-march of 1868, as she came in from town, Ercyline called to Mrs. Forrester. She received no answer. Mary Alice came running instead and said, "Gamma faw down," and took Ercyline by the hand and led her into Mrs. Forrester's bedroom. Mrs. Forrester lay in a heap on the floor, unconscious. Ercyline put a pillow under her head and covered her with a blanket. Then she scooped up Mary Alice. She wrapped another blanket around them both and ran the four blocks to the doctor's office.

Dr. Partridge took them back in his buggy, then went into the bedroom first, instructing Ercyline to ask her neighbor, Mrs. Lewis, to come assist him.

Mrs. Forrester had suffered a stroke and was in a coma. She seemed doll-like lying so still in the bed. Dr. Partridge told them, "There is nothing else to be done except to watch her carefully and call me if or when she becomes conscious again. Mrs. Lewis is a good nurse. She'll help you care for Mrs. Forrester. You can depend on her."

Ercyline accepted this verdict stoically and set about rearranging the household schedule. She cared for her friend as tenderly as if she had been her own mother. Mrs. Lewis took the two-year-old Mary Alice, crying for her "Gamma", to her own home for a few hours each day so that Ercyline might have time to bathe and care for Mrs. Forrester. Mrs. Forrester recovered just enough to be conscious of her surroundings, and to be fed from a spoon, but never enough to speak.

"Her eyes look so spooky," Ercyline told Ernest. "Like she wants to tell me something. They follow me all around the room. I think she smiled a bit at Mary Alice but I'm not sure."

Mary Alice spent a great deal of her time sitting on the sickbed playing with the sock doll Mrs. Forrester had made for her. She crooned to the doll and chattered away at her "Gamma". She stroked the thin gray hair, kissed the withered cheeks and patted her folded hands.

One morning in June, Ercyline found Mrs. Forrester lifeless. Ercyline would miss her very much, as she had shown them so much kindness and affection.

Though Mrs. Forrester's papers showed ownership of a cemetery plot, no funds were found for her funeral expenses. The undertaker agreed to delay his fees until the proceeds from the sale of the house were available. Ercyline struggled to keep control and showed only an armor of calm and efficiency through the funeral.

After the funeral, Ernest and Ercyline returned to the house. They found it full of neighbors and food. Though this did not surprise Ernest, it was another new experience for his wife. When she realized that this was the way of the townspeople to express sympathy for their loss, it was too much for her emotionally. Pushing Mary Alice into Mrs. Lewis' ample arms, Ercyline fled from the house into a nearby copse of cottonwood trees. There, Ernest found her, weeping.

"It's alright, Girl," he told her, holding her tightly and passing her his handkerchief. "Go ahead and cry. You loved her. I understand. It's alright to grieve. It really helps to cry." He too had been holding in the grief he felt for the loss of the woman who had shown so much unselfish kindness to them all. They cried together for a few minutes, then Ernest went back to play host, while Ercyline stayed in the woods until the guests had all gone.

Ernest called upon the Chief Selectman of the town the next day. "Have you a buyer for Mrs. Forrester's house yet?" he asked. "If you haven't, my sister-in-law would like to rent it."

The man shook his head and drawled, "Nope, not yet, though a few folks have asked about it. Mrs. Beebe can stay on to take care of the place until it's sold. We can set a five-dollar-a-month token rent, if that meets her approval."

"I have my sister-in-law's permission to act for her. We accept. May we ask for a two week notice before a new owner takes possession? What will happen to Mrs. Forrester's furnishings and personal belongings?"

The selectman looked up quickly, as if the thought had not occurred to him. "Don't know as the committee has decided on that yet. We'll trust Mrs. Beebe to take care of what's in the house. I suspect the new owners will want the furniture. As for the personal items..." He stroked his beard, "Whatever your sister-in-law doesn't want might be sold for charity. It would be a favor equal to... say...

a month's rent if she would take an inventory of the contents of the house so we can think about setting a value on it."

Ernest agreed, shook hands with the man and left. Ercyline accepted the news with reservations. "What'll we do when it's sold? Where will we go?"

"I don't know yet. I have some thoughts on it. Perhaps something will turn up before you have to move."

On through the summer, Ercyline stayed at home with Mary Alice. The little girl was sad most of the time. She was lonely for her "Gamma". There was no one to talk to through the day. She spent hours outdoors when the weather allowed, or sat in a corner hugging and talking to her stocking doll. Ercyline was sad, too, but kept busy with the millinery work that Ernest brought to her from the shop. She paid little attention to her daughter - glad that she was quiet and undemanding.

One day in August, 1868, Ercyline approached her husband with trepidation. "Ernest, we're going to have to do something before long. Figuring back to my last bleeding, I think there's going to be another baby come late next winter."

There was no reaction from Ernest, just a very tense silence. Then he stalked out the door, slamming it behind him. He had tried to meet his responsibilities the way he had been taught, but this was more than he knew how to face.

He disappeared for a week. On the eighth day, two men came carrying him to Ercyline's door. His clothing was dripping wet. Reeking of alcohol, he hung between his husky escorts. Ercyline was aghast! She directed them to what had been Mrs. Forrester's bedroom.

One of the men helped her to undress Ernest and put him in the bed. There he lay, only semi-conscious at times, raving at others, but unable to rise from the bed. The first few days, he was only slightly fevered, but when the fever rose sharply Ercyline sent Mrs. Lewis' son for Dr. Partridge.

"My gawd, he does it right," said the little doctor. "Not only does he fall in the creek drunk and catch pneumonia, but he's got the darndest case of the mumps I've ever seen. And they've dropped on him too. It's been going around town lately. You'll have to keep cold cloths on his forehead and his private parts until his fever breaks. Try to get as many fluids as you can into him. I'll ask Mrs. Lewis to come spell you off. You're going to be very busy until the fever breaks."

"Doctor, I don't have the money to pay you or Mrs. Lewis. Ernest hasn't been bringing in much since school let out. If he's too sick to work at the store, we'll only have what little I can bring in from my millinery work. What am I going to do?"

"Mrs. Lewis won't charge you, I'm sure. She's a good Christian woman. Perhaps someday, in some way, you can repay her kindness. I can do without. The mayor pays me plenty for treating his wife's many imaginary illnesses."

To Ercyline's surprise the neighbors who had been so thoughtful at the time of Mrs. Forrester's death rallied to her aid again. Some brought her food, others took care of Mary Alice for half a day. Someone slipped away with her laundry and she found it folded neatly inside her kitchen door without her being aware that it had been missing.

Ernest's fever hung on for more than two weeks. When Dr. Partridge came out of the bedroom to announce that the crisis had passed, Ercyline's knees grew weak with relief.

Though his fever was broken, Ernest seemed unable to gain strength. He lay in bed pale, thin and listless. No amount of coaxing persuaded him to eat more than a small bowl of gruel. Ernest knew it was time for school to open and a new teacher would be hired. Mr. Simms had long since hired a new clerk.

The pittance that Ercyline could earn making hats at home was their only income. The severity of his illness and its aftermath was preying on Ernest's mind. Again, he was trapped by his own mistake in blindly running away from a new problem. He had failed now in his weakness. He could not maintain a train of thought long enough to find another solution. In sleep, he found temporary escape from his hopeless situation.

The doctor was puzzled. "Mrs. Beebe, I just don't have any experience with this sort of thing. All we can do is try to stay cheerful and encourage him to move about and to eat more."

The boardinghouse keeper requested the removal of Ernest's personal effects. Ercyline put his clothes in Mrs. Forrester's closet. The other boxes of books and papers, she put up in the attic for the time being.

More than a month later, Ernest was still lethargic and mentally unable to cope with the simplest of matters, when the Chief Selectman appeared at the door.

"Mrs. Beebe, Ma'am," he said, introducing himself, "I'm right sorry to tell you that this house has been sold. The new owners know of your husband's condition and are willing to extend your notice to a full month. I'll have to ask you to make other arrangements by this time next month." He tipped his hat and strode off down the road.

Ercyline was panic-stricken. She went to Ernest's bedside to give him the news. He looked dully at her and shrugged his shoulders. "Do what you think necessary. I don't care." He turned away and fell asleep.

Ercyline didn't know what to do. Then she remembered what Hilda had said, "We must have faith." So she called on the preacher and asked for prayer.

"We've been doing that ever since Ernest got sick," he said, "But maybe we need to take more concrete action at this point. It occurred to me that he might have relatives who would be willing and able to help. Look through his things and see if there are any letters that might aid in your search."

Ercyline started going through a box that she had retrieved from Ernest's room at the boarding house. She found a letter from his uncle in Illinois, and read:

> My Dear Nephew,
>   It is good news that you are doing so well and curbing your penchant for gambling.

News of people and events followed. The last paragraph was apparently a repetition of previous letters.

> Just remember, dear Ernest; should you ever
> find yourself in dire straits resulting from other than
> unrepentant sin, you may feel free to call upon me for any
> aid you might require.
> Your devoted uncle, Minot Beebe.

Ercyline had no experience with writing and sending letters, so she enlisted the help of Mrs. Lewis. She wrote:

> Dear Mr. Beebe; I just read your last letter to my
> husband, Ernest Beebe. You said that he could ask you
> for help if he needs it. Ernest has been very sick for a
> long time. Our house has been sold and we have to move
> out next month. Ernest is still too sick to help me find
> a solution. He is unable to work yet. We have no money,
> except a little bit I get from making hats.
> I do not know what Ernest will say about telling you
> this. Please, Sir, would you help me decide what to do?
> Our little girl is two and a half years old and I am going
> to have another baby next year. For the children's sake, I
> have to ask for your help.
> Yours truly, Ercyline Beebe

Chapter Four

THE PLANTATION

Within two weeks, a large carriage pulled by a handsome team of horses stopped at the gate. A Negro footman in livery jumped down to open the door. He let down a step for the passenger; a sandy haired version of Ernest, but twenty years older and slightly shorter. The man stood stretching the kinks of travel-weary muscles while he appraised the house. Then he opened the gate and limped up to the stoop. He rapped gently on the door with his silver-headed cane.

Ercyline hurried from the kitchen to open the door. The rich but conservative garb of the man facing her and the luxurious carriage behind him were beyond her experience. "Y-yes, S-sir," she stammered, "C-can I h-help you?"

"Good day, Ma'am," replied the gentleman. "Is this the home of Ernest Beebe? I am his uncle Minot. I have come to inquire after his health. I have recently received a letter from his wife."

"Oh, my, do come in, Mr. Beebe! I'm Ercyline. It was my letter. Ernest is still very sick. He doesn't know that I wrote to you."

Ercyline stepped back to welcome Mr. Beebe into the front room, then excused herself to see if Ernest was awake to receive his visitor. Minot followed close on her heels. Just inside the bedroom door, he stopped and stood for a moment, to allow himself time to adjust to the sight of the emaciated remnant of the healthy young man he'd last seen five years before. He greeted Ernest heartily and shook his hand.

In a dull monotone, very unlike his normal quick speech, Ernest returned the greeting, adding: "Uncle Minot, what are you doing here?"

"My boy, I heard that you were ailing. Since this is the lull in the harvest season, I thought to come and see how you fared. Now I see that you are not at all well, and obviously in need of assistance. I shall go to see your doctor and ascertain how soon you may travel.

You belong in the care of your family. I will see to it and return this evening."

Ernest raised his hand in protest, but his uncle shushed him quickly. "It is evident that you cannot cope in your present circumstances. Your poor devoted wife seems quite careworn. I'll brook no arguments. You shall come home with me to recuperate."

Minot turned and left the house, entered his carriage and rode toward town. When he had seen to accommodations for his footman and driver he registered at the better of the town's two hotels. After a refreshing nap and reasonably good meal, he inquired for directions to Dr. Partridge's office. It was nearby, so he walked.

"Good evening, Doctor. I am Minot Beebe of Linnville, Illinois. I understand that you have been attending to my nephew Ernest. May I have a full report Sir? I have stood in loco-parentis to him since his parents passed away when he was a lad."

The doctor was impressed with his visitor's kindly demeanor and obvious cultivation. "I'm pleased that you've come, Sir. Your nephew is in bad straits physically, mentally and financially."

Minot frowned. "What has been the problem in his recovery? I understand that quite some time has elapsed since the crisis of his illness passed. I was appalled to see his condition when I stopped by this afternoon."

"Well, Sir," replied the doctor, "I can't really say. He was strong and healthy before his illness. That probably accounts for the fact that he survived at all. Why he has not progressed may be mental. I'm not trained in psychiatry. It doesn't help matters any that he won't eat enough to get his strength back either. The kindness of their neighbors is the only reason that they have food at all. I suspect that Mrs. Beebe is not getting enough rest or food, in order to make sure her family is taken care of. She is showing signs of deficient diet as well as extreme fatigue. I have only the greatest admiration for her devotion to Ernest's care."

Minot agreed, "I could see that she looks fatigued. I will see that she gets rest and care. When do you think Ernest will be able to travel? My intention is to take them to my home in Illinois, where he can recover in more familiar surroundings."

"I would say that a move just now, though risky, is just what the young man needs. Any stimulation to bring him out of his physical and mental lethargy."

"Risky, you say?" queried Minot. "In what way, Doctor?"

"Mr. Beebe, your nephew has been through a very serious and prolonged illness. He is very weak. It will no doubt be at least several months before he regains his former health. The rigors of a long journey may be more than he can withstand. But it may be that the change is what is needed to save him."

"Under what circumstances could he be safely moved? What precautions should be taken for a journey just over two hundred miles?"

Dr. Partridge toyed with the fob over his ample belly before answering. "That's a good distance to travel. If a litter could be improvised in a closed carriage, a fifteen minute stop for rest from the jolting of the ride every two hours or less, travel not more than six to eight hours a day would be reasonably safe. Perhaps the fresh air alone would stimulate his appetite. It would be an arduous journey for all concerned. I'd say that in another week he should be able to make the trip."

Minot thanked the doctor and set out briskly for his nephew's house. He found Ernest more alert than he had been in the afternoon. Ercyline was dressing Mary Alice for bed. The child's clear voice, speaking in well-enunciated words, pleased Minot. He was fond of children and had two daughters still living at home. He was taken with the little girl's intelligent face and alertness. Her bright, dark eyes studied him seriously and attentively as he talked to her. And she responded with enthusiasm.

Once Mary Alice was tucked away for the night, Minot took a seat in the sick room and outlined the plans for the removal to the plantation. "You have exactly one week to pack your belongings. Today is Thursday. I have business in Jefferson City and will return here on Tuesday to see to the final arrangements for our journey.

Your obligations to Dr. Partridge, Mrs. Lewis and the selectman will be taken care of before we leave."

Permitting no further argument, Minot changed the subject and soon left to return to his hotel.

Ernest was disturbed about this proposal, yet lacked the vitality to cope with alternatives. Ercyline was exhausted but elated at the thought that her husband would no doubt recover his former health after they reached Linnville. She set about packing their meager belongings.

Before he left town, Minot arranged for construction of a removable litter to fit the carriage.

When he arrived at the gate early the next Thursday morning, Ercyline had her household organized. Their belongings were stowed atop the carriage under a tarpaulin. The litter was carried into Ernest's bedroom by the driver and the footman. Ernest was placed upon it and carried outside. Stowed feet-first along the front to back axis of the carriage, the litter was reasonably comfortable and minimized the effect of the rough roads. Ercyline, Mary Alice and Uncle Minot had plenty of room, and could change seats at will.

Mary Alice enjoyed the changing scenery along the way. She napped on the seat, holding her father's hand.

The journey was an arduous one, as Dr. Partridge had predicted. Despite the awkwardness of removing the litter on each night's stop, Ernest did not mind. The doctor had also been correct in assuming that the stimulation of the trip would do more good than harm. On the third day, he began to converse with his uncle, and suffered Mary Alice to climb up by his side. He laughed when she sang in her off-key voice.

On the last morning, as the carriage drove up to the door of the inn to load its passengers, Ernest turned to his uncle. "Please, Uncle Minot, I'm feeling so much better." His voice was almost plaintive, "I think I'll be alright sitting up this morning. You said we'd be home before noon. It will be so much more pleasant to see familiar landmarks from a natural angle, rather than ninety degrees off. I can lounge back a bit and put my legs on the opposite seat so I won't be sitting completely upright."

Minot looked at his nephew with a frown. He understood his feelings, but Dr. Partridge had been explicit in his instructions.

"I'll have to refuse you Ernest, for your own good. This journey has been a risk and I don't want to take any chances now that it's almost over. I think we can put something behind your head and shoulders to raise them a bit, but that is as far as I'll bend the doctor's rules."

Ercyline and Uncle Minot folded two of the carriage robes for a prop, and Ernest settled back with a sigh.

Ercyline had fallen asleep and wasn't aware of the journey's end and the approach up the cinder drive to the graceful plantation house. Half asleep and exhausted, she was helped up the stairs and installed in a room that amazed her. Except for hats, she had never seen such ruffles and feminine trimmings. She did not know until several days later that it was the room of the eldest daughter, then away attending a young ladies' finishing school in St. Louis. At last she had time to rest after the long ordeal of Ernest's illness and the trip.

Ernest was carried into the spacious bedroom he had occupied as a lad. Three Negro women, who had known him in his youth, took over his care.

A young white servant girl became Mary Alice's constant companion and nursemaid in the third floor children's quarters.

A few days of rest, sleep and good food brought to her on lacquered trays, soon had Ercyline feeling the need for some exercise. She dressed in her best calico frock one cool morning and ventured from her room. Too tired to notice much on her arrival, she marveled now at the gorgeous colors in the long rugs centering the hallway. Her progress was slow as she stopped to gaze at each of the paintings hung along the walls.

Upon entering Ernest's room, she found him sitting in a large wingback chair, his feet up on a hassock. Though still weak, he had been able to walk with support across the room. He introduced Ercyline to the middle-aged Negress fussing over him.

"Mam Ginny, this is my wife, Ercyline. She's been very good to me in my illness. I owe her a debt beyond repayment for her faithfulness. How she bore up under the burden, I'll never know."

The woman curtsied and smiled conspiratorially at Ercyline. "Miz Beebe, you've done well with Mr. Ernest. He *was* always a trial to see to."

"Pleased to meet you, Mam Ginny. I thank you for taking care of him since we came. I'm sorry I haven't been to see him myself. I guess I was just too tuckered out."

Mam Ginny bobbed her excuses and left the room, saying, "I'll be back shortly, Mr. Ernest."

Man and wife looked at one another in silence. Finally Ercyline said, "Well, Ernest, you must be feeling better, sitting up in a chair and all. Are you eating more? You're looking a bit more fleshed out."

"Yes," he replied, "The trip seemed to do me good. Mam Ginny and the others have really kept after me. I'm still quite weak and can't seem to keep my thoughts on one subject for very long, though.

"And how have you been? Have you seen all of the house and grounds? This must all be strange to you."

"Well, no; I've been asleep most of the time," she replied. "I guess I was just too worn out myself. The Colored girls have been good to me, too. This is the first time I've been out of that pretty room. I never saw such fancy things before.

"Your uncle Minot brought Mary Alice to see me day before yesterday. He told me to take my time and rest. He's got a girl named Edith to look after her. They put her in another room he called a nursery. I've heard her laughing in the hall."

"I know," said Ernest, "Edith brought Mary Alice to me yesterday. She looks well and happy. It would seem that we've neglected her too long a time. She was shy with me at first. I guess I *do* look different in this setting."

Ercyline pulled a small chair to face Ernest while they talked. "Who are all these people? There's the girl who's taking care of

Mary Alice and two Negro women who come to my room and won't even let me smooth up the bedcover. They brought me real good food on a pretty tray that stood up like a bridge over my legs. Is the White girl part of Uncle Minot's family? Do the Negroes live in this house, too?"

Ernest had to chuckle at the open wonder on Ercyline's face, "No, no; Edith is a house maid who takes care of any children that are guests here."

"A house maid? What's that? What does she do if there's no children here? Does she work for money?"

"House maids are employees," he told her, "That means they are paid for what they do. They get a room to sleep in and all their food and their working clothes for free. They do all the work, such as dusting and cleaning and taking care of the family's clothes. Some of the Negroes live in the house, or rather in a part of the house that's built on behind the kitchen. All of them are called servants."

"You mean they're paid to do what Uncle Minot's family doesn't want to do?"

"Well, yes, partly. But this is a big house. It takes more than just a few people to do everything that needs to be done."

"Oh, my! Servants to do for us? I never thought of such a thing!" Ercyline had difficulty wrapping her mind around the situation. "This can't go on forever, though. You'll get well, and then what's going to happen to us Ernest? We can't stay here without doing something to earn our way. Uncle Minot's good to us, but we can't be beholden to him forever."

"Never mind, Girl. Just let me get back to feeling better. Then we'll work out some means for repaying his kindness. Go on outside while the weather is pleasant. Look around and learn about the plantation. Uncle Minot is in no hurry to push us out, I'm sure. This place was my home for years. He's been like a father to me.

"Now, would you help me back to the bed? I'm very tired. I think I'd like to sleep for a while."

Ercyline took her husband's arm. She tucked him in and received a kiss in thanks. Then he lay back and closed his eyes. She met Mam

Ginny coming up the stairs, and told her that Ernest wanted to sleep a while.

Mam Ginny thanked her, then added, "It'll do Mr. Ernest good to sleep. Miz Beebe, would you like me to show you around the house?" At Ercyline's nod, she turned and accompanied her along the hall and down the stairs.

The two women met Minot at the foot of the staircase. He dismissed Mam Ginny and offered to escort Ercyline on a tour of the house. The quiet grandeur of the plantation house was almost too much for Ercyline to absorb. The spacious rooms, tall windows, rich draperies, paintings and massive furniture were true wonders to her. The dining salon alone left her awestruck. There was a very long table, many high-backed chairs and three silver candle holders.

"Do you have *that* many folks for meals, Uncle Minot?" she asked.

He laughed heartily and reassured her that the table was used only when there were many guests. "We have a smaller dining room that we use for just the family, my dear. Come and see for yourself."

He led the way to a set of double doors and ushered her into a pleasant, sunny room. Cheerful and well lighted, it was much more colorful than the dark high panels of the salon.

Uncle Minot next led her to his library. Books! It seemed that every inch of the walls, except the tall windows and the two doorways, were covered with books! Ercyline walked around the room, afraid to touch the fine leather bindings with their gold lettering. One whole section was allocated to Bibles, concordances, commentaries and other Christian books.

"Sakes alive, Uncle Minot, I never knew there *were* so many books. Do you read them all yourself?"

"Well, most of them I have read during my lifetime," he chuckled. "Some of them were my father's and some were his father's before him. We all have brought some from the university. Others have been added as we find their subjects of lasting interest. Upstairs, on the third floor, is a classroom with many children's books. Please feel free to borrow any of them, either room."

"Oh, no! Thank you Uncle Minot. Ernest has brought me lots of books since he taught me to read. I never thought to see so many, though. I think I'd better start upstairs at first. These are too smart and thick for me!" Her eyes shone with anticipation.

A musical sound rang through the house just then. "Well, there's the luncheon bell. Come along Ercyline; you may as well meet what members of the family are at home."

Ercyline held back. "I've never had a meal in such a fancy room. All those forks and such; I wouldn't know what to do with them."

Uncle Minot took her arm and guided her on. He bent his head and smiled down at her. With a twinkle in his eye, he told her, "There's a secret to that, my dear: All you do is wait until the others have begun, watch carefully then do as they do. It'll come easily, you'll see."

They entered the room to find two pretty girls, one thirteen and the other fifteen, and an older woman already seated. Uncle Minot placed Ercyline at his left, then made the introductions.

"Ercyline, this mischievous scamp on my right is my youngest daughter, Imelda. Watch out if she starts tossing those yellow curls. It usually means she is about to throw a tantrum or is planning a joke on you. Next to you is my second daughter, Elizabeth. Under that copper hair is a sense of humor and a hot temper, though she is a dutiful girl. At the foot of the table is our indispensable Mrs. Mayton. Without her, the house would fall apart and the girls run wild.

"Ladies, may I present Ernest's wife, Ercyline. She has been through a difficult time, caring for Ernest. She deserves our gratitude for a task well done. I charge each of you to make her feel welcome, comfortable and a true member of our family."

As each of the ladies inclined her head and smiled her greeting, Ercyline became shyer. The girls were dressed in sensible, serviceable, well made but feminine gowns that were colorful and youthful in cut. Mrs. Mayton's well-fitted, soft grey dress was more severely cut. Her warm dark eyes appraised the newcomer thoroughly:

She saw a plain young woman only two or three years older than Elizabeth; obviously ill at ease. It would take a lot of polish to fit her into this setting. Her heart went out to the young woman. The girl looked as if she could use a bit of mothering; and pregnant again, too, unless Mrs. Mayton's eyes fooled her.

She hoped that the new little one would be more physically attractive than the homely waif upstairs. Not that the little thing wasn't bright as a new penny. She was going to be a challenge. Edith had reported that Mary Alice was into everything; not from malice, just intelligent and curious, though she could sit quietly for hours over something that interested her. The child was a study in contrast.

Chapter Five

THE DREAM BABY

Ercyline gradually overcame her shyness with the family during the next six weeks, while Ernest recuperated. When he was strong enough to come downstairs for meals, she started retreating into herself again; perhaps even more. The table conversation sparked around her husband. The subjects were generally over her head, and she withdrew into silence. Mrs. Mayton attempted to include her whenever possible, but Ercyline found herself more and more overwhelmed.

Mrs. Mayton found Ercyline in the children's classroom one afternoon. She was reading from a book in the section for fourth and fifth-graders.

Aha, so this was at the root of it all! She thought. The girl was less educated than she thought.

"Miss Ercyline," she said quietly. "I saw you coming out of the colored children's classroom the other day. You have really made an effort to become acquainted with the plantation. Mr. Beebe is pleased about it.

"It has come to my attention that the colored teacher has too large a class and could use a part-time assistant. Perhaps you could ask Mr. Beebe if you might spend an hour or two a day with the children." Mrs. Mayton hoped that this suggestion, if carried out, would encourage Ercyline to go further in her own education.

Ercyline looked surprised, then thoughtful. "I'll think about it," she replied.

Later that week, Ercyline approached Mrs. Mayton and asked for needle and thread to make repairs in her own and Mary Alice's garments.

"Do you sew?" asked Mrs. Mayton. "I had noticed that your garments are well made; never suspecting that you might have made them yourself."

"Oh, yes!" Ercyline brightened. This was something she could do well. It gave her self-esteem a lift. "My friend Hilda taught me, much better than what my granny ever could. I can make hats, too. I learned in a shop and worked there part-time for a little over a year."

Mrs. Mayton was quietly pleased with this information. Ercyline had not had the courage to follow the suggestion about the school. The housekeeper began to ask Ercyline's help with mending articles about the house. The girl eagerly volunteered her services where needed.

"You don't know how much this means to all of us," Mrs. Mayton told Ercyline. "Since Emily, who did all our dressmaking, married and moved to Kentucky with her husband, we have had only an inexperienced Colored girl to help with the sewing. We've had to go to Linnville, to a dressmaker, who hasn't always done satisfactory work.

"Elizabeth and Imelda are very hard on their clothes. Those two can wear out or outgrow dresses almost as fast as we can replace them. I just don't have time to keep up with it all. I'm sure Mr. Beebe will agree, if you care to take on some of our sewing."

Now, Ercyline felt that perhaps she could be more than a shadow in Ernest's light. The inactivity was beginning to be boring. Walking about the plantation, attending church services with the Beebes, reading and helping Edith with Mary Alice's care were not enough.

With a completely sufficient diet for the first time in her life, her spare frame was filling out some. The child within her grew, too; it had begun to stir. She would not feel like a beggar asking for maternity dress material for herself.

For the first two weeks in December, an air of subdued excitement had permeated the house and the Colored servants' quarters. Ercyline was curious, but too shy to ask. On December twentieth a swarm of servants, colored and white, invaded the house. Evergreen boughs appeared on mantles, stair rails and over the doors and windows. Holly branches with their shiny red berries superseded flowers in table vases. Mistletoe clusters hung from every chandelier and just inside the tall double front doors.

When she could stand it no longer, Ercyline asked Ernest about these goings-on. They were preparing for bed when she inquired. Just a few days before, she had been moved into Ernest's room.

"Of course, I should have told you", he replied. "The Beebe household always makes a big to-do at Christmas. Aunt Caroline, before her death, had charged Uncle Minot to keep the custom for the girls' sakes.

"Annabelle will be home from school tomorrow. She's the real beauty of the family. I don't know how she has stayed single this long. She's the most enthusiastic holiday celebrant of them all."

Ercyline brightened. "Oh good, I've wanted so, to meet her. Her room is so pretty and dainty. I'm sure she must be that way, too."

Ernest continued, "Uncle Minot has decided, because of my illness and your pregnancy, to cancel the usual enormous at-home party on Christmas Day. It will be just family and a very few close friends this year. On Christmas Eve, there will be a feast for the family, and later a tree to be trimmed in the large living room. There will be gifts for everyone. At midnight, the colored folks come to the front lawn to serenade us. Then Uncle Minot will distribute gifts to all of them."

"Gifts for all the Colored people, Ernest?" Ercyline couldn't imagine that many gifts. "Uncle Minot is so kind to get presents for so many people."

"The girls will probably be away at balls and parties a lot, until Christmas Eve. Once Christmas Eve comes, the family will stay home and celebrate together with gifts, special foods, the Christmas Story and carols around the piano.

"I'm looking forward to Christmas this year, now that I'm not mad at God anymore. I made a profession of faith as a child, but turned my back on God when my parents died. I know now that God's answer to your prayers, and your faith brought us through my illness, and Uncle Minot's faith and devotion to God and family is the reason we're here."

"Oh! I'm so glad, Ernest! I'd been wondering how you could be so cool about my becoming a Christian when your whole family is so devout.

"I never dreamed that Christmas could be such a big deal. Aren't we invited to any parties? I've never been to a party. What are they like?"

"No, we're not invited outside the house. It's not considered proper for a woman past four months in pregnancy to appear at parties. After the baby is born, perhaps we will go to some. Besides, I'm not really quite up to such things as yet. Be patient. You'll enjoy Christmas here, you'll see."

Annabelle arrived at the plantation in a flurry of baggage, hugs and kisses. She was a tall young woman, and she sparkled; conversing gaily. She had time for smiles and a kind word for everyone. Her greeting to Ernest was not more or less affectionate than that to Ercyline.

All through the Holiday Season, the door knocker rattled frequently as a multitude of swains arrived. Mary Alice was the recipient of hugs and stories and delighted introductions to her young suitors. These gallants soon learned to carry candies in their pockets because Mary Alice's regard was equated with favor in the eyes of Annabelle.

On Christmas Eve, Mary Alice was allowed to join the family at dinner in the brightly lit and decorated dining salon. Edith had coached her well. In her prettiest dress, made for the occasion by Mrs. Mayton and her mother, she was the calmest and most dignified member of the company.

When the late dinner was over, the family retired to the living room where the twelve-foot tree awaited the boxes of decorations. Every member of the family was involved in arraying the tree and singing while the girls took turns playing the piano. Mary Alice was carried to the top of the tallest ladder and afforded the honor of placing the glittering star on the topmost spine. Then everyone gathered around Uncle Minot as he pulled out the big family Bible and settled in to share the traditional reading of The Christmas Story.

"Uncle Minot," said Ernest, "would it be alright if I read the passages this time? I have decided to stop blaming God for my parent's death and turn back to my faith."

Everyone cheered and hugged Ernest and asked him what brought this change about.

"Credit goes to Ercyline and her friend, Hilda, who shared the gospel with her. She attended church services and read her Bible faithfully before and during my illness. She had the whole Church praying for me and for our deliverance from the mess I got us into."

"Well, I guess that qualifies you to do the honors," Minot admitted, as he passed the old family Bible over to Ernest.

As Ernest finished reading and said a prayer, rolling carts of hot punch and coffee, colorful snacks, cookies and cakes were brought in. The house servants carried in mounds of beribboned packages, and stayed to share the bounty with the Beebe family.

Mary Alice went from one adult to another, helping each one to unwrap the wonderful crackly papers. The whole company delighted in festooning the little girl in the ribbons. The mittens, bonnets and dresses that she received were less meaningful to her than the fun of scuffling through the boxes and papers that covered the floor around the chairs.

Edith carried the sleepy child to the nursery at eleven o'clock. Another round of punch was passed before the sound of carols was heard out on the lawn: It was the colored servants' contribution to the festivities. While the songs regaled them all, gifts were passed among the singers. When each had received a bright package, and each family a basket of fruit and candies to add to their next day's feast, the Negroes faded away into the darkness, their songs growing fainter and fainter.

Ercyline was as excited as Mary Alice on Christmas morning. Ernest and Ercyline ascended early to the nursery to watch Mary Alice's eyes when she found her first china doll. Ercyline had spent hours, advised by Mrs. Mayton, sewing an extensive wardrobe for the blue-eyed doll. A red-haltered hobby-horse shared the limelight with the doll. It galloped with Mary Alice's enthusiastic cries from one room to the other. The little family kept to their own quarters until the light supper was served in the evening.

After the holidays, Annabelle returned to finishing school in St. Louis. The house, though it was full of people, seemed colder and emptier without her cheery presence.

As Ernest's strength increased, one or another of the young women of the household accompanied him on walks about the plantation. The crisp air soon put color back in his face. However much he ate, though, he did not return to his former robust appearance; neither did his strength or the quickness of his wit. At twenty-six, he had the look and manner of a man ten years older.

Walking about the plantation's woods on a sunny day in mid-February, Ernest and Ercyline came upon a small deserted cottage nearly overgrown with rose bushes and weeds. The thick fieldstone walls and deep eaves caught her interest. She begged Ernest to explore it with her.

"Not yet; let's inquire first. No telling how long it's been empty. Possibly it's not safe. The floors and beams could give way and bury us both. I think we should ask Uncle Minot to tell us something about it, and if it's within his boundaries. I have forgotten about it, if I ever knew."

At dinner, Ercyline told the family about finding the cottage. The brightness of her eyes and voice told Uncle Minot that something more than enchantment with the house itself was behind her enthusiasm.

"I know the cottage of which you speak. It *is* on my property." He promised to inquire into the matter soon. He insisted that one of the plantation foremen, Josiah, who knew something of carpentry, should inspect it first. Within a few days, Josiah pronounced it safe. Uncle Minot suggested that the three of them explore it the next morning.

At bedtime, Ercyline said, "Do you think that Uncle might let us live in that house if it can be fixed up for us? I'd feel a lot less beholden if we had our own house and earned our keep. I don't feel right owing him so much. He's done a lot for us already."

The thought had never crossed Ernest's mind. Feeling completely at home here where he had lived for many years. The idea of obligation hadn't occurred to him. "Suppose we let this matter wait until we find out if the cottage can be renovated. It could take weeks to make it suitable to live in."

Ercyline could see that Ernest needed time to adjust to this idea. At breakfast, Uncle Minot announced that a carriage would be waiting at ten o'clock to take Ercyline, Ernest and himself to the cottage. Josiah drove the carriage. He was pleased that he had arranged the removal of tangled vines and weeds from the walls and the path to the door.

The door sagged open to show light flooding the surprisingly spacious rooms of the cottage. There was a partition to set off the kitchen. It formed a dining ell to the roomy main area. A narrow staircase led up to two low-ceilinged bedrooms; one larger than the other. Dormer windows brightened both rooms. The wide-plank floors were laid in a pleasing diagonal pattern.

Ercyline was as excited as a child. Uncle Minot, with twinkling eyes, broached the subject. "I presume you have ideas for this place as a home for yourselves? I hadn't thought about it until recently.

"Josiah, have you a crew available to see to cleaning this place up so that we may see its real possibility?"

"Yes Sir, Mr. Minot; that I do. Thought you might have that idea. I can have some people here in the morning. Give us a week and you won't know it's the same place."

"You have an appointment one week from today to approve or disapprove of your future home," Minot told Ercyline and Ernest. "I think we can find furniture stored away at the main house to make it quite comfortable. What do you say, Ernest? Do you feel able to become a householder?"

Then he looked thoughtful. "Ercyline's time is near. Perhaps we should arrange the move after she has recovered from giving birth. Spring is a good time for a new beginning."

A week later, the young couple gladly accepted Minot's offer and looked forward to moving into the charming cottage.

Ten days hence, Minot summoned Ernest to his library. "My boy, I have a problem: Imelda and Elizabeth need more preparation for finishing school. Annabelle has told me in which subjects she felt least prepared upon entering the academy. Mrs. Mayton really hasn't the time nor the education to take any further part in their training. Also, the school for the coloreds needs organization. Would you consider supervising courses of study for your cousins, as well as reorganizing the colored school?

"Since my grandfather's day, when it was still illegal to educate slaves, there has been a school on this property. Better educated people are more productive and happy, and they make the plantation more efficient. We have always had a harmonious way of life here. We must continue to see that our people get the best schooling possible.

"There would be a stipend for your services and free use of the cottage."

Ernest asked for a few days to consider the offer. His ability to maintain a train of thought was improving. However, he was beginning to wonder if he would ever regain his intellect. Perhaps preparing lessons for his cousins would be an intellectual stimulation. The Colored school should be no challenge, he thought to himself.

Before he could announce his acceptance of the offer, Ercyline woke him before dawn. It was mid-March and the flowers were starting to bloom, the trees were awakening from their winter sleep and the birds were starting to reappear.

"Ernest, I think it's time for the baby. I promised I'd send for Mrs. Mayton. Birth is a messy business, and I don't want to spoil the nice bedding."

Ernest; flustered and half asleep, stumbled out of bed to pull the call bell cord. He dispatched the sleepy houseboy who answered to awaken the housekeeper. Mrs. Mayton sent for Mam Ginny and immediately took charge. She sent a bleary-eyed maid for pads and linens, hot water, soap and towels.

Mam Ginny arrived just in time to hear the first lusty cry of a nine-and-a-half-pound boy. She had only to tie and cut the cord and clear the afterbirth. Her assistants cleaned up the bed while Mam Ginny oiled the baby, wrapped him and presented him to his father for appraisal. Ercyline and the baby were settled and smiling in record time.

Here was Ercyline's dream baby. He was blond and rounded of limb; a handsome baby. Even at birth he was a recognizable copy of his father.

The household rejoiced. In the morning, Edith brought Mary Alice to see her baby brother. She fell in love instantly. Uncle Minot congratulated all three members of the little family. His daughters oohed and aahed extravagantly. With Uncle Minot's permission, the child was named Carson Minot after the son he had lost in the war.

A strange coincidence occurred within forty-eight hours of the birth. A letter from Washington, D.C, bordered in black, was delivered to Uncle Minot. His son's burial place had been found near a cabin in the West Virginia Mountains. He had been wounded in one of the final battles of the war. Crawling in a daze from the battlefield, he had been found by a back-woods family who attended to him until his death several weeks later.

The illiterate family could not read the papers taken from his uniform pockets. When a circuit-riding preacher, new to the area, visited a nearby settlement in late 1887, the family turned the papers over to him. It was nearly a year later before he found the papers, forgotten in the bottom of his bag. He sent them on by mail to the War Department.

Bureaucratic delays in finding the grave and confirming testimony to authenticate facts accounted for further delays in locating Carson's home address.

Two weeks after the letter arrived, the Beebes held a memorial service and reception for family, friends and neighbors in the large living room of the plantation house. Immediately after the service, Uncle Minot arose and faced his guests.

"Ladies and Gentlemen. I thank you all for sharing this poignant time with us. We appreciate your sympathy, however, we must be about the business of the living. In this house, there has recently been a gift given to us all; a new Carson. My nephew Ernest has consented to making this the occasion for dedication of this new life, his son. Pastor, will you now take over?"

Elizabeth and Imelda stepped forward with Ernest and Ercyline to present the baby for dedication. Mary Alice was allowed to stand with them, dressed in a new, lace-trimmed black velvet dress. Mrs. Mayton had helped Ercyline choose a becoming gown in dove grey for her first presentation to the society of Linnville. It had a wide white collar which flattered her dark complexion. A new coiffure, piled high atop her head, set off her long slender neck and newly slender figure. The assembled guests noted her charming reticence. Not one was aware that it was actually a terrified awe of all these strangers.

Chapter Six

THE WONDER CHILD

April 15th was a lovely day; perfect for the Ernest Beebe family's move to the cottage. Over Mam Ginny's protests, Ercyline had been back and forth for three weeks overseeing the setting up of the household. Josiah's crew were busy, indeed: A trio of colored women had swarmed the house with brooms, mops, rags, soap and water. Behind them came a group of men with whitewash and shellac. Meantime, a crew set about cultivating the land around the house; marking it out into lawn and flower beds. Ercyline had a difficult time persuading Josiah to set aside an area for a vegetable garden.

"But Miss Beebe, Mr. Minot told us that wouldn't be necessary. We have more than enough from the truck gardens at the main house to take care of everyone's kitchens."

Ercyline stood, hands on hips, a don't-argue-with-me expression on her face. "Josiah, I'll deal with Uncle Minot. I do so love to work a garden! The last two years, I've had no place to have one. Now, you just set off the space I marked with those sticks. If you'd be kind enough to plow and rake it for me, I'll take care of it on my own from there."

His face broke into a sweat of indecision. Her piercing scowl finally overcame his determination. He just hoped Mr. Minot would understand how strong this young woman's will could be.

That evening after dinner, Ercyline cornered Uncle Minot and let her wishes be known. "If I can have some seed and sets, I'd be mighty grateful, Uncle. Would you please tell Josiah that it's alright to leave me a garden space? There's such a satisfaction to growing my own foodstuffs."

"We'll see that he works you a fine garden area." Minot patted her arm kindly. "You don't need to grow food; but I see you have your heart set on it."

With Mrs. Mayton's advice, Ercyline refused the finer, **larger** furnishings in the attics and storerooms of the plantation house. "I would feel more at home with the smaller, simpler things, Uncle," she said. It's a stone cottage, not a fine house. I'd feel crowded with the larger pieces."

Ercyline chose to use her own simple kitchen utensils, since she would again be cooking for her family. Also, she refused the rich draperies, a little worn, that were offered to her to be cut down to fit the smaller cottage windows. She made her own simple hand-woven kind, like those in the Negros's cabins. They were coarse but colorful; more in keeping with the rough-textured, whitewashed plaster walls.

On the Sunday afternoon before the move, Imelda and Elizabeth begged to visit the cottage. Ercyline and Ernest had not permitted them before this; using the excuse that they wanted to wait until it was ready for guests.

The family, including Uncle Minot and Mrs. Mayton, walked down the lane to the cottage. They chatted merrily along the way. Ernest stepped forward to open the door. "Come along, Mrs. Beebe. You shall be the first in, so that you may greet your first guests as lady of the house." He bowed gallantly and took her elbow, guiding her across the doorsill.

Ercyline's eyes widened and she clapped her hands to her face. Beside the hearth was a pile of pretty packages!

"Surprise!" shouted her guests as they crowded into the room. A fire burned in the fireplace and a kettle sang on the crane over the flames. The deal table in the dining ell was set with a lace cloth, new flower-patterned china and simple silver flatware. Candles glowed on either side of a low bowl of spring flowers. More flowers were set on the mantelpiece and sideboard.

Ercyline caught at the back of a chair to keep from falling as she wept with joy. "When did you do all this? What have I done to deserve it? Ernest, why didn't you tell me?" She was stunned by this show of the family's regard.

Imelda and Elizabeth led Ercyline to one of the big chairs by the fire and insisted that she open her gifts. There were pretty towels and runners, hand embroidered by the girls, crocheted doilies for the tables, ruffled pillow slips, additional tools for the kitchen, jars of preserved fruits, jams and jellies. Ercyline had never had a party all her own: She was faint with happiness.

On moving day, Minot announced that he was sending Edith with the new household for a time, until they were settled in with the two children. A cot was set up in the small bedroom for her, so that she could tend to the little ones' needs at night. Ercyline was of mixed emotions about this. A servant for her? This was something she had never imagined.

Edith had spent her early years at the plantation house, in the kitchen. She taught Ercyline how to cook dishes which were beyond her experience. Edith also had a natural affection and understanding for children, but she could not lessen the strong favoritism the young mother showed toward Carson.

When Edith, after three months, returned to the plantation house, Mary Alice crept into the baby's crib at night to quiet his first sign of crying. She found a spare sugartit and carried it in her pocket to pop into his mouth when he even frowned. Ercyline carried the little boy on her hip most of his waking hours, cooing and chuckling at him. She rocked him to sleep at night, singing odd little nonsense lullabies.

Mary Alice showed no jealousy at the favoritism her brother demanded and got. She adored the baby. Though Mary Alice could clearly enunciate "Carson", she dubbed him "Carsie", and the family followed suit. The nickname was to stick with him throughout his childhood.

A fringe-topped wicker baby carriage was found in a plantation attic. It was newly painted, and presented at the cottage. It became a common sight for Ercyline, Mary Alice and the carriage to parade up to the plantation house two or three days a week, as Ercyline's services were required in the sewing room. Edith was delighted to take over the care of the children while their mother was occupied.

On their arrival at the house, she was automatically released from her usual routine during their stay.

Ercyline had a white servant girl and two of the Negro girls as apprentices in the spacious, many-windowed sewing room under the eaves. Imelda and Elizabeth came often to sit and work with them. The Beebe sisters had been trained in fine embroidery, needlepoint, tatting lace and crocheting ever since they had outgrown the nursery. Here was the opportunity for Ercyline to learn yet another set of skills. She had an inborn talent for needlework of all sorts. She soon outshone the girls in speed and excellence in every phase of these arts.

At home in the cottage, Ernest devoted hours to reading. Often, as Ercyline sat playing with Carsie or plying her needle, Ernest read aloud to her or taught Mary Alice nursery rhymes. In vain he tried to teach mother and daughter to sing simple songs, but neither of them could carry a melody, though they both had an excellent sense of rhythm.

Suddenly, one evening, Ernest discovered that Mary Alice, at three and a half, was not just parroting the simple rhyme he was teaching her. She was sitting on his knee as he held the book. He paused to look up at Ercyline, and heard Mary Alice continue on with the words. Wondering if it was merely by rote, he deliberately chose another simple story he knew she had never heard. He began reading the first sentence, then allowed his voice to trail off into silence. Mary Alice; who had seemed to be repeating the words as he read, continued on. If she reached a word she could not fathom, she pointed to it and asked, "Papa, tell me, please?" then read on after he helped her.

Both parents were thunderstruck! This was an unheard-of development for a child so young! Henceforth, Edith was asked to let Mary Alice read any of the books that Ernest placed on a particular shelf in the nursery classroom. She was allowed to take them home. She read them over and over until she could recite them. Uncle Minot started sending to Springfield or St. Louis for copies of the little girl's favorite books. He presented them to her with bookplates marking them as her own.

In this one area, Mary Alice was possessive; she jealously guarded her books from Carsie as he became old enough to reach for them. She forgave him for dismembering her china doll and breaking the hobby horse in the next few years; but flew into a rage if he handled her books.

Carsie was two and Mary Alice five, when they disappeared from the rear yard of the cottage one mid-morning. Ercyline had gone inside for only a moment to stir a kettle on the fire. She thought they were playing their favorite hide and seek, so made no effort to look for them for close to thirty minutes. She went on working in her garden until she began to feel uneasy, and called out for Mary Alice. She got no answer. She called louder, but here was only silence.

Alarmed, she ran about the yard and checked the house, thinking that perhaps they had tired of their game and had fallen asleep. She found no trace of the children. Panic set in; she abandoned the search and ran to get help. An hour later, one of the Negro hands came upon the brother and sister in the orchard. Black head and blond lay face down (chins on hands) watching a line of ants demolish some cherries and carry the bits off to their nest. He tucked one child under each arm and toted them home.

Ercyline was so upset that she shook Mary Alice; then held her at arm's length and demanded to know why she had taken her brother so far away from the house.

Mary Alice looked squarely at her mother. In complete seriousness, she answered, "But Mama, you were playing in your garden. Carsie saw a line of ants and wanted to follow them, so we did. The cherries were at the end of the line. We weren't lost. We knew we just had to follow the ants to get back home."

Weak with relief that the children were safe, Ercyline gave them lunch and put Carsie down for his nap. She confined Mary Alice to the living room until Ernest's return. Mary Alice found a book and read it happily; completely unaffected by the restriction.

On Ernest's return that afternoon, Ercyline told him of the children's misadventure, and quoted Mary Alice's remarks. He broke into a hearty, infectious laugh, and soon had them all laughing in accompaniment.

"Ercyline, my Dear, I know it was wrong in your eyes; but don't you realize that this was an indication of intellectual curiosity? Mary Alice was taking care of Carsie, satisfying her need to know, and teaching Carsie at the same time."

He sat down, so he would be at the girl's eye level. He called her to stand in front of him, then explained to her that her mother, as all mothers should, needed to know where her children were at all times. "It's a protective sense that parents have. God has charged us to watch over our children - to take care of them. Do you understand?"

"Yes, Papa," Mary Alice answered solemnly, "When Mama plays in her garden, we must tell her where *we* want to play."

Ernest and Ercyline looked at one another over the head of their surprisingly wise child: She understood the situation better than they thought she would.

A few weeks later, while Ercyline was "*playing*" in her garden again, Mary Alice politely asked permission for her brother and herself, "Mama, may we pick some of those berries behind the hedge? They're very good. Carsie and I are hungry."

Ercyline looked up; knowing there were blackberries around the perimeter of the yard. "Of course you may, but don't eat too many. Carsie will get a tummy ache and we'd *all* be unhappy then, wouldn't we? I'll go in and get lunch started."

The children strolled off hand in hand toward the hedge as Ercyline rose, brushed the dirt off her hands and went inside. When she had finished fixing lunch, she went outside to bring the children in. She listened for their voices; as they usually chattered like magpies when they were together. Mary Alice, alone, understood Carsie's gibberish. Ercyline stepped through the gap in the hedge where she knew the berry canes were. The children weren't there! She ran around the corner of the hedge, then to the other side of the yard. There she found them lying, face up, under a bush. They were reaching up to pick some odd orange-colored berries. A flash of memory brought back something her grandmother had told her about these particular berries.

She screamed, snatched up Carsie, grabbed Mary Alice's hand, and ran for the house, calling to Ernest, who was reading in the living room.

"Ernest, come quick! The children have been eating poison berries. Get some soda and warm water, quick! We'll have to force them to drink it until they vomit! I just hope it isn't too late!"

Ercyline was so distraught, and Ernest so anxious to assist her, that Mary Alice could not persuade them to listen to her. She fought the attempts of her father to pour the strong sodium bicarbonate solution down her throat. Finally, in desperation, she stomped as hard as she could on his slippered foot.

Ernest let go of Mary Alice and roared in pain. Over Carsie's cries, she yelled. "Leave us alone! Brother and I have been eating those berries for a long time! They are not bad for us!"

Both parents stopped, open-mouthed. While nursing his sore foot, Ernest asked, "How did you know they weren't poison? Who told you?"

"The birds did, Papa, and the baby squirrels. They eat them all the time. We tried them, too; they taste good. We've never been sick from eating them."

The soda water treatment was forgotten. The children had asked permission. Though there had been a misunderstanding; they hadn't disobeyed. Obviously there was no danger, since they had eaten them before.

Ernest asked his daughter to lead him to the berry bushes. He picked several twigs with both leaves and berries. After lunch the two walked hand in hand up to the plantation house to visit the library. A thorough search of several books on botany confirmed what Mary Alice already knew. The berries were edible, though in some areas they were falsely believed to be poisonous.

Chapter Seven

THE ANGEL AND THE DEVIL

That day's adventure, or misadventure, depending on one's outlook, started a new phase in Mary Alice's life. She didn't neglect the books in the children's library, but she often picked twigs or dug up whole small plants to take to her father. They made their pilgrimages to the botany books with the loot. Uncle Minot and her father made a game of teaching Mary Alice the common, as well as the Latin names of each of her discoveries.

Ernest bought his daughter a leather-bound notebook, and encouraged her to copy the names of the plants from the books. Sometimes she grew impatient with the "funny squiggly letters", as she called the italics. They were much more difficult to copy, but she did her best. He found that she was also tracing the outlines of the leaves and growth patterns onto the same page with her childish version of the print.

When her sixth birthday had passed, and the adults realized how responsible Mary Alice had become, she was allowed the run of the plantation. She only had to inform the person in charge of watching Carsie of her destination. She poked her slightly oversized nose into every nook and cranny. She helped the Negro children gather eggs and learned how they were laid. She saw the hatching of new chicks and the birth of horses, kittens and other farm animals.

Excursions with the colored women taught her which plants were used for dyes, which for medicines, tonics, scents, spices, or drying for winter bouquets. When animals were slaughtered for food, the girl stood by, wide-eyed, but not dismayed; she understood the reason for it.

Uncle Minot remarked one day, when he was visiting the cottage, "The child seems to have boundless curiosity. I have questioned her about matters she asks to have explained, and I'm convinced that she really understands. It will be interesting to see how much she retains."

That autumn, Mary Alice looked forward to trips into the woods to gather nuts. An all-day picnic for the plantation children was planned for each trip. Different groves of trees made for a diversity of locations for the outings. There were butternuts, black walnuts, chestnuts and hazelnuts. Each called for a holiday as they were ready for harvest. Autumn was a wonderful time for all the children.

There weren't many white children on the plantation; these were the offspring of the relatively few white servants in the house. Outwardly, any distinction or prejudices between the two races were non-existent. There were subtle differences, however. Ernest discovered that the inadequate tutoring by the parents of the white children was less effective than the education being given the colored children. He suggested the establishment of one school for all. Here, he met with objections from both sides.

The Negro parents feared that their young would become uppity if they were schooled with the whites. In turn, the white parents' objections were founded in a growth of *"familiarity breeds intermarriage."*

Ernest found himself with supervision of two separate schools. Just where Mary Alice and Carson would fit in was a problem. They were neither of the servant world nor on a level with the children of the master of the house. He solved the problem over initial objections from all quarters by establishing the Negro school's curriculum after the basic three Rs, adding special studies in horticulture and agriculture. The other school dealt more with skills the children would encounter in maintaining the plantation house or pursuing another career. According to their abilities and aptitudes, some children were put into groups that were racially mixed for only part of the day.

Mary Alice's thirst for learning, from the age of seven on, was both voracious and omnivorous. By completing her assigned lessons in half the time allotted, she was allowed to spend the remainder of the time according to her current interest. Thus, she absorbed a practical knowledge in every phase of both schools.

Having read virtually every book upstairs multiple times and borrowing some of the appropriate books in Uncle Minot's library, Mary Alice, at ten, was given the full use of the shelves in the big room. Uncle Minot and Ernest guided her choices carefully. This scenario continued for several years.

For some weeks after her twelfth birthday, Mary Alice was unusually quiet and thoughtful. Then one day, as if a burden had been lifted from her, she requested a conference in the large living room. Uncle Minot, Mrs. Mayton, her mother, father and Annabelle sat together, expectantly.

"All right, Young Lady," said Minot, with a thinly veiled puzzled expression mirrored by the other four adults, "Would you please tell us what is the purpose of this meeting?"

Mary Alice got up from her chair, squared her slender shoulders and stood as tall as she could manage. "Mama and Papa, I don't want to hurt your feelings, but I would like to come and live in this house if Uncle will allow me to, and if Mrs. Mayton and Annabelle agree. Now that Elizabeth and Imelda are married, there are empty rooms. I would like to be here, nearer to the center of all the things I like to do and would like to learn.

"On the days that mama isn't here, I can substitute for her in the sewing room. Mrs. Mayton and mama both know that I am almost as well trained in sewing and millinery as Mama, and I'm learning the fine needlework. I want to know more about many things. I would also like to spend more time with Annabelle, learning social graces. And being closer to the library would help me, too.

"Papa, you know I can help you in the schools if I'm here all the time. I can even help the slower students after you've gone home.

"This way, too, Carsie can have the small bedroom at home to himself. It's inconvenient, now that I am almost grown, to have him leave the room while I change clothes. Carsie is old enough to want more privacy, too.

"I would like all of you to think about it for a few days and discuss the matter. I will abide with your decision."

She took a deep breath and asked to be excused from the room.

"Wow!" said Minot. "That was a long speech from a young girl. She must have been thinking about this for some time. No wonder she hasn't been her usual, cheerful self, of late."

He paused, looking thoughtful. "She has some good arguments there. Other than the actual separation from the life at the cottage, Ernest and Ercyline, I see no objection. However, she is your daughter. You would be seeing her almost daily, in any event. You would, of course, be the arbiters of any problems that might arise."

Ernest and Ercyline, both looking a bit dazed, nodded their heads in agreement.

"Mrs. Mayton," he continued, "what about you? What are your thoughts?"

"It's not my decision, of course, but the child is no trouble, indeed, quite the opposite. She is often an asset to me. I can trust her to take messages, for one thing. She has even attended to matters for me more quickly than I could myself these last two years, since stair climbing is becoming difficult for me."

Annabelle was next to speak. "Father, I can see the child's point of view. She is maturing rapidly and ought to have a room of her own. If she's really interested in the social graces, it would be my pleasure to teach her. And as Mrs. Mayton says, Mary Alice can often be a big help to us."

Ernest and Ercyline requested time to discuss the matter in private for a day or two.

Annabelle smiled to herself at the flattery used by Mary Alice in hinting that she admired and would like to emulate her. Since her sisters had married, she had become the chatelaine of the house. For no reason apparent to herself or anyone else in the family, she had never married. Swains by the dozens had pursued her, but found their mates at her parties. Suitors still called on her, but now they were most often widowers. At thirty-one, she was more ripely beautiful than in her youth. Maturity had sharpened her wit and mellowed, even further, her thoughtfulness and warm heart; though she never met the man who could capture it. Even she had no idea how this had come about. She merely accepted, graciously, her life as it was.

The discussion at the cottage was long and serious. Mary Alice was called in to repeat her reasoning. Ernest felt that she must understand the reality of her station in life.

"Mary Alice, you must realize that, though you admire Annabelle, you can never hope to be a true daughter of the house. We are merely living on their bounty. Your chances for further university education are non-existent. Uncle Minot does not owe you that, and we cannot afford it. I can lay out courses of study for you and test you on them, but your educational level, no matter how high, can never be accredited without transcripts and diplomas from established schools. There are few places where a woman is valued in intellectual circles. There are even fewer career choices for you. You must examine your own reasons for this proposal very thoroughly."

Mary Alice slept fitfully for several nights. The possibilities of the range of learning to which she could aspire versus the chances of application of that learning spun through and through her mind. She made her decision and approached her parents.

"Mama and Papa, even if I **never** have the opportunities to apply what I learn, I **dream** of the things in this world to know. I feel that

I must learn all that I can, so that no matter what is required of me, I can do it. I really do think that, in the main house, I can learn even more than what is in books."

Ernest's concern was that his daughter would aspire to more than what she could hope to attain. Would her spirit be crushed in disillusionment? Ercyline's concerns were in quite another direction. Mary Alice was the only person who could control Carsie.

In his early years, he had learned to manipulate the people around him with tantrums, tiresome pleading and outright disobedience. As he grew older, the problem increased. The childish behavior had been so rewarding that he had never matured emotionally. Now at the age of nine, he was seldom in school. Many times Ernest had literally dragged him into the classroom kicking and yelling objections. The first moment that his father/teacher turned his back, the boy was out of the room and out of sight.

He had a following of both white and Negro fellow truants who roamed as they pleased. No amount of punishment meant more to them than the challenge of getting away. Carsie was a big-boned, tall boy; stronger than boys two or three years older than he; therefore, he was the leader.

Some boys, attracted by the glamour of freedom, joined the group for a short time. They soon dropped out when they experienced the brutality meted out to those at the bottom of the pecking order.

Not satisfied with freedom to fish, swim and laze about, the pack of boys evolved into hoodlums. They terrorized animals and bullied other children. They obtained whatever they wanted by frightening younger children into procuring it for them. Threats of bodily injury for tattling kept their victims demoralized and silent.

Mary Alice moved into the plantation house and was no longer available to assist Ercyline in minimal discipline of Carsie. Ernest's attempts at physical punishment were waylaid by Ercyline's pleas for mercy for the boy. She was repeatedly duped by his fawning promises to "never do it again".

His misbehavior accelerated after Mary Alice moved out of the cottage, so that Carsie was no longer allowed to attend family or social functions at the plantation house. It became impossible to take him to church services. He delighted in disrupting the company at dinners or children's parties, so he was banished from them, too. Ercyline became so upset that she agreed to Ernest's escorting Carsie to a boys' school in Springfield. It was noted for strict discipline and reformation of boys such as Carsie. The group of truants disbanded in a matter of weeks.

One month after his departure for the school, Carsie walked into the cottage with a triumphant sneer on his ruddy face. He told a wild tale of cruelty and deprivation. "I just told them I was going home, and walked out."

On that same day, a letter was delivered to Ernest at the plantation house. It was from the headmaster of Carsie's school.

> Much like a magnet, your son drew to himself four of the worst troublemakers in his dormitory. They succeeded in terrorizing their classmates. One of the smaller boys had to be sent to the infirmary with a broken arm and severe bruises. The culprits were confined to quarters, but managed to subdue the upperclassman set to monitor them. The dormitory room was vandalized and money stolen from the monitor.
>
> Your son and two other boys have left the school campus. We can only hope that they have returned to their homes. Your son will not be considered for further enrollment in this institution.

Disregarding Ercyline's plea that Carsie had merely been homesick, and that allowances should be made, Ernest thrashed Carsie thoroughly and sent him off to his room without supper. The following morning he was gone, out the window on a rope made of his bed sheets. Within two days, the truant band was reunited, and set off on new, even more depraved exploits.

With Minot's permission, a meeting of the parents of the band was called by Ernest. It was agreed that the gang should be rounded up, and a plan for control of the boys was formed: Each boy was to be accompanied to class six days a week by an adult member of his family: a parent, grandparent or older sibling. The family member would stay in the classroom for half a day. After lunch, the boys would be escorted, each to a different place, and put to hard physical labor. By suppertime, they were too tired to sneak out of their sleeping quarters.

On occasion, one of the band would manage to escape from the labor crew. For each half day of absence, a full day of labor was assigned. One by one the boys began to be proud of their labors and vied with one another to see who could accomplish the most in the half-day period. Their school work improved for fear of assignments to full day labor; the penalty for low grades. The parents agreed to lavish praise for periods of good behavior and better test results.

Ernest arranged for a long talk with Ercyline and their pastor, after which she agreed not to interfere with Ernest's discipline of Carsie. Eventually, she came to be a passive participant in his discipline.

Residence in the plantation house was all that Mary Alice had anticipated. While she studied, tutored household students and spent afternoons helping out in the sewing room, she continued to develop her knowledge and skill in the fine arts. While investigating the duties of the servants and staff, she mastered each of their fields of work, one by one. She kept a notebook for each exploration.

The laundry of bed linens, towels and coarser cotton garments of the household was done in the yard by the Negroes. It was the task of the household women to care for the fine table linens and the wardrobes of family members and related items. They were experts in smoothing and ironing what articles were done in the house.

Mary Alice found this department interesting until the heat and weight of the sad-irons was introduced. A fire in the small stove in the laundry had to be kept going no matter how hot the weather, so that the sad-irons could be heated. During the time of her study the first coal heated irons were brought from St. Louis, by Annabelle. This was a help, but it was mid-summer and the heat was stifling.

Mary Alice talked with the laundress and then with Mrs. Mayton. The result was that the ironing was done in the cool of the very early mornings. The level of respect for Mary Alice went up several notches in the servants opinions.

Observation of the Kitchen was an on-going project. Minot had been spoiled by his wife, he said. He asked of Mrs. Mayton that the menus be widely varied at all times, as they had been when his wife Caroline had ruled the house.

Mary Alice learned the art of meal planning and made a point of being in the kitchen when dishes with which she was not familiar were being prepared.

Annabelle had brought with her a personal maid from St. Louis. She was a woman in her mid-thirties when May Alice made her the object of observation. Annabelle tolerated this intrusion on her privacy in good humor. The maid, Jenny, had an outstanding talent for hairdressing, so that Annabelle became the envy of the ladies of Linnville when she appeared in the latest of elaborate coiffeurs.

Among the talents Mary Alice learned from Jenny was the art of arranging flowers into wreaths and from human hair. It was the custom to cut short the hair of women who suffered from chronic headaches. Jenny made the wreaths and presented them as gifts to their owners. Mary Alice enjoyed this new craft, and soon became as expert as her teacher.

In exchange for Mary Alice's assistance in some of her duties, Jenny took time to initiate her pupil into the mysteries of a ladies toilette. She taught her to do her own luxurious hair in a more becoming and grown-up style. This became a subject of some discussion with Uncle Minot and her parents. Whether Mary Alice was old enough to put up her hair was the subject of a conference. Uncle Minot's opinion was that she was mature enough for this momentous step. Along with this, would come the lowering of her dresses to ankle length. Her parents reluctantly conceded, but required her to wear mid-calf dresses and unpin her hair when she went home to the cottage on visits.

"My girl," said Ernest, "you must look at yourself in regard to your surroundings. In the main house you are becoming a young woman, but in this house you are still our little girl. Your mother and I feel more comfortable when you are dressed according to your position in our family."

Chapter Eight

THE BUTTERFLY EMERGES

"Mr. Minot, Sir, I need very much to talk to you about Miss Mary Alice." Mam Ginny had stopped her employer in the yard. "She's asked to accompany me and my helpers on our nursing rounds. She must have been reading some good bit of medical subjects. For a girl of fifteen, she seems to know a lot about medical matters. She's asked to go with us to learn first-hand what she knows only from books. I told her that I would have to talk to you about it first."

Minot stood thoughtfully, combing his fingers through his thatch of iron-grey hair. "Come walk along with me to the orchard if you have the time. We'll talk this out. I need to know what sort of cases you're handling now before I can decide; then I'll have to speak with her father about it, too."

Mam Ginny nodded and fell in step. She outlined the simple illnesses that were her current concern. Minot agreed that these seemed proper enough for Mary Alice to observe, but asked Mam Ginny to wait until he could talk with his nephew that afternoon.

Ernest's permission was granted. Mary Alice seemed quietly pleased, though she was inwardly ecstatic. She felt that Mam Ginny would be more impressed if she restrained herself. She began the first of many volumes of medical notes that very next day.

Over the next two years, as more complex cases occurred, Mary Alice acquired a sound nursing education under the nurse/midwife's careful watch.

The spring of her seventeenth birthday, there was an epidemic of influenza that was more severe than any Mam Ginny had ever seen. She and her assistants were working long hours over their patients. Mary Alice was delegated her own cases to care for. She had only the rare supervision that the midwives could spare from their own rounds.

Mam Ginny's chief assistant approached her during the second week of the siege. "Mam Ginny, Miss Beebe's patients are getting better sooner than all the rest. Did you give her the least sick ones to care for? We're all wondering at how fast they're out of bed."

"No, Miss Mary Alice is a competent nurse; as good as any of you. I had no time to consider the type of cases I gave her. I'll look into it later today. Thank you for telling me about it."

Mam Ginny sought out Mary Alice and asked to see the patients under her care. All but one of the patients assigned her were out of bed, and Mary Alice had taken on the care of other members of their families or immediate neighbors who summoned her.

"I'm sorry, Mam Ginny, that I didn't tell you about the others; they just happened. I gave them a tea I brewed from a plant I know about. It grows wild in the pine grove. It made their bowels flux quickly and then return to normal. They didn't vomit anymore, either. I gave them your medicine, too. Their fevers dropped in a few hours and they felt much better. So many others got sick so fast that I didn't have time to tell you.

"Just now, I was coming to find you and tell you that my first cases are doing so well that they don't need me anymore. Their families can see to what little care they need. I can take on some of the newer cases, so the other nurses can rest a bit."

Mam Ginny was perturbed at this unauthorized treatment, but she decided that Mary Alice was right in her evaluations: Her patients had recovered much faster than anyone could expect.

"What was the plant you used to make the tea?" she asked. "Did you read about it? If not, how did you know to use it?"

"I don't know its name. I've never found it in the medical books. Ever since I was little, and Carson and I played in the woods, I've seen sick animals eat the leaves and get well again in an hour or two. I asked Carsie to get me some leaves on his way in from the fields. I made the tea and gave it to the patients. It seemed to clear the malady out of their bowels and soothe their belly cramps. I should have told you, but we've all been so busy that I haven't had the chance to see you."

Mary Alice hung her head, waiting for the torrent of criticism that Mam Ginny was known to unleash on presumptuous assistants. The silence became unbearable. The girl cocked her head and looked up to gauge the start of Mam Ginny's anger. She found the old woman's face twitching with a quizzical smile.

"Don't you ever do such a thing again, young lady. It's true that you're white and a member of Mr. Minot's family, but..." There was a pregnant pause, "I am the head nurse and midwife in these parts, and responsible for the care of all the sick. I might be colored, but I am the one who has to answer to the doctor."

She smiled broadly, then put her arm around the girl's shoulder. "After I've made my own rounds, you and I are going off to the pine grove to get more of those leaves for all the others. Go on up to the kitchen and tell the cook to send her gallon tea urn to my cabin. I'll meet you there."

Mam Ginny walked away shaking her head, with a spring in her step that hadn't been there for many a day. Mary Alice almost ran up the graveled walk to the kitchen. She was giddy with relief.

Several other similar situations came about as Mary Alice cared for patients. Each time, she was careful to tell Mam Ginny about it first, and described the treatment and effects. Some of the other nurses resented this young white woman who advanced so rapidly in Mam Ginny's regard. Suspicions were, among some circles, that Mary Alice may be a witch; how else could she heal diseases that no one else could? Mary Alice gave all the credit to God.

Within a year, Mary Alice had become indispensable to Mam Ginny, and was accorded the respect and privileges of a qualified nurse/midwife.

For her eighteenth birthday, Minot presented Mary Alice a letter of acceptance for one year at the Young Ladies' Academy in St. Louis. It was a dream she had never expected to realize. Ernest was pleased with his uncle's generosity but doubted the wisdom of the idea. He felt that his daughter might either be snubbed by the daughters of St. Louis society or return home with airs beyond her station in life.

The sewing room buzzed for weeks in preparation of a wardrobe for the tall, full-bosomed, but slender young lady that had emerged from the cocoon of her childhood years. Her slightly oversized Roman nose was considered a mark of aristocratic beauty. She had the sloped shoulders and swanlike neck so aptly suited to the high-collared day dresses and the low-cut evening gowns dictated by current fashion.

The only flaws precluding real beauty were her dark, sallow complexion and her wide, thin-lipped mouth. Artful patting of cheeks and biting of lips could add color, as cosmetics were considered unsuitable for young ladies. By far her best feature was her large, intelligent black eyes, fringed with long dark lashes and framed by perfectly formed eyebrows; expressive eyes, but known to snap in anger. Uncle Minot's favorite joke was that if her angry glances had not been filtered through those thick lashes, the recipient of the glance would surely be reduced to a small pile of ashes on the spot. Too, her smile was a delight to see. Annabelle often remarked that when Mary Alice's smile lit her face, it also flooded the room around her with brilliance.

In September of 1884, Annabelle chaperoned a nervous and excited Mary Alice to St. Louis. They had a delightful week introducing the country cousin to the wonders of the city. They enjoyed theaters, musical evenings, afternoon teas, morning walks along the river front and a day trip aboard a paddle-wheel steamer. There were also carriage rides through the city. Mary Alice was still wide-eyed when she was presented to the Dean of the Academy.

Here again, was another world to experience; a world of bells, routine, ritual and females by the dozens. Unaccustomed to the company of young women of her own age on so intimate a basis, Mary Alice found herself on the edge of groups. She was too mature for the giggling cliques and too inexperienced for the discussions about men. She was completely unfamiliar with the world of urban society and her defense was to wrap herself up in a world of books, available in the school's vast library.

Before the end of the fall term, Minot sent for Ernest. He had before him a letter from the Dean of the Academy. "Well, Ernest, it would seem that we have done almost too well by your young lady's education. This letter arrived this morning. I think you should read it."

Ernest took the heavy cream-colored sheet from his uncle. After a formal salutation, the Dean had proceeded immediately to the matter at hand.

> Mr. Beebe: We were pleased to accept a fourth young lady of your household to our campus in September. However, we now find ourselves at a loss as to what to do with her. Ernest glanced up from the letter with a look of thoughtful questioning. "Go on", said Minot with a twinkle in his eye. "it gets even more interesting."
>
> We find, upon testing your niece after but two weeks of classes, that her level of education is equal to or beyond what we could offer her. Her knowledge of demeanor, deportment and social graces is developed to the fullest, and admirably so. Her intellect is astounding.
>
> The only point lacking is one in which we cannot assist, since it is impossible to devote her entire day to a matter that comes only with experience in social intercourse.
>
> She has little in common with the young ladies with whom she is now dwelling. Her maturity, otherwise, is far beyond her years. We suggest that she be withdrawn from the academy at the Christmas break.
>
> Miss Beebe has been an interesting and refreshing challenge to the faculty. Unfortunately, she has met the challenge and bested us.

Ernest put the letter back on his Uncle's desk and sighed, "Well, it would seem that we both underestimated our girl. What will we do with her now?"

Minot chuckled. "You know, my Boy, I have three-daughters-worth of experience. I say we expose Mary Alice to a wider field of social life in the town and let Annabelle advise her. She's a handsome young woman. It should be but a very short time before some fine young man discovers her charms. Bring her home, by all means. We shall have a Christmas ball as an unofficial debut."

Ernest travelled to St. Louis to escort his daughter back to the plantation. There was a warm family dinner to welcome her home.

Carsie was subdued but elated at the return of his beloved sister. He had very much missed her visits to the cottage and the talks they shared on the walks back to the main house. Carsie had learned that hard work and the praises he received from his parents and Uncle Minot were far more rewarding than the camaraderie and mischief of the pack of delinquents he had led before. He had given his life to Jesus during Mary Alice's absence and was thinking about going to seminary after finishing his studies at home. He was as intelligent as his sister but his talents and interests were in a different direction. He was a natural leader.

At the Christmas ball, Mary Alice stood in the reception line inside the double doors of the big living room. Annabelle had invited a number of young men from Lynnville; some not from the most prominent families. Their older brothers or cousins were not on her own or her sisters' debut guest lists.

"After all," she reasoned, "Mary Alice will have no dowry from cousin Ernest. Perhaps Father might provide a minimal one. The parents of young men of good prospects would be dubious of an alliance with the daughter of pensioners."

A holiday visitor accompanying a Lynnville gallant caught Mary Alice's eye. The young men were somewhat tardy arrivals and she had more time to chat with them and evaluate what she saw. Her eyes had widened involuntarily when she looked up, up. She was tall; five feet and eight inches and wore two inch heels. Frank Walden towered above her; six feet three or more. He was impeccably dressed and his yellow mane was combed in the latest fashion. A well trimmed reddish moustache framed his flirtatious smile.

Frank was instantly attracted to this tall, dark beauty. Her innocence and interest were betrayed by her downward looks and shy smile.

He was an expert in the science of seduction. Matters concerning women from the age of fourteen to forty had caused his expulsion from two colleges. His holiday visit with his classmate from the state university was an evasion of parental tirades due to the third expulsion, and for the same reason as before; women found him irresistible. He was handsome, charming, gallant, an expert dancer, and had a semi-trained melodious tenor voice. He had acquired enough education between expulsions to discourse wittily on many subjects. Parents of his friends, until they learned of his faults, were happy to have their sons and daughters associate with this personable young man of good family, who neither drank excessively nor gambled.

Luckily, he had received his quarterly allowance from home before the university's letter to his parents had reached its destination. He had wired his family of his invitation and acceptance of holiday hospitality. That he'd neglected to say where he would be visiting was a tactical oversight.

During the ball at the Beebe mansion, Mary Alice was the envy of the other young ladies eager to practice their wiles on Frank. He danced once with each of them as duty prescribed, but every free dance was signed on Mary Alice's card. Her eyes hypnotized him only a bit more than her slender figure and bounteous bosom attracted him. She was gay and charming. She danced well and her conversation was more than the empty chatter of most of the town girls he had met until then. Her obvious intelligence would be a challenge. He planned and discarded several modes of seduction as fast as his opening gambits were checkmated, one by one, in a most charming and apparently innocent manner.

Through twelfth night, Frank was Mary Alice's frequent escort to social gatherings of several kinds. He found himself to have feelings for Mary Alice that he hadn't previously experienced. All the other girls and women he'd dated before had been merely ramparts to be stormed to prove his self-image as conqueror.

Just after the New Year, Frank's classmate Bill became ill with a respiratory ailment that proved resistant to all treatments prescribed by his doctor. The young man fell into an emotional depression that the doctor feared would countermand any good that medical science could do. Bill's parents begged Frank to stay on. His sunny disposition and witty banter seemed to supply a lift of spirits for their son that nothing or no one else could do. He accepted the invitation because he wanted an excuse to stay near Mary Alice and away from his parents.

Hoping that a show of penitence would alleviate what he hoped were weeks of worry, Frank finally wrote to his parents in February of his decision to stay on as long as needed to help his friend. No answering letter arrived from home. In early March, there was a message requesting that he visit the office of a Lynnville attorney. In the law office, he was presented a fearsomely formal document that stunned him. The paper informed Frank that he was disowned and disinherited by his family.

Head down and shoulders sagging, he left the office. He walked for hours trying to assimilate this dreadful state of affairs. Hadn't they always forgiven him after a time? Wasn't he always welcomed home, if not with open arms, with warm greetings? Hadn't the family always returned to their usual cordial way and made no further mention of his escapades? What now? What was he to do? For now he was welcome to stay on, unquestioned, as long as he was a help to his friend.

That night, he didn't return to Bill's house. He felt the need to assert his manhood, so went to a brothel where he found himself unable to perform. His love for Mary Alice haunted him. She was the one he wanted to be with, but she was a proper Christian lady whom he respected.

After he left the brothel, he walked around in deep thought until after breakfast time, then went to the Beebe manor to see Mary Alice. She could tell immediately that something was wrong. He wasn't his usual cheerful self, and he looked like he'd been up all night.

"Would you take a walk with me?" He said "I need to talk to someone and can't think of anyone else I can trust with this information."

She got her coat and took his arm. Once they were out of earshot of the house and found a place to sit down, he took a deep breath and slowly told her what had transpired the day before. Before he knew it, he had poured out his entire sordid past.

Mary Alice was sympathetic but dismayed at the revelation that the man she had fallen for had such a dire reputation. She told him that she would have to ponder this information for a fortnight and get back to him. "But in the meantime, why don't you go talk with our pastor? Maybe he can guide you as to what to do in light of this development."

"I've never been a religious man," he said, "but if that's what you recommend, I'll try it. I value your opinion. You probably don't want to hear this in light of what I just told you, but I have fallen in love with you, Mary Alice. I would do anything to win your favor back." He rose, kissed her hand and went his way, leaving her to her thoughts.

A week later, Mary Alice was pleasantly surprised to see Frank sitting next to the pastor's wife on the front pew at church. They made brief eye contact, but neither made any effort to speak to or even approach the other.

Uncle Minot and Annabelle made note of this but didn't broach the subject. They had observed her quietness and fallen countenance ever since their last meeting. They assumed that the two had had a lover's quarrel of some kind.

Ernest and Ercyline had remained home that day, as they were feeling a little under the weather. All of them had assumed that Mary Alice and Frank would be announcing their engagement before too long. Several more weeks went by, during which time, Frank met many times with The Beebe's pastor and surrendered his life to God.

His friend Bill began to recover his health. Frank had been a steady source of strength and cheer. Bill's father was a lawyer, and had offered Frank a job as a clerk. But Frank wasn't interested in that line of work.

Mary Alice found herself engrossed in a whooping cough epidemic that consumed her time and energy, so that she didn't get back to Frank, as she had said.

Frank grew restless without a challenge or Mary Alice's company, so he packed his bags and headed for the train station figuring, after not hearing from her for this long, that she must have decided to discontinue their relationship.

Broken-hearted, Frank said farewell to Bill at the train station in Springfield and boarded the train. He had decided to go west, to Oregon territory. Half a continent away, there had to be opportunity for a new start.

Chapter Nine

THE BIG ADVENTURE

Frank entered the railroad car at the rear and paused to assess the seating possibilities. The car was well over half full. Halfway up in the car, in a window seat, he saw an attractive slender neck above the seat back. It was topped by a full, dark chignon and a feathered hat. Frank strode down the aisle and swept off his hat. He smiled most winningly and asked, "Miss, is this seat taken, or might it be too bold to ask to occupy it?"

The lady turned from the window and Frank found himself looking squarely into the soft black eyes of Mary Alice!

Frank collapsed into rather than sat on the seat.

He was speechless for a minute. He couldn't believe his eyes! Her smile told him everything he needed to know. He took her hands in his and they sat looking into each other's eyes while he regained his composure. Then he broke the silence, "I thought I'd lost you forever. How did you know where to find me?"

"Never mind how. We are together and on our way to share the rest of our lives. Whatever your destination is, we'll make a home there for ourselves. Just sit quietly for a bit and then tell me where we're going."

Frank looked seriously at her. "I have no concrete plans. My thought was to go to Oregon. There have been reports of a booming economy there. A man should be able to find a reasonably good position somewhere. Are you sure you're ready to face the uncertainty? I have very little funds except train fare to the end of the rails at the Idaho/Oregon border. From there I hoped to earn my passage down the Columbia River to Portland. The problem is that I don't have enough money to take you with me once we reach Chicago."

She smiled and squeezed his hand, "Uncle Minot and Father gave me money in lieu of a dowry. I have enough to pay my way and a little extra for food and to set up housekeeping wherever we end up. I must warn you right now, though, that I will make the decisions on when and on what to spend it. We'll have to be careful of what we have. But we're both young and strong enough to work it out when we get to Oregon."

It was a tiring day's journey to Chicago. At the terminal, they had no trouble finding the right ticket window to buy passage to Duluth, Minnesota, where they would change trains again to the end of the line. They had less than two hours between trains, and whiled away the time with a light dinner at a coffee shop in the station.

The Duluth-bound cars were more comfortable than those of the branch line from Springfield. The coach in which Frank and Mary Alice rode was not as crowded, and they were able to find facing seats so that they had freedom of movement.

By morning their initial awkwardness had vanished. Their youth and renewed air of romance charmed their fellow passengers, who took them for newlyweds. The lovers decided to go along with the illusion.

Though this train was more comfortable with its upholstered seats, it wasn't long before the heat of the prairie day dictated that some of the windows be opened. Immediately, soot blew in to cover everything and everyone with a gritty gray coating. The passing flat landscape grew tiresome. To relieve the monotony, the passengers started making friends.

Someone began to sing a lullaby to a fussy child. It was picked up by someone nearby and then by a majority of the rest. Frank soon became the unofficial song leader. The singing helped them all to forget the misery of the journey for a few hours.

The young couple started playing games with some of the restless children so their parents could take a break. They also took turns telling stories to the youngsters.

Mary Alice was pleasantly surprised to see this side of Frank's nature. He was a child among children as he capered along the car leading a game of follow the leader. A bag of peanuts bought from the roving food vendor provided an hour of entertainment as Frank taught the children to toss the nuts into the air and catch them in their mouths.

Duluth finally appeared out of the black of a rain-drenched night. It was late and the food vender hadn't appeared with his box lunches at the dinner hour. On-going passengers stormed the little restaurant to purchase what they could of portable food in the hour between trains.

For this next and longest leg of their journey, the cars were more primitive. Wooden seats with no padding were crowded together allowing only a minimum of leg room. A pot-bellied stove took up a great deal of space in one corner of the car. There was no water available except a ten gallon tank with a spigot for drawing drinking water. A tin cup hung from a hook on the wall next to the tank. Toilet facilities were minimal.

Most of the children were carry-overs from the Chicago train and had found playmates by the next day. Frank and Mary Alice had some time to talk quietly to each other. They planned to find a minister to marry them at the first opportunity.

Part of that day there was another round of singing. It became a game of thinking of songs with the names of the passengers. It developed into a hilarious session. When it came to Mary Alice, there were Mary songs, but no one knew an Alice title.

Suddenly, Frank's face brightened. "I know an Alice song. The first line of two stanzas are 'Alice, you are my chalice, however, the rest of the song is not fit for the ears of ladies and children. Let me see...'" In a few moments his quick mind composed a parody of three nonsensically romantic verses that had everyone applauding and laughing.

When the children started to tire, someone started singing hymns. Those who knew them joined in, and the mood changed. The stage was set for witnessing and Bible stories.

"Frank, I've been thinking," mused Mary Alice later, as most of the passengers were going to sleep, "Mary Alice is a childish name and too many women are named Mary. Would you feel uncomfortable calling me Alice?"

"Now I know we're attuned," he said. "I'd been thinking about that very thing. Mary is my grandmother's and my sister's name. It might be a good idea to get a little variety in the family. Alice it is!"

From that moment on, Alice it was. To her death, few people knew otherwise.

On the east side of the pass through the Rockies the train was stopped by a rock slide ahead. The railroad water tower and wood yard for the train were but a few hundred yards from a group of buildings that were just short of deserving the appellation "ghost town". None of the false-front stores and shacks had been painted for decades. Some leaned crazily against their neighbors as if for mutual support.

The conductor came through the cars with an announcement. "Ladies and gentlemen! The slide ahead won't be cleared and the tracks repaired for approximately six hours. There's not much to see in the town but it will afford a diversion of sorts to those of you who may choose to leave the cars while we're waiting. There will be three long blasts of the whistle in warning. You'll have sufficient time to return before we roll."

Most of the passengers were happy to leave the crowded train for a bit, to stretch their legs and get relief from the hard bench seats. Alice and Frank loitered behind the rest.

They approached a bearded man who was leaning against a building nearest the edge of the town. "Tell me Sir," said Frank, "is there a court of any sorts in town? We would like to apply for a marriage license."

The man looked up at the tall stranger. "Nope, no court. Thar be a J. P. up the street, though. You'll hafta look close to see the letterin' on the front of the buildin'. It's almost all sandblasted off from the goldang wind always blowin' 'round here."

Frank thanked the man, and he and Alice strode off arm in arm up the dusty street. Nearly halfway along the row of dilapidated storefronts they found the faint remnants of a once gaudy sign. It read: J.D. GOLDEN, JUSTICE OF THE PEACE (licenses, registry agent, deeds and claims validated).

They had to watch where they stepped across the boards of the rotted porch. Frank reached to open the door. The glass pane had long since been replaced with boards. So out of plumb was the sill that he had to lift up on the handle to push the door inward. A cracked brass bell attached to the door clacked to announce their entrance.

An old man, heralded by a blast of stale whiskey, stumbled through a door in the rear. His once white socks below and long john shirt above his wrinkled trousers were grey and stained. He squinted his bleary eyes and peered through the gloom until he located the intruders, "Whut can I do fur ya, Sir n Ma'am?" His hoarse voice was almost unintelligible.

"Good afternoon, Sir," Frank replied. "We were led to understand that you are authorized to issue marriage licenses? The young lady and I wish to be married immediately."

"Yeah, is that so?" The old man glowered at them as if people who wanted to be wed were some sort of suspicious oddities. "Well, I guess I kin take keer o' that."

"Hank!" he bellowed, in a voice calculated to crack the sand-pitted glass at the front of the store. "Come out 'ere. These folks'll need a witness to a hitchin!"

Another old man, even dirtier and smellier than the first, came around the door frame. He was barefoot and wore nothing above the waist. The door frame was all that kept him from falling.

"Wait," said Frank hurriedly, "We would prefer a Christian ceremony, if possible. When we have the license, we would appreciate your directing us to the nearest minister."

"Wahl, that'd be a fur piece to go, young fella. Last preacher we had left town four, five years ago. He just give up tryin' t' save whut few sinnin' souls were left. Ain't had 'nuther willin' t' bury hisself in this gawd-fersaken hole. Looks like if ya wanna git hitched t'day, I'm all ya got available."

The two young people looked at one another. They shrugged their shoulders in unison and turned to the old man. "All right, I guess you'll have to do. Where do we sign for the license?" asked Frank.

After a couple of minutes of fumbling through a stack of papers and ledgers on a lopsided roll-top desk, the old man unearthed a battered book marked "Registry of Marriages". He blew the dust off the cover, placed it on a rickety table and opened it to the last entry dated several years before.

"Just sign 'ere on the nex' empty line, both o' ya. Put yer age an home address on the nex' line..." He handed Frank the stub of a pencil. "Sorry... ain't had no ink fer a year or two."

Frank and Alice signed the registry, while the man fumbled further into the desk for a small book. He blew its dust off and sneezed. He opened the small book and held it tipped toward what small amount of light came in through the window. His nose two inches from the print, he intoned a garbled version of a ceremony.

"There!" he pronounced as he closed the book, "yer hitched by the 'thority o' the State o' Montana. That'll be two bucks fer the registry an two bucks fer me. Yu kin toss Hank four bits fer his trouble, too." Then the two old men signed the registry book as official and witness.

Frank and Alice stood for a moment, confused, "When do we get our copy of the certificate?" Frank asked.

"Tell ya; been outa the fancy c'tif'cates fer a couple years. I'll send a r'port to the cap'tal. Then ya kin write to 'em n they'll send ya one. It'll take a while, though. I kin write ya a note an sign it, that'll haf t' do ya fer now."

"But wait, what is four bits?" Alice wanted to know. "Is a bit a special coin in this state?"

The two old men looked at one another and then the Justice cackled. "Well, Miss, I mean Missus, yu'd best get usta that. In th' gold n silver minin' days, banks out 'ere in the West couldn't keep 'nough small change; too many folks movin' in all at once. They got t' cuttin' silver dollars inta eight pieces. Two bits was worth a quarter, four bits fer half a dollar, an so forth. There's still a lot o' them 'round, even if they ain't legal no more. Folks got t' callin' the legal coins two an four bit pieces. Git used to it or folks'll know yer greenhorns."

He pocketed the money Frank counted out and held out his hand to both of them in congratulations. Both old men turned back to the doorway, smacking their lips in anticipation of more whiskey.

Out on the street again, Frank apologized to Alice for the shoddy wedding.

"Never mind, dear," she answered. "We're legally married now. It was sort of an adventure. Someday, we'll have a tall tale to tell our children about our unusual wedding." She went off into a fit of giggles that lasted back to the train.

Frank couldn't help but join in her laughter. "What a woman!" he thought to himself.

All the passengers were awe-struck by the views through the majestic Rocky Mountain range. They craned their necks to see the snowcapped crests on one side and Oohed with fear at the horrendous drop to the foamy rapids far beneath them on the other. The train seemed to cling precariously to the narrow ledges as it wound in hairpin turns up and down the mountainsides.

Down out of the Rockies, the train moved through the rolling western foothills. Suddenly, Alice glanced out her window. "Oh, my Lord! Frank, look!" she nudged his arm and pointed.

Roused from half sleep, he jumped, then leaned across her to see what had upset her so. "My Lord, is right! We'll never make it! It's not sturdy enough to carry the weight!"

The train was moving along the edge of a cliff. A dizzying drop below them, a raging torrent foamed and crashed around and between boulders as large as box cars. Ahead they could see a delicate span. The rails across it gleamed in the afternoon sun. The bridge looked as fragile as a spider's web.

The conductor entered the rear door of their car just then to see what had become almost monotonous to him. All the passengers were on one side of the car, their faces masks of horror. They seemed all convinced that they were doomed to die!

Taking a deep breath, the conductor roared, "Everyone, Attention! Will you please return to your seats?" He paused a moment until most passengers complied and the commotion died down. "We are nearing the new railroad bridge across the Snake River. The bridge is *completely* safe. It is considered a modern engineering miracle. Trains cross it every day. However... if *every* person in *every* car is hanging out the window on the same side, there could possibly be trouble. *Please* remain in your seats. You will *all* be able to see the river as we cross." He proceeded down the aisle, enforcing his command with courteous but firm urging and reassurance of stunned passengers.

As they crossed the bridge, every window was crowded with excited faces. Far below, the roar of the river added its booming to the echo of the train's passing. Sounds rebounded from the vertical walls. It was a terrifying noise, in contrast to the beauty and grandeur of the canyon.

A few hours later, the conductor again came through the train. "Huntington, Oregon in one hour! End of the line! Stage coaches are standing by to transport passengers to the Columbia River!"

Many of the passengers, including Frank and Alice, were surprised to hear the last part of this announcement. They had thought that Huntington was at the confluence of the Snake and Columbia rivers, when in fact it was a two and a half day's journey through partially mountainous terrain. Some, like Frank, were not prepared to pay additional stage fare.

Not long after they were off the train and milling about the station making inquiries, a number of roughly dressed men began circulating through the crowd. They homed in on obviously desperate people and deftly herded them to the end of the platform.

"Men, we're prepared to offer you the opportunity to earn your stage fare in jig time. We represent the Blue Mountain Logging Company. We are operating in the hills there behind you. A few weeks work in our camps will pay you enough to get you on your way. If you're interested and traveling alone, there is a wagon to your right, the green one, which will transport you to the camp immediately. You can go to work tomorrow morning.

"If you have families, the yellow wagons on your left will transport you, at no charge, to Bluetown, where we have housing, company-owned, to put them up. When you've got them settled, then we'll take you up to the camps later today."

The air buzzed with discussion and decision-making for some time as the logging company men circulated, answering questions:

"No Sir, you can't take your family up to the camps. The men sleep in bunkhouses. There are no accommodations for families."

"Yes Ma'am, the company houses aren't fancy but they'll do you for your brief stay."

"Yes Ma'am, we have a school, but it's closed now until September. You'll probably be in Portland by then."

"Yes Ma'am, we have a company store in town. You won't need funds. Your family's food and needs will be signed for and deducted from your husband's paycheck at the end of the month."

"No Sir, you'll have no expenses in camp. Your bed and board are free, above and beyond your pay."

"A dollar to two dollars a day is the pay, according to your job and the camp's production."

"Depends on the location of the camp you'll be assigned to, Sir. You may be able to see your family every Sunday or maybe only once a month if you're at one of the high camps."

No, I can't tell you which camp you'll be in. You'll have to wait until you get to headquarters to be assigned. Your family will be notified."

After a little while and some more discussion, six men climbed aboard the green wagon and were driven off toward the mountain, their baggage stowed beneath the rough plank seats across the wagon box.

Married couples and families drifted off in individual groups to talk over the opportunity offered. Frank and Alice strolled off hand in hand.

"Do you have enough money to get us both to the river, Alice?" he asked. "I think I can get better work there or work on a boat to earn our passage to Portland. Then we wouldn't be separated."

Alice looked at her husband seriously, her black eyes almost pierced his brain. "Yes, Frank, I do have *just* enough money to get us to the Columbia, but no more. I will *not* gamble with it. You'll have to take the job with the logging company for a short while. I'll be alright on my own in town. I'll find something to do to pay my own way, and you can save your wages for passage."

Frank attempted argument, but Alice was steadfast in her decision. They gathered their luggage and boarded one of the yellow wagons.

Chapter Ten

SUCCESS!

Contrary to what they had been told, the buildings in Bluetown were pitiful shacks. Unpainted and with broken windows, they were joined by a narrow boardwalk which had many missing planks. On the way up to the town, Frank and Alice had struck up an acquaintance with another young couple who had no children. The two women agreed to share one of the two-room shacks. At least they would have companionship while the men were in the camps.

One look at the ragged pads that served as mattresses on the rope-slung bed frames told Alice and Lillian what to expect. Alice lifted one corner of a pad and spread the ripped seam. Bedbugs scurried deeper into the moldy stuffing. They ordered Frank and Joe to throw the pads outside until they could be burned. They would use their coats and a lap robe Lillian had, if necessary, for bedding until new pads could be drawn from the company supply.

Two blasts of a steam whistle called Frank and Joe to the headquarters office for assignments. The two wives walked along so they could purchase food at the company store. Families stood saying forlorn goodbyes to their men, who were loaded aboard narrow wagons for the camps. Goodbyes were waved from both groups until the wagons faded into the forest.

Alice and Lillian braced themselves for a battle for new mattresses. Apparently, the company supply officer respected courage in women. They had no difficulty drawing replacements, and the officer promised to have them delivered to their shack shortly.

Foodstuffs in the company store were plentiful, but second rate and expensive. The two women bought only bare necessities; enough for two or three days. Alice sent her new friend back to the shack and found her way to the hiring office. She stepped inside the sparsely furnished room and looked around. With all the dignity she could muster she approached the most respectable looking of the four men seated at desks in the back. "Sir, my name is Alice Walden. My husband just left for one of your camps. Since I am alone, I wish to find work to occupy my time and pay my way while he is away. Would you please direct me to the proper person to whom I might apply."

The man looked up from the papers he had been scanning. "Why, I guess I'm the right person, Mrs. Walden. We sometimes hire women for certain jobs in town. I perceive that you're an educated woman, but what type of work can you do?"

"I am a seamstress and could serve as a secretary. My penmanship is excellent. Also, I am a qualified nurse and midwife. I have overseen household servants and I am an excellent cook. Any of these or whatever other position you may have to offer would be satisfactory to me."

The man scrambled to his feet. "I beg your pardon, Ma'am. A gentleman should not sit without offering a seat to a lady. Please do take this chair and rest yourself. May I introduce myself? I'm John Harney. I'm sure that we have something suitable for a gentlewoman such as yourself.

"Most important to us, but not a full-time position, I'm afraid, is a nurse for our emergency infirmary. The nearest doctor is in Boise, Idaho. Sometimes we have to send injured workers to Huntington on the train. If we had a nurse, she could accompany the injured men to make sure they get proper care on the trip. Would you consider this position, Mrs. Walden?"

"I might, however, I should like to see your infirmary first. I want to look over your facility and equipment and study your records." Alice was inwardly pleased at her success thus far. They must need a nurse desperately, she thought.

"Indeed, Mrs. Walden, do come along." He jumped up to escort her down a hallway and opened a door marked "INFIRMARY".

The outer room was, without a doubt, the gloomiest, most unsanitary medical she had ever seen. With dignity, she picked up her skirts, as if to avoid soiling them, and walked around the room, an exaggerated look of distaste wrinkling her nose. Mam Ginny would have been horrified at the idea of nursing in such a dirty place, she thought to herself.

"Mr. Harney! *This* is your infirmary? Who was my predecessor and how long ago did he or she leave, that this room has fallen into such a state? I cannot guarantee any kind of care in such... such... FILTH!"

Mr. Harney spluttered, "Mrs. Walden, I regret the state of affairs here. I had no idea the place was in such poor condition. I will see to it that someone is sent to clean it up as soon as possible." He was flushed with embarrassment. No answer was offered about any predecessor.

"I have just the person in mind, Sir," Alice said. A Mrs. Jonnason has come in on the same wagon with me. She is a conscientious worker and meticulously clean. I'm sure she could be persuaded to assist me in bringing order to this place. I do hope the other room," (she motioned) "through that door? Is in better condition."

The man rushed to the door as if to protect what was behind it from offending her sensibility. "I'm not sure, Ma'am. *Do* let me have a look first?"

"*Nonsense*, Mr. Harney, nurses are exposed to sights that make strong men cringe." She brushed him aside and opened the door. She scanned the room, "Mr. Harney, it's really not bad at all. Oh, it does need cleaning up, but it will be a small matter compared to the other room."

They turned and went back into the office area. "May I send Mrs. Jonnason to you in the morning for your approval as my assistant?" she asked.

"Oh, yes, *indeed*, Mrs. Walden, and by the way, is there anything else I can do for you to make your stay in Bluetown more comfortable?"

"Mr. Harney, there are *so* many inequities in the housing in Bluetown that it would take *weeks* to tell you about them all. However for now, I would like pillows and blankets for two beds and disinfectant to make my quarters habitable. After I have had time to assess the remainder of my needs, I will notify you."

"Yes Ma'am. I'll show you out and arrange to have the pillows and blankets delivered to your home within the hour."

Alice managed to maintain her air of dignity until she was out of sight of the headquarters building. Then laughter bubbled up from her toes until she was weak. All the way back to the shack, she alternately giggled and laughed aloud.

Lillian looked up from her bucket of sudsy water as Alice came in. She got up from her knees, leaving a puddle on the floor. "Alice, your face is so red! Are you alright? What's the matter?"

She rushed over to comfort her friend, who had collapsed on her bed; tears streaming down her face. "What is it? Has someone done something awful to you?" Lillian was frantic with worry.

Alice turned over so Lillian could see that she was shaking with laughter, not distress. She sat up, trying to control herself. "Oh, I *did* it! We're *both* going to have jobs! We'll be able to save our husbands' wages by using ours for living expenses. Mr. Harney thinks I'm a *great, fine Lady,* and he can't do enough for me!"

Using her best acting mannerisms to exaggeration, she recounted her meeting with the superintendent. The two young women rocked in each other's arms with merriment. They had a difficult time sobering up to receive the messenger with the bedding and disinfectant.

When he had left, Lillian conducted Alice on a tour of the shack. She showed her the cracks between the floorboards where the light shone through from under the house. There was no subfloor, just plain boards over the joists. Knots in the wood had fallen out here and there, leaving holes to admit even more drafts. By holding a candle next to the corners, they could see more bedbugs between the wall planks.

"Look!" Lillian showed her roommate, "Our *luxurious* household effects!" She pulled back threadbare curtains, exposing the rough, unpainted shelves.

"Oh no, not all this! How *privileged* we are!" Alice covered her mouth in mock amazement. "Four whole warped tin plates, three forks, one knife, six spoons and two tin cups!"

"With a hole in the bottom of one cup, Milady," giggled Lillian. "We must call the tinker to have it mended. Oh yes, and our utensils; fit for royalty!" She pulled out a huge, rusty cast iron frying pan and a tiny cooking pot that would hold scarcely two cups of fluid.

When they had finally managed to stop laughing, they set to work to make the shack livable. Alice drained some kerosene from a lamp. She soaked a cloth in the smelly stuff and poked it along all the cracks that might harbor the bed bugs.

Lillian finished scrubbing the floors. "We'd better not wash the windows." She said. "The dirt on them will serve to give us privacy until we can make some curtains."

By this time they were so exhausted that they ate a cold supper and fell into deep sleep as soon as the lamp was out.

The next morning, armed with rags, buckets, brooms, mops, soap and disinfectant supplied by Mr. Harney, Alice and Lillian launched an attack on the dirt of the infirmary. Alice persuaded Mr. Harney to provide paint for each room as it was cleaned. She presented him with a list of supplies for the examining room and bedding for the sick room's three beds.

As soon as they had conducted Mr. Harney and two other company officials through the shining new department three days later, the first patients arrived. Several mothers brought in children with infected, running sores. Alice treated them with lancet, poultice and bandages. Soon the condition became epidemic for both the children and their mothers.

Alice called on Mr. Harney. "Sir, this problem is becoming progressively worse. Some of the patients are running fevers.

"Would you care to accompany me on an inspection tour of the homes of the more seriously ill? We should determine the cause, if possible. We may lose some of these patients, and the town will have an unhealthy reputation. You may have difficulty in recruiting men off the trains or elsewhere."

Her dignity and persistence, by this time had the poor man completely cowed. Meekly, he followed her on a round of the shacks.

"Mrs. Walden, I had no idea conditions were this bad: Bed bug bites becoming infected cause these sores, you say?" He was viewing a fevered child whose body was more than half covered with running sores.

"Mrs. Jones, will you lift Jimmy off the bed for a moment?" Alice asked the child's mother. She spread a rip in the mattress to expose a horde of the shiny bugs. "Would you care to sleep in a bed as infested as this, Mr. Harney?"

He shuddered; too horrified to answer. In shack after shack, she showed him the conditions of the structures, as well as those of the tenants. Harney became more pale and sick with each visit. With over half the homes still uninspected, he turned to his guide. "Mrs. Walden, tell me all that is needed to correct this unconscionable state of affairs. I'll start reparative action as soon as I can get supplies. I'll write to the company offices in Portland, detailing what I've seen and ask for further expenditures. I'll call on you in the infirmary in the morning for a list of necessary actions."

Lillian was excited by the news. She, too, had been sickened by the sight of helpless children so afflicted. Together, they sat until the early hours composing a list of supplies and procedures to relieve the suffering of these hapless victims of the company's greed and neglect.

A few of the shacks were vacant, so Alice suggested repairing, disinfecting, and ridding these of pests, then moving the worst afflicted families into them as fast as possible. Each vacated shack was then worked over before another family was moved into it.

On the first Sunday, the men who worked in the nearest camps gathered in front of Harney's home. They chose a spokesman, who knocked on the door.

"Mr. Harney, we all want to volunteer our time to speed up the repairs on the houses. We're all angry and feel bad that our families have to live in these horrible places. We'll all work on Sundays to get our families into decent houses."

A roar of approval from the men told Harney that he was obligated to accept the offer. It would save on wages, too, he figured.

More could be done with his allotted funds, and faster. "Men, I'm glad to accept your offer. Follow me down to the storage yard. There I can issue tools and materials, and tell you which houses are to be done."

The men were glad to be doing something positive for their families. Results were startling and immediate. The air of resentment that had permeated Bluetown from the first day was lifted.

Unfortunately, Harney's funds didn't cover reroofing or painting. With the first fall rains, there were complaints of leaking roofs. Some of the families had to double up in the houses with fewer leaks. Alice and Lillian were among the first to apply for these repairs.

"Mrs. Walden, Mrs. Jonnason, I don't know just what to do. I'm over the limit I can expend now. I *do* have a number of tarpaulins, though not enough, to use on the worst roofs. If they are stretched taut enough, I suppose they will serve until the heavy rains start."

Alice spoke up quickly, "I remember something my mother told me. Even light canvas can be waterproofed temporarily if it's painted with boiled-down pine pitch."

Mr. Harney brightened, "That's it! I'm going to Huntington, or Boise if I have to, to get canvas. I seem to recall that there are barrels of pitch in one of the sheds in the supply yard. Tell me what else you'll need."

Writing an order as she talked, Alice promised, "I know the women will be glad to sew the canvas pieces together if it means dry homes for their children."

"I'll be on the road within an hour," he said. "I sure hope you're right. I'm putting my job on the line for this, Mrs. Walden. These poor families have been through enough already!"

"Mr. Harney, we'll all be grateful for your kindness." Alice and Lillian spoke as one, and their remark was echoed by the women who had come with them.

In reply to a sharp letter from Portland taking him to task for over expenditures, Harney replied:

We have found a direct correlation between the
improvement in the living conditions for the workers'
families and an increase in the harvest of logs. Apparently,
men who are not worried about their families' welfare
are more content and concentrate on working more
efficiently.

Nothing more was heard from the comptroller in Portland. The
bills were paid promptly to the Huntington and Boise firms who had
trusted Harney's word. Both he and Alice became heroic figures to
the employees and families of the logging company.

Chapter Eleven

STARTING A FAMILY

Over the summer of 1885 in Bluetown, Frank had been making a name for himself in the high camp. Since he was a big man, it was assumed that he was fit for strenuous labor. He was supplied with suitable clothing, leather gloves and boots, all charged against his wages, as he found out later. His pride wouldn't allow him to admit that he had never done anything more strenuous than tennis or horseback riding.

At dawn of the third day, when the bull boss clumped through the bunkhouse, rousing his crew, Frank was unable to rise from his bed. His hands and forearms were swollen, scratched and bruised. He had suffered excruciating leg cramps all through the night. The cook, who doubled as camp doctor, came to administer time-proven remedies to Frank and two others of the new men in similar straits. For two days, they were allowed to rest. The third morning, they were ordered out of the bunkhouse, groaning in protest, to limber up the tightened muscles with light duties.

The bull boss cursed them for not admitting at the start that they were not in good condition. They were docked five days' pay. At the end of the month, when Frank returned to Bluetown for two days off, he had but one dollar to show for his labors. Other men were similarly docked for other infractions. Men with three or more children found that they not only had no pay but were in debt to the company store for their families' expenses.

Frank's strength built up over the next few months through hard labor. He began to be proud of his new abilities and was made a crew boss because of his education. Other, older men of equal ability and strength, more experience but less education were at first resentful. Frank's sunny nature and sense of fairness, however, soon won them over. He was a lady's man, true, but he also enjoyed the companionship of men as well. He was popular with bosses and crews alike. He had the ability to lead men; to make them want to work harder for him. Frank worked along with them and asked no man to do a job that he wouldn't do himself. He encouraged his crew to join in after-hours recreation to lighten their loneliness and build their camaraderie. He also held Bible studies and prayer groups for those few who wished to attend.

In October, autumn ice clogging the water in the log flumes signaled the end of the high camp activities. Some men were moved to the lower camps and others down to Bluetown. This latter crew went out each day to the flume catch pond to load logs onto the huge wagons for transport north across the mountains to the Columbia River.

Joe and Lillian, thanks to her work with Alice, were able to move on to Portland at the close of high camp season. Frank was assigned to the catch pond for a time. He and Alice had the house to themselves through the winter. Alice had gotten pregnant on Frank's very first weekend home and was concerned that the wagon trip over the trail north would be too strenuous.

Alice had acquitted herself admirably in her care of injured loggers over the summer and fall. It had not been necessary to escort any of her patients to Boise, but her infirmary beds were frequently in use.

At season's end Alice and Frank called on Mr. Harney. "We would like to stay on over the winter Sir," Frank said. "My wife is too far along in her pregnancy to risk the trip north. We think it's safer for her to remain here for the birth. We've decided that I will stay on with the company for as long as you are operating in this area. But I'll have to have employment to tide us over the off-season."

"Walden," replied Mr. Harney, "I hear you have an excellent record in the woods. Your supervisor gives glowing reports. He was telling me that most of your education was wasted; that you are a born logger."

"Maybe so, Mr. Harney, but he was glad of the chance to use my education in figuring his board-foot production and writing reports. He's a good boss and a respected one. I wouldn't mind working for him again."

Harney grinned, "You shall, Walden, you shall. He's already asked for you, should you wish to stay on."

Alice interrupted the men's bantering exchange. "Mr. Harney, did you get the vouchers you asked for to further improve the housing?"

"Why, yes, Mrs. Walden, I did. I've been pondering how to start. There are so few men wintering over, and those are out cutting slash for cord wood for next spring's crop of families. Come to think of it, Walden, would you take on the job of painting and repairs?"

"I haven't done any of that sort of work before...," Frank scratched his chin, "but it might be an interesting challenge. I think I'd like to try. There would be more than I can handle alone, I'd guess."

Harney replied, "The men will be in from the slash when the bad weather closes in. You could go over what needs to be done and have the work organized and supplies in from Portland and Boise by the time the men are ready. I'll need preliminary estimates and final reports of work hours and expenditures to submit to the home office. Do you think you'd care to handle that part of it too?"

"Yes Sir, I'm sure I can. The other men will be as pleased as I am to have work over the winter. I don't think there'll be any problem recruiting them. Thank you Sir, for myself and for Alice," he said as they shook hands.

Frank and Alice left the office on this happy note. She hugged his arm as they walked to their house. "Frank, I'm so glad it's worked out for us this way. Are you sure, absolutely sure, that you want to stay with logging? It *is* a waste of your education."

Frank put his finger on her lips to silence her. When they had closed the door of their house behind them, he spoke, "Woman, I feel that my whole life has been wasted before I came here. I *love* this outdoor life! I love the feeling of using my hands and building my strength. I feel really *alive* for the first time!"

She could see by the fire in his eyes that he really meant what he said. "But Frank, we have to be separated so much of the time. Can't you manage it so that you're home more often? I get so lonely here by myself."

"I'll try to arrange it, dear, but I can't promise. I have to go where they send me. You know we'll never be rich, of course, but I have a feeling that logging is going to be my life's work."

Alice smiled back. "I'm glad that you like your work. I hope you always work where you feel happy."

"Alice, the separation is hard for you, I know. Do you mind living in these company houses, now that they've got them fixed up, I mean?"

"Oh, no. I don't mind at all. It's not Uncle Minot's plantation house, nor even my parents' cottage, but where you work is my home. Out here, I lie in bed at night and hear the wind through the tree tops, the rain on the roof and the creek chuckling behind the house. It's a beautiful place to live."

Then she snuggled up to him and purred, "Mr. Walden, my feet are cold. Come on ol' logger, let's eat and go to bed where it's warm."

Mid-February, 1886 brought to the Blue Mountains one of the worst blizzards anyone could remember. The snow was driven horizontally by gale force winds. Alice was snug and warm in her newly winterized and painted house. Frank had gone out on horseback with two other men to one of the lower camps on a hunting expedition. The mountain road was too treacherous for freighting in fresh foodstuffs. The few families wintering over depended on a supply of fresh game to supplement the canned and dried goods from the company store.

Alice woke before dawn to feel the first pull of birth contractions. She put on her slippers and warm robe and went to build up the banked fire. The heavy old cast iron stove that served for both cooking and heating was still warm. Looking out the window, she could see that it would be impossible to get to the infirmary or to the neighbors for help.

She sat down before the fire with a cup of coffee to assess what needed to be done if she had to birth the child alone. On the plantation, she had brought several children into the world, and there had been a few at Bluetown, too. The process didn't frighten her.

She put on a pot of water to boil up string and scissors. She had cloths for cleaning up and sterile bandages in a bag she kept packed for emergencies. She rummaged for her stack of hard-to-come-by newspapers and an old quilt to protect the bed sheets. On a tray, she laid out oil to clean the baby, soap, a cloth and a large bowl for water to clean herself afterward.

All she could do now was wait for nature to have its way, hoping that some neighbor would be brave enough to face the storm in time to assist her. Alas, it was not to be.

She lay on the bed, pulling with all her strength on the roped sheet harnessed over the head of the bed frame. The contractions (Mam Ginny had taught her the value of never referring to them as pains) rolled over her body in waves, leaving her faint with exhaustion and wet with sweat.

In one period of relaxation, she caught herself laughing aloud at the thought of a teacher at the academy. The old-maidish woman had intoned, "Horses sweat, men perspire, women glow."

She thought to herself; if the old girl was right, I must be lit up like the candle-covered Christmas tree in the big house living room!

The joke carried her over until the next contraction. At the deepest point of this one there was a sudden splash, then a moment of relief from the pressure. She congratulated herself for having provided padding to absorb the viscous waters. Almost without pause, she felt a commanding contraction; a feeling that her body was being lifted and squeezed as if by a giant hand. Just as the hand flung her down again, she heard the baby's first choking cry. She sat up, amazed to see the boy-child lying between her feet. Her body had expelled the child with such force that his feet were thrashing a full 10 inches from her birth canal.

In a moment of exaltation, she picked up the tiny boy by his heels and massaged his abdomen and chest, then his throat, in a series of downward, gentle strokes, until his breathing passages were clear of the mucous that dribbled from his mouth. The baby inhaled sharply and deeply, then vented a series of lusty cries. Tears of relief and happiness clouded Alice's eyes. Quickly, she groped for the pile of cloths on a chair by the bed and swaddled the baby close.

She rested for a moment, wiped her eyes, then sat up to check for the afterbirth. There it lay, throbbing between her thighs. Quickly, she picked up the cord and kinked it. Holding the fold in one hand, she reached to the chair for the two pieces of sterile string. With practiced hands, she tied one tightly, close to the baby's navel and the other about two inches beyond. Then with the sterile scissors, she cut halfway between them.

Reaching for yet another cloth, Alice folded it and placed it between her legs, pulling it close to her body. She felt a release of tension and accompanying fatigue. Picking up her baby and placing him to her breast, she pulled the coverlet up over both of them and slipped into exhausted sleep, thinking how proud Mam Ginny would be!

Bang! Bang! Bang! The noise filtered through to Alice's sleep-drugged mind. A woman's voice called to her through the reinforced plank door. "Alice! Alice! Are you alright! Alice!" Again the banging.

"Wait, wait," came from her throat, but so hoarse and weak that the visitor could not have heard it. Alice put the baby aside and groped for her robe. She stumbled out of bed toward the door, "Wait, wait," she called as she rested her head against the door. This time the woman outside heard her and stopped knocking. "Just a minute, let me rest a bit." Alice took a deep breath and lifted the bar from its brackets. She clung to the frame as the door swung open.

Rachael Merdy, who lived across the narrow street, hurried inside and closed the door behind her. She looked at Alice's face and saw paleness and exhaustion. In the room she saw the evidence; the bloody cloths and the chair beside the bed with part of its load toppled to the floor. Looking back at Alice, her eyes traveled to her abdomen. "Oh my gosh! You were all by yourself! Is the baby alright? Are you alright?"

She caught Alice as she started to slide to the floor. Rachael was too small a woman to attempt to lift Alice. Quickly, she ran to the bed and snatched up a quilt. She tucked it snugly around Alice, then went back to see to the baby. Determining that the sleeping baby was alive, she left to get help.

One by one, as they were summoned by Rachael, four women entered the house. They lifted Alice to her bed once they had restored it to order. The fire was rebuilt quickly to warm the cooled room. Before long they had the baby and Alice cleaned and warmed again.

One of them brought the new sleepy mother a cup of coffee. "Have you had any food today, Alice? How long ago was the baby born?"

"No time for food. My contractions started before daylight. I don't know what time it was, but I was so tired all I could think of was sleep."

Later, they all sat down for a cup of coffee. The house was back in order and Alice fed and asleep. "Thank goodness I looked out the window when the wind stopped," Rachael said. "I knew something was the matter when I didn't see smoke from Alice's chimney."

The group agreed on a rotation to stay with Alice and her baby for a few days. Each woman was glad to be able to repay Alice's kindness to the town.

The three hunters had been isolated by deep snows. They were comfortable in the cook shack of the lower camp, used as headquarters for the hunt. A deer apiece hung in an outer building. The snow continued to fall steadily after the blizzard stopped. It was a week before the sun broke through the canopy of snow clouds. The frozen deer were loaded on the two pack mules for the trek back to town. In places, the drifts were so deep that the men had to take turns dismounting and forcing the tired horses to break a path through for the others.

Little Carson Minot was ten days old before his father held him in his arms. Frank had come home and opened the door quietly to surprise Alice. She had been standing at the window, her back to the door. He was the surprised one when he saw her, slim again, racing across the room into his arms.

Little Carsie, as he was called for many years, was a good baby; small boned and shorter than would be expected from tall parents. He was a happy child.

By spring, when the lower camps were opened again, Mr. Harney called Alice and Frank to his office. "Walden, your supervisor has asked for you at the high camp again this year. If you'd prefer one of the lower camps, I'm sure he'll understand."

Frank looked at Alice. "Let us talk it over first, Sir. I'll give you an answer tomorrow"

"Meantime," said Mr. Harney, "I have a proposition for Mrs. Walden, too. Your infirmary won't be too busy at first. You are respected by the remaining families. Would you take on the assignment of quarters for the new families and see that they are properly settled?"

"Certainly, I'll be happy to. I'm glad that these new people will have a better start than we did."

Mr. Harney had the sensitivity to blush. "Mrs. Walden, all my days I'll be ashamed that I let the town get into such condition. I'll always remember you for giving me the opportunity to atone for my unfeeling disregard for all those poor people's misery."

Alice took little Carsie to the infirmary with her. A neighbor named Mary cared for Rachael's two children when their mother was called upon to assist Alice. Rachael had acquired some nurse training back East.

This year the injuries were more frequent than the year before. Twice Alice had to escort men to Boise. The first man had a large splintered piece of timber driven completely through his shoulder joint. He was in horrible pain throughout the twenty four hour journey. Alice had repeatedly requested medication to relieve the pain of the injured men, but the Portland office refused. Since she was not a doctor, they reasoned, she was not qualified to administer drugs. The fact that injured men had to travel over rough wagon roads or lie in box cars for hours before their pain could be lightened was of no concern to them.

The doctor in Boise was horrified when he saw the injured logger in deep shock. "Why was this man not given laudanum?" he demanded to know. Alice stepped forward, putting on an air of dignity and outrage to match the doctor's.

"Because, Sir, the home office of Blue Mountain Logging won't permit me to have any in the infirmary. This poor man has been suffering agonies with every slight bump or move for nearly two days! If he survives, it will only be because he was in superb health when he was injured!"

"And who are you, young woman?!" the doctor growled. "What do you know of laudanum?"

"I am Alice Walden, nurse/midwife in charge of the infirmary in Bluetown. Now I propose that you stop questioning my qualifications and get busy helping this poor man!" Her look pierced the doctor with a ferocity that sent him back to his patient's side in a rush.

Alice followed the stretcher and the doctor into the surgery with an air that defied anyone to question her. She scrubbed her hands and donned the voluminous apron proffered by a nurse. The doctor and an orderly had cut away the logger's shirt, leaving a border around the wood that had driven the fabric into the wound. By this time, the patient had been given laudanum and was drifting into sleep; his pallor ebbed somewhat. Alice was checking the man's pulse when the doctor realized that she was across the operating table from him.

"What are...?" the doctor began. Again she transfixed him with her piercing scowl. He didn't pursue the question, but turned back to his task. Alice had kept the man turned on his uninjured side, propped into position with folded bed rolls. The doctor noticed this precaution. He looked questioningly at Alice. Her nod told him that this action had been her idea. His answering nod showed his approval. With the patient fully sedated, the long process of removing the splintered shaft began.

Pauses in the procedure were necessary at intervals to allow for more of the laudanum to be administered. The patient had to be allowed to regain enough consciousness to swallow the sweet, syrupy medicine. When at last, after four hours, the patient was put to bed in the small hospital, all the operating personnel were drenched in perspiration.

The doctor turned as he washed his hands and removed his bloodstained apron. "Ma'am I apologize for my abruptness. My name is Justin King. May I ask yours?"

"Alice Walden, as I told you before. You were so angry at the time that I don't believe you even heard me."

He glanced at her left hand, and noting the wide gold band, he said, "Mrs. Walden, I am truly sorry that I upset you. I don't know where you were trained, but you are the best nurse I've ever worked with."

"Thank you, Dr. King, I'll treasure that compliment. In exchange, I want to ask you for a favor. Where can I obtain some laudanum in the event that I have other patients in great pain? Also,

I would like to ask why you didn't use chloroform to keep your patient asleep."

"First question first. I will personally see that you have a small supply of laudanum. It deteriorates in a matter of three or four weeks, so there's no point in you having more. Send word when you need more and I'll get it to you."

"And the chloroform, Dr. King? It seems dangerous to me to let your patient awaken to that degree then wait for the effect of the drug."

"Mrs. Walden, you haven't seen as many men die from chloroform suffocation as I did during the war. It should not be used except by trained personnel. We have no one here trained to use it; it's too dangerous. Ether gas is used back East, but it's too volatile to be shipped out here. And there are no facilities near here to manufacture it. I'll continue to use laudanum until ether is more readily available."

This bit of information was stored in Alice's memory and served her well in years to come. She left her patient in the hospital and boarded the next train to Huntington. Her breasts were aching; she hadn't been able to express enough milk to relieve them for very long.

Rachael had found a woman who'd agreed to be a wet nurse to little Carsie while Alice was away. The woman was a Godsend, but there was no substitute for a baby to drain her swollen mammary glands.

In early fall, Alice and Rachael lost their first patient. An entire family had come down with the same illness. Rachael first reported it. To be safe, Alice quarantined the house.

She had never seen diphtheria before, but Mam Ginny had told her about it. She also had read a not-too-technical treatise about it in Uncle Minot's library.

Frank came down from high camp on an errand of importance to Mr. Harney just at this time. He was horrified to find that Alice would risk contracting the disease herself, or worse, maybe bring it home to little Carsie. Alice reassured him that she was taking every precaution, and he was not to worry. He went back to camp in a somber mood, mumbling to himself about the possible consequences.

The mother of the family began to recover first, then the children, in order of their ages, from the oldest on down, turned the crises and began to get better. Only the infant of the family worsened. The dirty grey membrane formed inexorably in his throat. Twice Alice burned sulfur in a pan, cooled it and blew it through a paper cone into the child's throat. It slowed the pace of the ugly growth, but the tiny body burned with fever and wasted away. Both she and Rachael immersed the child's body in tepid water repeatedly in an attempt to abate the fever.

With a final strangling rattle, the baby lay still. Seeing the expression on Alice's face, the mother screamed and reached from her bed for her baby. Alice lifted the child to his mother's arms and turned away from the pitiful scene. She walked around the little house seeing to the comfort of her other patients. One look back at the mother cradling her baby and crooning to it and her control broke. She ran sobbing out of the house.

She walked along paths in the woods until the pressure in her breasts turned her toward Mary's cabin and her own son. She took him home and sat, tears coursing down her cheeks, long after he had finished suckling and gone to sleep.

Rachael came to find her after she had found the stricken family alone. "Don't worry, Alice. I'll go to Harney's office and arrange to send for the father. He's at high camp, so it'll be a while. I'll stay with them until he comes."

Alice's head snapped up; her detachment vanished. "No, it's my fault they're alone. You go to Harney and I'll go back as soon as I can leave Carsie at Mary's."

She changed her wet baby's clothes and left him at Mary's house, then returned to take up her duties. When the mother was asleep, she took the dead baby away. She bathed him, dressed him in his best gown and wrapped him in a lacy shawl she found in a cupboard.

Then she placed him in a wicker basket in an attached shed where the cool would keep him until his father made arrangements for burial. She went back in the house with a quavering sigh. Her duty was done. It was up to the child's father now.

Chapter Twelve

THE EPIDEMIC

Late fall's shutdown of the camps was the last for Bluetown. The logging company was abandoning this area. The clear-cuts had gone beyond what was economical for building more flumes.

Frank's superintendent sent him to Harney's office. "We're moving down the Columbia near Bridal Veil Falls, about twenty five miles east of Portland," Harney said. "Your boss has asked for you as his crew boss in the new area. Will you and Mrs. Walden come with us? We'll have need of her services there, too. We're building a new company town and would like her advice."

"I was hoping you'd ask me," said Frank. "I know I can speak for my wife. We'll be pleased to move with you. You've been good to both of us. We could hardly do better."

"That's good news," Harney said, "We'll notify you of the plans for the move as soon as we have our logistics all figured out."

The Columbia River Logging Company was built on the skeleton of the defunct Blue Mountain Company. For the move to Bridal Veil Harney took with him most of the supervisory personnel and a dozen loggers. The company housing was nearly completed; it would more than double the population of the little river town. Accessibility to Portland and Vancouver would attract loggers and their families, where they would feel less isolated than in most areas.

The Waldens arrived in Bridal Veil after a week's vacation in Portland sightseeing and shopping. It was a nice change, but they were glad to get back to the serenity of the forest.

Alice was immediately caught up in the arrangements for the new infirmary. Mr. Harney had sent for her directly from the riverboat landing.

"Mrs. Walden, the infirmary is in a separate building here. I hope it's large enough. After you've had time to pick out your new home, go look the place over. You have a free hand to order whatever is needed."

"Do you really mean that, Mr. Harney?! We can have any house we choose?" She turned to Frank. "I guess it really does pay to be loyal to the company. Let's go and see the houses." Then she grabbed Frank's arm and pulled him toward the door, calling over her shoulder, "I'll be back later, Mr. Harney, with a list of what's needed in the infirmary."

"Welcome to your new home," Mr. Harney called back. "May you find happiness here in our little town."

Alice and Frank chose a two-bedroom house a few steps from the infirmary, "So you won't have so far to walk in the rain," he said. "They say the rain here soaks you almost as fast as the river winds can dry you out.

"Can you put off your inspection of the infirmary long enough to entertain your husband for an hour or so, Mrs. Walden; after we've brought our luggage up, of course?"

"Why yes, Mr. Walden, if you can wait until I've fed and bedded down our son," she pretended to simper.

Frank picked up Alice from where she stood in the corduroy road, little Carsie on her hip. With both in his arms, he stepped inside. "I'm a little late carrying my bride across the doorsill, but the Bluetown shack didn't deserve that honor." Laughing at their own silliness, they began a four year residence in Bridal Veil.

As soon as Frank had his little family settled, he left for the first of the new camps to help put it in readiness for the crews. The climate was wet, but there were seldom extremes of heat and cold. In mild winters, the logging would go on the year round.

Alice's patients often came to her as victims of the "widow-maker" winds funneled by the river's gorge. They blew constantly, prematurely toppling falling trees out of control. No matter how careful he might be, a man was lucky to escape the widespread branches of the gigantic evergreens should he be in their paths as they fell. Serious injuries occurred more frequently here than in the eastern camp.

Rachael and Jim arrived not long after operations began at camp one. Rachael was once again hired as Alice's assistant. She was kept busier here. Alice's trips to Portland with injured men in the company's steam launch were more frequent than either woman liked.

Alice asked Frank about the number of injuries. "There seem to be so many men injured or killed. Is the equipment inadequate?" she wanted to know. "We worry about you two up there."

"No," he told her. "The equipment is the newest and best. It's just that the wind and the rain are so unpredictable. It's a risk we have to face up to. I try always to be careful for your sake and for Carsie's. Please don't worry."

"Frank, I *do* worry. I'm here in town, and get just as panic-stricken as the rest when the emergency whistle blows. I dread the rattle of the ambulance wagon as much as any wife in town!"

"Please, dear, don't talk like that. I'll be alright. You won't find me on that wagon. You know that."

"No, I *don't* know that!" She almost snapped at him. "I've seen the wives and children and what it does to them! The permanently disabled men and their families leave here with little hope for the future. The widows have none!"

In spite of Frank's efforts to reassure her, she was more distressed with each incidence of disability or death, but she tried to hide her feelings for his sake.

Alice made a trip down-river to Portland with a patient in early February of 1887. Her return was delayed by a storm which stopped all traffic on the river. While she was gone Carsie's wet nurse Jane became one of the early victims of a serious epidemic of influenza. Mary took over the care of Carsie and was forced to wean him. He was drinking all his fluids from a cup before Alice's long absence ended.

The heavy storm winds and torrential rains had closed both camp one and the newly opened camp two. Operations were abandoned for safety's sake. Frank came home to an empty house. He went to the infirmary in search of his family and found it crowded with seriously ill victims of the flu epidemic. "Does anyone know where my wife and son are?" he asked the clerk in Harney's office. "Things were so hectic at the infirmary that no one had time to talk to me."

Harney, looking pale and wan from his own light bout with the flu, looked up from his papers. "Walden, stay away from the sick ones; it's a mean illness. Mrs. Walden is in Portland. She went with a man downriver; he was pretty bad off. The storm has closed the wagon road with slides and the river's too rough for boat travel. She's been gone for a week."

"My son, where is he?" Frank asked. "Is he sick, too?"

"I don't know, Walden. There are so many people down sick that I can't keep track. Leave word at the infirmary for Mrs. Merdy; she'll know. It'll likely be a while, though; she's been a busy woman with all those sick people's care to supervise."

Frank left a message at the infirmary and trudged on home, his head feeling leaden. He went to bed without building a fire. The thought of food was nauseating.

"Frank, Frank? Wake up Frank!"

That wasn't Alice's voice, he thought. What's going on? He roused a little. His head felt as big as a balloon, a lead one. "Huh, who's that? Why is it so dark? I feel awful. Am I sick?" He opened his eyes and squinted. A woman was lighting a lamp, not Alice, who? She came toward his bed. "Rachael, what are you doing here? Where's Alice and the baby?"

"Frank, you've got a granddaddy of fevers. How long ago did you get back to town; with the rest of them at noon?"

"Yeah, tried to find my family. Where are they? Are they alright?"

"They're fine. You're the one who's sick. You haven't been in town long enough to contact this epidemic. Have you had any sick men at camp the last few days?"

"Dunno," he said thickly. "Can't think... Wait... fella from the tally office was at camp three days ago. Said he had a headache and felt drowsy. We went over figures for a couple hours in the cook shack. Fella's name's Hansen."

Rachael shook her head, "He was unconscious when he got back to town. He had a high fever. You probably got it from him.

"Now stay down," she said, as Frank attempted to sit up. "Just help me get your outer things off."

"No, no, gotta get up, gotta find Alice, and Carsie, too. Couldn't find 'em. You sure they're not sick?" He knew he was repeating himself, but couldn't stop.

"I'm sure. Alice is in Portland. She took a logger down a week ago. She'll be back as soon as she can. The baby's at Mary's. We'll just leave him there for now. You have to take care of yourself first."

Rachael started a fire for hot water. She found a bowl of broth in the cooler cupboard and heated it. With a little coaxing, she got Frank to take the broth and some tea. Then she changed the sheets and found a dry pillow. Frank's clothing was damp from perspiration. She figured he'd be fine if he kept that up.

"Now look, Frank, here's the chamber pot. I've put a bottle of water and a glass on the chair. I've got to get on to other folks. Sleep as much as you can tonight. I'll be by or send someone to check on you in the morning." She pulled the covers up, blew out the lamp and let herself out. He was asleep before the latch clicked.

Before Alice came home Frank was on his feet, although feeling weak, and just in time; Mary's family had begun to be ill with the flu. Rachael brought the happy little Carsie home to his papa. She also brought them food and milk from the store.

"Carsie's all yours now," she told Frank. "Every woman in town is either sick, helping me or taking care of someone else's children. Carsie is weaned to the cup now. You just cut up the same thing you eat into tiny pieces for him. There are plenty of diapers for night time and he wears underpants during the day. You'll have to watch him for signs that he needs to go on the pot.

"I'm on my way where I'm really needed. Good luck, Papa!" She left a bewildered Frank and a chortling baby to their own resources.

The storm raged on. It was a total of twelve days before the launch brought Alice back to her family. Alice first sought out her son. His wet nurse Jane opened the door at Alice's knock.

"Alice, it's so good to see you back. Rachael will be so relieved. She's been a tireless angel through all this sickness."

"All this sickness? There **were** a *few* folks with influenza when I left. What happened? Tell me, is Carsie alright? Where is he?" She pushed into the house.

Jane shrugged and closed the door behind Alice. "Calm down. I got the flu, and the younguns, too, so Rachael took Carsie to Mary. When **her** family got sick, Frank was well enough to take care of him. Go on home. Both of them are fine, but I'll bet Frank will be glad to turn the boy over to you."

With a word of thanks, Alice left Jane and hurried home. She burst in the door to find Frank sitting on the floor. He was rolling a ball to Carsie. The two of them were obviously enjoying themselves. Alice knelt beside Frank and held both of her men in her arms. It was wonderful to have her family together again.

When they had had enough of the joy of reunion, there was a spate of questions and answers.

"Frank, how is Carsie eating? My milk is almost gone. It'll likely take a while to refresh and I'll not have enough until then."

"Don't worry," Frank said. "He's all weaned. He drinks from a cup like a topper and I can't fix enough food to fill him. He'll weigh a ton in no time. But are you alright?" he asked. "You've been away so long. How did you fare in Portland? Where did you stay? What did you do?"

Alice put on the coffee pot while she answered. "The company paid for a hotel room. It was very fancy, eating in a restaurant. Oh, it'll be so good to eat home-cooked food again. I hate the smell of fried foods that absolutely permeated the place."

"How did you arrange for your expenses in town?" Frank wanted to know. "You were there quite a while. Did you have enough money?"

"The company has a contract with that one hotel and restaurant. Employees who are in town take a chit to the manager and charges are sent to the office. I didn't take any money along so I was stuck with eating the hotel food. Next time I'll take some cash so I can have a change once in a while."

"It'll be so nice to have this time together," Frank remarked. "We can have a regular vacation." He grinned. "I'll be happy to share the boy with you, too. I never did much of this before, and he's kept me busy, I tell you."

"Wait just a darned minute!" she said, backing away from her husband's open arms. "My job isn't done yet. In case you forgot, there's been an epidemic resulting in a lot of overworked women. I've got to get down to the infirmary and see that some of them get some rest. My vacation is over for a while. I'll stop by this evening for supper. I hope you set a good table, Mr. Walden."

With that, she went out the door, blowing kisses. At the infirmary, she caught Rachael just starting out on new rounds, her kit bag repacked with supplies. The two women greeted one another affectionately. Alice was concerned at the obvious fatigue in her friend's face and posture.

"Sit down a minute. I need to know all that's gone on while I was away. How many sick do you have now? I'll need a list of them and what needs to be done."

Rachael protested that she had to get to her patients. "You can stay here, Alice, and coordinate the rest of them. Each one of the helpers can give you a list of her patients, too." She quickly scribbled on a pad, the route of her rounds, and wearily got up from her chair.

Alice stopped her. "That will be enough for you today! I see you have no one bedded here so there can't be too many seriously ill. I'll take the list and bag. You're going home and to bed for a rest!"

"But Alice," Rachael protested, "there are six of us. We're all tired. I can't rest while others keep going. It wouldn't be fair."

"Nonsense! I'll see who's really sick enough and find replacements or something. Don't you worry; I can handle things."

Scowling in mock severity, Alice pushed her assistant out the door. "March! Go home! Git!"

In a matter of hours she had the patient load redistributed. The peak of the epidemic had passed and there had been no new cases since the previous morning. Time was the principal treatment now; other care was merely incidental.

No sooner had the two camps gone back into operation, than the terrifying shriek of the alarm whistle sounded. Though it was early morning, barely dawn, women came running to the infirmary to await the arrival of the ambulance wagon. Each woman in the crowd was as tense as her neighbor. Whose man was hurt or killed this time?

Rachael had spent the night in the sick room with a child who had been injured by a runaway wagon. She ran to the door and lighted a kerosene lantern while she awaited the wagon's arrival.

Alice came in the door, Carsie on her hip, as the wagon stopped. She reached the door in time to catch Rachael with her free arm as her friend fainted. The man on the litter was her husband Jim. His face was swathed in bandages, but there was no mistaking that tousled, coppery hair. One of the men by the door helped to lift Rachael to a bed in the sick room. Alice handed him a vial of ammonia. "Wave it under her nose so she gets a whiff of it. She'll come around in a few seconds, but keep her here. I'll send someone to stay with her."

Back in the outer room, she went to the door to hand the sleepy Carsie to Mary. She called out, "It's Jim Merdy that's hurt. Will one of you come in to stay with Rachael? The rest of you may as well go on home."

She turned as the men carried Jim into the infirmary. "Put the stretcher on the examining table, please. We don't want to move him any more than necessary."

When they had set him down, she asked one of the bearers, "What happened to him?"

"He'd just loaded a big log on a wagon. He was on top of it when it started to roll. He fell and a branch stub caught him across the face. Lucky the branch jammed on the wagon bed and kept the log from rolling further, else he'd been smashed under it. He was knocked out and hasn't come to."

Alice gently removed the makeshift bandage. Jim must have gotten a shock to his skull, too. If that injury wasn't too bad, he was lucky to be unconscious. The pain would have been horrible. His face was a purple mass and his left jaw-line laid open from ear to chin. The lower jaw was dislocated and sagged to the right.

Alice said a quick prayer, then carefully let the lower jaw droop and inserted searching thumbs into each side of his mouth. With her fingers grasping along the jaw line, she moved the bones cautiously. The grating feeling told her that both jaws were broken just below the hinge.

"Here, you," she instructed one of the bearers, "hold his head still. Put your fingers at the back of his head and hook your thumbs at the side of his eye sockets."

She pulled gently and felt the bones settle into a normal position. "Thank you, you did it just right. Would it bother you to hold him while I sew up this cut?"

The man gulped, his face pale, "Not if I can hold and not look; my stomach's a little touchy about seeing too much blood already."

"Fine, don't look. I'm going to move his head to the side and brace it. You hold his head in place... there, but don't touch the jaw. Do you understand?"

"Yes Ma'am, I can manage."

She spoke to the other stretcher bearer, "Please close the door and build up the fire. We don't want our patient chilled. You did well to wrap him warm on the ride down here from camp."

She cleaned the wound of bits of bark and slivers, washed it with clear water and sutured the ragged gash. He would have a nasty scar.

Bandaged tightly so that he could not open his mouth, Jim was placed, stretcher and all, onto the bed next to Rachael's.

Alice held her friend's shoulders so she wouldn't get up too quickly and faint again. "Hold on girl, he's unconscious. He doesn't know you're here. Now get up slowly, slowly. I'm going to send someone to find the launch crew. You can look at him but don't touch."

She gave Rachael a moment to croon over her comatose husband. "Now go home and pack a suitcase for a week. I'll write out the instructions on what to do when you get to Portland. This time I'll hold the fort here."

Rachael left to take care of preparations for her journey as a man left to summon the launch crew.

"Bring me word, please, when they have steam up and are ready to put Jim on board," Alice had instructed him." She packed a kit of necessities for Rachael's use.

When Rachael came in with her satchel, Alice had her sit down at the desk and read the instructions carefully.

"Now, that takes care of Portland. Here in the kit are fresh bandages. Don't disturb the present bandages if you can help it. There's an eye dropper and a vial of laudanum. Don't give him any unless he starts thrashing around and is still unconscious. If he wakes up and can stand the pain, don't give him anything but a few drops of water."

Two men from the launch appeared in the doorway. "What needs to be done to get your patient ready, Mrs. Walden? The boat's ready."

"Try not to move the blanket roll so that his head won't turn. Mrs. Merdy, here, is his wife and a nurse. She'll see to his care. But should she ask for help, don't hesitate." Alice fastened the stretcher straps over the blankets so that Jim couldn't uncover himself.

She embraced Rachael. "Take care and come back soon. I'll see to your house, so don't worry."

As the men and Rachael left, Alice went to comfort the whimpering Carsie. All the commotion had frightened him. She sent Rachael's attendant away. Cuddling the boy in her arms, she rocked him to sleep. Then she put him down gently and turned, with a sigh, to straightening up the infirmary, all the while saying a prayer for Jim and Rachael.

Fortunately, for the next week the infirmary was quiet. Very few patients came, and those merely for first aid. The injured child was able to go home within a day of Rachael and Jim's departure. Alice had time to herself, to rest. A runner from Harney's office brought her a letter from Rachael.

Dear Alice,

Jim is still only semi-conscious. The doctors say there was a brain injury of some kind. They have no idea when he'll be able to leave the hospital.

I've written to Mr. Harney that I'm taking a job here on the nursing staff to support us until Jim is able to work again. I'm afraid it will be a long time, if ever, before he'll be logging again.

When you have time, would you see to getting our things sent on to us? Mr. Harney has the address of the rooming house I've moved into.

Alice, you've been the dearest friend I could ever ask for. I'm going to miss you so much. Please write when you can.

Love,
Rachael

P.S. I hope a new assistant will be found for you soon.

On the heels of Rachael's letter came Mr. Harney and a representative from the town of Bridal Veil. Mr. Harney introduced his companion. "Mrs. Walden, this is Mark Henner. He's come to ask your help. The folks in the old town are in a bad way."

"Mr. Henner, what can I do for you?"

"Ma'am, the influenza spell you folks had over here has gotten over to our folks; probably from the school kids. Some of them have just dropped over in the street. We'd appreciate it if you'd come and help organize our folks' treatment like you did here."

"Mrs. Merdy did all that, I'm afraid. I wasn't here through the worst of it, but I'm sure I can do it for you. Do I have your permission, Mr. Harney?"

"Yes, yes, of course. That's why I personally brought Henner over to see you. If you're needed here, I'll send a runner to tell you."

Mr. Henner looked at both of them. "The folks in town will sure be grateful. Everything's just about at a standstill, it hit so fast. Thank you, Mr. Harney.

"Mrs. Walden, I've a buggy here at the office. I'll wait for you to get whatever you need and take you over to the town hall when you're ready."

"Mr. Harney," said Alice, "would you stop over to Mrs. Will's and ask her to care for my son while I'm gone? Meantime, I'll pack a valise and be right back."

She went home and filled a sack of necessities for Carsie and a valise for herself then returned to the street leading her son, who clung to her skirts. Mary was waiting for them and took the boy home with her.

Back at the infirmary, Alice turned to Harney. "I don't know what medication is available in town. After I've looked it over, and should it be lacking, may I send for some of our supplies? Our new stock came in on the launch that returned last week."

"Of course," Harney said, "don't hesitate. We'll send for more if need be. Go right along over and don't worry." He stood watching as the buggy drove off, his hand raised in farewell.

Henner stopped his buggy at the steps of the small storefront that served as Bridal Veil's town hall. A committee of men and women, ten in all, milled around the room anxiously. "Folks, this lady is Mrs. Walden," Henner announced. "She's the nurse for the logging company. Mr. Harney asked her to help us out, and she's willing."

He turned to Alice. "Now what do you need from us, Mrs. Walden?"

Alice looked around the room and picked out a table by the rear wall. She walked to it and turned to the room. "Ladies and Gentlemen, I'm happy to help you. First I need to know approximately how many of the households have sick people. Next, I'll need to know how many women, who are not sick, are willing to help out. Any woman who doesn't want to assist in nursing but who will care for the children of those who do should come forward.

"Mr. Henner, would you and those present see that this message is taken to every house? Does anyone know if there are any medical supplies in town and where they're stored?"

A stout man stepped forward. "Mrs. Walden, Ma'am, I'm the proprietor of the general store. Reckon whatever you need, if I have it, is yours to call on."

"Good, thank you, Sir. Ladies and Gentlemen, if you'll gather the information needed and recruit assistants, I'll meet you back here after I've seen what supplies are available."

Quickly, the room emptied; everyone was anxious to help. At Alice's request, Mr. Henner drew out a rough plat of the town. The houses were marked with symbols as reports came in.

Alice thought to herself how much easier it was when she knew everyone by his or her first name. The loggers' families and the old-town people didn't associate very much. The loggers were regarded as transients or foreigners by the townspeople. Except for tradesmen and the schoolchildren, the two groups seldom mingled. There had been no offers of help, Rachael had said, when the logging folks were so desperately ill.

In two hours Alice had a man at the table marking symbols and a relay of people carrying messages. As the women came in they were enlisted as nurses or for childcare. Alice sent the nurses' helpers out to place their children, then gathered the nurses together in the little hall. "If you are all careful to wash your hands between households and put on a clean apron before you enter each house, it's possible that you won't get sick. That you are not sick now is a pretty good sign that you may not be susceptible."

This announcement seemed to raise the morale of the women, as Alice had planned. Then she quickly gave each woman basic instructions. She took them, one by one, into assigned households and directed the care needed.

Some of her nurses and helpers fell ill in the next forty-eight hours. There had been almost too few to start with and the situation was becoming desperate.

Alice sent for Mr. Henner. "The spread of the sickness is worse than I'd anticipated," she told him. "Would you take a message to Mr. Harney for me? Ask him to see if some of the company women who helped Mrs. Merdy would volunteer to come over to assist me?" In an hour, Henner was back with the first of the volunteers and returned for a second load.

It was necessary to coordinate a constant shifting of child care and nurses as the epidemic progressed. Alice began to appreciate Rachael's generalship more and more as the days passed.

The townspeople were not as fortunate as their neighbors in the company town. There were eight deaths before the tide of illness began to ebb. Alice attributed it to the difference in population. There were older people in old town and the children were not as robust as those of the loggers. It was in these two groups that the fatalities fell.

As the crisis passed, old-town Bridal Veil began to come back to life. The streets were again peopled, as they had not been for two weeks. Alice and her volunteers were able to return home.

A few weeks later the townspeople sent an invitation through Harney's office: The logging town's people were bid to a celebration of gratitude. It was the first time that they were openly welcomed into old-town, other than by the tradesmen and saloon keeper.

The epidemic had taken its toll but had brought about a feeling of good will and understanding that lasted. From that time on the two towns were as one.

Chapter Thirteen

THE VISIT

In those three years away from her parents, Alice had always been a faithful and frequent correspondent. She reveled in the three or four letters that answered each of hers. Her parents, Uncle Minot, Annabelle and Mam Ginny shared her letters among them.

In the late spring of 1888, Frank came up the road from the office where the wagon had just deposited the crews for the weekend. "Hey, Alice!" he called as he stepped through the door, "a letter from Linnville! Looks like your mother's writing!" He held it behind his back as she came running. "Nope, got to pay the toll to your postman first."

She reached around him for the letter. He quickly lifted his arms high, waving it above her reach. Then as her patience grew short, he put his arms around her and lifted her off the floor. Round and round he waltzed, holding her tightly, humming a tune. In a minute his happy teasing song had her laughing with him. She flung her arms around his neck and kissed him.

He returned her kiss with fervor, forgetting to guard the letter. She snatched it from his hand, slipped out of his arms and ran across the room.

"You devil, I knew a kiss would disarm you," she giggled.

"Well, smart miss, what did you think I meant by 'paying a toll?' I got what I was asking for, didn't I? Now I'll go shave while you enjoy the spoils." Chuckling to himself, Frank took the kettle from the stove and poured water into his shaving basin.

Alice turned to the light from the window to read her letter. "Hurrah!" she yelled, startling Frank and waking Carsie from his nap. "The railroad is opening all the way to Portland in June. Mama, Papa and Carsie are coming for a visit! Now I'm sorry I fussed about the noise and dust of the track work all this year. Little did I know it was going to bring us such good fortune!"

Little Carsie sensed the joy in his mother's voice and ran to share it. She picked him up and danced over to Frank. "Grandma and Grandpa and Uncle are coming to see our boy. Oh, I'm so happy. How can I wait? I'll burst!"

"Calm down. Your face is as red as a rose. When will they be here?" Frank asked.

"I don't know. I just read that far and forgot everything else!" She shifted the boy to his father's arms and ran to pick the letter up off the floor, where it had landed. "Let's see, oh darn! No definite date yet. They have what amounts to a lottery for the first trains, and Mama hasn't heard yet. They'll write again as soon as they know.

"Listen to this. Carsie is planning to take a year off before entering college. He wants to know if you can get him a job with the logging company. They ask if you could request that he be on your crew so you can keep an eye on him. Mama worries about his safety.

"She says he insists on being called Carson now. When they forget and call him Carsie, he ignores them.

"Carsie, oops, Carson says he has some news to tell us."

"I can't say I blame him, Frank remarked. It is a rather childish sounding nickname; much more so than Mary Alice. I can't imagine what else could be happening in his life. It couldn't be marriage, as he is planning to stay here quite a while.

"I don't think it'll be any problem getting him on my crew, but I can't babysit him. I have too many other things to worry about on the worksite. He'll get the same careful oversight as any other new man. It should be easier starting out for him than it was for me. He's been working on the plantation and at the mission doing some pretty hard work, if I remember correctly."

A week later, another letter came: Wednesday, July 14th, was the day the results of the lottery had determined for the arrival of the Walden's guests.

Harney was generous in allowing them to check extra beds and bedding from the supply warehouse temporarily.

The weather had been fine and there were no injuries or illnesses to prevent Alice from meeting the train in Bridal Veil. She'd hardly slept the night before because of her excitement.

Ernest and Ercyline were dirty and on the verge of heat exhaustion when Carson helped them off the train; a little unsteady on their feet from days on the moving train. They embraced Alice and little Carsie joyfully.

The initial excitement of reunion subsiding, Ernest asked, "Alice, how close is the nearest hotel? We need to wash off a few pounds apiece of prairie dust, train soot and perspiration."

"Oh my, yes," echoed Ercyline. "*Heaven*, just now, will be a tub of *cool* water! Why didn't you tell us how arduous the journey would be?"

"Papa, Mama, please, not the hotel!" wailed Alice. "We have extra beds at home and I left buckets of water on the stove so you'll be able to bathe. Frank even rigged up a shower bucket surrounded by canvas for Papa and Carson. We've been planning for weeks."

"What an imposition we'd be, all of us in your little house? We couldn't do that! Frank will be unhappy with all the crowding, won't he?" asked Ernest.

"Of course not, what a thing to say! Besides, if you stay here in town, you'll be too far away. It's a long walk from here to our house. I borrowed a buggy from Mr. Harney to take us all back.

"Frank won't be down from camp until Friday night, so you'll have plenty of time to settle in before he gets home. Please say you'll come home with me! There's nothing to do in town, and we want you to stay with us, *really* we do. The hotel is not much more comfortable, and the only public bath is a tub in the back room of the barber shop two blocks away from the hotel. You wouldn't put Mama through that embarrassment, would you?"

After her parents agreed to go home with her, she turned to Carson. "Frank has arranged for an interview for you with Mr. Harney as soon as he gets back down from camp." She gave him another hug. "It's so good to have you here little brother, though you're not so little anymore. I *do* believe you're as tall as Papa now."

Carson put one arm around his sister and picked up little Carsie on his other arm. "Hello little fella. So, you're my namesake. We'll have lots of fun, you and I, won't we?" Carson tucked the little boy like a bundle under his arm and galloped off. Little Carsie squealed with joy as they bounced along to the buggy.

Alice deposited her family at her door. "Go on in and rest a bit. I have to return the rig. It's just a few doors away and I'll be right back. Carson, would you keep track of Carsie for a bit?"

"Mama!" said Carson in mock terror, "Look what she is dooming me to! We just get here and already she wants me to be a **nursemaid!**

"C'mon boy, let's play horsey." Then he grinned and swung Carsie onto his shoulders and trotted away around the yard.

Ernest and Ercyline went on into the house as Alice drove off. "What memories this place brings back," Ercyline said. "A lot like the first real house we had. The country here is prettier, though. I see Mary Alice has my green thumb. Not many houses we passed along the way had any flowers at all, and these houseplants are lovely, too, aren't they? I must say, I'm pleased."

Ernest looked around and spied a huge wash tub. "Your bath, Madam," he bowed and gestured as his eyes twinkled. Let's pull the blanket across the wire Frank has rigged for your privacy and you shall be cleansed, Milady. I see there is plenty of heated water on the stove. Hop in, and while you're soaking I'll go look for the shower Frank's fixed up for us men folks."

Ercyline wasted no time getting into her bath. Alice returned in time to show her father and brother how to operate the shower, then she went to pour warm rinse water as her mother emerged from the tub.

"Such a wonderful bath. The water must be very pure here. I never saw soap make such lovely suds. I can envy you this," Ercyline remarked as she dried her still-slender body. "Your father and I were noting similarities to a house we lived in not long after you were born. Primitive, but adequate."

"Mama, I'm so glad you didn't have to come to a place like the shack we lived in before. This is a palace in comparison."

"Don't apologize, dear. I've told you about the soddy dug into a river bank that was our first home. Our history seems to be repeating itself, in a way with you, doesn't it?"

Ernest came in, bringing his grandson, while Carson used the shower. "Mary Alice, I feel like a human again. I swear the water that ran off me could have been made into mud pies.

He turned to Ercyline. "Dear, do you think we'll have the courage to go through the ordeal of the return trip?"

"Oh, Papa, Mama, I'd be the happiest person in the world if you'd stay out here! Would you? Could you?" Alice was almost pleading.

"We'll see," her parents said almost in unison. Ernest added. "We could use some food, girl! Are you planning to starve us? The train food was unsubstantial and monotonous."

"Of course, Papa. If you'll put some wood in the stove, I'll get started on dinner." She busied herself with cooking, refusing Ercyline's offer to help. "Not today, Mama. You just rest. Tomorrow morning, I have to work at the infirmary for a while after you've come along to see my **PROFESSIONAL** OFFICE." She simpered this last remark. "You can come back here afterward and relive your early days for a while, grandson and all.

"If it's alright with you, I'm not even going to ask about your trip until Frank is here. If we wait, you won't have to tell it twice. We've both been waiting eagerly for Carson's news, also."

Light bantering between the four adults centered on "remember when" and playing with little Carsie until his bedtime. When he was tucked in, Ernest announced that they had been through the wringer for several days and were ready to turn in, too.

"I can see that you and Mama both look tired. Come on, Carson, let's go for a walk. They can have some privacy and we can talk about them," she teased. "Prepare to have burning ears, you two." She kissed and hugged them both, then took her brother's arm as they left.

"Now, tell me what you've been up to since I left Illinois. Have you been fighting off the girls or keeping yourself pure for Miss Right?"

Carson was pensive for a few moments. "There was one special girl. We thought about marriage, but her father forbade it. Do you remember Clarice?"

"Do you mean Mam Ginny's niece?"

"Yes, Father and Uncle Minot agreed that a mixed marriage, or any marriage for that matter, would not be advisable before going to college. We decided that they were right and called off the romance. That's why I'm planning to stay here for a while; to clear my mind before getting caught up in academics."

"It's probably for the best," Alice consoled, "But I'm sorry that it had to end that way. Hard work will keep your mind and body occupied, and the fresh, clean air won't hurt you either."

They walked on; Carson asking about her job and Alice asking about the college he planned to attend.

"Now brother," she said, "let's hie ourselves off to bed. I can see that you're tired, too."

On Thursday morning, they all walked to the company office, where Alice presented her family to Mr. Harney.

"Go along to the infirmary, Mrs. Walden. I know you have work to do. I'll show your family around the yard and bring them back to you shortly."

"Thank you Sir. I've work to do that needs concentration, and they'd be bored. I'm sure they'll enjoy the tour more under your knowledgeable guidance. I'll see you all in a little while."

Mr. Harney escorted the Beebes through the yards. "As you can see, we have a railroad spur now. We still raft the greater part of our products downriver to our mills, but these logs," he indicated a string of loaded cars, "these big ones are of such large radius and weight that they are unwieldy in rafting."

The Beebes stood in awe. The logs were so huge that only one could be carried on each flatcar.

Carson broke the amazed silence. "I didn't know trees grew that big." His voice was husky with wonder. "How do they cut anything so... so HUGE? Are there really saws that long?"

"Our son has spoken for us," Ernest said, in the same awed tones. "It's hard to believe one's eyes."

Ercyline finally found her voice. "It seems to me that it must be very dangerous work to fell such giants."

Mr. Harney laughed gently. "There are many thousands of such trees in these mountains. The men are very adept at their skills and they can drop a tree so neatly that there is no damage to smaller trees close around it. The little ones, we leave for future harvest. The top sections of these monsters are probably on their way downriver by now."

I'd certainly like to see how these big trees are handled." said Ernest.

"I'm sorry," Harney replied. "We never allow visitors in the harvesting area. On-lookers, not knowing the lore of forestry, can be a hazard to themselves, as well as to the loggers. There is to be a logging contest near here next month. If you're still here, you can get an idea of some of those skills. It's quite an affair."

Returning to his office, Harney offered his quests coffee and sinkers. "Sinkers?" asked Ercyline. "What are sinkers? It sounds rather unappetizing."

"Forgive me. It's a logger's name for doughnuts. The camp cooks make them from a cake-like dough, and they are huge. The loggers tease them that the doughnuts are so heavy, they'd sink if they ate too many and then fell in the water. These were made by my housekeeper. I assure you they're not true sinkers."

While his quests rested and enjoyed their refreshments, Harney told them of his admiration for Alice and Frank. "For a pair so young, the Waldens are exceptional indeed. Frank is held in high esteem by the crews and camp supervisors. Few men can work as hard and as long as he does. With his education and intelligence, he is indispensable at every level of responsibility. He has no enemies, only admirers.

"Your daughter, Mr. and Mrs. Beebe, is as indispensable as her husband. Her medical skills and sense of organization are beyond belief for one so young. She is always the epitome of dignity and ladylike behavior, I'm ashamed to say she has me wrapped around her little finger."

Ernest and Ercyline were pleased to hear those words of praise from a man of obvious authority. They beamed with pride all the way to the infirmary.

Alice had just finished working at her desk as they came in. She put aside her pen and record book with open relief. For half an hour she escorted them through her workplace, explaining her duties as they progressed.

"Do you always work alone, Alice?" asked her mother. "What happens when you have to be away?"

Alice told them of Rachael, and praised her abilities. "It's been difficult since she left. Luckily I haven't had to be away since. There are two women in town that come in to relieve me if we have sick folks overnight, but they aren't nurses. Things have been so peaceful lately that I fear a storm on the horizon. I do hope that a trained helper is found for me soon.

On Friday evening Frank walked in the door and welcomed his son and wife into his waiting arms. Ercyline blushed as Frank bowed and kissed her hand.

"Mr. Beebe," Frank nodded.

"Oh, now, how about making that Papa or Ernest; whatever you're comfortable with. We're family now and Mr. and Mrs. is just too formal, don't you think?"

"So be it; Papa and Mama it is," he said as he took Ernest's hand in a firm grip. "Alice and I would like to hear about your trip. We'd like to compare it to ours. Were the cars comfortable? What route did you take?"

"Go ahead, dear." Ernest sat back, enjoying his after-dinner coffee. "You tell them. Truth is, I was asleep a great deal of the time. The click of the rails and the train motion do that to me."

"Were you asleep, too?" Ercyline answered.

"I think he's just sleepy now after eating so much of that delicious stew. Lordy, we haven't had venison stew in more years than I can remember. Are there many deer close around here?"

"Oh, yes, Mama," answered Alice, "That's why we have to fence off the garden; to keep them from eating it all up. They come right up to the house. Sometimes they clatter up and down the road at night."

"If Frank has the time, your father will be going hunting, methinks. He's getting too lazy in middle-age to go hunting in the woods back home alone. And Carson has been too busy.

"Back to our trip. Yes, the seats were comfortable, but all the way from Chicago in the same car; the upholstery got so dusty that we had to vacate the cars twice while they swept them out. The seats sent out a cloud of dust whenever we sat down. It was terrible. We could barely breathe. And no facilities to wash anything but our hands and faces. It was unbearably hot, too."

For a time, they laughed together and compared experiences. Then Alice and Frank exchanged a glance.

"Well, might as well out with **our** news," she said, "I didn't tell you because your letter arrived before I had a chance to write. We decided to wait until you got here. Grandchild number two is due in November. We hope you're pleased."

All the Beebes answered at once in a babble; each one's remarks drowning out the others'. "Hold it!" Ernest called the meeting to order. "One at a time. Of course we're pleased. I think a girl would be nice this time. Maybe a brunette, in contrast to the little fellow's sandy-haired fairness?"

Ercyline piped in, "Maybe the children would as soon it be another boy. Whichever it is, dears, we'll be delighted for both of you."

"What'll you name this one," Carson piped in, "Does Frank have some family names that he'd like to use?"

"We talked about it a bit," Frank answered. "We decided on Ercyline for a middle name for a girl, if Mama approves. But we want you three to choose the first names, whether boy or girl."

They all sat thinking for a few seconds. "May I propose Hilda?" Ercyline said. "She was such a wonderful Christian woman and my first and best adult friend. She led me to the Lord and taught me so many other useful things as well. Maybe a daughter will be blessed with her sunny disposition and her love of the Scriptures."

Ernest looked thoughtful. "I had a favorite teacher named Ida. How about we compromise and call her Ilda (with a long I)?"

"You know, of course, that people will want to pronounce it with a short I," Alice reasoned.

This time Frank spoke up. "If she's as assertive as her mother," he said with a quirk of his eyebrow, "she'll have no qualms about correcting them."

They all smiled and nodded approval.

"I think Frank's family is being left out of this, don't you?" Carson said. "You don't have any bitter feelings toward your parents, do you Frank?"

"No. I deserved the treatment I got from my family. I realize that now. I think, with Alice's and your approval, I'd like to name a boy after my father and give him my mother's maiden name, also. How does Henry Cody Walden sound?"

"Very masculine and distinguished," his mother-in-law commented. "I vote for Frank's choice."

"All in favor, say 'aye'," Ernest ordered. The motion was carried unanimously. "So be it, Ilda Ercyline or Henry Cody, it will be. That's enough brain work for the evening. It's been a busy day for all of us. I declare this meeting adjourned. I'm going to bed."

Chapter Fourteen

BECOMING A MAN

The wagons left on Monday morning, before dawn, taking Frank and Carson to camp. Had it not been for the respect Mr. Harney had for Frank, Carson wouldn't have had a chance to work; in mid-season the roster was full.

Frank had gone to Mr. Harney, asking humbly, "If you'll put the lad on at minimum wage, I'll find a job that will keep him out of harm's way until he proves his mettle."

He could only pray and watch him as closely as possible.

So that he and Carson would have some privacy to talk, Frank arranged for them to ride to camp on the supply wagon's tailgate.

"Carson, I'm going to lay it out for you. You'll be starting out at the very bottom. We can't have you risking your life or anyone else's because of your inexperience. You're going to fetch and carry to start. If you prove dependable, you can move on to more responsible jobs. You've got to keep your head out of the clouds. You'll have the double burden of being a young greenhorn and my brother-in-law. Be prepared for some razzing from the crew."

"All right, Frank," Carson said. "I've worked in the fields for Uncle Minot since I was about ten. I'm used to hard work. I'm not proud. I started off my life on the wrong foot, but God turned me around. I won't let you down."

"You'd better not!" Frank replied with a twitch of his eyebrow. "Alice will never forgive me if I let you get yourself killed!"

Carson grinned and held out his hand. Frank grasped it warmly and tousled Carson's blond curls.

The subject was changed. The rest of the conversation consisted of Carson asking questions and paying close attention to the answers.

Carson adapted to the work fairly rapidly. He worked willingly and cheerfully. In the evenings, he and Frank worked together; teacher and pupil. "Good Lord," he remarked. "These trees are

magnificent! It's an awesome and terrifying thing to see them come
crashing to the ground. The tearing of the last fibers as they fall
sound like screams of agony."

Frank stood thoughtfully for a minute. "It's not the *noise* that
bothers me. Just think of the hundreds *of years* they've stood,
weathering wind and snow, heat and cold, outliving all other living
things. I feel so.. so.., how can I say it? humbled and insignificant. My
lifetime is but a *moment* compared to theirs."

"I know just what you mean," Carson said. "Do you suppose the
other men stand and wonder at the endurance of these giants they
fell so routinely?"

"Your guess is as good as mine," Frank said. "They haven't said
as much."

In odd hours between his duties, Carson was put to work lopping
branches off of fallen trees. One day the good-natured ragging of
the other men got to be too much for him. "Petersen," he called to
the most persistent of his hazers, "I'll challenge you and beat you
lopping. You're lazy and take it easy every chance you get. Let's see
you prove you've got a right to tease me!"

"Done," answered Petersen, "first thing tomorrow morning!
We'll ask Walden to leave the last downer tonight, and I'll show you a
thing or two."

Frank tried to dissuade them, but Carson's dander was up; he
was determined. The other men knew what the outcome would
be. Petersen was an expert. His apparent easy actions were due to
experience. He could accomplish more with economy of motion than
other men could with speed and exertion.

"All right; Beebe, Petersen!" Frank called out when they had
assembled the next morning, "Here's your downer!" Frank indicated
that they should start, one on either side of the huge fir when he
dropped his hand.

Let the lad observe and learn humility and to control his
temper, Frank thought. He wouldn't listen to me, so let him take the
consequences.

He dropped his hand. Whack! thud! chop! The chips flew right and left. Petersen worked with his usual deceptive ease and finished his side in gig time, while Carson strove with frantic concentration. He wasn't aware that Petersen had put down his axe and was lounging against the butt of the tree, laughing silently to himself at the boy's flailing actions.

A sudden burst of derisive laughter from the crew finally penetrated Carson's concentration. Little more than halfway along the huge bole, he stopped and looked up. The lack of chopping sounds puzzled him, until he turned to see Petersen's half-sneer.

"Whatsa matter, city boy? Slackin' off, are ya? Now you know how a man works. Go get Walden to dry behind your ears before you dare an old hand again."

The other men slapped Petersen on the back, laughing as they went off to work.

Red-faced, Carson realized his folly and asked Frank for forgiveness.

"Well, boy, you've learned a valuable lesson today. I warned you that every new hand gets initiated. You're going to be judged by your response to this. Take this tally back to camp and take the rest of the morning off to think and pray about this. After lunch, pick up your axe and finish lopping that downer."

The rest of the day there were a few snickers from the crew just within earshot of Carson. That night, between the bunkhouse and the dining hall, Carson pulled Petersen aside and apologized for his behavior. "I guess I haven't gotten my temper completely under control yet. I'll stay in my place and out of your way from now on. Can we be friends?"

Petersen shook on it and told the other men to lay off of Carson. From then on he was treated with civility and included in the after-hours recreation.

On the next weekend in town, Ercyline greeted Carson with a shriek. "What happened to your face? Have those brutes of loggers hurt you?!" she turned to Frank. "We trusted you to look after him, not let him be beaten! How could you allow such treatment of new men?!"

"No, Mother," Carson interjected. "It's not like that at all. It's a dangerous environment, and sometimes the fellows get to horsing around in the evenings. Sometimes you get an accidental boot, or fall against a stump. It's nothing at all unusual; just a bit of roughhousing to break up the monotony."

Ernest turned a questioning eye to Frank behind Ercyline's back. A nod and an upward twitch of Frank's eyebrow confirmed Carson's story. Quietly, Ernest offered a congratulatory handshake to his son.

August came to Bridal Veil in a drizzly, cool rain. Day after dripping day, the clouds crept down the mountain delivering their watery load on the town. It was necessary to keep the lamps burning most of the day to see to daily tasks.

Ernest and Ercyline both developed severe colds. The day Ernest found mildew in his slippers was the last straw. "Alice, your Mama and I are just not cut out for this climate. It's young folks' country. We think it's best that we go back where we belong. I'm going down to book seats on the train as soon as possible. We'll say our goodbyes to Carson and Frank this weekend and be on our way."

"Papa, no, not yet, you just got here! There's good weather yet to come and autumn is beautiful here in the gorge. You'll get acclimated; wait and see. Wait at least until school starts the first of September. Mama talk to him. Make him stay!"

Ercyline's arm encircled Alice's shoulder. "We'll miss you, as we know you'll miss us, but we talked about it already. We made this decision together. We must go home, don't you see? We'll come back to visit you in two or three years."

It was difficult to tell which of the three was closest to tears, but Alice could see that her parents had made their decision and she must accept it. They knew that Alice's life would not be easy. However, knowing that her marriage was sound and she loved her work, they could leave with few misgivings.

Early Monday morning's farewells to Frank and Carson were solemn. Ernest and Ercyline were leaving both their children behind. It was a difficult time for them.

"Frank, I'm so glad that Carson is fitting in and enjoying his work," Ernest told him, "Mother and I appreciate yours and Mr. Harney's cooperation. We know you'll be a good influence on him. Maybe he'll get over Clarice so he can keep his mind on academics next year. Thank you for taking care of my family. It's good to know that they're in capable hands."

The little house was abuzz with packing, preparing picnic foods for the trip, kisses and hugs. On the buggy trip to Bridal Veil station, Ernest and Ercyline were quiet and held each other close.

Another tearful goodbye and they were on their way home. For how long? Alice wondered. The trip wouldn't get any shorter and probably no easier. Her parents weren't getting any younger, either.

Alice was becoming concerned when no word of her parents' return trip arrived in five weeks. She haunted the office whenever she was going on or off duty at the infirmary.

At the end of September a letter arrived. Its borders were black. Bystanders in the mailroom, knowing its portent, offered their sympathy. She was too apprehensive to do more than lift her hand in response to their words of concern. The infirmary was the nearest place where she could find privacy. The letter was in her mother's handwriting.

Dear Mary Alice:

You will have seen the border, so I had better tell you first that it's for Uncle Minot. He was returning from a business trip to Springfield and collapsed just as he stepped off the stage in Linnville. The doctor was there to meet someone and got to his side just as he died. He passed away so quickly that he had no warning, or so the doctor said. It's a comfort to know that he's in Jesus' presence now.

134

He was buried next to Aunt Caroline. Imelda and
her husband John arrived here the day before the funeral.
Elizabeth, Daniel and the children came the next
morning.

There were, it seemed, hundreds of people here. I
have never seen a funeral so well attended. Annabelle had
intended to have the ceremony in the salon. The last few
years, she has insisted on calling it the salon. She says that
the term large living room is too old fashioned.

At the last hour, the casket was carried out to the large
veranda so that everyone could be close.

It was a lovely funeral. Most of the cut flowers and
plants, Annabelle had sent to the old soldiers' home
afterward.

We had to scramble to find enough food for everyone.
There were so many more folks than we'd expected. It was
quite a task. We were all grateful that so many came to
show respect for dear Uncle Minot.

Alice had to stop several times to wipe away her tears and
recompose herself before she could continue.

Annabelle had borne up well under all the
responsibility for the funeral and taking over the
administration of the estate. She has lost some weight,
though.

John and Imelda stayed on for two weeks to help
Annabelle. Elizabeth and Daniel stayed only for the
reading of the will, then had to return to get their children
ready for school.

Alice hesitated as she turned the page. "Why hasn't mama made
any mention of papa so far?" She thought it strange that *he* didn't
write this letter.

The letter continued:

> Uncle Minot's will left a token bequest for the two
> younger girls because they both married well-to-do men
> and had no need of funds. He did ask that Annabelle let
> them have whatever articles they wanted from the house
> as mementos.
>
> The rest of the money and assets, as well as the
> plantation itself, he left to Annabelle. Her choice of co-
> administrator of the estate has to be approved by the
> family lawyer and Uncle Minot's financial manager,
> jointly.

Alice thought to herself, Mama usually doesn't write such long
letters. Usually, Papa is the one to write "books", as he calls them.
Ah, here it is:

> Your father took no part in all this. Indeed, his grief
> at Uncle Minot's passing has caused a setback in his
> recovery.

Alice wondered what she meant by "his recovery". They had
colds when they left, but nothing serious. Then read on:

> I'm sorry to tell you of his illness. You know Papa
> hasn't been physically strong since before Carson was
> born, when he was seriously ill.
>
> The cold from which he had almost recovered when
> we left you, worsened on the trip. A snow slide ahead of
> us, in the mountains, stopped our train for thirty hours.
> We had no heat after the wood in the car was used up.
> Some of the passengers wanted to get wood from the
> tender. The conductor had quite a time holding the men
> back. If we'd used that wood for heat, there wouldn't have

been enough to fire up the boiler to get us through the mountains and to the next fuel and water station.

Everyone bundled up in their extra clothes to try to keep warm. The cold air was hard on your father's weak lungs, and he was quite fevered. We had to go clear to Duluth before we could get him to a hospital. The doctor said he had pneumonia.

Alice sighed as she remembered how much her father hated to be ill and how much her mother fussed and worried over him. The letter continued:

We were in Duluth for two weeks before papa was allowed to leave the hospital and move to the boarding house where I was staying. His doctor wouldn't permit him to come on home yet. He said there was too much risk of contracting another infection on the train. We were allowed to come home a week later. I had to arrange for a wheelchair to get him from the Duluth train to the Springfield train. Fortunately, we didn't have a long wait in that drafty station.

Mam Ginny insisted that we stay in the main house when we got home so she could keep a closer eye on him. We haven't moved back home yet. We'll have to wait until your father is fully recovered, I guess. Mam Ginny can be forceful when she's concerned about a patient, as you well know.

Papa says to give you his love and our regards to Frank.

With love to you and Carson and kisses to the baby.

Love,
Mama

In the usual autumn flurry of illnesses among the children in the weeks after school started, Alice had little time to dwell on the sad news from the plantation.

As September ended, came the arrival of the east winds down the gorge. Its attendant injuries from the camps were so much a drain on Alice's energies that she sent her half-trained aides to Portland with two severely injured men.

These emergency trips were no longer made aboard the launches. The cabooses attached to the logging trains, fitted with comfortable bunks for the crews, were utilized as ambulance cars by agreement between the railroad and the logging company. The trip to Portland was much shorter and safer than the river trip.

One morning, the third week in October, Alice was unable to rise from her bed. One of the injured men's wives, who had no children, was staying with her overnight. The woman had become hysterical when she had not been allowed to accompany her husband on the train. Alice had invited her to stay, ostensibly to help with Carsie, but actually to help keep her busy.

Grace roused at Alice's call, "What is it? Are you sick?" she asked.

"I'm not sure yet. I got so dizzy when I started to sit up. Will you help me? Just move slowly. Ooh, let me down again. The room is floating and I feel so bloated. Look, my hands are swollen. Lift the covers. I want to check for swelling in my feet and ankles."

Grace folded back the quilt and sheet. Alice was too weak to lift her leg. "Please help me? Would you lift it up so I can check? Oh my, look at that; it's puffed up. Push your finger into the flesh just below my ankle, please? See how the dent stays white and doesn't spring back?"

"What can I do?" Grace asked, anxiously.

"Before Carsie wakes, will you find something to put under the foot of the bed? It needs to be elevated about four inches."

After Grace did as Alice instructed, she told her, "I'll need to limit fluids until I can get one of the herbs from the dispensary to help carry off the excess water from my body."

Grace was busy for a while caring for Alice and Carsie and preparing breakfast. When she had everything in order, Alice asked her, "Would you take Carsie with you and get some medicine from the infirmary for me? Stop on the way and ask Helen to go with you to let you in. She'll give you a jar marked 'herb mix, dropsy remedy'."

"Are you sure you'll be alright while I'm gone, Alice?"

"Yes, I'm sure. Helen will get the key from the office, then lock up afterward. Please don't worry."

Reluctantly, Grace bundled herself and Carsie against the chilly October morning and left.

Alice's mind was struggling to figure out a duty roster for her aides to cover for her in the infirmary. She couldn't seem to hold a train of thought. She cursed herself for not having Grace leave her a tablet and pencil.

With only a token sharp knock on the door, Mr. Harney pushed into the room. "What's wrong, Alice? Is there anything I can do to help?"

"No, no, stop fussing so. It's nothing serious. I'm sure Grace will stay with me. It'll be good for her to have something to do to keep her mind off of Andy."

"What do you mean 'nothing serious'? Mrs. Allen said you were too sick to get out of bed. Shall I arrange to send you to Portland to see a doctor?"

"Oh, please! Do calm down!" She paused. "When you came in, did you call me Alice?"

Mr. Harney spluttered, "Did I?... I... suppose I did."

"I don't need to go to Portland. I'm in the last month of my pregnancy, if you'll remember: Goodness knows it's been obvious enough. This problem arises sometimes. I'll have to stay home and off my feet for a while.

"My aides will be able to handle things quite well, I'm sure. I'll supervise from here. I've sent for Helen Daws to come here this morning, so we can keep the situation in hand. Please don't worry."

Reluctantly, Harney left, looking a little less upset.

There ensued a period of idyllic Indian summer weather. No "widow maker" winds blew and the skies were blue and cloudless. The infirmary was virtually empty. Alice's aides brought her one or two patients for diagnosis, but there was no need for her to feel guilty about deserting her post. Except that she was forced into idleness when the weather beckoned her outdoors, Alice was content. The herb tea lessoned her edema somewhat, so she was able to be out of bed for short periods, as long as she propped her feet up when she was sitting. Her knitting needles clacked busily, making warm winter garments for Carsie.

When Frank came home for a weekend, he teased her. "Look at you; holding court like a queen with her ladies-in-waiting; people in and out all day! You'll be so spoiled you won't want to go back to working again."

His eyes belied the concern that his gaiety tried to conceal. He tried, manfully, to cover his true feelings. The effort was not lost on Alice. Before he left for camp he protested that perhaps he should stay behind to care for Carsie and to be with Alice in case of the birth.

"Nonsense," she protested, "I bore Carsie entirely by myself; and this time I'll have Grace to care for Carsie and the baby. I have three capable women, all well-trained, at my beck and call and within a few minutes arrival. Besides, husbands are generally useless at a birthing anyway. The next time you come home you may be holding your new son or daughter. For now, your role is breadwinner," she teased. "Now skedaddle or you'll miss the wagons."

He kissed her longingly and ran out the door just in time to hop the tailgate of the last wagon.

Chapter Fifteen

ARRIVAL AND DEPARTURE

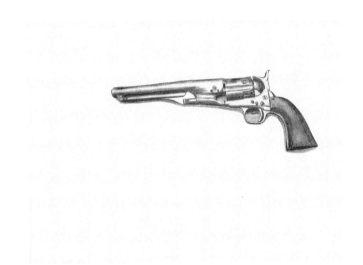

In mid-November, Grace received word that her husband Andy was recovering well. She was torn between making a trip to Portland to visit with him and her sense of obligation to care for Alice and Carsie.

"But, Alice, what if you're alone when the baby starts to be born?" Grace fretted until Helen and the other nurse helpers held a planning session for eventualities. Only then would she agree to leave.

Mary's eldest daughter, Sarah Jane, agreed to stay with Alice at night. A responsible twelve-year-old, she had cared for her younger brothers and sisters most of her life. Carsie was fond of the girl and comfortable with her. She was to take the little boy home with her after she had prepared breakfast for them, and then go off to school. Alice's aides took turns dropping in to check on her needs.

Grace left with a lighter heart. "I'll feel a lot better now, knowing that you're well-cared-for," she told Alice. "I'll be back in a few days, maybe with Andy. Take care of yourself and don't stay up too long at a time."

She kissed Alice and hugged her, lifted Carsie for a quick embrace and went to catch the train, already whistling its warning on the siding.

At dusk, Indian summer fled with the onslaught of winter's first storm. Torrents of rain accompanied by gale winds soaked the towns on the shore of the iron grey river and whipped the waves into froth. The spume resembled tossing manes and had been dubbed "river horses" by the Indians. These deceptively small waves could make boats rear and kick like horses, too.

From her door Alice stood watching the majestic power of the great river below the town. This river was as wild during a storm as the craggy hills behind her on the Oregon shore. In calm times it rolled along in imitation of the bare rounded hills across on the Washington side. Though it was not as great a river as the wide expanse of the Mississippi she remembered from her few crossings and the riverboat ride she had taken with Annabelle, the Columbia had an untamed quality that fascinated her.

"Alice!" She jumped at the voice. "What are you doing standing there in the open doorway? You'll catch your death!" Helen took her arm and closed the door behind them. "Off to bed with you. What were you thinking, standing there like that?"

"The river is so beautiful in the storm. I couldn't resist taking a few minutes to enjoy it." Alice allowed herself to be divested of her dressing gown and tucked into bed. "Sit down a minute. I'd like you to do me a favor if you have the time."

"Sure, just let me put on the coffee pot and we can sit and chat while it brews." Helen bustled about, setting the room to rights, building up the fire, cleaning the coffee pot and filling it. Then she pulled up a chair. "Now, let's hear what you have in mind."

Alice smiled warmly at her friend and helper. She was a dear soul; her heart as big as her full-blown figure.

"Well, I've been thinking that I may not be able to get to the infirmary for the birthing. This dropsy happened before I had time to prepare everything here. Would you please round things up for me? Carsie came so quick; I'm sure there'll be no time after the contractions start."

"Of course I will. Let me get you a pillow to put behind your back so you can enjoy your coffee. Now tell me where everything is and I'll get it all ready."

The next half-hour sped by in pleasant chatter as the clop of Helen's heavy, mannish shoes moved back and forth.

"There, in that trunk under the window," Alice said, "the last item, that old quilt, yes, the blue one. My friend Rachael gave it to me. She said it wasn't worth packing along when she left Bluetown. It served to absorb the birth waters when Carsie was born. I couldn't bear to part with it when we came here."

"Well," Helen puffed from her exertion, "If that's all, I'll have another cup of coffee and rest a bit."

The two women sat chatting merrily for a while, then suddenly Alice sat bolt upright. "I forgot something! Helen, that flat rectangular pan, the heavy one in the cupboard next to the stove, would you get it out and wash it? We'll need to boil those cloths and dry them for packing. And the scissors and cord should be boiled and wrapped in one of the cloths, too."

"Lordy, Girl, calm down! You haven't had any signs yet, and you're as fidgety as a hen on the nest." Helen did as Alice asked and hung the cloths to dry on a cord strung above the stove, while the scissors and birth cord were boiling. Later, she put the packages away in a cupboard, ready for use.

No sooner had Helen gone than the door flew open again. Frank burst in out of breath. "I met Helen down by the office; she said you weren't well. What is it?!"

"Quiet down; it's just some edema; water collecting under the skin; nothing to worry about. It's made me a little weak and I've had to stay in bed. I'm a little better now. It's merely something that happens sometimes just before a birthing.

"Now sit down here and give me a kiss. I promise I won't break. Now, how about you? Did the storm close the camps down again? Is that why you're home in mid-week?"

"Yes, we had a few big ones blow down. One of them caved in a corner of the bunk house. So, here we are. I'll probably be here to see the baby born this time. Is it soon, do you think?"

"Probably; I've started getting some early signs. I haven't told anyone, but I've had a few twinges of false labor twice, so it won't be much longer."

Alice looked toward the door. "Where's Carson? Didn't he come down, too?"

"Yeah, they brought the whole camp in. We made quite a caravan down the mountain. Carson stopped to visit a friend. He'll be along shortly to get cleaned up. One of the younger fellows wants him to meet his sister this evening. We'll get our pay later today."

Frank went off to bring his son home. The two came galloping up the road, laughing together; their hair flying in the wind. Carsie sat on the bed playing hills and valleys with the quilt folds while his father made supper. It was a happy evening for the little family.

Carsie was tucked in, willed to sleep by his father's bedtime song. "How blessed I am," Alice said aloud, watching them. "Four years married and still crazy in love with my Prince Charming."

"You're blessed?" Frank quipped. "How about me? You put up with being alone most of the time. There aren't many women who hold down a job and take care of a house and child, too. I'm the lucky one; and more in love with you every year.

"It's been a long day and we both need some sleep. Is there anything I can get for you before we turn in?"

"Is the teakettle still hot? I should have a cup of herb tea before sleeping, to keep the edema down."

Frank got up. "Doggon it, Woman! I no sooner get through doing up your dishes, and here you want me to dirty some more!" He pretended to grumble as he prepared a tray for the tea. Engrossed in his teasing, he jumped as he heard a sharp sound from the bed;

half groan, half shriek. He spun around, the tray with the cups in his hands. "What's the matter?"

Alice looked up at him with her brightest smile. "Guess what? You're going to be a papa again, tonight! Let's get cracking! There's a bit to do to get ready!"

"Oh my God!" He dropped the tray and stood agape, staring at her.

"Frank!" she almost shouted at him.

He shook his head as if coming out of a trance. "What do we need to do? Tell me, quick!"

Waiting for another contraction to pass, she set him to work. "First, help me to a chair. You'll have to get the bed ready."

After he had seated her, she put him to stripping the bed and padding it, ready for the waters and blood. "Now, help me back to bed. There are strips of sheeting in that end cupboard and some packages wrapped in brown paper.

Bring the small table over here by the bed and put the packages on it. Now loop a length of the sheeting over the head rails so I can get hold of the ends.

"Now go! Get Helen up here quick! I'll be alright for a few minutes. Just call her, but don't wait for her. Get back here as soon as you can."

In an incredibly short time he was back, out of breath, stumbling over the door sill in his haste. "Helen's coming. She was already in bed. She had to put on her robe and slippers. Are you all right? Hold on, I hear her coming."

Helen burst through the door without knocking and headed straight to the bedside. Looking around, she directed, "Frank, will you get a lamp and hang it on the rafter by the foot of the bed? I'll need more light."

"Ooh!" Alice pulled the sheet strip in a spasm, her arms cording with the effort. "Helen, just in ti-i-ime!"

Frank stood bug-eyed as Alice's body arched. Helen pushed him out of her way and threw back the covers.

"Well!" She said in mock disgust. "What did you need me for?"
She reached for a cloth from the table and plucked from the bed a
squalling baby girl. Wrapping the baby tightly, she laid her at Alice's
side, opened the pack of cord and scissors.

In a minute, she handed Frank his daughter "Take her over
by the fire and keep her warm." Then she turned back to Alice.
"Afterbirth and all, I see. Always did say you were efficient, Alice.
Now let me clean you up, then Frank can hold both his girls while I
redo the bedding."

In a trice she had everything in order, the baby bathed and put to
Alice's breast. "Well what're you waiting for, Papa? Get a wiggle on!
There's broken china and the floor is wet. Get them cleaned up while
I get your wife a cup of herb tea."

Carsie came in from his small bedroom, rubbing his eyes.
"Mama, Papa, I heard some noise." He stumbled sleepily to his
mother's side. "Ooh, my baby; it's here! Sister, Mama? Is it my
sister?" His eyes popped wide open as he climbed up on the bed to
peer at the red-faced bundle in the crook of his mother's arm.

Frank picked up his son and sat down on the bed with the little
boy on his lap. "You have a beautiful little sister." In an aside to
Alice, "I suspect she'll be a bit prettier when she's looking a little less
boiled?"

Helen brought Alice's tea, and Frank picked up the baby, putting
her in Carsie's eager arms. "Here you are, Son. You're the eldest, and
from now on you're to help take care of your sister, and protect her,
always."

"Yes, Papa, she's *my* baby. I love her. Look Mama, she's looking
at me! She loves me, too!"

Little Ilda Ercyline was indeed looking directly at Carsie. At that
moment there was forged between these two tiny beings a bond of
spirit that held them closely all their lives.

"Come on, Son, time for bed. Mama and Sister are tired. You can
hold her again tomorrow."

When Frank had put the drowsy little boy to bed and tucked him in, he returned to find Helen had gone quietly. Both Alice and the baby were sound asleep.

That winter, Carson grew restless in town with nothing to do. Little Ilda's crying got on his nerves. A few times, he went hunting in the hills with some friends. He didn't have enough seniority to take part in the repair crews. As a result, he started playing pool in the evenings, though he never drank or gambled with the other men. Sometimes he stayed out late, not getting home until after Alice and Frank were asleep.

Early February brought a particularly vicious storm. Frank and his crew left for camp reconnaissance as soon as the storm eased. One morning, when Frank had been gone several days, Alice awoke to the sound of his building up the fire.

"When did you get in? Was there a lot of damage? Are you going to have to go up again? Come see Ilda. She's awake now. I'll feed her as soon as I come back in from the outhouse." She got out of bed and put on her robe and slippers.

Frank held open the door for her and kissed her as she passed him. "Hurry back. The coffee's done and I've got some of your cinnamon rolls in the oven to reheat." He went to get the baby from her cradle and stepped into the room to wake Carsie and Carson for breakfast. Carson's bed was unruffled! He hadn't slept at home. That was certain!

Alice came in the back door and whispered to Frank, "Go look out on the road." She took the crying baby and put her in her cradle. "Carsie, come and talk to Sister. She gave him a sugar tit to hold for the baby then shut the bedroom door. Crossing the room to the front window, she stood beside Frank, looking out at the road. "What do you suppose is wrong? Why are they here?"

Two men stepped onto the porch, then knocked softly on the door. Frank told Alice to stay inside, then opened the door and stepped out. One man said, "We're here about Carson." Frank put his finger to his lips as he closed the door. He stepped off the porch and pulled the men aside. "I fear you have bad news. His bed hasn't been slept in."

The man spoke softly. "There was a fight down at the saloon last night. One of the men pulled out a gun and started shooting wildly. Carson was hit. He was dead before he hit the floor. The sheriff heard the commotion and came running in just then. The man turned toward him, and the sheriff shot him dead.

"I'm so sorry. He was a good kid; had a lot of potential. They took him to the church. You can see the preacher about him."

Frank thanked them. They said goodbye and left.

Frank took a deep breath as he reached for the doorknob. As he entered, Alice hurried over to him. She was shaking with worry. "I heard them say something about Carson! He's not here! Where is he?! What happened to him?!"

Frank sat her down and recounted the story the men told him. She was stunned. Before she could react, Carsie came running in from the bedroom. "Mama, Sister's crying. She pushes away the sugar tit. She won't stop crying. Please, Mama, come take care of Sister?"

All talk was suspended until after the baby was nursed and Carsie finished breakfast. Neither Alice nor Frank had any stomach for more than coffee.

Frank went to see what he could find out about the night's happenings and to make arrangements for Carson's burial. There was no mortician in the small town, so Carson would be buried in the churchyard cemetery within two days.

That night Alice couldn't sleep. "What are we going to tell Mama and Papa?!" She sobbed in Frank's arms. "They trusted us to take care of him!"

"I'm sure they won't hold us responsible," he consoled. "We did what we could. He made a poor choice and someone else made an even worse one. It was an accident. I'll send a telegram tomorrow."

The whole town was very sympathetic toward the little family. Alice didn't have to cook or go to the infirmary for two weeks; there was such an outpouring of love for them.

Bad weather held on through to the end of February of 1889. Frank and a small crew of men went back to camp for short periods to repair damages wrought by the winter storms.

It was three months before Alice could muster the courage to write to her parents.

Dear Mama and Papa,

I'm sorry it's taken so long for me to write you. I couldn't find the words to tell you my grief at Carson's death. I know it must be as hard for you as it is for us.

He told me he planned to attend Moody Bible Institute when he returned home this summer. I know you were very proud of him, as was I. He proved himself to be a man after God, though he had his faults. Don't we all?

He got restless with nothing to do and put himself in harm's way. I'm so sorry we failed you and him. I hope you can find it in your hearts to forgive us.

Other than that, we are all fine here. You should see the baby. She is surely going to be a big girl; she's growing so fast. Carsie dotes on her. He can sometimes soothe her when I can't. He loves to hold her in the rocking chair and sing to her. Her big brown eyes follow him everywhere.

It's been a mild spring with few illnesses or injuries in the infirmary. My garden is growing as prodigiously as the children.

With all my love,
Alice

Chapter Sixteen

A BRAVE FACE

Spring of 1889 was a joyous time for the Waldens. Carsie grew tall and slender. At three years, he was starting to read nursery books sent from the plantation and ordered from Portland.

Carsie and Ilda, then eighteen months, were inseparable. They were happy children, laughing and clapping their hands at the progression of clouds across the blue sky. The sweep of swallows over the water at dusk fascinated them. Ilda held onto her brother's hand, her sturdy legs trudging gamely where his longer legs led. Her brown eyes and his brilliant blue ones were equally curious of the world around them. Their father's tenor voice was an eagerly anticipated joy to them both. When he was at home, they often begged him to sing. Their sweet baby voices piped along with his.

One May morning, "Auntie Helen" came to awaken them. "Come along children, quietly. Mama has a surprise for you, hurry!"

Wide awake at the promise of a surprise, they padded into their mother's room. "What's the surprise, Mama?" Carsie ran to climb on the bed and helped Ilda up beside him.

"Look, Darlings, see what I have for you?" Alice pulled back the little blanket. "A new baby sister. Isn't she pretty?"

The children begged to have the cover lifted so they could examine her. They counted her tiny fingers and toes. "Look Sister, how teensy they are. Does she sleep all the time, Mama?" One question followed another as the two inspected the baby.

"She'll be awake more, later. She's tired now from her hard work to get born. Later, she'll open her eyes and you can watch her. Go now and get dressed. Auntie Helen will fix your breakfast today."

"Aren't you going to eat with us, Mama?" Carsie was puzzled.

"Come Mama, breffus now. G'up now." Ilda pulled at her mother's hand.

"Not this morning, Sister. Mama is tired, too. We both need to sleep for a while."

Grace Leah was their "halfway" baby. Her hair was neither dark nor light, her skin neither ruddy nor fair. Her eyes were grey-green with golden flecks. She was neither sturdy like Ilda nor slender like Carsie.

"She's our 'changeling child'," Frank decided. "She's fussy and demanding attention, yet she doesn't like to be picked up and cuddled like the others."

"She's a lazy baby," Alice noted. "Even when nursing, she acts as if it's too much trouble. See, she follows movements but never smiles. It's as if she's only interested in observing, but doesn't want to participate."

Frank was summoned from camp that September; Mr. Harney greeted him cordially.

"I hope you're in the mood for a move, Walden," he said. "I've a proposition to put to you. Have a seat and I'll explain."

Frank pulled up a chair to face the superintendent. "It must be pretty important to get me down off the mountain in mid-week."

"It is, I promise you, perhaps even history-making. When you came downriver, do you remember the portage at Dalles City?"

"Yes I do. It was the first town I ever saw built on solid rock; and all uphill. There was blasting for a building foundation while we were there."

Harney sat back and folded his hands over his slight paunch. "The company has contracted for timber rights in the mountains behind the city. Because of the ruggedness of the area and its distance from the river, it isn't practical to take logs out by road. We've got crews out building roads for supply wagons."

"Roads for supply *wagons*?" Frank's left eyebrow flew up nearly to his hairline. "How do we get the logs out then?!"

"Wait a minute, let me finish!" grinned Harney. "The first logging won't be started for several miles out of town. It's desert country up to there, and nothing but sagebrush and greasewood in the way.

"So the solution, Walden: We've already started the biggest and eventually the longest flume ever known. We figure it'll be about fifteen miles in length. We'll start logging out on each side of the flume as it's built. There's plenty of water in the hills to keep it going. It will be a challenge!"

Frank's eyes were alight with enthusiasm. "Where do I fit into all this?"

"We'd like you to go in with the first logging crews to clear out timber for the road and the flume-way. Road crews will follow you and flume construction crews behind them. You'll need to get going as soon as possible."

"Will the flume carry the logs to the river or to a rail yard?" Frank wanted to know.

"Neither; here again, something new for our company. We've bought out a small lumber mill. We'll expand and handle the whole operation ourselves, from felling the trees to finished lumber."

"Wow, this *is* big news! When do I start?" Frank could barely contain his eagerness.

"You'll need to get up to Dalles City tomorrow to meet with your new superintendent. Before you actually get on the job, you'll need to take time to arrange quarters for your family. We have a boarding house leased out for the men until some decision is made about housing for their families. As for you and your crew; you'll be staying in tents and moving them along with you as you progress with the clearing."

Frank sobered a bit. "I don't know how Alice is going to take this. She's grown so fond of the hills and the forests here. I remember how she shuddered at the look of the bare brown hills on both sides of the river as we came through."

"Well, you go on home and break the news to her. You might mention that there's a substantial raise connected with this job. That might help cushion the shock a bit. I'll talk to her later about her replacement here."

Frank left the office as if in a fog. His mind was filled with questions. How was Alice going to react to the news? This job would be an undertaking for giants. Problems and their possible solutions whirled in his mind.

Alice looked up from her sewing and rose to greet Frank. "What is it? I wish you could see the expression on your face. Something big is about to happen, I'll wager."

"I knew you'd sense it, Alice. You can read me like a book."

She stood with her arms crossed, a stern look on her face. "Alright, page one: You've just come from Harney's office; I heard the wagon over an hour ago and you've always come straight home before. It had to be something official to bring you down in mid-week.

"Page two: Your face is all creased up in thought and you wouldn't look directly at me as you came in. So it has to be news that you're not sure I'll like.

"Page three isn't clear yet. You'd better sit down and tell me about it before the children wake from their naps."

He sat slowly and deliberately on the kitchen chair and ran his hand through his hair. "I have some good news and some maybe-not-so-good news. How would you feel about another move?"

Her face brightened at the prospect. "Oh Frank, you don't even have to ask. We've been here over two years now. I've had itchy feet for some time. If that's all you're worried about, don't. Wherever you go, I'll follow, even if it's just a shack. I'll clean it up, hang some curtains and make it a home for us. Now tell me the rest. Where do we go from here?"

He stood up, walked a few paces and turned to face her. "I hate to tell you this, but do you remember the barren hills around Dales City? That's where you'll be living. The longer I work this job, the longer intervals I'll be away from you all. It may be years before it's all done.

"It's a good job; a real challenge. Harney thinks I'm the right man to do it. There *is* a good raise in pay to go along with it."

Alice stood and came over to him. She put her arms around his neck and looked deep into his eyes. "My dear, when will you learn that you are the center of this family? You go where you need to go and we'll follow."

She pushed him into his big, comfortable chair and sat in his lap. "Now tell me all about this new job and the when, why and how of it."

Frank heaved a sigh of relief and related the rest of Harney's story. "I'm to go into Dalles City on the train tomorrow to get the lay of the land. I'll have to find housing for you and the children. Then I'll go up on the supply train to where the first logging will start. I'll know more about it then.

"Harney's giving me authority to hire my crew, subject to the agreement of the superintendent in the office at Dalles City. They hope to get a good start before winter sets in."

Alice gave him a kiss and got to her feet. "I guess I'd better start some supper, then start thinking about a packing schedule for the move. We've accumulated a lot of things in two years that we can leave behind."

She heard Grace stirring and the other two singing together softly, as they always did before coming fully awake. Their singing seemed to be a bridge between dreams and reality for them.

Dalles City was still growing rapidly at the time Frank arrived. No housing was available. Many families were living in tents. There were long waiting lists for the shoddy housing that was springing up; houses not likely to last long in the extremes of the climate and the ever-present strong winds that were a fact of life here.

Frank had some difficulty finding the company office, up a steep flight of stairs, over a merchandise store. The superintendent and Frank might have been father and son, they were so much alike in color, height and build.

Frank introduced himself and offered his letter of introduction from Harney. While Arnborg read the letter, Frank had time to look around at the spartan plainness of the room. Its small, uncurtained windows looked out on the corner walls of the neighboring buildings. A plain deal table and three chairs made up the entire furnishings.

Putting the letter down, Arnborg looked up. "Please, sit down. I've been waiting to meet you. Harney's letter recommends you highly."

He turned and bellowed, "Lotta! Bring Mr. Walden a cup of coffee!"

Frank took a seat by the desk, but jumped up as a striking brunette entered. She carried a small tray. "Brought one for you, too, Peter," she said, speaking with a slight accent. Probably Scandinavian, Frank thought.

After a long conference with the superintendent, Frank jumped aboard a logging train going to the end of the flume and on to the area where real log clearing would start. He estimated that the logging crews would not be needed until mid-October.

The desert growths were a minor barrier to the contractors, but the terrain was a difficult one. Blasting of solid rock was necessary in some places and shifting sand complicated others. The flume traversed some steep hillsides in long swooping arcs. The radius of the curves had to be large enough to allow the huge logs to shoot down and around without catching and jamming. Clearing a jam was time consuming and very dangerous for the men. Logs that were propelled by the force of the water and gravity would often shoot out over the top of their earlier fellows, crushing men working to clear the jumble.

Back in Bridal Veil, Frank reported to Harney's office. "With your permission, I'd like to go back up with the survey crew. They're about to start into the timber country. I'd like to know a lot more about what we'll be getting into.

"However, that's not the big problem for me, personally; for my family I should say. Mr. Harney, there *is no housing* for new families in Dalles City. People are living in *tents* and coming in faster than new houses can be built! I don't know just what to do about it."

"If you've no objections," said Harney, "Alice and the children can stay on here for a time. It's really not that far by train, so you can visit easily. I've had no success in finding a replacement for her, so we *do* need her to stay on here, anyway. Talk to her. It's your decision.

"Your gear has been sent to your home, and you can set your own schedule to start. You have a free hand, working with Arnborg, just when you'll start actual logging. You'll be busy with your plans between now and then."

Again, Frank went home with a sinking heart. "Alice, I don't know how to tell you," he started. "There *is* *no* place for you and the children to live in Dalles City." He described what he had found there. "Mr. Harney wants you to stay on and keep your job here for the foreseeable future. We'll be apart for longer and longer intervals. Maybe you'd be happier here. I'll put in for one of the houses up there if you'd like me to. It's your decision."

Alice looked squarely at her long-faced husband. Standing in the circle of his arms, she searched his face for an answer before she spoke.

"I feel that we'd be better off here, in familiar surroundings. You are so tied in knots with your interest in this challenge, I couldn't deny you, nor could I add to your concerns by moving the children into such uncertainties. We'll stay on here."

Frank stood holding her for a long minute. Two excited little bodies, hurling themselves at his legs, broke the tension.

"Who are these two little Indians?! Mama, have you traded my little darlings for a couple of ruffians?!"

"Papa! Papa! Papa!" sang Carsie and Ilda, as they led Frank to his chair and swarmed over him with hugs and kisses.

At the sound of a sharp cry, Alice signaled that she was going to tend to little Grace.

"Come along, you two scamps; Papa's going to take you to the store. Scoot, get your hats and coats!" Out the door they went, singing and skipping down the road.

Alice sat in the rocking chair, Grace suckling quietly at her breast. The tears dropping on her face were of little concern to the baby.

Weeks at a time! Alice *knew she* could manage, but what would they do without Frank for months at a stretch? She would have to keep herself and the children busier than ever. Reasoning did nothing to stem the tide of tears streaming down her face.

Chapter Seventeen

THE TRAIN WRECK

Until the heavy snows of January, 1890, Frank was able to come home for a day or two every two or three weeks. He walked in the door on Christmas Eve.

"Surprise everyone, Santa's here!"

Immediately, he was surrounded and bowled over. "Hey, wait! You'll crush the goodies!" He lay on his back like a big bug, smothered by hugs and kisses, squeals and loving words, pretending not to be able to turn over.

When the reception quieted and the door closed, he was allowed to take off his mackinaw and was led to his favorite chair and helped off with his boots.

"What did you bring us, Papa?" Carsie's blue eyes were dancing.

"Pwesents? Papa, pwesents?" piped Ilda.

"We'll have to wait until morning and see, won't we?" Frank looked over the children's heads, his eyebrow quirked at Alice, in question.

"Hurry off to get your nightclothes on, children. Ilda, you can wear your new red one tonight. Scoot!" She patted their bottoms as they passed. Then she sat on Frank's lap and gave him a long passionate kiss.

"What do you say Alice, maybe let them have the ones I brought before bed, then in the morning they can have what you sent for?"

"I think that would be alright, but you'll have to tell them stories and sing quiet songs to get then unwound before they'll sleep."

"Done! It may be awhile before I can do it again. It'll be my dearest pleasure."

"Oh, no, Frank! Do you mean you have to go right back up?"

"Not until Friday's noon train. We're supposed to meet the supply wagon Saturday morning. The Indians say that there's bad weather due. The superintendent says he'd rather have us snowed in up there where we can keep on working than snowed out down in town."

Baby Grace was wide awake. Her big, long-lashed eyes shone with the infectious excitement of the others. Carsie and Ilda had returned, pulling their pajamas on as they came.

"Here you are, Sister, a Cellilo Indian doll to play with." Frank helped her unwrap the package. It was a beautifully carved wooden doll dressed in a beaded, fringed dress and moccasins.

"Papa, s'booful," Ilda's eyes went soft as she cuddled the doll.

"Look at that; a Madonna already, at two," Frank whispered to Alice.

Carsie stood back quietly and smiled affectionately at Ilda.

"Hmm," said Frank. "Seems to me I had something here for you, Son. Where do you suppose it went? Did you knock it out the door when you all bowled me over earlier? Let me see?"

"Shall I look outside, Papa?" asked Carsie gently, getting up from his place by the big chair.

"Wait, let me look first." Frank pretended an elaborate search all around his chair. "Do you suppose...? Here it is under the chair! Come on over here, Son, so I can help you with it." Frank pulled out the package wrapped in brown paper and laid it on his lap.

His usual calm manner almost forgotten, Carsie reached for the string and tugged mightily. But it was too stout for his four-year-old fingers. "Please, Papa, would you cut the string for me?" His eyes shone brightly in the lantern light as he followed the progress of his father's hands.

With deliberate slowness, Frank drew his pocket knife. He made a show of deciding which of the three blades to use, pulled at the chosen blade as if it were stuck, then quickly snapped the crossed strings. The bundle popped open. Fringed and beaded deer-skin cascaded at Carsie's feet.

"There you are, my little tawny-haired warrior; a real Indian jacket and moccasins!" He looked up at Alice. "They're a little large, I think, but he can wear them longer."

Carsie picked up the jacket and slipped it over his nightshirt, then stepped into the moccasins. He turned around, arms outspread to give everyone a good view.

His face turned very serious as he looked straight at his father. "I'm not sure this is the right thing for me, Papa. I wonder if I'll learn to like it." As he finished the sentence, his left eyebrow shot halfway up his forehead, but his face didn't change otherwise.

"What, why wouldn't you like it?!" Frank's eyebrow raised in echo of his son's. He turned to see what was up with Alice. She had put Grace on her lap and was choking with laughter.

"What goes on here? What's so funny?" Frank was puzzled. He turned back again to find Carsie giggling uncontrollably, as he flung himself into his Papa's lap.

Alice got control of her laughter and wiped at her streaming eyes with a corner of her apron. "If you could have *seen* the two of you! Those *eyebrows;* like father, like son. Carsie's just like you; he'd rather tease than eat. All you had to do was watch that eyebrow to know he was putting on an act."

"Teasing me, eh boy?! We'll have to take care of that!" Quickly Frank flipped the giggling boy over and pretended to paddle him. Then he lifted him into a bear hug. Alice, Grace and Ilda laughed at their antics.

Other, smaller trinkets came out of a small pack behind Frank's chair. When the last one was opened and admired, Ilda yawned and rubbed her eyes. "Sisser sweepy, Papa. Sing a song, pwease, Papa?"

Both children climbed into his lap and cuddled down against him. The vibrations in his chest as he sang soft songs: Silent Night, Adeste Fidelis and others, soon had them both sound asleep. Alice finished nursing the baby, put her down and took Ilda from her father's lap. Frank rose from his chair, cuddling Carsie in his arms, and together they tucked the sleeping little ones into their beds.

Two hours later, the small Christmas tree decorated with handmade ornaments, two loving parents tumbled into their own bed, too tired for lovemaking.

Christmas afternoon was gay, with neighbors dropping in. The roasting turkey perfumed the air. Coffee and tea accompanied a platter of Alice's by-now-famous Poor Man's Fruitcake for all to share.

Overnight, a soft snow fell. It came quietly in huge airy flakes. An even ermine-like cloak covered the whole town.

That was an enchanted Thursday. The snow was perfect for making snowmen and snowballs. Every man, woman and child in town was out in the clear cold air. Halloos, laughter, the rumble of men's voices, chatter of women and piping of children filled the town the day-long. It was a day out of a fairy tale; a magical time to be recalled for years.

On Friday morning, the snow was gone, melted away in a warm rain that had tiptoed in during the night. Frank awakened early that morning; he wanted as much time with his family as possible before the train took him away, possibly for months. The children slept later than usual, so there was a time for sleepy caresses, awakening desire and a burst of passion before the day began.

Breakfast was eaten in an air of forced gaiety by the parents. They had decided to prolong the happy moment for Carsie and Ilda until the last minute.

Toot, toot, toot, toooot! The emergency whistle blew the entire populace out-of-doors. Word came that there was trouble at the train shed.

"Sarah Jane!" Alice called to Mary's daughter. "Can you come over to stay with the children? I'll be needed if there are any injuries."

"Of course I will." She ran to tell her mother, then returned, her skirts flying, to coax the two little ones back into the house for a game.

Alice and Frank ran with the others to the tracks. A handcar stood on the main track. A man in a brakeman's work outfit was standing beside it.

"Trouble at the switch." He was pointing eastward, speaking rapidly; repeating this one sentence over and over.

Someone cleared a path for Alice to the man's side.

"What is it, what trouble?" She asked him.

"Trouble at the switch," he repeated again.

Alice shook him, repeated her question and got the same response. "Hold him," she told Frank. Then she slapped the man's face sharply, first on one side and then the other. "He's in shock," she told those who gasped at her action.

The man stood absolutely still for a moment, staring into her eyes. Suddenly his face changed, and he shook his head as if rousing from sleep. "Oh, Ma'am," he moaned. The train's derailed! A boulder on the track. Lotta people hurt. Engineer and foreman may be dead. We crawled over all those logs to get to the engine. Found the hand car on a side rail. Other feller helped me get it on the main tracks. He was hurtin' too bad to help me pump. *Please,* somebody get some help up there!"

Frank yelled out, "Someone get the yard foreman here, fast!"

Alice looked around. "Helen!" she called, spying her in the crowd, "Would you get this man to the infirmary? Give him hot tea, lots of it, and keep him warm."

A prayer meeting was organized by the women and older children.

Soon the portly yard foreman arrived. "What's wrong?" He puffed. Then he saw Frank and came up to face him. Quickly, Frank told him the brakeman's news.

The foreman shouted out orders immediately, "Hey Joe, round up every man of the yard crew and anyone else you can find! Get 'em here on the double! Tell 'em to bring axes and pry bars! Tom, unlock those hand cars on the siding. We'll need 'em all.

"Ma'am, no tellin' how many injuries up there. We'll tow the small flat car up with the small switch engine to bring 'em down."

"We'll need a closed car," she said. "Injured people in shock need to be protected from the cold. While you get your engine warmed up, I'll go to the infirmary and get what I need.

"Frank, will you and three or four other men come with me to bring back the supplies? But first, run home and get our heavy coats and hats."

162

The emergency crews scurried off to retrieve the needed items and people. The hand car crews started for the wreck, to survey the conditions and do what they could to clear the way for the main body of rescuers.

At the dispensary, Helen and Alice bundled up blankets and handed them to the men. "Take these down and wrap them in canvas so they'll stay dry if it should start raining again." Quickly, she packed bandages, antiseptics, laudanum and some instruments into her bag. Just then, Frank arrived with their coats, which they struggled into as they ran back to the train shed.

Stakes had been installed into the sockets along the sides of the flat cars, and cable rigged between them for handholds. Over twenty men were aboard the flat cars when they pulled out of the yard. Someone handed out rubberized coats to protect against the wind and any possible rain. The tiny switch engine crawled at an agonizingly slow pace. It was built for power, to push the log cars, not for a race against time such as this.

In ten minutes the switch engine came to a halt behind the line of hand cars. Water seeped from the collapsed boiler, turning to steam as it reached the burning wood and coals scattered out from the overturned engine.

Screams and moans could be heard from the two passenger cars and the caboose at the other end of the train, several hundred feet away. Men were working with axes to cut a path through the long pile of huge logs, which lay at every angle where the impact of the sudden stop had broken them loose from their cars, scattering them in every direction.

Men from the flat car swarmed forward to tackle the jumbled logs. Some sort of clear way had to be made to allow rescue crews to get to the injured people.

A man in rail man's clothes came toward Alice. His head was crudely bandaged with his bandana. She stopped him.

"Have you come from the passenger section?"

"Yes, Ma'am. Lots of folks hurt pretty bad. The other car's still on the tracks, but folks are shook up and a few are cut from the broken window glass. I had a ***devil*** of a time getting over those logs to get back here. I didn't know if anyone had made it through."

She led him to the switch engine. Calling up to the driver, she told him, "As soon as we can get these tarpaulins and blankets off the flat car, go on back to Bridal Veil station. Have someone telegraph back to the nearest stations east; the first one that has an engine and a closed car of some kind; to send it here as soon as possible. The injured can be moved to a hospital to the east a lot faster and safer than we can carry them through the log jam and on to Portland."

"Yes, Ma'am, on our way!" The engineer started the switcher moving as the last supplies were removed.

Alice went back along the line of hand cars. She met Frank at the head of the line. He was stumbling and his face was ashen. Just as he reached her, he wretched violently.

"What is it, dear?" she said as she steadied him. "What did you find?"

He attempted to answer, but didn't get past "The engineer," before he vomited again. "Don't make me say it for a minute. It was too awful!" He wrapped his arms around himself to stop his shaking.

He walked the twenty feet to the river bank and rinsed his face and mouth in cold water before he could speak.

"I'll probably have nightmares for a long time. The engineer was over half-buried in hot coals. The... whole thing was... too... ***horrible!***"

"Is there nothing we can do, then?"

"No, thank God he died just as I got to him; he was burned too badly. I just... can't... stand the thought of it."

He held her for a moment, then dropped his arms and squared his shoulders. "Alice, I'm going back and help get a way cleared through the logs to those poor folks. I'll be back for you as soon as we can get you through."

Half an hour later, a young man came back to Alice. "Mrs. Walden, your husband is helping to get the last logs out of the way.

He's bigger and stronger than I am and said I could help more by coming for you."

The man took Alice's arm as they made their way past the overturned log-carrier cars. Men were still swarming over the first wrecked passenger cars; pulling the dead and injured out through broken windows. The other car and the caboose stood still untouched. Some injured passengers who had fought their way out were walking about in a daze. Some had started walking back along the track and had to be forcibly returned.

On the bank at the near end of the first broken passenger car, Alice found an Indian woman. She was sitting stoically quiet; her left leg twisted at an odd angle and badly burned from just above the ankle to mid-thigh. Her face was set, as if in a trance, but her hands were clenched so tightly that her nails had cut into her palms, causing blood to run down her wrists.

"May I help you?" Alice asked gently, as she wrapped a blanket around the woman's shoulders. "I'm a nurse. I'm here to help."

The woman slowly turned her head. Through clenched teeth she answered, "Go help the others. I can wait."

"Perhaps you can, but you're first in line. I'd like to give you something for the pain and then I'll get some help to set your leg and bandage it."

"Don't need medicine," the woman said. "My people have a way to put pain away with our minds."

"Perhaps you can, but you are in shock and could die from it. I promise that the medicine is not going to do anything but make you more comfortable."

Something about Alice's voice reached through to the woman. She nodded, "Alright, I will take your medicine. You have a good spirit."

Alice lifted the woman's head and spooned in the laudanum. While the drug was taking effect, two men who were passing recognized Alice and stopped.

"Do you need any help, Mrs. Walden?"

"Yes, could you find some boards from one of the wrecked cars, long enough to make a litter and a splint for this poor woman?"

"Aw, she's just an Injun," the younger man said.

The older man punched him in the arm. "Never mind your opinion. The lady said 'find some boards'; we find some boards." He pulled his companion away.

Alice bandaged the burned leg lightly while the men were gone. Then she showed them how to roll the boards up in the sides of the blanket to make a litter.

"Now, before we move her, reach one of those smaller boards to me," she said to the older man. "Can you hold her under her arms while I pull on this leg to set it?" Good. When I say so, you (she indicated to the other man) quickly put that board along her leg and hand me this roll of bandage beside my knee."

When Alice felt the bone ends fitting together, she said "now." The young man placed the board as he was told. "Now come over here and hold her foot; so. Don't move it or ease the tension on it." Quickly, she bandaged the splint tightly to the ankle and foot. She did not, because of the severity of the burns, dare to bind the splint elsewhere.

The two men carried the woman to the passenger car and found a place to put her down on one of the makeshift bunks.

"Thank you," Alice said to the older man. "You are most kind." Then to the other man: "I hope you never need help from an Indian." She gave him a stern look; the kind that her father used to tease about.

The younger man flushed, lowered his eyes and left the car, cap in hand. His companion stayed to help cover the woman with a blanket, and then carried the extra boards away with him.

In all, Alice treated thirty-two patients. Because the cars were last in line and were cushioned from the initial crash, only fourteen people were in need of hospitalization when they reached Dalles City. One of the least seriously injured women was a nurse, so as soon as the engine hooked up to the caboose, Alice left for home on one of the hand cars. Frank stayed for twenty four hours to help clear the track.

It was New Year's Day before the track was completely cleared. A part of the track bed had to be rebuilt, and several rails, with their ties, replaced before normal service could be restored. Frank left on one of the first eastbound cars.

Three times in those days, Frank had nightmares about the engineer. The fireman's body was never found. It was supposed that he had either been thrown into the river and drowned, or else buried under and consumed by the spilled coals of the engine's fire box.

Chapter Eighteen

TORN APART

In March of 1890, Alice was shopping in Bridal Veil while Sarah Jane watched the children at home. Leaving the General Store, Alice was window dreaming on the street toward home.

"Good day, Mrs. Walden. Haven't seen much of you since the flu epidemic. Guess we've both been too busy, eh?" The mayor cum owner of the feed store doffed his hat respectfully.

"Good day Mr. Henner. Are you wearing your Mayor's hat today or your businessman's?"

"Neither, I'm afraid. Today my hat fits the chairman of the school board. I nearly ran you down; my thoughts were elsewhere. We've a real problem here with our school system."

"So I've heard," Alice remarked. "Some of the older children and their parents have been telling me about it."

"They have? What do they say?"

"The parents are concerned that their children are losing interest in school. Then too, some have found out that our elementary school isn't accredited for entrance into high school. Neither Portland nor Dalles City will accept them."

"That's the gist of it. There's another side to it, though," he added.

"I suspect what it is, but tell me about it."

"The other side is lack of funds to hire better qualified teachers and build a high school. We have an increasing number of students from the company folks. They're all renters, of course, and don't pay property taxes. The company owns its own land and isn't carried on the town rolls."

"Perhaps we can get the parents together and come up with a solution. Give me two weeks to get something organized," Alice told him.

She sat up late with paper and pen for several nights that week.

On Monday afternoon, she left the infirmary and was on the way to pick up her mail. Sarah Jane met her halfway, "Mama told me to pick up your mail, too. She's with your children."

"Thank you, dear. I *am* tired. It's been a busy afternoon. I don't know what I'd do without you and your mama. I'm glad she's at my house; I've something to talk to her about."

Sarah Jane walked along with Alice until their homeward paths diverged. "Goodnight, Mrs. Walden; I'll see you tomorrow after school. I wish I didn't have to go; I don't get much out of it. My teacher isn't much older than I am and it's hard to act respectful, for the younger children's sake, of someone so close to my own age."

"Goodnight, Sarah Jane. Take care."

The house was warm and smelled of fresh coffee. Mary was holding baby Grace against her shoulder. Carsie and Ilda were sitting at her feet, hanging on her every word as she read a story from their children's Bible.

"Hello, Mary dear. Don't you have enough of your own children to take care of without tending to mine, too?"

"Pour yourself a cup of coffee," Mary told her, "and read your mail while I finish this story. Just a couple more pages to go."

"Thanks, I will. I've been longing for a cup all day. There just wasn't time to brew a pot today."

Alice sat down with her coffee and looked through her mail. There were some circulars from Portland stores and the usual short letter from Frank. He said it made him homesick if he wrote too much or too often. He'd written that the mail came by snowshoe carrier because the drifts were so deep.

At the bottom of the pile was a letter from Linnville. She put it aside to read later, when the children were in bed and the house was quiet.

Just then, Mary called, "You'd better come take the baby. She's fussin' at this old dry cow. I'll see about fixing some supper for you all."

"No, Mary, get yourself a cup of coffee and sit down for a bit. I'll get the children some milk to tide them over until supper. I need to talk to you."

She sat Carsie and Ilda at the table with milk and a cookie, then put Grace to her breast.

"It's the school situation. You know how unhappy the students and parents are about it. How do you feel about getting a meeting together to talk about a solution to the problem?"

"**Something's** got to be done," Mary answered as she finished her coffee. "I'll help pass the word for you, if you can get Mr. Harney to let us use the fire hall for the meetings."

"Thank you Mary. That's a good idea. I'll talk to him tomorrow, and we'll see what can be done."

After the children were all tucked in for the night, she sat down again at the table with her letter.

> Dear daughter, if I had the proper stationery, this letter would be edged in funereal black.

Alice braced herself for what came next.

> I really don't know where to start to tell you; so much has happened here in the last few weeks. Perhaps I'd better start with the conditions that started it all.
>
> We had an exceptionally dry fall and winter here. Everything is tinder-dry. There was a constant wind that made everyone irritable. Two weeks ago there was a terrible thunderstorm. The sky, at midday, was as dark as night. The lightning flashed in sheets across the sky. In midafternoon, it touched down and ignited the haystacks. They flashed into infernos as the wind whipped the flames and picked up bits of the burning hay.
>
> Before we were aware of the danger, the roofs of the barns, the carriage house and the houses in the rear yard were all on fire.

Alice shuddered at the mental picture. Her mind's eye recalled the hollow square arrangement of the yard dwellings and the carriage house.

> Everyone turned out and formed bucket brigades. New hay flares landed faster than the previous ones could be doused. It seemed nothing could stop it.
>
> Finally, Josiah ordered that the roof of the main house be wet down, too, so that it wouldn't catch fire. It was a useless decision. Fires started in corners, on window sills and in doorways. As the roof burned, the wind lifted the loosened shingles and carried them along.
>
> To make a long story less so, everything is gone, burned to the ground. Yes, even the plantation house. People formed lines to get the valuables out of the house, but the burning hay ignited that, too. It was just too much for even the large number of people living here.
>
> Annabelle slipped away in the confusion and ran back into the house to retrieve something. The burning staircase collapsed on her.

Alice put down the letter. Her vision was blurred from the tears streaming down her face. She took a deep breath and composed herself as she wiped her tears away. The letter continued:

> Our cottage was far enough removed from the fire to be spared. Neighbors took in most of the plantation people. We had Edith and some of the house people here at the cottage, sleeping on the floors for a week.
>
> Elizabeth, Imelda and their husbands took in as many of our people as they could. Most of the Negroes found jobs elsewhere in the county.
>
> There are some business assets to be accounted for, still. The lawyers and the court are in probate now, to literally dissolve the entire estate.

Your mother and I will stay on here until spring, at least. We are sure God will supply a solution for us. The Church has been in prayer for us.

I'm sorry that this letter had to contain so much terrible news.

The letter was signed with her father's usual flourish.

Alice cried and prayed herself to sleep that night. Her dreams were happy ones of her childhood. She had nowhere to go but forward now. She'd left her home, but no matter how far she'd traveled, she always thought of the plantation as her home. That anchor was gone now. Her beloved mentor, Annabelle, was dead. The graceful plantation house, the library that had played such an important part in her intellectual development, destroyed, her childhood friends, both colored and white, scattered to the winds.

She awoke with a cleansed mind. God had given her peace that everything would work out; that she would be the new anchor for her family, including her parents, somehow.

Mr. Harney granted the use of the firehouse, with the condition that he be allowed to attend the meeting. Word was passed among the company families. On the appointed night the fire house was crowded with the majority of the company wives and those loggers who were in town.

The red fire wagons were banished from the high-ceilinged room for the evening. Voices echoed and the smell of horses and harness oil from the adjoining stable scented the air. The volunteer firemen, dressed in whipcord and red suspenders, stood around the walls as if guarding their sanctum.

By informal agreement, Alice presided. Mr. Harney and the mayor sat with her facing the room. With a nod to one of the volunteer firemen, who touched the alarm gong for attention, Alice opened the meeting.

"Friends, we're all here for one reason; to decide what we can do to help solve the school problem in Bridal Veil. I'm going to ask the mayor, who is the chairman of the school board, to explain the problem to you. Mr. Henner, you have the floor."

In his easy-going, person to person manner, he related the problem of insufficient tax money available versus the number of students.

"We all know that the company is going to be opening a saw mill next to the yard soon, which will bring in more families with more children and thus more crowding in our classrooms.

"Company land and housing is outside our town limits and the company doesn't pay taxes except a minimum for services the town supplies for you. We're open to suggestions from you folks. We need your help."

Arguments and suggestions flew about the room with no feasible plans put forward. Mary's husband, Burt, stood up to be recognized.

"My wife and I talked this over before we came, and we decided to offer to pay whatever's fair for our younguns'. We can't afford much, but we want them to get a good education. Now that's our idea. You folks can go along with it, or if anyone can come up with a better idea, we'll go along with it."

The room buzzed for a minute, then several people, one at a time, stood in agreement with Burt.

Alice stood and thanked Burt. "That was a very good idea. I think it's no more than fair. Mr. Mayor, what do you think about it; will that suffice?"

"Thank you for your support," the mayor said. "I'll take it up at the next school board meeting. Now that leaves one more problem. Since we're expecting more students, we'll need to build a bigger school and a high school as well. That will require a lot of money. We'll have to take that up at the board meeting next month, also."

Mr. Harney stood up. The room went quiet in respect for this man they recognized as their advocate for the company.

"Folks, I can't promise anything, but I'll put in a good word with the Portland office. Once the saw mill is operating, I'm sure that we can provide the lumber for the buildings at a more than fair price, since it will benefit our people."

The firehouse erupted in applause. The mayor nodded his thanks. When Harney was seated, one of the loggers jumped up. "I fer one'll be there t' help with the buildin' whenever I'm down fer the weekends. Are y'all with me?"

A roar of deep voices rose in agreement, accompanied by whistles and foot stomping.

Alice stood and signaled for the gong. In the ensuing quiet, she thanked Mr. Henner, Mr. Harney and the loggers, then adjourned the meeting.

Before leaving, the mayor asked Alice to attend the next school board meeting in April to represent the company families.

After Sarah Jane went home, Alice sat down to write her parents about this turn of events.

Dear Mama and Papa,

I'm going to propose that the school hire teachers from the state normal school. That will require that we hire a principal with some experience in reorganizing curriculum to make the school here certifiable to the state.

Papa, if I can get them to agree, would you be an applicant? You did such an outstanding job of reorganizing the plantation system. I'm sure that the same type of thing will be applicable here.

Please do think about it. I'll send you what information I can get from the state capital on standards. Then, if and when they decide to do it, you can send a letter of application.

Alice's letter arrived like a thunder-clap at the stone cottage. Ercyline was enthusiastic. She had liked the Oregon country, particularly the river gorge. The idea of living in a town again and near Alice and the grandchildren was a welcome one.

Ernest was thoughtful for many days. He had not been in the habit of making important decisions for his life ever since they had returned to the plantation more than twenty five years earlier. His life had been ordained and orderly. He had been safe and secure in his position on the plantation.

"Our world has been torn apart," He told Ercyline as they sat by the hearth. "I don't know but that I'm too old to be uprooted."

Ercyline took his hand. "We *will* be uprooted soon, in any event. Only God knows what the courts will decide, or who will buy this land and our home."

"I suppose you're right," he sighed. "Perhaps I could draw up an outline of what I did in reorganizing the plantation's system. I do believe that I kept it up to modern standards."

"There you go, thinking constructively already. Why don't you get started on it tomorrow? Then when Alice sends you the papers from Salem, you can revise your outline to fit their standards."

"Do you really think I can do it? Do you still have that much confidence in me?" he brightened, "Ercyline, this is the most encouraging thing that's happened to me in a long time."

"Whenever you set your mind to a task, you've always done an admirable job," she answered. "I think the change will be good for both of us. We've been growing like a couple of old mushrooms here. There's nothing like a new adventure to put the zest for life back in a body!"

And so it was decided. The arrival of the papers from Salem heralded a flurry of writing and rewriting. As soon as Alice wrote that the town had decided on the idea of a superintendent of schools, Ernest sent off his letter of application, endorsed by the school board in Linnville and several prominent friends of Uncle Minot.

Chapter Nineteen

THE PRINCIPAL

On a warm day in early July, Alice had been shopping at the general store and was starting for home when she heard a man's voice, "Mrs. Walden! Mrs. Walden! Wait a minute!" The mayor, panting from the heat and the exertion of moving his considerable bulk, came running up behind her.

"Your suggestion for a school superintendent is about to be fulfilled!"

Her fingers crossed behind her, Alice offered, "Congratulations! Have you decided who your man will be?"

"A man admirably suited for a reorganization plan, it would seem from his letter and recommendations: a Mr. Beebe from Illinois. We agreed that his qualifications were *outstanding*!"

"That's good news, Mr. Mayor. When will he be arriving?" Alice was hard-put to contain her excitement.

"We've asked him to be here by the first of August, if possible. That will give him nearly six weeks to get the first stages of change in the works."

"Thank you, Mr. Mayor. I'd better get along home and start preparing for my guests. Good day, Sir."

"Prepare for guests? Are you expecting folks from out of town, Mrs. Walden?"

"Yes, indeed! Mr. and Mrs. Beebe will be staying with us until you have living quarters arranged for them," she grinned mischievously.

The mayor looked puzzled, "What...?"

"Mr. Ernest Beebe is my father. He and Mother will want to get reacquainted with their grandchildren before they settle in town."

The mayor let out a hearty laugh, "You are a ***devious*** woman, Mrs. Walden! I guess I'll see you in August when your parents arrive."

"Of course, Mr. Mayor," Alice smiled as they parted ways.

Two weeks later, Alice left the children in Sarah Jane's care while she went to meet her parents' train.

"We've burned our bridges behind us, Alice!" her father said as he stepped off the train.

"Indeed we have, dear." Ercyline took his hand to steady her step down from the vestibule. "Your father is ten years younger in anticipation of a new adventure. He's been walking on air!"

"That's because the butterflies flitting about in my stomach are keeping me aloft," he answered.

"What are you worried about, Papa? The townsfolk are fine people, and anxious to help you get started, you'll see. Now come along; the children have been so excited, they barely slept last night. I confess that I didn't sleep much, either. Hopefully, we'll all sleep well tonight. There's a small reception planned for tomorrow night, to acquaint you with the school board and the teachers. You'll need to gather your wits for the questions you'll be asked."

Ernest won over his neighbors with his charm. Ercyline, in her quiet way, had no trouble fitting in with the ladies. While her husband met and made plans for action with the school board in the next few days, she was busy settling into the small house that had been provided for them. The ladies of the town had stocked the cupboards with food. Until their own household effects arrived by train, their bare necessities were loaned to them.

"The plantation property is still in limbo," Ernest reported. "The girls told us to take whatever we wanted from the cottage and arranged for funds enough to pay freight for our household goods. The lawyers gave me two thousand dollars in exchange for a quit claim to any inheritance."

"I *knew* there would be provisions made for you from the estate, Papa. Imelda and Elizabeth have written to me of their affection for both of you."

"We're certainly grateful," Ercyline added. "We'd have been near destitute without their generosity."

And so Ernest became engrossed in his new career. Ercyline spent a great deal of time with her grandchildren. Both were quite content, as was Carsie, who strutted hand in hand to first grade class with "my grandpa, the Principal!"

The school and its students thrived under Ernest's care.

That winter was mild, affording more visits from Frank than the previous one. These extra visits probably had something to do with Alice conceiving again in February.

Early that same month, Bridal Veil acquired the services of a fine young doctor. Thomas William's dark, ruddy complexion and stocky physique harkened back to his welsh miner ancestry. He came to their town by recommendation from his brother, a logger who had told him of the rugged beauty of the country, the fine, friendly nature of its people and their need of his skills.

He and Alice worked together amicably. She was thankful to have medical help so close. It eased her burden as well. The town had grown so large, that at times it had been difficult for her to keep up with the medical needs of its populace, in spite of her helpers.

The months passed without incident until September. Again, Alice was beset in the last weeks of her pregnancy, with edema.

Frank was worried that this time the edema seemed to be accompanied by a mental darkness. He could no longer tease her into a change of mood. With her reluctant consent, he called upon Dr. Williams to examine her.

Sarah Jane was with Alice and the children when the doctor rapped on the door on a Tuesday morning in late September.

"Dr. Williams, please come in. Mr. Walden told us to expect you." She took his coat and hat and hung them on pegs by the door before she led him into the bedroom.

"Mrs. Walden: Dr. Williams to see you."

"Hello, Doctor, it's nice to see you again. We haven't had much need for your services this summer, have we? What may I do for you?"

"You do for me? Dear lady; one look at your face and hands should convince you that it's my services that are needed here. May I further examine you?

"All right, but I don't think it's really necessary. Frank is such a worrier under that cheerful face he shows the world. I went through this with my second pregnancy, but had no problems with the first and third."

The doctor pulled back the coverlet to expose her grossly swollen feet and ankles. He tried to hide his worry.

"May I examine your abdomen, please?" He pulled the covers over her legs and, with her help, raised up her gown. "Just as I thought, you have eclampsia. This is more than just edema, Alice. What have you been doing for it, besides raising the foot of the bed?"

"I have an herb mixture that makes a rather unpleasant tea, though it works very well as a kidney stimulant."

Dr. Williams further tested her for reflexes and taughtness of the abdomen. "I see that you've been careful of your diet. Your fingernails and eyelids show a nice deep pink. There's no sign of anemia.

"Young Lady: would you bring that lamp closer? I need to check for possible distension and dilation of the cervix."

Upon examination, he exclaimed, "Well! I see we might have a problem here. When do you estimate the term of this pregnancy?"

"About the first or second week in November, if I calculated correctly."

"We'd better prepare for a surprise then. There is a slight dilation **now**. Eclampsia often precipitates early delivery. If you've not delivered by the end of this week, I'd like you to come and stay in the sick ward behind my office. That way I'll have more equipment to deal with a premature infant."

"Do you really think it'll come to that? My previous deliveries have been spontaneous. In fact, **explosive** might be a better description."

"It may well be again, but we have first to think of the child's welfare. Promise me that you'll come or send for me the **minute** you have even a twinge of a contraction."

"I promise. Thank you for being so concerned. I'm sure everything will be just fine. Just wait and see.

"Now, will you have a cup of coffee? Sarah Jane has inherited her mother's talent with a percolator."

Doctor Williams patted her hand and rose from his chair by the bed. "No, thank you, I have two other calls in this part of town."

Over the next six days, Alice's depression deepened. It was as if a miasma of dread hung over the house. On Friday, she noticed a red stain in her gown as Sarah Jane was helping her with a sponge bath.

"Honey, when you're through feeding the children, will you go over and ask your mama to see about getting me into town. I think it's time for me to go to the clinic, and I may need some help."

Helen sent word ahead to the doctor and borrowed a small wagon from the yard. One of the men came to drive Alice into town. She found she was too dizzy to stand alone. The men struggled to get her into the wagon gently. Helen bundled her warmly against the cool September evening.

The doctor was waiting for them. He and the driver carried Alice inside. No sooner had she been settled into bed, than the first contraction came. It was a strong one, and Alice gasped out in surprise.

The doctor's wife, a nurse herself, came running. She was nearly bowled over by her husband's headlong rush through the door.

"That must have been a strong contraction! Was it the first one?" he asked.

"Yes, Thomas, but it was something different than before."

Quickly, he examined his patient. "Katie," he said to his wife, "bring the obstetrical pack over here, then take the receiving blankets in the kitchen to warm them. Put that small basket on the oven door and line it with blankets. We're going to have a tiny one."

Dr. Williams pulled up a table for the pack of instruments and went to wash his hands.

It was a difficult delivery; Alice labored long and hard. "It seems we have a breach presentation," the doctor told Alice between contractions. "I'm having no luck turning the baby."

For six hours, they struggled, before the little boy made his appearance. He was very thin and had a full head of black hair.

"Give him to me!" Alice begged.

"Not this little fellow, Mama! He needs suction to clear his breathing passages."

Application of a syringe to suction the mucous was of no avail. A sharp swat on his bottom brought no reaction either.

"Katie, do you still have that tub of rinse water in the kitchen?" At her nod, he rushed the baby out of the room. He plunged him in and out of the water several times before a cry, more like a faint mew emerged, as the tiny chest began to expand and contract, at last.

"Here you are, Katie. Wrap him up tight and tuck him into that basket. We'll have to keep the fire going all night to keep him warm."

Alice was almost out of the bed before the doctor got back to her. "Get back in that bed!" he roared. She was too weak and surprised at his unusual outburst to argue, and did as she was told.

"Is he alright? Is he alive? I want to see him!"

"No, you can't. We can't even weigh him yet. Katie is watching him every minute. She'll see to him. You need to rest. Lie back now and sleep."

As he pulled the covers up to her chin, her eyes closed and she fell into a deep, exhausted sleep. She barely even stirred when, an hour later, Katie came to bathe and dress the flesh torn by the baby's buttocks-first exit.

Thomas Williams was iron-willed under the mild manner he presented to the world. "Alice Walden, I don't care if you *are* a nurse. You are *not* leaving this bed until I say you can. Don't even *try* that fierce glower on me. Lie down!"

"We'll need some of your milk." Katie said. I'll help you express some. The little fellow is too weak to suckle yet. A few eyedropperfuls at a time is all he'll be able to manage."

On Saturday night, Frank came to see his new son, and chuckled. "Alice, they've got him all swaddled and tucked into his basket, until all that shows is his rather large nose and a shock of black hair. What have we produced this time?"

On his way out, he stopped in at the doctor's examining room. "Dr. Williams, what happened with this birth? Alice looks awful. Her color is so grayish yellow. She insists that I ask you when she and the baby can go home."

"I know, Frank; it's like trying to hold back the ocean. She's a strong woman but doesn't realize how much this ordeal has taken out of her, nor how much blood she lost.

"The little fellow will need to be kept tucked up warmly and fed every hour for a month. She's much too weak to attempt that for several more days, at least.

"Is everything all right at home? Are the other children being taken care of properly?"

"Everything is fine at home. Her parents live in town, and my mother-in-law has taken them to stay with her for as long as necessary.

"Keep her down as long as you can. She's strong-willed and will want to cart the baby off home as soon as possible."

Alice's recovery was more rapid than Tom Williams expected. He persuaded her to stay on for a few days, gradually taking over the care of the baby.

Finally, the day came when Henry Cody was taken home to meet his brother and sisters. Ercyline came each day from town to care for the little family while Alice used most of her returning energy caring for "Little Tucker", as he was tagged.

Ercyline had given him the nickname when she noticed that Henry would not sleep and was fussy unless he was swaddled closely and tucked firmly into his blankets. "Tucker" or "Tuck" became his family nickname for all of his life.

He was a strange baby; quiet, and watching every move around him, except when being changed or bathed; then he howled with a fierce temper. His black eyes were small and crowded close at the sides of his narrow beak. His greedy mouth was a wide, lipless slit. Through childhood, he was endlessly hungry, yet always thin and short for his age.

Tucker's violent birth had a farther-reaching effect on his parents. A freak of healing made sexual intercourse impossible for over three years. It would be several years before Alice became fertile again. This was not an easy time, but they drew strength and patience from God's promises that He was with them and had a plan for everything that occurred in their lives.

Chapter Twenty

THE INDIAN WOMAN

On a cool spring morning the year after Tucker's birth, a wizened old Indian woman knocked on Alice's door.

"Are you Spirit Woman who helped Indian girl at train wreck many moons ago?" she asked Alice.

"Yes, I tended to the wounds of a young Indian woman. What can I do for you?"

"Ka-teen-ha is daughter of my son. Her hurts are healed and bones are strong but she has much pain and cannot stand or walk straight like Cellilo girl should. She not find husband. Cellilo men no want crooked-walking girl."

"I'm so sorry. What can I do to help your granddaughter?"

"Ka-teen-ha say you have good spirit. She think maybe you can help crooked leg. Can you help her?" The old woman stood quietly on the doorstep, her black eyes soft with concern and hopefulness.

"I don't know, Old Mother. I'm not a doctor. Perhaps if I see your granddaughter, I could give some advice."

The old woman turned and beckoned to a figure standing in the shadow of a tree. Alice started, as a woman stepped forward. The left side of her body was pulled down and twisted as she walked. Pain had marked her once pretty face into a sorrowful mask. There was little resemblance to the woman at the train wreck.

"Do come in, both of you." Alice seated the grandmother. "Ka-teen-ha, would you lie on the bed, so that I may examine your leg more closely?"

The young woman did as Alice asked. When Alice had finished the examination, she offered her guests some refreshments.

When she had learned all she needed about her patient's history, she asked the old woman, "May I keep Ka-teen-ha here with me for a time? I want to take her to visit a doctor friend of mine. He is very wise and might be able to help her."

Ka-teen-ha waited respectfully for her grandmother to speak. The old woman nodded her head.

"You can do me a great favor, too," Alice turned to Ka-teen-ha. "The young girl who has helped me care for my children is leaving soon to go to school in Portland. I'm in need of someone to care for them when I'm working at the dispensary."

"Yes, yes!" The young woman's Indian stoicism broke. "I will do whatever you say!"

She turned to her grandmother. "I will stay with this spirit woman."

The old woman rose, bowed her head to Alice and placed a hand on her granddaughter's head in blessing. Without a word, she walked from the house and down the road. Ka-teen-ha stepped outside and brought in a rawhide bundle containing her sleeping pallet and personal effects.

Alice sent word to Dr. Williams, asking for a consultation in her home. He came later the same day.

"I would have brought my patient to you, Doctor, but you'll see for yourself why I didn't want her to walk all that way."

"Where is this young lady that concerns you so?"

"Ka-teen-ha, please come here!"

Thomas' eyes narrowed at the sight of the girl as she came into the room. "What has happened to you that you walk in such pain?"

"Mrs. Walden can tell you better than I can, at least the start of it all."

Between the two women, he heard Ka-Teen-Ha's story. Gently, he examined the grotesque, crippling scar tissue.

"You know, Alice, I worked for a time in a mining town. There was a fire in one of the shafts, and I saw crippling like this."

He turned to Ka-teen-ha. "I think we can help you, young lady. You'll suffer a great deal of pain for many months, but you may be able to walk straight again. I can do nothing about the appearance of the burn scars, however."

"I will do whatever you say, Doctor. You are her friend. I trust you."

And so Ka-teen-ha was settled into the only vacant corner of the children's bedroom and became a member of the Walden household. The children grew to love her, and she them.

She observed and respected their Christian practices, but held fast to her Indian religion; excusing herself when the discussion got uncomfortable for her.

Fractions of inches at a time, Dr. Williams' incisions to ease the pulling of the scar tissue and Alice's therapy sessions began to show results. Each bit of improvement brought a gradual lessening of the ungainly posture and gait of their patient. Alice's admiration of the young woman grew stronger with each passing month.

Just at that time, the lumber mill started operations and the company issued a new policy. Employees who wished to repair or enlarge their homes could do so on their own time. The mill would supply the lumber but the men would have to do the work themselves. A rush of applicants descended on Mr. Harney's office over the next few weeks. Frank was among them. The Waldens' house was a bit crowded already and the addition of Ka-teen-ha made an expansion essential.

Through May, the individual projects proceeded very slowly. The men had only Saturday afternoon through Sunday to work on their homes, and rumbles of discontent began to roll through town. In camp during the week, some of the men gathered in the bunk house. One of the men spoke up, "It'll take 'till hell freezes over to get my house finished! What's the use of the free lumber if we don't have time to use it?!"

"Walden, you're the educated one around here! Do you have any ideas?" said another.

"I sure have, in fact, I've been thinking about it for quite a while. Every time we've worked together on a project we've gotten a lot done. Why not now?"

That Saturday evening, with Frank as its spokesman, a committee presented themselves in Harney's office.

"It was a good winter harvest this year, Sir. You've got the mill pond chock-full. Can the mill keep working for a while on a slightly reduced log supply? We have an idea for getting more done on our houses, if it's possible."

"Actually, we were thinking of either laying off a few men or shutting down for a month or two next winter." answered Harney.

The committee nodded agreement among themselves as Frank answered for them. "We think we can help each other and solve your problem, too. Supposing some of the men who are building, say the equivalent of a crew from each camp, take a week off in rotation. It would cut down your overproduction and the men could help each other get their houses finished."

Harney smiled and banged his fist down on his desk. "Done! I don't like laying men off. You've solved it for me. I'll set up a schedule during the week and you can decide by lot which men will be off each week. I'll see you this time next week, right here!"

As soon as their extra room was finished, Ka-teen-ha helped Alice move the little girls' beds and belongings.

"This is a larger room than the boys'. There will be space for all four children to play in here, Alice. That is good."

"They'll have to wait for their playroom, though," said Alice, "It'll be too crowded for a while.

"Look out!" Alice pulled Ka-teen-ha away from the doorway as Frank came through carrying a bed frame.

"Here you are, young lady," Frank stated, "a double bed frame for you. You'll sleep more comfortably now. Here's the rope and there're the holes. You two get busy weaving the rope into the frame, while I go to the store and get the pad for it."

"For me? But Alice, I'm just fine on my pallet."

"Nonsense, besides, the girls are outgrowing their little beds. We'll move them into the big bed when you go home. So you see, it isn't a luxury at all."

Later that night, when Ka-teen-ha and the children were in bed, Alice told Frank, "I wish you could see how brave that girl is. The pain of stretching the scar tissue with heat and massage must be excruciating. She grits her teeth and sweats, but never cries out in pain."

By November of that year, 1892, Ka-teen-ha was ready to return to her people. She was able to do the continuing therapy on her own.

On the first anniversary of the day she had left, she knocked on the Walden's door once more. She was greeted by cries of welcome and children's arms entwined around her. Alice's clasp was equally warm. As they stepped away from their embrace an odd chill passed across the younger woman's face.

"You look just wonderful; so straight and tall! I never realized just how pretty you are. But something's wrong, I can tell. What is it?"

"I've come to ask you to come to my grandmother's funeral. She died yesterday and it was her wish that you be there as she goes to our ancestors. Can you get away for three or four days?"

"I don't know. When does the ceremony start? I'll have to see whether my mother can stay with the children that long. What have I done to deserve this honor?"

"Grandmother was so sure that you could heal me. She prayed to the Great Spirit for you every day after I came here. You were in her mind and in her prayers, continually.

"Please say you'll come, Alice, I want you to meet my people and them to meet you."

Ercyline was overjoyed at the chance to spoil her grandchildren for a few days. Alice would be home again before Frank came home on Saturday.

On the station platform upon their arrival, a sturdy Indian brave dressed in unadorned deerskin met the two women. Ka-teen-ha introduced him, "Alice, this is my brother, Ka-ma-tahn."

"It is my honor to meet my sister's friend, the Spirit Woman. Our family will always remember you for what you have done for Ka-teen-ha." He turned and led them to a small cart hitched to an Indian pony. "I hope the trip to Cellilo will not be uncomfortable for you, Mrs. Walden. This was the only wagon available. We were not sure if you could ride bareback. It is our custom, in time of grief, to put aside all unnecessary things."

Seated on the piles of fur robes, the women sat at the rear of the cart. Ka-ma-tahn squatted at the front to drive the pony. It was well past midnight when they arrived at the Indian village at Cellilo Falls. The cedar-bark-roofed huts were dark, but lights flickered through the oil-skin covered openings in the longhouse walls.

"Come, Alice, we will let you rest tonight. Tomorrow will be the start of Grandmother's journey to our fathers." Ka-teen-ha led Alice to a small hut warmed by a fire. Smoke rose through a hole in the roof. At one side was a fir bough-filled pad covered with robes. In a corner, covered with beautifully woven blankets, was a cot, whose mattress and pillow were rabbit skins.

"One of my sisters or I will stay here with you at all times. Our presence is required at the longhouse, but we can be excused to attend honored guests."

No sooner had Alice settled into the bed than a slender, attractive young woman entered. She introduced herself, "I am Ka-teen-ha's younger sister, Ka-soo-nee. We are happy to have you with us." She settled down on the pallet on the ground.

At mid-morning, after a light meal, Ka-teen-ha led Alice to the longhouse. Alice told herself that the term "longhouse" was certainly appropriate. About twenty feet wide, it was perhaps sixty feet long. The side walls were but four or five feet tall, but the center of the curved roof was quite high and the interior surprisingly light. Several small fires along the center line kept out the chill of the November morning. On a platform near the center of the building was a crude coffin covered by a brightly colored blanket.

Ka-teen-ha introduced her friend to her parents and other members of the family. Everyone sat on the hard-packed dirt floor. A blanket was brought for their guest and, though she protested, folded for a seat. It was explained that honored guests were expected to use them. Ka-teen-ha sat beside her and quietly explained the activities of the day.

"The blanket on the coffin is to keep Grandmother warm on such a cool day. This evening, more blankets will be added."

Drums and Indian flutes were playing softly all day, accompanying a procession of singers, who relieved each other in turn.

"They are telling the story of Grandmother's life," Ka-teen-ha explained, "She was a good woman; wise and strong. In her youth she was beautiful. Many braves sought her hand."

Throughout the day, members of the family and friends came and went at intervals. No food was eaten. "It would not be polite to eat in Grandmother's presence, as she cannot join us," Ka-teen-ha explained.

On the second day, members of the family and friends began to carry clothing, household goods, blankets and jewelry into the longhouse.

"What are they going to do with these things?" Alice wanted to know.

"These are all the things that Grandmother owned, used, or even handled regularly. They must all be given away. Nothing must be kept to bind her to this world. She must be rid of all things of this earth before she is free to go to her fathers."

People of the village came to pay honor to the dead woman. Most of them carried off articles from the display at the end of the coffin.

Suddenly, a shriek broke the solemnity of the room. Ka-teen-ha's mother and an aunt pulled a sobbing young girl through the door.

"My young cousin is disrespectful. She has not yet learned the dignity of a woman."

"Why does she carry on so? Is her grief so great?"

"Yes, but that is not why she cries out. Watch and you will see."

The women forced the girl to kneel beside the coffin and held her. An older man (her father, Ka-teen-ha said) used a steel knife to cut the girl's long braids close to her skull. She hid her face in her hands and sobbed more loudly as the thick braids were laid before the coffin. When the women released her, she jumped up and ran outside.

"What was that for? The poor child! Was that really necessary?" Alice was concerned for the girl.

Ka-teen-ha explained. "Grandmother was fond of my cousin. She used to say that she once had beautiful, thick hair like hers. She spent hours combing and braiding Ma-ho-mah's hair. Since Grandmother cared for it with her own hands, it must be cut off and disposed of. I objected to this practice, but my mother and Ma-ho-mah's parents said it must be so. I will give her a pretty shawl that she has admired to cover her head until her hair grows out."

Toward evening, Ka-teen-ha's father came over to Alice carrying a bundle of rawhide over his arm. "Spirit Woman, my mother wanted you to have this. She made it herself when she was younger." He laid it before Alice and turned to leave. Alice started to protest, but Ka-teen-ha held up her hand to stop her.

She knelt before Alice and opened the folds of the rawhide. "Grandmother liked this skirt and wore it for special times and when she was picking herbs or berries. It is heavy, and protected her body from branches and thorns. She said you were a woman of the forest. In a way, she is giving you her protection, too."

The skirt was mid-calf length on Alice, due to her longer legs. The waist was laced, so that it could be adjusted to the wearer. It had two large pockets with fringes of colored seeds strung along the bottom edges.

Alice was moved by this act of kindness and affection. "I'll keep it always and remember your grandmother and you each time I wear it, Ka-teen-ha."

That evening it was explained that the ceremonies would continue for seven more days. Ka-teen-ha told her friend that she was not obligated to stay for the remainder of the time. It was arranged that she be taken into The Dalles in time for the noon train.

Along with the skirt, Alice was given her choice of several trinkets for her children. She made good use of the rawhide skirt. It didn't wear out during her lifetime. One of her granddaughters inherited it and wore it for many years after Alice passed it on to her.

Chapter Twenty One

THE OTHER SIDE OF THE COIN

Tales of November's Indian funeral were added to the Walden's family chronicles, to be told again and again on rainy nights. Soon, Christmas stories replaced them. The children were dancing with anticipation of their father's return from The Dalles on Christmas Eve day. The noon train whistle sent them scampering to the front window. They watched eagerly for his long-legged, bundle-laden frame to appear on the road. Just after they tired of waiting and left the window, there was a rap at the door. Carsie rushed to open it. His bright smile faded; the visitor was a neighbor who was one of the Dalles flume crew.

"Mama, it isn't Papa," Carsie called over his shoulder.

Alice came frowning to the door. "What're you doing here, Hank? Have you news of Frank? Did he miss the train?"

"No'm" was his answer. "Frank didn't come into The Dalles with us. He was out with a crew of surveyors and timber cruisers. We had a heavy snowfall the last few days and we figure they're holed up somewhere until the storm's over. They've plenty of food and supplies. We couldn't look for them in the storm. We just barely made it out ourselves. Don't you worry none, though; they're all experienced woodsmen and know how to get by."

"Thank you, Hank. We appreciate your coming to tell us. Merry Christmas to you." Alice closed the door and turned to the children. Their faces were maps of disappointment. She had to hide her own.

Carsie's gentle words shook her out of her despair. "It'll be alright, Mama. We can just wait and have our Christmas when Papa gets home. It'll be just as much fun. Besides, we'll have two Christmases, one with Grandma and Grandpa tomorrow, and one with Papa, later."

As usual, on Christmas Day, neighbors stopped by fairly early to share coffee, cocoa and cookies and exchange gifts.

Their gaiety was a little forced as they pretended that there was nothing different. Each family said a word of assurance as they left.

In mid-afternoon, carrying Tucker, Alice shepherded the older children through a light snowfall to her parent's home.

"Won't Grandpa and Grandma be surprised that Papa isn't with us?" Carsie's eyes twinkled. "Let's tease 'em and say he's gonna be late."

What a sweet child, Alice thought. He's trying so hard to cheer us all.

"It won't work, Son. Grandpa knows about your eyebrow."

"Oh pooh! Why can't I control it, Mama? It gives me away every time!"

"You should be glad that you have something of your father's that no one else has."

"Ouch! Mama, that boy threw a snow ball at me!" Ilda was brushing powdery snow from her collar.

"Come on, Sister!" Carsie shouted, "Let's throw some back at him. He's bigger, but there are two of us." The snow was powdery, and the inexpertly-made snowballs flew apart in the air, but it was great fun. Three-year-old Grace tried gallantly to keep her ladylike dignity as she walked at her mother's side. Finally, she could stand it no longer and stooped to pick up a mitten-full of the white fluff. After several attempts to form a snowball, she gave up and marched back, chin in air, to her mother's side, until they arrived at the Beebe's.

Tactfully, Ernest removed the extra chair and place setting, while Ercyline helped remove coats, hats and mittens.

Dinner over, Ernest sat back with a satisfied sigh and leaned over to Carsie. "I like this, don't you, Boy? All these pretty ladies to ourselves for once. When your Papa gets back, we'll have to share them. Meantime, let's enjoy it." Carsie sat back in imitation, but his agreement was not so hearty.

Snow fell heavily all afternoon and evening. Ernest stepped out on the stoop after dark. "Alice, come look. No one else is stirring. It looks like you're snowed in for the night. It ***will*** be a diversion for the little ones, to take their minds off their father's absence."

"What a great idea! I've no desire for wading through that stuff in the dark toting Tucker. He's getting heavy to carry and the footing may be slippery. I accept!" She was glad for the diversion herself, though it did nothing to allay a sense of foreboding that she couldn't shake.

Carsie and Ilda delighted in helping Ercyline make cookies. Ernest read the Christmas Story to them. Grace and Tucker found new corners to explore, and made forts from blankets and chairs. Alice was grateful to sleep late while Ercyline doted on the children.

On the third day, Ernest called to Carsie, "Come on, Son, let's go over to see if there's a letter from your papa. We both could use some exercise." The two set off, frolicking through the winter landscape, throwing snow at one another and laughing. They returned with a customarily short letter from Frank:

> Dear Family,
>
> Sorry I can't be there for Christmas. I will see you all about January seventh. It's a long story, so I'll wait until I get home to tell you. I'm alright; don't worry.
>
> Love to all,
> Frank

"Well!" exclaimed Ercyline, when Alice put the letter down, "Frank certainly doesn't tell you much! Are all his letters like this one?"

"Yes, Mama." Alice smiled at her mother's frown. "He hates to write letters. He says he has to repeat everything when he gets home anyway. His letters tell me when he's coming home and that he's alive. I have to settle for that."

The little family stayed until New Year's Day, when the snow finally cleared enough to allow safe passage back home.

On January eighth, Alice was on her way home from the dispensary just as the evening train from upriver whistled its arrival. She thought she might as well go to meet it. There was a chance Frank was coming in. She and the train arrived at the station at the same time. The conductor jumped down to place the metal steps, then mounting them, reached back into the doorway as if to assist someone out of the car. A chill ran through Alice's spirit and she began to run. A quick check of momentum prevented her from crashing into Frank as he hopped off the step on his right leg. The other foot was bandaged and his leg bent at the knee. He reached back to get a pair of crutches.

Alice waited until he was balanced on both crutches before she spoke, "Mister *alright* Walden I presume? What have you and your foot been up to?" She stepped back as Frank held his arms awkwardly to embrace her. Her look, half concern, half annoyance, momentarily stopped him.

"Hey! I'm here, hale, hearty and homesick! Is that any way to greet a long lost husband?!" Frank smiled wistfully as he took a hesitant step toward her.

At that, Alice broke. With tears in her eyes, she walked into his arms. "I've had a vague feeling of dread since Christmas Eve. I knew something was wrong, but I kept telling myself not to be a silly goose."

Then, after a long hug, she wiped her eyes. "Come along home; you'll have time to tell me about it on the way." She picked up his valise.

"You'll have to go slow; I haven't learned to make very good time with these things yet," Frank said as he hobbled along beside her.

Frank made as light of the story as possible as he unwound it on the way up the hill.

"A couple of surveyors, two timber cruisers and I got caught in a blizzard and holed up under a bluff. We were dragging in fir boughs to make a shelter when a good-sized snow slide caught me and sent me tumbling down the hill. I wound up with my left foot in a creek. A small tree wedged me in so I couldn't move. My head and right arm were above the snow, so I could yell and wave. It seemed like hours before the others found me and got me out. Lucky I had my heavy boots on. My foot got mighty cold where it broke through the ice."

"So that's why the bandage? What did you do for the foot?"

"One of the cruisers got some snow and rubbed it gently on my foot until they got enough snow melted and heated up. They soaked some undershirts in the warm water and wrapped them around my foot. I never had anything hurt so much in my life. What a way to spend Christmas!

"The others made a travois out of fir branches as soon as the storm let up. They towed me out to camp behind our pack mule. From there, we rode the ponies into The Dalles. Arnborg helped them carry me to the doctor."

"How bad was it by then? Did the doctor let you see your foot?" Alice was trying to keep calm, but found herself shivering from anxiety and concern as she thought of the possible aftermath of severe frostbite.

"The doctor said it was second degree frostbite and that all the outer layers of skin came off when he uncovered it. He really took after it. He said it could get gangrene if I didn't take care of it. I told him I wanted to come home; that I had the best nurse in the country to take care of me. So here I am, and you are elected to spoil me until Dr. Williams says otherwise."

By the time they reached their house, Frank's face was white with pain. He was grateful to sink into the big chair and hold court for the curious, happy children swarming around the cushioned box which elevated his foot. A drop or two of laudanum eased him through the evening.

The spirit of Christmas had come to the Walden's at last!

Three weeks later, a valise and a canvas-wrapped bundle arrived from The Dalles. It was Frank's gear sent down from the flume camp. Alice clucked her tongue over the smelly clothing. "Didn't you ever wash anything out? Whew!

"What's this bundle?" She started to pick it up. "It's heavy!" She dropped it quickly, as Frank exclaimed, "Nosey Parker! If you'll just wait a minute, I'll show you." Frank pulled the bag to his chair and undid the intricate lacings that held the canvas together.

"For heaven's sakes, Frank! What are *you* doing with a shoemaker's last and tools?"

"Ole Swenson, who was cook's helper in camp, gave it to me. He was planning to quit at Christmas and go back east; said he wouldn't have any more use for it. He's been teaching me boot and leather repair for the last four or five months. I calculated I could make a little extra money with it and save a bit on our own shoes, too."

Alice looked through the smaller tools stowed in pockets sewn in rows inside the canvas carrier. "I saw the cobbler's shop back home but it was **nothing** like this. You've never said a word about it all this time."

"I thought I'd surprise you once I knew how to use it all. You never know when something like this may come in handy."

"Right now, it will!" Alice jumped up and soon returned with a pair of Carsie's shoes and one of Ilda's. "Carsie has been walking to school on these soles. They're so thin, as Mam Ginny used to say, 'He could step on a coin and tell if it's heads or tails!' Three eyelets in Sister's shoe are missing, as you can see."

"Well, nothing like starting right off. Yep, I've got a piece of leather that will do for half soles, and these eyelets may be a little different, but not so one would notice. My *first* job outside of camp!" He patted Alice's bottom suggestively. "I do hope there's appropriate compensation forth-coming."

"There just **might** be," she purred, "We'll wait and see how good a job you do." She pretended to slap Frank's hand away as she turned to ladle water from the stove reservoir into the dishpan.

"That shoe repair outfit was a God-send," She told Helen later. "Frank hates to sit still with nothing to do. He can work with it and still keep that foot up. Dr. Williams said it would be a month or more before it heals enough to take all the dressings off and walk without crutches."

"What a good idea!" Helen snapped her fingers. "With our large brood, we've always got a pair or two in need of fixing. That'll help you a bit, too. With Frank's income cut off, you'll be needing some extra money."

Frank, when approached with the idea, was at first reluctant to accept pay. "These are our friends, Alice. How can I charge them, when they've done so much for you and the children while I was away?"

"I know how you feel, dear, but we will be needing *some* sort of income for a while. My pay from the dispensary isn't enough. Also, I've been thinking that you could watch the children while I'm at work. That way I won't have to pay Helen's girls, too."

Ercyline heard of two widowers' families in town, who needed washing and ironing done. In a few days, Alice was extremely busy after dispensary hours. With her own family's laundry, her outdoor clothes lines were constantly laden in good weather. Wires strung in the big bedroom were substituted on rainy days. Fortunately, the late winter and spring that year were mild. She was able to use the lean-to shed in the yard for the washboard, and to boil white clothing over the fire pit.

"It reminds me of the laundry shed and lines back home in Illinois," she told Frank, "except that here, there's only me to keep them going."

"Alice, you're working too hard. You'll be down sick, and then what'll we do?"

"Nonsense; I get so restless in the winter when I can't work outside in the garden. All this is good to keep me active. I'd get fat otherwise, then you wouldn't love me anymore," she pouted.

"*You* get fat? Look at *me*!" Frank patted his belly. "You'll have to cut down on my food, or I'll be a barrel before I can get back to work."

Mid-March, in Dr. William's office, Frank was told to "get off your duff and find a job or you won't be able to get through the door."

"What do you mean, 'find a job?' I'm a lumberman."

"Not anymore, you're not; not unless the lumber company agrees that you can work in the woods only in warm weather!" Thomas' firm voice left no doubt of his sincerity. "I'm telling you, if you work anywhere that your foot gets even chilled, you will suffer the pains of hell. From now on you'll work down out of the mountains, preferably at an inside job where your foot will stay relatively warm."

Frank collapsed into a chair. This was a blow he had never thought could happen. He had planned to be a woodsman the rest of his life.

"Alright, I guess this is one more time when I'll have to trust God's promise that 'All things work together for good to them that love the Lord'," he sighed.

Frank walked into Harney's office with a face of optimism and a lump of pessimism planted firmly where his stomach was accustomed to being. An exchange of pleasantries over, Harney sat back, "What's the problem, Walden? You don't seem your usual cheery self. How soon are you heading back for The Dalles?"

"That's my problem, Harney. I'm not. The doctor says I can't take this foot up where it's cold; and I'd have a *devil* of a time going up there without it! What I need is a low-land job. Is there anything available here at the mill?"

The superintendent's involuntary change of expression told Frank the answer before he spoke. "I'm sorry, Walden. We're overmanned now, and I may have to lay off a few men for a while. It's been so wet that we can't get logs to the flume. Mud slides have shut down the roads, so we're getting short in the mill ponds.

"Why don't you let me ask around? I'm going to a meeting in Portland later this week. With your top work record, if there's anything open, you'll have a job. We'll hate to lose you and Mrs. Walden, but if it is to be..." his voice trailed off as he stood and shook Frank's hand in a strong grip.

Alice was finishing packing the wagon Frank had made for delivering laundry as he came up the road. "Who else, besides Dr. Williams, have you been talking to?" she asked. "Thomas told me that if your foot was as healed as he expected, he wouldn't need to see you again. I can tell you've had other news, probably not so good."

Then she turned to their oldest son, "Off with you, Carsie; trundle your wagon on down to O'Malley's and hurry back.

"Come on in the house, Frank, and get that foot up. You were favoring it a bit as you came up. Is it hurting some? What did Thomas say?"

"Oooh, it feels good to get off my foot. If I had a cup of coffee and a piece of that cake, I might be persuaded to tell you all about it."

"Coffee yes, cake no. I declare Frank, you're worse than the children. It's too close to suppertime, and you **don't** need the cake." She patted his belly as she handed him the earthenware mug. "Just half the milk and half the sugar, as usual, too. You can't eat like a lumberjack when you're not working like one. Now tell me all about it while I get supper started."

Frank was silent for a minute before he told her of the news. He had been rehearsing the proper way to tell her all the way from Harney's office.

"Well, it looks as if my itchy feet are going to get scratched, doesn't it?" she said as she put the food in the oven. They've been bothering me since before you went to The Dalles. I was all primed for a treatment then. Here's where I start putting into action all the moving plans I made then." On her way to the pump, she gently kissed his cheek. "Don't worry, I've got a good feeling about all this. Something told me it was past due."

Two weeks later, Alice was leaving her office at mid-day. "Oops! Excuse me, Alice." Said Mr. Harney. (It was one of those silly situations in which she was pulling the dispensary door open at the same time he was pushing at the other side.) "I just got in from Portland. On my way to the office I thought to stop by and ask if you'd send Frank down to see me. I have a bit of good news. But I'll hold off and let him tell you himself."

"That's **cruel** punishment to a woman's curiosity, but I guess I'll survive. I was just on my way home to have noon dinner with the family. Frank's getting to be a fair-to-middling' cook these days. I'll send him over right after he eats."

"Thanks, it'll give me a chance to wash off the train soot before he comes in. Good day, Madam." With a flourish of his hat, he bowed deeply and they parted ways.

Alice's curiosity was at a boil before Frank came grinning in the door that afternoon. "I'm off to Oregon City tomorrow to sign up for a job in the lumber mill. It starts in three weeks, Harney says."

"Oregon City? That's south of Portland on the Willamette River, isn't it? What kind of job?"

"I don't really know yet. Harney says it's a starter and won't pay too much, but the pay will improve as I learn the ropes. It's in West Lynn, across the river from Oregon City. I'll go down that way Sunday and talk to the company supervisor Monday morning. I'll be back Tuesday or Wednesday."

Through the open doorway of the big room, Carsie and Ilda caught the gist of Frank's "going away". They came running through the doorway. "Papa, please don't leave us again! Please don't, Papa!" they begged. Grace came in behind them and stood back, observing the tumult. Her stance and closed expression told her parents what Carsie and Sister were saying, and just as eloquently. Little Tucker stood expressionless, holding Grace's hand, clueless as to the meaning of all these goings-on.

"Sorry little ones. It's got to be that way. I'll be back as soon as I can."

Keeping his promise, Frank came in the dispensary door Wednesday at mid-morning. "Alice, I got the job! No more laundry for you after June first!" He picked her up in his arms and waltzed her across the floor, disregarding the smiles of several patients waiting for attention.

"Frank, stop it! This is no place for tom-foolery!" Alice blushed furiously as she struggled to free herself.

After a few more steps, he stopped, put her down and bowed to the applause of his delighted audience. "Thank you, ladies and gentlemen. As for *you*, Dear Lady," he raised the hand which he had kept captive and brushed it with a kiss, "I will see *you* at home *later*." He swept out the door, leering suggestively at his embarrassed wife. With a quirk of his left eyebrow, he vanished through the door.

That evening, with the children tucked in for the night, Frank and Alice sat down to talk over their plans.

Frank started, "I found a house to rent, with one bedroom, a sort of alcove that we can use for the girls' bedroom and a loft for the boys. It'll be available after June first. The current renters want to stay on until school is out. Guess that'll be better for us, too, won't it? I sure hate to go alone again. It's been grand to get reacquainted with my family."

"Never mind, Frank, we know it'll likely be the last time for a while. I'll keep them busy helping me pack up. I'll miss you, too. This is the longest time we've been together since we got married. We've gotten so spoiled. Not only that, but moving away from my parents will be hard, too."

"Close enough to visit regularly, though," Frank interjected.

"That will help some," Alice said as she cuddled close to him.

Dr. Williams found a practical nurse, a newcomer to Bridal Veil, to take over at the dispensary. She started on Monday, May twenty sixth. Alice worked with her a short time each day until Thursday. She found the young woman pleasant and efficient.

On Friday, Alice packed the last of her dishes and cookware into a barrel. She sorted and put a three-day supply of clothing in suitcases before packing the rest of their clothes in paper boxes. Her father came to help carry the suitcases to his home, where they would stay overnight. Frank would load their goods and drive them, in a hired wagon, to their new home the next day.

Chapter Twenty Two

RATS AND BEDBUGS AND A BEAR, OH MY!

A long two days after the tearful farewell to the Beebe's, Carsie and Ilda jumped down off the wagon's tailboard. Carsie turned back to help Grace and Tucker down. "Is this our new house, Papa? It's not as nice as our old one."

Carsie had voiced what the lump stuck in Alice's throat prevented. Back to Bluetown again, she thought. The lean-to kitchen on the left side seemed about to lean away. The roof was covered with tar paper, torn in several places. Two of the windows had cardboard nailed up to replace broken glass.

Frank came hurrying to her side after hitching the horses to a tree. One look at his tight-jawed wife was all that was needed. "C'mon, ol' girl, it's really not *that* bad. We'll soon get it set to rights. The housing agent is due this afternoon to see about getting the repairs done."

Alice made no reply. She squared her shoulders and shook off Frank's proffered arm. She walked to the door as if she were on her way to a tumbrel and the guillotine. Her heart rose to join the lump in her throat as she stood surveying the shambles inside the door. She stopped in her tracks and her knees grew weak as she surveyed the house's interior.

"It looks like they had a bar-room brawl in here before they left!" Broken furniture and glass littered the floor. "The dust is as thick as smoke, and it reeks of urine, beer and only **God knows** what else!" Alice stepped gingerly into the room. "Don't let the children in until I clear out the glass and filth."

"It's a wonder the house didn't burn down," Frank said as he righted the pot-bellied heating stove lying on its side.

Later, Alice wrote to her parents:

> It would take a ream of paper to list the damages and filth in the house. I just can't bear to recount them for fear of crying.
>
> We cleaned out the front room enough to put up our beds, then went to a restaurant for dinner. I would have been afraid to step into the kitchen, much less trust the crazy-angled, rusty stovepipe. I told Frank he'd better report it before the whistle blew the next morning. I would have marched down to the office myself if the crew hadn't arrived by noon. The Bluetown shack was a palace by comparison.

For a week, Frank lit lanterns at night and with a borrowed .22 rifle, shot at rats that kept them all awake. He made a slingshot for Carsie and taught him how to use it. There seemed to be herds of them skittering and scratching in the rafters and under the house. With traps, slingshot and gun, they eliminated most of them within a week. Alice killed others with poisoned meat placed well out of the reach of the children. It was to be a never-ending battle for all the time they lived in West Lynn. In spite of the efforts of the company and the tenants of the mill district, the rats continued to plague everyone.

By the time the house was put to some semblance of livability, bed bugs had made their appearance, and fleas! They came by the millions. Alice grew to hate the house and the company town so much, that she fumed whenever she spoke about it thereafter.

"Now that the family is going to be together all the time and there are several nearby, I think it's time that we started attending church again," Frank said one evening. "Have you heard anything from the neighbors about the churches in town?"

"I've had the same thing in mind. I met a woman in town and got to chatting with her. She says there's a small non-denominational church just down the lane that her family attends. I'll find out when the services meet." She gave him a quick peck on the cheek and went to tuck the children into bed.

The next Sunday, they attended the little church. It had been converted from a salt box house. From an inverted U shaped frame at the end of the gable hung a rather small brass bell; its tone was clear and rich. The congregation was proud that their bell had been brought around The Horn from New England. It had served several churches before they had acquired it.

Inside, a young man as tall as Frank greeted them. "Good morning! I'm Stephen Thatcher, the Pastor. Welcome to our little church."

"Thank you, Sir," Frank gave the proffered hand a hearty shake. "We're the Waldens. We haven't been in town long." With a smile and a quirk of his eyebrow, he added, "We thought we'd give you folks an audition today."

The pastor grinned broadly, "I do hope we get the role and the production has a long run. And this is Mrs. Walden, I take it? Welcome, Ma'am. What a fine looking family. We have a Sunday school for the older children, starting in...." he paused as he took a watch from under his coat..."about fifteen minutes."

He beckoned to a buxom young woman nearby. Bettina, dear, this is Mr. And Mrs. Walden and their children. Folks, this is my wife Bettina. She can take the children to their class."

Tucker was holding onto Grace's hand, as usual. Mrs. Thatcher gently detached him. "I'm sorry Mrs. Walden. We don't have a class for the tiny ones. You'll have to keep him with you in the Chapel." The three older children left in Mrs. Thatcher's wake. She looked back, puzzled. Later she remarked that she'd expected the little boy to cry or make a fuss at being left behind.

"We seldom have that problem with him." Alice told her. "He's our quiet one. He either goes along with whatever is expected of him, or goes off by himself."

They all enjoyed their first experience at the church and soon joined the congregation. The building was homey and the congregation friendly. Brother Stephen preached God's Word from his heart and Mrs. Thatcher charmed the children, so that they all looked forward to Sunday mornings.

It wasn't long before Carsie and Ilda made professions of faith and were baptized.

The family was some months in West Lynn before Alice had a chance to become acquainted with her neighbors. Long hours of work were needed to reclaim the house from its deplorable condition and transform it into a home. The move was early enough in the year that she was able to put in the cuttings and potted plants that she had brought with them in the wagon. She and Frank worked every spare moment to prepare the backyard garden for sowing vegetables. Alice had a small spot for a cold frame to force annual flower seeds. Frank found an almost intact window to use as a cover for it. In a very short time, her vegetable garden was flourishing and the front yard was a riot of color.

"This winter, could we transplant some of the rhododendrons we saw along the road from Portland?" she asked Frank. "Their delicate pink is *so* cheerful. *Anything* to brighten up our section of this dreary neighborhood."

Through the summer, Sunday afternoons were given over to rambling around the area, hiking into the woods and swimming lessons for the children in a nearby pond. Abandoned orchards were made note of for future fruit picking.

In August, Frank came home, almost running. "Guess what? Jim and Becky Ingeborg have moved into town! He got laid off at the mill in Bridal Veil and got on here. Let's have a party!"

It was their very first planned party. Neighbors, through the years, had dropped in uninvited. Sometimes the occasion would end up as a party, but never had they planned one. Their scope of acquaintances was wide, but their close circle, narrow. Loggers and mill workers were more prone than most other groups to heavy drinking and gambling. Since the Waldens did neither, their opportunities for socialization were limited to mostly church members.

The party was set for four o'clock on Saturday. For two days, Alice was busy baking breads and pies. Their guests, the Ingeborgs, Pastor and Mrs. Thatcher, two other couples from their church and two couples from the mill would bring the rest of the food. Friday afternoon, Alice looked at the clock as she took the last pan of rolls out of the oven.

Time to get Tucker up from his nap and start supper. She covered the rolls with a dish towel and went to see if Tucker was awake, but his cot was empty! Alice looked all around the little boy's favorite hiding places indoors, then outdoors. There was no sign or clue where he might be. The yard gate was latched.

By that time she was beginning to panic. When it came to her children, her usual calm competence was a thin veneer. Then she realized that the other three weren't about either. They'd been playing in the yard, earlier. Where to start looking?

She ran down the street calling them, "Carsie! Ilda! Grace! Tucker!" over and over. Everyone she saw, she questioned. Some older children scattered out to help in the search.

Toot, Toot, Toooot! The sound of the switch engine pierced through her body. Could they be down in the train yard?! The road ran parallel to an embankment, which was nearly even with the cab of the main line engines. The deeper tone of the big train's whistle and the prolonged clang, clang, clang of its brass bell alarmed her even more.

Around a slight bend in the road, she saw Carsie, Ilda, Grace and half a dozen other children. They were sitting at the top of the bank, their legs hanging over into space. As she arrived behind them, her footfall obscured by the sound of the train, she saw them raise their arms to wave to the engineer. At that moment a number of small objects came flying over the brink of the cut. The children scampered up and ran to gather them.

One of the brightly wrapped bits landed at Alice's feet. A boy made a dive for it and became entangled in her skirts. Most of the children had seen her by then and stopped, surprised, where they stood.

"What's this all about?" Alice tried to keep her voice calm. "What are those things?"

At that, all of the youngsters came to her, holding out their hands to show her. Out of the babble, she chose an older boy to speak.

"The engineer of that train smiles and throws candy and lollipops to us every day when he goes by."

Alice's breathing slowed as her heart quieted. "How long has this been going on?"

"Since the fourth of July." Answered the boy. "A bunch of us were out here that day, laying in the shade, and waved at the engineer. He waved and rang the bell and tooted the whistle at us. The next day he threw us some candies."

"Alright, he's gone now. I want you all to go home and tell your parents about this. They'll want to know. Maybe they'll want to find a way to thank the engineer."

The others wandered away, waving goodbye to Alice and her children. Suddenly it came back to her. How could she have forgotten?! "Sister, take Grace and go straight home. You can pick some strawberries from the garden for after supper."

When the girls were out of earshot, she put a hand on Carsie's shoulder. "Tucker's gone; I don't know where. We've got to find him. You go with the girls and then look up the road beyond the house. I'm going up by the switch yard and see if he's watching the trains."

Carsie scooted back along the road. As Alice hurried on, a man appeared over the rise ahead. In his arms, he held a screaming Tucker.

"Oh, my Lord; is he hurt?!" She ran to the man and held out her arms for her wayward toddler.

"No Ma'am, but he gave us all a scare, and the whistle of the switch engine set him hollering. We came around the end of a car and there he was, standing *smack dab* in the middle of the track, with the switch engine heading *right* for him! Tony ran and plucked him off the rail. I recognized him as one of yours and was just coming to bring him home. How'd he get so far from home?"

Alice rocked the sobbing little boy in her arms. "I have no idea. I thought he was asleep, then found he was gone. Thank you all for saving him. We'll keep a closer eye on him from now on."

She arrived home on shaky legs, thinking what could have happened. That evening she asked Frank to put a different, and more complicated latch on the gate, at a height where Tucker couldn't reach it.

On Saturday, the yard was teeming with adults and children. The men set scrap planks across saw horses and log rounds for tables and benches. The food was plentiful and hearty. The shady cool of the yard was conducive to a leisurely meal. Of course, everyone ate more than was good for them. The men sat back against the house, replete, or lay about on the mossy ground as the children played and the women put away the extra food and cleaned up the tableware.

Just before dusk, Pastor Thatcher reached for the fiddle case he'd slipped in unnoticed. Jack Smith, from just up the road, went home for his concertina. In the light of a full moon, Frank's strong voice led the singing between square dance sets. The children, one by one, fell asleep on their parents' coats and shawls. At last, the dancers exhausted, the group rested and sang old sweet songs and gentle hymns until it was long past time for sensible people to be out.

After church the next day, Pastor Thatcher pulled Frank aside. "I noticed Carsie was fascinated by my fiddle last night. Bettina and I talked after we got home and thought to put a question to you. We had a son, once. He got the fever when he was ten and the Lord took him home. We had bought him a child-sized fiddle when he was seven. If he wants, would you let me give *your* son lessons for *my* son's sake?"

"I think it would be a wonderful experience for him," Frank said. "I'll talk it over with Alice. The only thing is, we can't afford the lessons just now. We may have to wait a while before he can start."

"*Pay* me for it?!" the preacher exclaimed. "Who said anything about *pay*?! It would give me the greatest pleasure to teach an intelligent youngster like yours. He has a good sense of rhythm and a strong, true voice. Music is his talent. He mustn't be cheated out of it. Please urge Alice to let me teach him."

So, for an hour twice a week, Carsie went uptown for fiddle lessons. Sometimes Ilda went with him. Bettina longed for children of her own. "The Lord hasn't blessed us with any," she said. Now and then, the Thatchers kept the two children over for supper. After the meal, they gave them voice lessons. It was a real treat for Carsie and Ilda to go home and teach their father what they had learned.

The warm weather held through September. During the summer, the children had found a huge blackberry patch down a logging road.

After the children were in bed, the first Saturday evening in September, Alice asked her husband, "What do you think about going for a picnic after church tomorrow, Frank? You've been working on the house and helping me in the garden all your spare time. We can go out to pick blackberries for jelly; maybe put some up for pies, too."

"Alice, can't you ever think of maybe *just* a picnic? Who told you picking blackberries wasn't work, too?" He paused a moment. "Come to think of it, if I close my eyes I can *almost taste* fresh blackberry pie. Let's do it!"

The children each carried a pail with a sandwich and some milk. Most of the way, Frank carried Tucker in a makeshift backpack. He also carried a blanket, "To snooze on while the rest of you work," he told them. They all laughed, knowing he couldn't help but be in the middle of everything. He was always unhappy when he was idle. The rest of the food and supplies were in Alice's basket.

"Papa," Carsie's voice held a note of concern. "Timmy told me there's bears around here. Bears like blackberries, don't they? Do you suppose we'll see one?"

"I doubt it, son. Bears are more afraid of people than we are of them. The only time they'll bother you, is if they're frightened or protecting their young. We'll just sing and make lots of noise, so they'll stay away."

They found a wide shade tree under which to spread their blanket, rest from their hike and eat lunch. On the edge of a wide meadow, there were low clumps of blackberry brambles dotting the landscape; surrounded by late daisies and magenta fireweed. Alice taught the children to make daisy crowns for their hair, while their father told them stories of the logging camps.

"If we're going to get our berries and be back home in time for supper, we'll have to get a wiggle on!" Alice tickled Carsie, Ilda and Grace to their feet. "I spied a big clump of berries around a tree over there. Anyone want to help me?"

Nope," said Frank, "we're going to pick these low bushes in the sun. That way we'll have an excuse to quit, for cooling off once in a while. You go on ahead."

Alice retraced their way for a bit, until she found her heavily laden patch. She planned to start in the shade and follow on around as the shadow moved.

After a while, Frank and the children, with berry-stained faces and hands, decided to retire from the sunlit meadow for a cooling drink. Carsie set off ahead to find his mother and persuade her to join them.

Alice's bucket was three-quarters full when she heard a rustling to her right but out of sight. She thought it was probably Carsie or Sister choosing this cooler spot and went on picking. Moving over a step and reaching up, she froze. There stood a bear on his hind legs, his head on a level with her own. The bear blinked his eyes and made a low rumbling noise, startling Alice out of her trance.

"EEEYOWW!" she screamed. Throwing her bucket into the air, she spun around and ran in terror. With a noise halfway between a squeal and a roar, the bear lumbered off in the opposite direction. Not twenty feet from the berry patch, Carsie stopped, wide-eyed at the noise. Alice, in her panic, didn't see him. They collided and fell into a heap.

Frank and the others heard the scream and saw the bear loping across the field. "Stay here! I'm going to see if your mother is alright." He tore through the long grass and undergrowth in the direction from which the bear had come.

He found Alice sitting on the ground comforting the sobbing Carsie, her own scare forgotten in her concern for her bruised and frightened little boy.

"Did the bear hit Carsie?" Frank asked her. His voice startled both of them back to reality. Alice began to shake at the same moment that Carsie broke into his hearty laugh.

"Papa, you should have *been* here!" he managed to choke out between gales of laughter. "Mama and the bear: It was *so funny!* I wonder which one was scared the most." He clasped his stomach and rolled over and over on the ground, laughing helplessly. Frank was caught up in the boy's infectious laughter. He helped Alice up, and standing with his arms around her, he rocked her back and forth.

"Oh, you *men!*" She struggled to get free. "I could have been *killed* by that bear and you're *laughing* about it! Don't you have *any* concern about *me?!*"

Frank and Carsie exchanged glances and went off into more helpless laughter. Sobering somewhat and between frequent bursts of chuckles, Frank told her, "Carsie's right; I wonder who was more scared. If you could see yourself..." His glance caught the shiny bottom of the upturned pail. He retrieved it and held it so that she could see her reflection. At that, Alice joined their merriment.

"Poor bear! I almost scare myself!"

"Poor bear!" Carsie echoed. "Mama, your face looks like it's got Indian war paint on it, with all that berry juice smeared all over it!

Your hair sticks out every which way! Bet that bear thought you had that icky stained hand up in the air to hit him: Poor bear."

"Anyway, boy, we found out your mama's a fibber. She says she doesn't eat any of the berries while she picks. How else could she have berry juice on her nose and streaked down her chin."

He turned to Alice. "But how did you get that stain across your forehead?"

"I don't know; unless I reached up with my wrist to wipe off the sweat and push my hat back off my face. A berry cane pulled it over my eyes a while ago." She looked up, "Where *is* my hat?" Looking around, she saw it had fallen into the midst of the scattered berries.

The three of them returned to the others for a cooling drink. The younger children giggled over the story of their mother's escapade. They all helped to salvage most of the spilled berries before they started home.

This was the last of the summer's fruit: It was canned and placed in a colorful array on shelves in the cellar.

In November Carsie came in the door from his violin lesson. "Mama! Papa! Only four months of lessons and Pastor wants me to play the fiddle for the Christmas service! Can I, please?!"

Alice looked questioningly at Frank, who glanced up from his book. His eyebrow arched up in assent. "I don't see any reason why not. I'm sure you'll do us proud!"

"Are you sure you're ready, Carsie? Won't that take a lot of extra practice? We don't want you to neglect your school work," his mother added.

"It'll be alright, Mama. Pastor says all my lesson time will be practice. And he's letting me bring the fiddle home next week, so I can practice a little every night, too."

"That's fine, Son. We'll help you all we can. You'll be the star of the program, won't he, Mama?" Frank hugged Carsie to his side.

Ilda and Grace had parts in the Christmas program, too. Ilda was one of a chorus of Angels and Grace, dressed in green, with a holly crown, was to carry a candle.

Frank had joined the choir and had his own songs to practice. One night, Carsie stopped in the middle of his fiddle practice, "Papa, everyone's in the Christmas program, except Mama."

"Neither is Tucker," Ilda added, "but he's too little."

"Who says Mama's not a part of it? Who's making all your costumes? Who's dipping all those candles?" Frank reminded them. "Who's going to be holding Tucker up, so he won't miss anything?"

"And baking cookies for the party after the program?" Alice chimed in. "Just because I'm not going to be up in front of everyone doesn't mean I'm not part of it. Almost everyone in the church is doing something. That's partly what church is about; to help each other."

"I'm sorry Mama. I guess I just wasn't thinking," Carsie said, as he hugged his mother.

The Christmas program was a great success. The children all left the church clutching net bags of candy canes, cookies and Christmas oranges.

Before New Year's Day, a mild epidemic of influenza struck the company town and Alice found herself in harness again, nursing. Becky Ingeborg took on the care of the Walden children in the daytime, while Alice had to be away. Most of Alice's pay was in barter for services. The majority of mill families had one or more members who were skilled in a craft of one kind or another, but little money.

Later that winter, Frank had opportunity to do some leather repair at work. He was on hand one day when a heavy leather belt, essential to the running of some of the mill machinery, snapped. Gradually, the mill came to a halt, as the idle machinery caused a backlog on one end and a shortage on the other. The foreman let out a string of curses. "***Now*** what'll we do?! That was the ***backup*** belt, until a new one comes down from Portland next week!"

"Wait a minute!" Ingeborg was standing nearby and spoke up. "Walden works with leather in his spare time. Maybe he can jerry-rig it until the new one comes."

Frank got extra pay whenever the belts needed repair after that. He would examine the belts after the mill shut down at night and repair those that were weakened. He was promoted from his original job outdoors as a "catter" or "pond monkey".

The new inside job, grading cut lumber, was easier and better for his left foot. "Finally, I'm fed up with getting dunked in the cold water when a log decides it doesn't want to get pulled up the bull chain into the mill!" he told Alice.

"And I know how painful that can be on your bad foot," she sympathized.

Chapter Twenty Three

THE PRETTY MUSHROOM

Later that year, as the Waldens were walking home from church, they crossed paths with one of the mill hands, who greeted Frank, "Hey, Fat, that's a nice lookin' family you've got there." Frank waved an answer as his face flushed.

"What did he call you?" Alice asked.

Frank stammered a bit before he could reply. "I guess I have to confess. You'd hear eventually anyway. Since I've been working inside, and with all this weight I've put on, some of the hands have started calling me 'Fat'. I don't relish it, but it's stuck, and so I've got to make the best of it or else lose some weight."

Alice's eyes sparkled, "And I suppose *my* good cooking is getting the blame? We'll have to see about cutting out third helpings for you. Then you *and* the grocery bills can both be cut down to size."

Alice watched Frank's eating habits a bit more carefully for a time. "Though you have lost one double chin," she told him a month later, "your pants still fit as tightly as ever."

On a Saturday night a few days later, he was standing in the tub in the kitchen after his bath, pouring clear water to rinse off the soap. Alice noticed, with concern, that his normally slender ankles were slightly puffy.

"When you get your nightshirt on, sit down on that chair and let me have a look at those feet," she told him. When he did so, she took his size thirteen feet on her lap for examination. "When did this start?" she asked. "I should have noticed, but I'm usually busy straightening the house while you bathe."

"I don't rightly know. Seems like my feet have been bothering me since I started putting on weight. I never noticed that there was any swelling. It must have come along so gradually that I wasn't aware of it."

Let's try some of my herbal tea for edema for a while. It tastes pretty bad, I'm sorry to say, and you'll be urinating a lot more than usual, but it should help. We need to keep this under control or it'll become permanent. I can't think what could be causing it. I'll do some studying about it."

Each time Alice handed Frank a cup of the herb tea, he complained, "Do I **have** to? It's worse than castor oil! Isn't there anything else for this?" The tea helped both the edema and the weight loss, somewhat, but Frank remained heavy.

That autumn brought a bumper crop of fruits and vegetables from the garden and the old orchards. Alice, Becky and the girls kept busy canning, drying and making preserves in their spare time.

That winter was mild and snowless. Spring came late after a wet, gray, depressing three months. Spring weather arrived just in time for Easter, which was a real treat for the children. Alice made them all new Easter clothes, and fancy hats with flowers and bows for herself and the girls.

Reverend Thatcher greeted them with a big smile, "You brought to mind a family a geese, coming down the road with your heads held high. You all look so nice this morning!"

When Easter was over, Alice got busy with gardening and readying Carsie's and Ilda's summer wardrobes. Tucker got Carsie's hand-me-downs after several years and some altering, but Grace was into Ilda's dresses as soon as her sister was out of them.

In late spring of 1896, through mismanagement and breakdown of old machinery, the mill began to cut back on work. As a result, men were laid off one or two at a time.

Frank's foreman came to the house one evening in July. "There's bad news ahead, Fat. The word's out that the whole shebang will be down in two or three months. I want my crew to be warned ahead of time so they can look for other jobs. We'll be cut back to four days a week by August first. That'll give you two days a week to look around."

With Harney's and his foreman's recommendations, Frank soon had work promised in a shingle mill on the outskirts of Oregon City, to start the day after Labor Day.

"We've not much time, just two and a half weeks, to get resettled before school starts," he told his family. "I'll be starting my new job that same day."

The next day, Frank went alone to the shingle mill. Inquiring at the office and among the workmen, he found a suitable house set back on a wooded lot. It needed some repairs, for which the owner was willing to trade two months' rent.

Frank was laid off after work on Thursday, August 26th. "Hallelujah! Twelve days to get that house livable!" he called to Alice as he came in the door. "How are you coming with the packing? I can take a few things over every day in a cart that a fellow is lending me."

"I'm far enough ahead that we'll have Sunday after church and Labor Day to get moved," she answered as she dished up their evening meal. "You better call the children in from the yard."

"Carsie, get Tucker washed up for supper! Girls, come on in!" Frank called.

"Whoa!" he stopped them at the door. "Let's get your shoes off first. Where did you ever find mud to tromp in?"

"Oh, that's not hard to do, Papa," Carsie piped up. "Remember the low spot where Grace and Tucker picked a bunch of skunk cabbage for a posey for Mama last spring? There's lots of mushrooms down there now. Can we have some of them for supper, Mama?"

Alice dropped her serving spoon and whirled around, "*Mushrooms?!* You picked *mushrooms?!* Did any of you eat any?! Where are they?!"

Carsie held up his bandana. He had tied the corners together to make a pouch; it was bulging. "We have all different kinds, Mama. We knew you didn't have time to go get them yourself. Tucker started to eat some but I wouldn't let him. You said last year not to eat mushrooms unless you gave them to us."

Alice and Frank both heaved an audible sigh of relief. "Are you sure the others didn't eat any?" Frank asked him.

"I don't think so, Papa. I asked the girls, and they said they didn't. I tried to watch Tucker, but he was sorta pouting and wouldn't talk to me after I took one away from him."

Alice's heart sank. Tucker was a secretive little boy. He often went off by himself, setting the whole family hunting for him. No matter how carefully he was watched, he managed to slip away.

"Alright everyone, sit down to supper. Tucker, you come here." She took the little boy into the alcove and held him on her lap. As usual, he squirmed to be let down. "No, you sit here and look at me!" Alice held his head so he faced directly at her. "Now, tell Mama; did you eat any of the pretty mushrooms? Some of them are *so* pretty, it's hard *not* to. The orange ones look like the peels of Christmas oranges, don't they? They can make you *terribly* sick if you eat them, though. Did you try one of *them*?"

"No, Mama." He hesitated. "It was one of the brown ones with the pretty ruffle around it."

"Will you show me one like it?" She was fighting to control her panic. "Come, I'll dump them on a towel and you can show me the pretty ruffles."

Though Frank looked up in question as Alice and Tucker passed the table, she avoided his eyes and smiled at the children. "I'll be with you in a minute," she told them. At the sink, she spilled the mushrooms out onto a towel on the counter.

"*That* one, Mama, just like that one." Tucker looked up at her with the nearest his little face could muster toward enthusiasm. His expression returned to its usual stoic appearance as he saw panic in his mother's eyes.

Alice got up, put him on the chair and went to mix a glass of warm water with three tablespoons of soda and a pinch of an herb from her box of medicaments. "I'm sorry, Son, but this *must* be done. The pretty ruffled mushroom will make you *very* sick if we don't get it out of your tummy quickly. You'll have to drink this, right now."

Seeing his eyes going dull and his face starting to turn grey, she knew she would have to resort to extreme, even cruel methods to save his life if she didn't persuade him to take the medicine.

"Frank, will you come here and bring your tea cup with you?" When he did so, she pointed to the cup. "Papa has to take his tea every day or he would be very sick. It doesn't taste good, does it, Papa?" Frank screwed up his face as he drank a bit of the tea.

"You see," she told Tucker, "Papa knows that if he doesn't take the medicine tea, he'll get sick. You must be as brave as Papa and drink this so you won't be sick."

"Tucker looked intensely into his father's eyes. He reached for the cup and took a tiny sip and spat it into the sink. "Ugh!" he said, "Bad!"

"I know, Son," Frank looked squarely into the little boy's eyes, "but I *have* to drink it to stay well. *You'll* have to drink the glass of medicine Mama has. Be a good, brave, big boy, and take it all down."

Back and forth, the child's eyes swung from Alice's face to Frank's several times. Seeing their love and concern for him, he quickly took the glass from his mother's hand and downed it all. Brave and determined as he was, Tucker was only five. He gasped and began to cry. His hoarse voice startled them all, as his bawling filled the room.

Alice picked up Tucker, threw a shawl around both of their shoulders and bolted out the door. At her gesture, Frank returned to the table and the other three children.

In an instant, Tucker began to vomit explosively. The acrid fluid carried bits of mushroom with it. He continued to gag and choke for several minutes before he collapsed in Alice's arms, limp and almost lifeless. His stomach was still churning, but was completely evacuated.

"What happened, Papa?" asked one of the children. "Why was Tucker sick?" asked another. "What did Mama give him to drink?" The questions flew from the astonished children at the table.

Frank picked up his fork. "It's all over now. He's going to be all right. He ate a poison mushroom. Mama had to get it out of his tummy before it made him sick. Let's finish supper now and surprise Mama by doing the dishes and straightening the house. This ought to be a reminder for you three not to eat anything until your Mama says it's alright."

Their usual cheerful natures returned and all four were soon singing at their tasks. Alice slipped by and up to the loft with Tucker over her shoulder.

When Carsie came up to bed, she told him, "Put on your nightshirt and go sleep with Papa tonight. I want to keep an eye on Tucker. Ask Papa to bring a cup of warm milk pretty soon. Tucker will need it in a bit. He's starting to wake up."

When Carsie and the girls were settled in bed, Frank came to the loft with the milk. "I'm surprised that you didn't get milk for him right away; that's what I've seen you do before in cases like this."

"I would have, but he fainted from shock. It's not a good idea to force fluids on an unconscious child, or anyone else for that matter. Their swallow reflex doesn't work. The fluids might go into the lungs and cause pneumonia."

"How is he doing? Are you going to stay with him all night, as Carsie said? Is Tucker *that* sick?"

"I don't know. I'm satisfied that all of the contents of his stomach are clear, but I don't know how much of it had started to digest. If he'd eaten it on a full stomach, I wouldn't worry so much. We'll have to wait a day or two before I'll know for sure."

"Hey there, Boy," Frank said, as Tucker opened his eyes. "Starting to wake up? How about sitting up for this nice, warm milk Papa brought you? You should be really hungry by now."

Tucker pushed the glass away with a wavering hand. "No more medicine."

"This isn't medicine, Son. It's just warm milk. It'll make your tummy feel better. Just a taste to start?" Alice held the glass to his lips.

Like a puppy, he lapped a drop with the tip of his tongue, experimentally. "Mm," he murmured. "Good, more."

"Just a little bit at a time, Son," Alice coaxed. "Your tummy will throw it up if you drink too fast. That's it, slowly now."

When the glass was empty, Tucker pushed it away. "Sleep now, Mama. Want to sl..." His voice faded off and his eyes closed before Alice got his head on the pillow.

"I'll go down and get into my nightgown if you'll stay with him a minute, dear." She gave his hand a squeeze and went down the ladder.

In the morning, Frank poked his head over the top of the ladder. "Is everything alright with our boy? Did you sleep at all? I didn't hear any noise during the night."

"Of *course* you didn't. You don't have a mother's ear. In fact, if the *house* fell down, you wouldn't wake up!"

"Not last night! That Carsie sleeps like a whirling dervish. Whew! I got an elbow here, a knee there, his head dug into my spine. What a night! Remind me not to do that again."

"Aha! Now you know what *I* go through when you come home extra tired. Carsie sure is Papa's boy, acrobatic eyebrow and sleep habits, too. Revenge *is* sweet, my dear! Watch while I gloat," Alice chuckled, then kissed his cheek as she passed. "Let me go get dressed and have some breakfast while you stay with him."

"Do you think it would be alright to take him downstairs?" Frank asked. "It would save you a lot of running up and down that ladder."

"Yes, please. We can wrap him in a blanket and put him on Carsie's cot while you bring Tucker's cot down. Then bring him down. It'll be good for him to be with the family."

Tucker was listless most of the day. Since he was ordinarily a quiet child, Alice was not *too* concerned.

Carsie had gone with Frank to Oregon City to work on the new house. The girls played quietly or helped Alice with packing. She sent them outside to play after lunch.

Tucker slept after his meal of chicken broth and bread. Alice glanced at him now and again as she passed his cot. Twice, she stopped to stroke his forehead, checking for fever. Hearing a noise as she emerged from the cellar trap door in late afternoon, she saw that his face was white, his back slightly arched and his arms and legs extended and stiff.

"Oh, no! He's convulsing!" she said aloud, then ran to the door to call Ilda. "Come here, quickly!"

Ilda came running in from the yard as Alice moved Tucker onto the floor.

"Go take the bucket and get some cold water to put in the tub," she instructed. "Then get the warm water from the stove cistern to add to it. Hurry, we've got to get his fever down!"

Ilda did as she was instructed, then stood wide-eyed in near panic. "What else can I do, Mama?"

"Would you please refill the cistern and check the fire while I get Tucker ready to go into the tub. Can you lift the teakettle?

"Yes, Mama. Should I refill it, too?"

"That's my girl. Yes, please." Alice stripped off Tucker's nightshirt and wrapped him tightly in a cotton blanket to control any flailing of his limbs. She tested the water temperature, then lowered the boy's rigid body into the tub.

"Sister, would you go next door, please, and ask Mrs. Nelson to bring any hot water she might have on hand? Tucker will need to have the water warmed again before our kettle boils."

Skirts flying, Ilda dashed out the door. She returned with the neighbor on her heels. Each of them was carrying a pail of hot water.

"What's the trouble?!" Anna asked, "Ilda said Tucker was sick!"

Alice explained the problem.

"I've got my big kettle heating to can some string beans, but they can wait," Anna said. "While I'm gone, honey," she told Ilda, "get out your Mama's big kettle, put it on the stove and fill it. I'll be right back."

Grace and Ilda were sent to Anna's house to stay with her children. The two women took turns, one holding Tucker in the warm water, the other putting cool cloths on his face and neck. Twice, when he stopped breathing, Alice picked him up and bent him over her leg. She slapped his back sharply a few times, until his sigh told her that his lungs were working again. Nearly two hours passed before normal color returned to his face. Alice could feel his body begin to relax. In another fifteen minutes, she lifted him out of the tub, unwrapped and reswaddled him in dry blankets that Anna had put on the open oven door to keep warm.

"For the second time, a warm tub and oven-heated blankets have saved his life," Alice told Frank when he and Carsie came home for supper.

Carsie's cot was brought down to the living room for Alice to sleep on. For three days and nights, Alice never ventured more than ten feet from Tucker's cot. She noticed, on the fifth day, when Tucker was looking at a picture book Ilda was reading to him, that his left eye wandered away to the side, while his right eye stayed focused on the book. He was still listless and content to be tucked into a quilt atop the load on the cart on moving day.

"We'll have to get him to an eye doctor in Portland as soon as he's well enough to travel," Alice told Frank one night after the children were abed. "I don't know whether his eye can be helped but we have to try."

Chapter Twenty Four

THE GINGERBREAD HOUSE

Moving day was exciting for the family. Carsie and Frank were the only ones who had seen the house. Many of their possessions had preceded them, as Frank and Carsie made their daily trips to get the house ready. The borrowed horse clopped across the planks of the bridge and down the cobble-stone streets and the wagon rumbled in harmony.

At the south end of town, the cobbles gave way to packed gravel and dirt. Near the mill, Frank turned the horse to the left, up the hill and away from the river.

Tall fir and cedar trees crowded in on both sides, their branches making a dark green tunnel over the road. A quarter of a mile along, Frank turned into a rutted drive.

"Where's the house, Papa?" Ilda asked excitedly. The others echoed her question.

"What would you say if I told you it's a *"gingerbread house"*; you know; like the witch's house in Hansel and Gretel? *It* was hidden away in the woods, too."

"Oh, Papa!" practical Grace chided. "Gingerbread would melt in the rain and fall down!"

"We're here!" Carsie yelled as they rounded a knoll. He jumped down to run on ahead. The girls clapped their hands in delight when they saw the house.

"Oh, Frank, it's charming!" Alice squeezed his arm. The brown-shingled house was sheltered under tall firs, its outlines gleamed with fanciful white trim. The shutters and door matched.

"*I* painted them, Mama!" Carsie beamed. "Do you like it?"

"It's lovely! You do good work, Son!"

Alice explained that the term "gingerbread" was used for the fancy-cut curlicues and scalloped trim. Carsie was most interested in the subject and even mildly embarrassed at the effusive compliments about his work.

"I'm sorry to say that the interior is not as fancy," Frank admitted. "The builder must have spent all his money and time on the outside and ran out of both before he could get to the inside." He stepped ahead and opened the door.

With so many of their things already inside, most of which Frank and Carsie had already unpacked, the house seemed warm and inviting to the children. They scampered about, finding their own quarters in the double loft. The girls' dollhouse and other toys and some of their clothes, hung on nails, identified the front end of the spacious loft as their room. The other end, partitioned off by colorful quilts strung from wires, held Carsie and Tucker's belongings. The main floor was one large space, divided off into rooms by skeletal framework.

Alice tried to hide her disappointment from Frank. "I'm sorry, dear," he said. "We'll get these walls finished little by little as we can get the boards. With winter coming on, we needed to get the outer walls done first. For now, we'll line the walls with newspapers."

Only then did Alice notice that the outer walls consisted of bare framing. The spacer boards and the inner surfaces of the shingles, light peeking through here and there, were all that protected them from the elements.

She took a deep breath and forced herself to be calm. "Did the landlord make any offer of materials for the finishing work?"

"*Well*... he sort of hinted at it, but I think he's a bit of a skinflint. He said to go ahead and get what we need, and he'll give us two months' rent for it."

"Oh Frank, you just never have enough spunk to argue for your rights! It will cost us all we've got, beyond bare necessities to do all that! Is two months' rent all he agreed to for all your work?"

Frank's fair complexion reddened noticeably. He gave her a weak smile, then turned to the door. "Come on, Carsie! Sister! Grace! Let's go and get some of the stuff from the wagon! We'll have to get everything off the cook stove and get it in place if Mama's going to get our dinner tonight."

He turned back to Alice. "Hank Engen is coming up this afternoon to help me carry the stove in. We'll have it set up in plenty of time. A hot meal is going to taste good. It's clouding up and it smells like rain.

As if on cue, as soon as he left for West Lynn to return the horse and cart, it began to rain.

"Mama!" Ilda came running to the top of the stairs, "come quick! We've got to move our bed! The roof's leaking right over the middle of it!"

Just in time to hear, Carsie came in the back door with an armload of stove wood. He hurried to help. "Omigawsh, Mama, come help me move our beds, too! Mr. Scroggins didn't tell Papa the roof leaks when he was by last week. Papa and I were putting some new boards in the floor that day."

"Scoot downstairs and get the chamber pots. They're in a box by the door. That'll have to do for now," Alice told him. "We'll have to be on the lookout for other leaks, too."

When Frank came in the door after dark, he stopped in mid-stride. "What the dickens is all this?!" His eyes followed the line of bowls and pots around the room. "Are we playing a game?"

"Yes, musical drips!" Alice walked over to stand before him. "Isn't it *charming*?! We've had *such fun* this evening!" Her stern expression and hands-on-hips stance told him that "*fun*" was not at all what she meant.

Just then he heard a series of plinks and plunks. It had begun raining again. "Oh, no, *that* many leaks?! I thought I saw one or two the other day, but in the rush of nailing new shingles on the walls and replacing so many dry-rotted floor boards, I just forgot to check them again. Scroggins is going to hear about this!"

"He'd *darn* well better hear it from you or he'll *certainly* hear it from *me*!" Alice snapped. "What can be done about it now?"

"Nothing tonight; it's too dark and wet. It would be too dangerous. We'll have to wait until tomorrow. There are some extra shakes under the house. I'll get at them first thing in the morning, and then I'll get more scrap shakes from the mill to finish sealing up the wall holes."

On Tuesday morning, after the rest of the family had set off to work and school, Alice put on her shawl and bonnet. Tucker was left at the Engen's for the morning. She walked into Oregon City and found a junk dealer on the edge of town. She bargained with the scrawny middle-aged owner for several bundles of old newspapers. She told him that Frank would be in to pick them up later that afternoon.

At the owner's bellow, a young woman slouched out of the shack that served as a dwelling and an office for the junkyard. "C'mere, Mattie and heft these here bundles o' paper fer the lady. You can stack 'em up over there by the shed 'til 'er man can come get 'em."

Alice noted that, close up, the girl was younger than she'd first thought. Alice thought to herself that the girl might be pretty if she were cleaned up. Aloud, she said, "I'll trade you a dress and shawl for your daughter in even exchange for the papers, if she helps me take them home in that wheelbarrow over there. That way she can get her clothes and bring the barrow back. It will save my husband a trip here."

The man snorted, "Daughter, ha! That slut'd been booted outta here long time ago if'n she's my girl. Ain't no use anyhow, 'ceptin' to warm my bed and cipher fer me."

"It would be more seemly for your business if she were decently dressed and cleaned up a bit, don't you think?" Alice spoke matter-of-factly, as if it was of no real concern to her.

The girl approached them as Alice spoke. She reached out and gingerly fingered the fringe of Alice's shawl. "It's purty, ain't it? I could work a lot better when it's cold if'n I had a warm shawl like this," she whined. She looked sideways at the man, half fearful, half flirting.

"Ah, go on wit' the lady and git yerself lookin' human," the man growled. "Do y' s'pose y' might get 'er scrubbed up a bit while yer at it, Missus? It's gettin too cold for her to go down t' the river bend, and she's gettin' a bit gamey lately."

"I'm willing to try... if you'll throw in that slab of wood there. My husband could make a nice desk out of it for our children."

"Well... I s'pose. Here, Mattie, y' can push the barrow, and the lady can carry the slab."

Back at home, Alice put water on to heat for Mattie's bath. "Take your clothes off and I'll toss them out," She told the girl. Let me have a look at you before you get in the tub." The ragged dress was Mattie's only garment. Alice clucked her tongue and shook her head. The girl's body was black and blue in many places, new welts stood out on her buttocks and shoulders, her scalp was nearly covered with lice and she was covered with flea bites from head to toe.

"You poor child! Have you no way to clean yourself down at the yard? Did no one ever show you how to get rid of these vermin?"

"No'm I just had 'em all my life, far back's I can r'member."

"If you had no more care than that, then how in the world did you ever learn to read and cipher?"

"An old man took me in one winter when I's little and my folks died. He didn't beat me much and traded a toss in the bed with me now 'n again for feedin' me. 'He said 'e were a perfesser 'til 'e got lung fever and couldn't work no more."

"He taught you to read and cipher?" Alice asked.

"Yes'm: It come natural t' me, and I kept on practicin' and readin' everthin' I could git aholt of. I can't cipher much, but ol' Andy don't know no better. I got a warm place t' sleep and near 'nough t' eat."

Alice sighed; pity for the girl welled in her throat.

Deloused, treated for the flea bites and scrubbed nearly raw, Mattie was fitted into one of Alice's old dresses, tucked and hemmed to fit her shorter, gaunt frame. Alice found her a few pair of clean underwear, a shift and some winter stockings. "Maybe I can do something about your shoes," she added. The soles of Mattie's shoes were worn nearly through and they were laced with twine. Alice found two scraps of leather in Frank's supply and cut them to fit inside the shoes.

"Thank y', Ma'am! I really 'preciate it. Don't think I ever felt this good in my life!" When Mattie left, she was almost dancing down the road.

"There's not a lot more I can do for Mattie just now, but if opportunity comes, maybe I can find a better situation for her," She told Frank that evening.

As soon as Alice had glued several layers of newspapers around the walls, she remade curtains from the supply in her trunk. "Hand-me-downs from every house we've lived in," she told Frank. "Could you string some wire across our bedroom alcove on which to mount these long ones?"

"As usual, you've made this place into a home, Alice. You *do* have a talent for it. Although I was beginning to think we were going to have a pot of paste stewing on the back of the stove all winter. It is a deal warmer.

"The children will learn to read faster, too. Have you noticed how they walk around the house reading from the newspapers? They were having so much fun reading the other night, they forgot to ask me to read a story until bedtime."

During the papering, Alice had stolen a few minutes to write to Dr. Williams. She described Tucker's illness and resulting eye problem and asked his advice. His reply was:

> Take the boy to St. Vincent's Hospital in Portland.
> The condition you describe as "wall-eye'" is properly
> called exotropia. It is caused by nerve damage in the brain.
> The nerve and muscle may have been weakened during his
> difficult birth and aggravated by the convulsions from the
> poison mushroom.

Alice read the letter to Frank that evening and said. "I'm going to write to the hospital for an appointment for Tucker."

"Let's hope they can help him, "Frank answered. He's been through a lot in his short life."

The hospital's children's department answered in a few days. Alice and Tucker set off early on a Monday morning. They walked into Oregon City, to the train depot.

"Tucker, come here!" Alice called half a dozen times when he wandered off.

"Wanna see the train," he repeated each time he returned from the end of the station to peer along the tracks for a first glimpse of the locomotive. His lack of facial expression and leisurely pace belied his eagerness.

When the engine did come in, hissing, screeching and thundering, Tucker ran, screaming, to hide in Alice's skirts. Alice had to carry him, still sobbing, on board the train.

When they got to Portland, a horse car, clanking along its tracks, took Alice and Tucker to the foot of the hill, very close to the hospital. They were admitted to an examining room almost at once.

"Grampa?" said Tucker, when the doctor came into the room.

"Why, yes, I *am* a grandpa," came the answer, "but not *your* grandpa. Maybe I'll be your *extra* grandpa. Is that alright with you? Come on now, up on this high stool, so I can see your eyes better."

"You *do* look very much like my father," Alice told him. "The children haven't seen him in some time and they miss him. It's fortunate that you resemble him, otherwise you might have had difficulty with my son. He has always been our "touch-me-not" child. He takes a long time to get acquainted with strangers."

"Let's see your eyes, Henry," Doctor Gunderson put his hands out as if to cup Tucker's face between them. Tucker jerked back and nearly fell off the stool.

"Whoops!" Alice caught him. "I forgot to tell you; he refuses to answer to anything but his nickname, Tucker."

"That's fine. Tucker boy, I'm sorry. Can we be friends again?"

Tucker looked so doubtfully at the doctor, that Alice took him on her lap and sat on the stool. "You'll be alright, Son. The doctor just wants to look at your eye. He won't hurt you, I promise."

Slowly, gently, the doctor examined Tucker's eyes. When he had finished, he sent the boy off to another room with a nurse.

"Mrs. Walden, in your letter you told me his medical history and that you suspected exotropia. I'm afraid you are right. There is only one treatment for it and I can't offer you much hope. Sometimes it even weakens the other eye. He would need spectacles with a lens that will help pull the eye into line, but he will have to wear a patch over the good eye, which could weaken it. It's your decision."

"Would he still need the glasses without the patch, Doctor?"

"Not at this point, but should you decide not to try the patch now, I would recommend an examination every six months to check for damage. There's not enough known about this condition to offer you more encouragement."

"Thank you, Doctor. I'll talk to my husband and let you know of our decision." Alice shook his hand and went to find Tucker.

The older children were anxious to know the results of Tucker's day. They were as disappointed as their parents.

After the children were in bed, Alice related Tucker's reaction to the train. "Obviously, he'd forgotten about his earlier encounter with the train," she told Frank.

Frank and Alice sat talking by the fire for a long time that night. They decided against the patch because of the risk to the other eye and the distinct possibility that Tucker wouldn't use it or the glasses, anyway.

On Tucker's next visit to Dr. Gunderson, Alice asked to see the Sister Superior before they left. She was directed to her office.

"Good afternoon Mrs. Walden is it?" The kindly-looking, tiny woman stood up as Alice entered. "Is there something I can do for you?"

"For *me*, no. I have a young woman acquaintance who is in a *most* unfortunate situation. Perhaps you could help *her*."

Alice told her Mattie's story. The wizened old Nun sat back for a moment with her eyes half closed. "We *do* hire a number of unfortunate young people here in many departments. For most, we offer room and board and a very small salary. Could you bring the young woman into town one day, so that I may interview her?"

Alice was happy to have found a chance for Mattie to have a decent life. She spirited the young woman away from the junkyard on the same pretext as before. In two days, Mattie was cleaned up, led to the Lord, and taken to Portland to work in the hospital. Alice hugged and kissed her at the door.

Mattie was nervous but excited at the chance for a new, better life. She hugged Alice goodbye, with tears of gratitude in her eyes.

Alice's heart was light as she made her way back to Oregon City.

Chapter Twenty Five

GOOD NEWS AND BAD NEWS

On a lovely, warm evening in May, 1897, the children were all playing outdoors with the Engen youngsters. Not a minute between homework and bedtime could be wasted. Their merry shouts echoed through the woods.

Alice and Frank had pulled two chairs out onto the stoop to share the twilight peace. Suddenly, she sighed deeply, "Frank, what would you say if I told you I think I'm pregnant?"

Frank sat upright as his eyebrow arched. "I'd say you'd better check in with a doctor to be sure. We don't want any complications like those you had with Tucker. What makes you think you could be? You don't seem to have gotten any heavier, and you haven't had any monthly flow since before he was born. It *would* be strange."

"I don't really know; my waistbands have gotten a little tight, for one thing. Then there's just a feeling a woman gets. I've never showed much until after the babies started to move, so I'm not sure."

"Why don't you go to the clinic at the Oregon City Hospital in the next few days? All the children, except Tucker, are in school, and you don't have any nursing cases just now."

"Perhaps I will." She paused for a moment, "I'm not sure if I *want* to be pregnant or not. Four children is a nice-sized family and I'd be happy with that, wouldn't you?"

"Yes, I guess so, but if it is to be... We'll make out all right. Now, *I've* got a bit of news for *you*.

"I got a letter from Harney today. I held it back from the rest that I picked up at the post office, just to think about it for myself."

Alice glanced up from the sock she was darning, "What is it; a change in work again? I can't think what else Mr. Harney would be writing about. He's not given to casual letters."

"Yes it is, and I wonder if you'll approve. It sounds good, but it'll mean that I have to go on ahead for a while and leave you and the children again."

"Why, is there no housing for families? Where is the job?"

"You guessed it. Last question first. It's on the west slopes of the Blue Mountains. They're getting ready to send in the surveyors. The timber cruisers report rich timber stands; enough for several years. They want me to join the survey crew and help start up the logging camp."

Alice concentrated on her needle in silence for a minute. "When will you go and when can we follow?"

"Harney said to write to them immediately, so I won't know for sure until I get an answer. I think it means right away. They're starting to build a mill first, then a new town with housing for families in the fall. That means you and the children won't be able to come join me until next spring."

"Does Mr. Harney say it'll be worthwhile, in salary, I mean?"

"It's the best I've been offered so far and I won't have to be in the camp through the winter. Once it's set up and operational, I'd go down to the river and help get the mill operations started."

She looked deeply into his eyes, "I'd say by your answer that you want to go. Will it be as hard for you to go away from all of us again as it will be for us to be without you?"

Frank looked over at Alice again, as if startled. "Oh, my dear, of *course* it'll be hard!" He rose from his chair to kneel at her side and put his arms around her. "It'll be the hardest thing I've ever done. But with the possibility of another child, we'll need a better income. I'd hate it if Carsie had to quit school now to help out. And you ***know*** he'll insist. Easy going as he is, once he sets his mind on something, there's no stopping him.

"My principal worry is you. What if you have another complex pregnancy, as you did with Ilda and Tucker? I should be here with you then."

"***That*** settles it!" Alice put her darning in the basket by her feet. "I'll go into town tomorrow and find out for sure!"

She carried her chair inside, saying over her shoulder, "It's time for the children to come in. Will you call them?"

The next day, Alice walked to the Oregon City Hospital after leaving Tucker with Mrs. Engen. She registered at the clinic for examination. A young doctor came into the exam room soon after she'd been seated by a nurse. He was reading from the application as he entered the room. His attitude was condescending.

"You say here, Mrs. Walden, that you are a nurse. I find it *strange* that you are not sure of your pregnancy. How is that? Especially since you had four previous confinements!"

Long before Alice completed her previous history of births, his manner changed. She could feel his mood shifting to compassion.

"I beg your pardon, Ma'am. My attitude was unforgivable. I'll send a nurse to help you prepare for examination. I'll be back shortly."

His manner was gentle as he confirmed her pregnancy. "Be sure to come back if you have any complications. Please ask for me." He extended his personal card. "Will you be giving birth here at the hospital?"

Alice laughed out loud. "Doctor, if there are no complications, there won't be *time* to get to the hospital. Spontaneous doesn't *begin* to describe my first three deliveries. Should I develop eclampsia again, I promise to come to you." She offered her hand in friendship.

On the way home, Alice mulled over what she should tell Frank. He felt that he should take the job for the money's sake as much as he wanted to take it to get back up in the woods. Would he refuse to go if she told him about her pregnancy? She didn't want them to be separated for over a year any more than he did. How would the children react to news of his leaving? She had plenty of time to decide, as it was a long walk home.

It was not until everyone was in bed that Alice and Frank could talk. She waited for him to open the subject, "Well, my dear, what did the doctor say?"

"He confirmed my suspicions. I *am* pregnant, but he foresees no problems. I'm sure it would be alright for you to go on ahead. In any event, I'll write to Mama. I've no doubt that she'll come to be with me when my time is near."

"But how do you know when that is? You never regained your cycle to know when conception took place. What makes you so sure everything will go smoothly this time?"

"Don't worry. If I have any problems, or when the baby starts to drop low, I'll write Mama to come. Besides, I can calculate the baby's arrival date by the start of the movements. The only concern I have is the children's' reaction to your going away again. They'll be heart-broken. How will you tell them?"

Frank was silent for a moment. "It *will* be hard. They're bright youngsters, though, and they'll understand. I'll write to the company's temporary office in Weston and get confirmation before I tell them. There is no sense in upsetting them if nothing's going to happen."

In a little over a week, Frank received a letter from the Milton Freewater Company in Weston. He didn't open the letter until after supper when the older children were studying at the table and Tucker was practicing his alphabet. He read it and handed it to Alice.

They wanted him to come to Weston as soon as possible. The letter stated that the survey crews would be starting out about June sixth.

When she had finished reading it, she looked to where he stood by the stove. His left eyebrow quirked in question, then he looked toward the children and back to her.

Alice nodded, then mouthed, "As soon as they're finished," then went on with her sewing.

Suddenly, Carsie looked up from his homework, "Papa, Mama, something's wrong, I can *feel* it. What is it?"

"Not really wrong, Son," Frank replied. It's just that Mama and I have some good and some not-so-good news for you. Finish your studies, then we'll tell you about it."

By that time, the conversation had attracted the attention of the other three. Nothing would do but that they know all about what was going to happen. They all got up from the table, pleading for answers.

"All right, you *scalawags*! Come on over here by my chair so we can all be comfortable." Frank sat down in his chair next to Alice's. "Mama, do you want to tell them your news first?"

Four pairs of wide eyes and four small heads swiveled toward their mother, question marks all but written in the air above them.

"How would you like to have a new baby brother or sister this fall?" Alice asked quietly.

The reactions were as varied as the children before her. Eleven-year-old Carsie looked concerned but pleased. "It would be fun, in a way, Mama, but won't it put a crimp in our hiking for a couple of summers?" He looked thoughtful, then continued, "But that's alright; we'll just have to go without you or stay here and help with the baby."

Ilda's round face lit up as she clapped her hands, her curls dancing as her head nodded approval. "Oh, Mama, a new little baby? What fun; like a real live baby doll to take care of!" At nine, she was the "little mother" to Grace and Tucker. She had a natural need to take care of small people and creatures of all kinds.

Grace sat quietly; her solemn grey eyes looking from one member of her family to another. "I would like another girl," she stated matter-of-factly. Then she got up and went to sit on the bench facing them all. "What's *your* news, Papa?" Her manner was serious beyond her seven years.

Tucker, always the stoic, simply shrugged his shoulders. He rose and went to sit beside Grace. The contrast between these two was more than even Carsie and Ilda's. His dark coloring and homely, craggy, six-year-old face, against her tall, lithe frame, fair coloring and delicate features made it hard for people to believe that they had the same parents.

"*Your* turn, Papa! Tell them!" Alice said, smiling to herself as she watched the range of reactions among their children.

Their attention returned to their father.

"I don't know if my news is so good. I have a new job coming up next month. It pays better than at the shingle mill, so we can afford the new baby." Again, the four heads nodded approval. "But... and this is the not-so-good news, it means I'll have to be away from you all for... maybe a year."

The three older children moved to be nearer their father. "Oh, no, Papa!"

"I'm trying to get a newspaper route this summer. That'll help with the money, then you won't have to make more." Carsie's disappointment was almost painful to watch.

"Do you *really have* to go, Papa?" Ilda and Grace asked, almost in unison.

Tucker, as usual, merely shrugged his shoulders. Alice wondered if anything, short of a train, would make him react.

"Look at it this way," Frank consoled, "When school lets out next year, you can all move over there to Eastern Oregon to be with me. We'll be *real pioneers*! There will be a *whole* new town *way* out in the woods! We'll be a *long* way from any civilization. Think of all the hunting you boys and I can do together! We won't have to buy any meat; *just* like the early settlers. There are *all* kinds of *wild animals* and birds to learn about. Maybe..," (he put his finger to his temple) "maybe we can even have a *log cabin* to live in! How does *that* sound?!"

By this time, Carsie was dancing up and down. "Really, Papa?! Is it *that* wild there?! Can I have my own rifle?! Can we help you build the cabin, too?!" Then his voice quieted suddenly. "A whole year, though. That's a long time. We'll miss you so much, Papa. And Mama will be lonely, too."

Alice chimed in, "If we get busy and get the rest of our garden in, so Johnny Engen can water it for us, then we can go on the train with Papa as far as Grandpa and Grandma's for a visit. School will be out in a few days."

This announcement brought delighted exclamations from the three. Tucker had already turned back to his slate, his nose wrinkled up in concentration as he wrote in his laborious scrawl. Alice's and Frank's eyes met, after they had both noted Tucker's actions. Both sighed and shrugged their shoulders.

School was out the last Friday in May. The next day, the family trekked into Oregon City to catch the train for Portland and Bridal Veil. Frank would have two or three days with them before he went on to Pendleton, the nearest station to the proposed railroad spur into Weston and eventually to the Milton Freewater mill town.

Chapter Twenty Six

THE SEPARATION

With Frank's absence, Alice felt the mood of her family change. The children were old enough now to be more sensitive to new situations. They knew their father wouldn't be home on weekends, as he had been in Bridal Veil. There was no happy climax to look forward to at the end of the day, as it had been when he came home from the mill. The lack of his lighthearted laugh and clear tenor voice left a void for them that she couldn't fill.

"We'll all have to find the good things of our days to talk about at dinner from now on," she said after one particularly gloomy mealtime. "Let's all remember the happy things and try to look forward to the good times we'll have when we're with him again."

Carsie and Ilda were the first to begin singing again and encouraged the others to be more cheerful. Their natural optimism soon took over. Alice recognized the degrees of change and felt her heart lift with theirs.

A week after their return from Bridal Veil, Carsie received a letter from the newspaper saying that no vacancies in paper routes existed in their area but that his name would be kept on file. Alice saw his disappointment, though he tried not to show it. When his chores were done the next morning, he quietly walked off down the road alone. Alice puzzled over this. He was the most obedient and thoughtful of the four. It was not like him to go off this way.

"Sister, did Carsie say where he was going?" Alice asked, as they were working in the garden.

"No, Mama. He told me to keep an eye on Tucker and that he'd be back in a little while. Then he washed up and went off."

In an hour, Carsie came back, breathless from his run up the hill. "Mama," he panted, "I've got a job at the mill for the rest of the summer. Mr. Engen introduced me to Papa's foreman and put in a good word for me."

"Oh, Son, not the mill! You're too young and it's so dangerous around all that machinery!" Alice felt her heart crowd up into her throat. "Please God, give him a few more years to be a child before he's trapped in the world of the mills," she prayed silently.

"It's only sweeping up and carrying messages. I told Mr. Swenson that my Pa showed me how to use the froe to cut shake seconds from the cedar butts and how to sharpen the blades. He said, 'maybe later'. I can start Monday, if you'll write a note that it's alright with you."

Alice slept very little that night. What would Frank say? Would he approve? But then, he had said, "When Carsie makes up his mind...." When she did finally fall asleep, she dreamed of the dangers and the rough men into whose midst she was sending her son.

Carsie had little appetite in the morning. His big blue eyes followed her every move until she spoke. "I'll give you a note for Mr. Swenson, Carsie. I'm not really happy about it, but maybe it's for the best. Besides which," she teased, "you'd be underfoot all summer if I didn't. So go be a big, important wage earner if you really *must*."

"Yippee!" Carsie jumped up, nearly upsetting the bench and Grace with it. He skipped to Alice's side to kiss her cheek. "Wait'll I tell Carl Engen. He'll bust, absolutely bust!" The door almost pulled off the hinges as he yanked it open and flew off without the note. He returned for it a few minutes later, a little embarrassed and out of breath.

Alice made it a point to be working in the front yard as Carsie came walking slowly, painfully up the drive Monday evening. Poor child, she thought as she watched him trudge along, his head down, as if it was just too much effort to hold it up.

He looked up as he came near. When he saw her, he squared his shoulders and grinned with obvious effort, his eyes lacking their usual sparkle. "Hello, Mama! I'm a warrior home from battle, like Ivanhoe! Do you have a crown of laurel for my brow?"

"I hadn't thought of it that way or I surely would have. However, I do have a warm dinner of flapjacks and sausage; thy favourite, Sir. Dost think thee'd like a hot bath to sooth thy weary bones, Milord?"

She dropped a mock curtsy. "Even Ivanhoe bathed before he supped."

Carsie couldn't help but giggle along with Alice, in spite of how he felt.

In her next weekly letter to Frank, she wrote:

> Carsie fell asleep at the supper table. I roused him
> and steered him up the ladder to bed. He undressed so
> slowly and painfully, I could have cried; poor boy. I don't
> think he was aware that he fell onto the bed without
> his nightshirt. I was tempted not to wake him Tuesday
> morning, but I knew he'd be mortified to be late to work.
> He was almost around the bend in the road before he
> could walk normally.

Carsie fared better after the first two weeks, and was soon able to manage the walk with lessening fatigue. For several weeks though, he went to bed immediately after supper. The other children missed him terribly, but they were proud of him and willingly took over his chores to show it. Alice never heard them complain.

On Saturdays and Sundays, when Carsie was home, he helped in the garden and played with the others as if work did not exist. Alice planned picnics, visits with neighbors and forays into the woods whenever possible, to make his weekends into escapes from the mill world. She mourned that his violin case gathered dust in the corner of the loft.

The third week of August brought a letter from Frank that said he was ill with tick fever:

> I'll be off work for quite a while. I'm so weak that I
> can't stand up. One of the men I work with is a native here
> and knows how to treat this illness. I'm staying in a cabin
> behind the cook shack. The only worry I have is that I
> won't be able to send you any money until after I get back
> to work again. It's good that Carsie is working and that

you can eat out of the garden for a while. Do you have any nursing cases right now?

Alice answered his letter, assuring him that all was well, although it would be a tight squeeze, financially.

Thank goodness, only Tucker and Grace needed new shoes for school, she thought. I'll take the children down to the river for fishing on the weekends to keep them busy.

She had no real worries about Frank; he was still young and strong.

While talking with the children about the start of school the next day, Alice's arguments and a direct order did no good: Carsie threatened to skip school and find a different job if she told Mr. Swenson to let him go.

"We need the money while Papa is sick. Sister can bring my lessons home and I can do them after work," Carsie squared his jaw in determination.

Alice kept her composure during their waking hours but wept in the unguarded hours of the night. Her dreams were of Carsie's bright mind and the wasted years ahead. Somehow she knew he would never go back to school.

At the end of September, Alice was mending while Ilda and Grace were washing the supper dishes.

"Mama?" Sister's usual hearty voice was soft. "When is the new baby coming?"

"Soon, I think. Babies aren't very predictable; maybe by the middle of October. Grandma will be here by October seventh."

"Will you go to the hospital, Mama?" Grace asked, "Suzie's mama went to the hospital to have her baby."

"I don't think so, but maybe we should talk about it after you finish the dishes, so we can be ready just in case the baby comes before Grandma does."

On Saturday, Alice got out the familiar equipment and Grace and Ilda made the newspaper pad. They delved into the battered trunk for the old quilt Alice had never gotten around to discarding. While the string, scissors and bindings were boiling on the stove, she told the girls what to do in case the baby came early.

"Grace, you'll go over to tell Mrs. Engen, and take Tucker with you if he's awake. Both of you stay there when she comes over here. If Tucker is asleep, we'll just let him alone. Just like your father, a storm could knock the house down and he'd sleep through it."

For the next week, Alice and the girls rehearsed their roles every other day. At three o'clock in the afternoon on Tuesday, October fifth, Alice felt the first contraction. Quickly, she set out the things she would need. Between short stops for ensuing contractions, she built up the fire and prepared her bed. At first, she considered trying to get to the Engens', but a quarter mile might be too far. Carol had no equipment, and trying to carry even a minimum would be difficult.

She barely got to the bed during a heavy contraction. The next one was the last and Alice bore her ten pound son as she had borne Carsie, alone. This time she was not as exhausted. "An old hand at the game, I am!" she said aloud, while she tied and cut the cord. She pulled up the blankets to await the children's homecoming. She found herself smiling in anticipation of their reactions.

Ilda and Grace came in the door giggling. Tucker was a few steps behind them grumbling, "Girls!"

"Mama, Mama, are you here?!" A note of alarm crept into Ilda's voice as it rose in pitch. "Mama?!"

"It's alright, I'm in the bedroom! Come in and close the door! I have a surprise for you!"

All three came, half running, into the corner.

"The baby! You've had the baby! Oh Mama, It's *beautiful!* Can I hold it?" Ilda's excitement made her almost dance about.

Grace stood, wide-eyed and quiet.

"I suppose you got another *silly* girl," Tucker said, as if nothing out of the ordinary had happened.

"No, it's another brother for you. See, he has lots of black hair like yours, Tucker."

"Oh, well, that's alright then. Can I have an apple, Ma?" He turned and went to find the fruit. Then he sat down with a book.

"Sister, will you start supper? There is some stew meat and vegetables, already cut, in the cooler. Grace can keep an eye on it while you go and send Mrs. Engen over. You'd better stay there with her children until Mr. Engen gets home.

"This baby sure made a hash out of all our plans, didn't he?"

Ilda started supper while Grace stayed with Alice. She stared at the baby. "Mama, is it really another boy?" Her tone told her mother that a boy was *not* what Grace wished.

"Yes, Honey; he's a beautiful baby, too. You and Sister can help me take care of him, now that you are big girls."

Grace came nearer and pulled the blanket back from the tiny face. "Ooh, he *is* pretty, Mama; not like *Tucker* at all! I hope he's more fun, too."

Alice chided, "Grace, it's not very kind to keep reminding Tucker of that. He *is* your brother after all, and we love him.

"Now, would you go check if the teakettle is full? I hear it boiling. Mrs. Engen is going to need warm water to bathe the baby. Get the wash pan and some towels out, too, please."

"Yes, Mama. I'm glad the baby came. Too bad it's not a girl, though."

Carol Engen came in the door, breathless. "I hurried as fast as I could, Alice. Ilda said you'd had the baby by yourself. You should have told me. I'd have been here to help!"

"There was no time to tell you, Carol. The labor was less than thirty minutes from start to finish. I knew it would be fast, so couldn't risk the walk to your house.

"I'd appreciate it if you'd clean up the baby, though, and then help me get myself and the bed straightened up."

Carol put a pan of warm water on the table, took the baby from Alice's arms and unwrapped him. "You even tied and cut the cord?!" she exclaimed, "all by yourself!? I don't know as how I'd have enough sense to do all that."

"You would if you'd done it as many times as I have. I was all alone when Carsie was born, too. And besides, I **AM** a nurse."

Carol shook her head in amazement as she bustled about. "What are you going to name this little boy? Did you and Frank decide before he left? Oh, my, he is just *too pretty* to be a boy!"

"No, I purposely didn't bring up the subject," Alice answered, "His name is Frank. It's about time we had one with his father's name. His papa can give him a middle name when he gets around to it."

"I'll help Grace finish fixing dinner before I go," Carol said as she put the soiled linens in a box to take home. "Is there anything else I can do for you, Alice? Are you comfortable?"

"I could use a cup of tea, if the teakettle got refilled. Why don't you sit down and have a cup with me? You've been flitting around like a honey bee since you got here."

Carol checked on Grace's progress with supper, fixed two cups of tea and pulled a chair to Alice's bedside. She sighed, "Oh, so *that's* what it feels like to sit down!"

When she had finished her tea, she asked Alice, "Do you think you'll need me to stay 'til your mother comes? When is she arriving?"

"Thanks, no: Mother will be here before noon, the day after tomorrow. She's taking the late train into Portland and then the first train out to Oregon City. She can hire a buggy to bring her here.

"I can keep Ilda home. She's capable; and a couple of days out of school won't hurt her studies much."

"Your mama will be surprised, won't she?" Carol chuckled at the thought.

"Not a bit. She delivered me all by herself, *and* she was only fifteen! She knows about Carsie, so it's an old story for her."

True to Alice's prediction, Ercyline calmly took over the reins of the household. Her firm hand kept Alice down for all of two days, against her many protests.

On the ninth day after little Frank's birth, Ercyline packed her valise. "There's no reason for me to stay, Alice. You're doing as much as before. Your father needs more mothering than *you* do."

Chapter Twenty Seven

ALICE IN WONDERLAND

Through a series of letters from Milton Freewater and Weston, Frank kept Alice up-to-date on the progress of his tick fever. It was a fairly severe case.

> Martin told me that if I'd gotten the Rocky Mountain Spotted type, they'd have taken me in to the hospital in Pendleton. As it is, I spent some time in a boarding house in Weston. I never felt so weak in my life!
>
> Alice, you've given me another son and I'm pleased that you've given him my name. Thank you for not going with 'Francis Marion', like my parents did. I swear, they named me after my aunt Frances, and I got teased about it a lot.

He returned to work just a few days after his namesake's birth. In November, Alice wrote back:

> I'm sad, as are the children, that you can't come home
> for Christmas, as we had planned. Between the time I
> had to take off for little Frank's birth, and your illness,
> there just isn't any money to spare. I'll do my best to make
> it a happy time for the children. Maybe we can get up a
> neighborhood party to keep us all busy.

"So many mill people are transient," she told Carol Engen, "Why don't we find out who doesn't have family nearby, and if there are enough, I'll ask Swenson and the superintendent for permission to use part of the mill floor for a party. None of our houses is big enough for more than twelve or so people."

The Engens were from Minnesota and had no extended family nearby. "What a grand idea!" Carol was enthusiastic. "Back home we always had folks in from miles around. I really miss all the big Christmas doings!"

An hour before dark on Christmas Eve there was a knock at the door. Carsie ran to answer it. "Hello, Mr. Ingeborg. Mama, look who's here!"

"Come in, come in! Get out of the cold!" Alice said, wiping her hands on her apron. "What brings you over here? Did you bring Becky along? This is a wonderful surprise!"

"More of a surprise than you know," he told her. "I've got a wagon outside. Pastor Thatcher said I was to bundle you all up and bring you to West Lynn for supper and the Christmas Eve party. He told me not to take 'no' for an answer."

Even Tucker whooped in delight at the invitation. "Can we go, Mama, please?!" the four clamored, gathering around her.

"I don't know; there's so much yet to do before *tomorrow's* party!" Alice's face flushed with pleasure at this unexpected turn. The children's delight soon won her over.

"All right, all right, shush, you'll wake the baby.

"*Do* come in, Jim, and have a cup of coffee to warm you while we get ready.

"Well, children, I guess you'll get your Christmas gifts early!"
Alice went to get the new dresses she'd made for the girls and
bright flannel shirts for the boys. "I'd planned for you to wear these
tomorrow," she told them, "but this is a special occasion. Scoot
upstairs and get changed."

Half an hour later, bundled in quilts on a pile of hay, the Waldens
left for West Lynn. Bettina fed them a bounteous dinner before the
services began.

"And now, my friends," Stephen announced from the pulpit,
"We have an unusual and special event for Christmas Eve. We are
celebrating the birth of the Christ Child. How fitting then, that we
should celebrate the arrival of our newest member. Alice Walden, will
you bring the baby forward?"

Alice flushed with surprise and stood up. Carsie nudged her with
his elbow. "Go on, Mama; they're waiting for you."

"Alice; would you permit Bettina and I to be godparents for your
child?" Stephen asked, as she stood by the altar.

"I am honored, and I know Frank will be, too. We can have a
dedication service after Frank gets home."

At the end of the service, Stephen took Alice's elbow and steered
her to the front door to stand beside him as her friends filed out with
congratulations. One by one, they piled packages at her feet. "For the
new baby," said one. "Knew you'd need 'em after six years. Tucker's
duds are probably gone by now," said another. Flurries of hugs and
handshakes later, Alice's knees were trembling, until she could hardly
stand. Stephen brought a chair, as Carsie closed the big door.

"Alice, I don't know what we would've done if you hadn't come.
We counted on your children coaxing you. Folks have been busy for
weeks planning this."

At these words, Alice looked up, her face streaked with tears. "A
body never realizes how many friends one has until something like
this happens!" she said. "My, I don't know how long it's been since
I've been this overcome!"

After a moment, Bettina took her hand and coaxed her up.
"Come along now and have a cup of coffee. There's hot chocolate for

the children, too. You'll need it to fortify you against the cold on the ride home." She led them all to the parsonage to await Jim Ingeborg's return from taking his own family home.

Upon investigation, early Christmas morning, the packages from the Church held some new and some not-so-new clothes, and toys for all the children, as well as cookies, nuts, breads, Christmas oranges and venison jerky. "My goodness, I won't have to make more clothes for the baby until he's four! There are all sizes. How wonderful our friends are!"

Alice soon had the children putting away the wrapping paper, then sat them down to breakfast. After they had finished eating, she told them to get ready for the party at the mill while she did the dishes.

By one o'clock, people began arriving at the mill. The men had cleared the floor after work the day before and set up planks on saw horses for the food and drinks. Alice wrote to frank that night after the children were asleep:

> There were at least fifty people. There were more than enough bachelors to keep the daughters dancing. Besides Carsie's fiddle; he'd practiced for weeks; there were two mouth harps, a guitar and a concertina.
>
> I never saw so much food! Everyone had a good time, and the loggers were good about not drinking heavily. I hate to say, I sat in a corner with the baby and wished with all my heart that you could have been here. I hope you had someone to be with today.

The rest of the winter and spring went on without fanfare. The Walden family went on with their lives, praying every night for their reunion with Frank.

On the morning after school was out at the end of May, Mr. Engen came to take the family to the train station in Oregon City. Alice had sent the few needed articles of furniture and their other belongings to the freight office the day before. Frank wrote to her that he had a stove, bed frames, table and chairs. Mysteriously, he never mentioned what kind of house he had for them. Alice's curiosity was piqued, but he continued to ignore any questions about it in his letters. On the train, her mind went back over Bluetown, West Lynn, and the unfinished shell they had just left. Frank just didn't seem to have much sense, or else not enough backbone when it came to such things.

What are we getting into this time, she asked herself, and prayed for a pleasant surprise.

Three glorious days with Ernest and Ercyline passed quickly, as the family visited with old friends and Mr. Harney. Then on Saturday they were off to Weston, where Frank would meet them. Alice was hopeful that their belongings awaited them there.

The children, except for Tucker, were delighted with the rickety, narrow gauge train from Pendleton to Weston. Little Frank was lulled into a deep sleep, so that Alice checked him several times to make sure he was alright.

Alice heard Frank's hearty "Whoop!" as he came running down the station platform. The children swarmed over him before Alice, carrying little Frank, stepped down to the platform.

"Hey, you rascals! Get off me!" he mock scolded them. "How can I get to your mama without stepping all over you?!" He untangled them gently, giving each one a hug before setting them aside.

"Here, Mama, give me the baby." Ilda took the squirming child from her mother, as Alice stepped longingly into Frank's waiting arms.

Frank picked Alice up and kissed her soundly, whirling her around. "Old lady," he said as he put her down and held her at arm's length, "you're even prettier than I remember. It's so good to hold you again!"

"The feeling is mutual," She agreed.

He embraced her once more and held her close for a long quiet moment before he turned to pick up his youngest son.

"Now **this** is what I call a handsome lad! And a husky one, too. Look at that mop of black hair and those big eyes! Alice, will you look at those long eyelashes? This boy is going to break a lot of hearts before he's even grown!"

The train to Milton Freewater was not meant for passengers. The Waldens rode with all their household goods on an open car meant for finished lumber. A wagon awaited them beside the mill in the tiny town. Mountains crowded the flanks of the unfinished company houses lining the single street. The mill dominated the landscape. Its tall stacks spewed smoke and steam into the otherwise clear air. Already, a pile of sawdust loomed taller than the storage sheds and stacked lumber around it.

"I hope the ride to the house is short," Alice sighed. "I'm still vibrating from the train ride."

"It's not in town, I'll tell you that! I knew you wouldn't want to be hemmed in. You'll see when we get there." Frank's smug expression broke into a grin as he drove the wagon along the street. They passed the company store, some small shops, post office, saloon, the livery stable and smithy, then left the town itself and started up a narrow road which became steeper.

"I know! I know!" Carsie began to laugh. "It's a log cabin! Did you build it yourself?! Did you leave some of it for us to help, Pa, did you?!"

"You've got it right, boy. I knew you'd guess pretty soon. Wait until we come around this bend."

The cabin faced east, into the morning sun. Tall firs shaded it from the south and west sun. Alice stared with her mouth agape. "Frank, it's beautiful! What a view! Such a lovely setting and a good-sized house, too!" Alice held her breath, wondering about the inside. "You've really been working hard. Did you have lots of help? Those logs look heavy."

"I sure did. We have a slew of old friends here from Bluetown, Bridal Veil and a couple from West Lynn, too. Everyone was wonderful. The women brought food; just like a barn raising. Be prepared; we'll owe them a party when we get settled."

Everyone piled out of the wagon, but Frank called the children back, "I want your mama to see it first. Come, *Milady,* and enter your ***castle***." He flung open the door and doffed his hat as he ushered her into a whitewashed room. Alice stepped through the door with just a hint of hesitation, bracing herself for possible disappointment. Her eyes widened in pleasure. The room was spacious enough to serve as living room, dining room and kitchen.

"And a big, stone fireplace?! Oh Frank, it's lovely, and so light, too! I've never thought of a log cabin as being anything but dark." She walked from one large window to the next around three sides of the room. A huge three-paneled one looked out over the valley, with a glimpse of the river below. "A window over the sink, too?! I've always felt closed in with only a blank wall to stare at while I cook and wash dishes."

"I know, I've heard you grouse about it. I ***really did*** hear a few things you've said through the years." Frank strode to a door in the fourth wall and flung it wide for Alice to enter their bedroom.

"It's beautiful! Oh, Frank, I could kiss you!"

"Well, what are you waiting for?" He grinned, and welcomed her into his arms.

They turned to the front room again to find four silent children waiting for them.

"But Pa, there's no rooms for us. Is that what you left for us to help you build?" Carsie's expression was half curious, half eager.

"Nope! Look here in the corner. You just pull this rope... and presto!"

The children's mouths dropped open as a panel in the ceiling opened and a set of folding stairs descended into the room. At the top, a wall divided the attic into two rooms.

"The white one is for the girls. Boys don't need so much light to primp, eh, fellas?"

The four scampered up the stairs to inspect their rooms and choose their beds.

"Hey, come on down here!" Frank's voice boomed up the stairs. "There's a lot to do yet! We've a wagon to unload before we can start living in this house!"

"Get the pots and pans in here first, while I get the fire going," Alice called as they went out.

"Not to worry; there's a treat in the wagon. We'll bring in the dishes and utensils first." Frank brought in a basket that Alice knew was not one of hers. "Some of your friends fixed up a picnic meal for tonight. You don't have to cook until tomorrow."

Alice started to tear up, "Frank, this is the best homecoming, yet. Even the Bridal Veil house, though it was new, was not as nice as this one, nor did it have such a glorious setting. I'm so happy, I could sing!"

"Don't, Mama, please! We'll sing and you can dance," Carsie laughed. "Your singing hurts our ears."

"Oh, it does, does it?! Well, now I know how to punish you when you're naughty!" she teased back.

The beds made up and essentials unpacked, Alice sat down with, "Whoosh, it's warm in here! After supper I'm going to need a bath, when and if I have enough energy to build a fire and get water heating. I think everyone's going to need one."

"If you'd rather have a shower, I've rigged one like the one we had in Bridal Veil," Frank said offhandedly as he carried a box of clothes up to the attic rooms. "Rest while I get the fire started."

"A shower? Oh, there's nothing more refreshing! Thank you dear."

"Me, too, Papa!" Carsie called down the stairs. "I'll pack warm water for you first, Mama, and then put more on for myself and the others. I've still got train soot and dust all over me."

"Me, too," said Tucker. "Men take showers and girls take baths. I'm getting too big for the tub, anyway."

"We want to use the tub." the girls agreed.

After dinner the girls stacked the supper dishes and took them to the sink. "Papa, where'd you put the pump? I went out back a while ago and didn't see one; or is there a creek nearby?" Ilda asked.

"Better than that," Frank answered. "You were upstairs while Carsie was filling the kettle and the stove reservoir. I put the dish rag over it to hide it. Tah dah!" He flipped the rag off of a faucet over the sink.

"Running water?! Grace, come look! We won't have to pump or pack water anymore. Running water in the house; and this far out on a mountain!"

Grace and Tucker came running and took turns opening and closing the spigot.

"Where does it come from, Papa? I didn't see any pipe out back," Ilda went to the back stoop to look again, "Why there's even a faucet out here to wash up!"

"There's a stream about two hundred feet up the hill; plenty enough water for all our needs. There's yet another tap for the shower, and one for the garden," Frank added.

"We're getting so fancy, I'll have to unpack my satin dress to keep house." Alice minced across the floor, picked up a teacup and held it with her pinky finger perked up in the air. She drew a cup of water and sipped grandly. "*Delicious*, my dears, an excellent quaff."

The children giggled at these rare comic antics from their mother. Then each copied her actions, while Frank fell into his big chair, laughing.

"Come down off your high horses, your majesties. Remember, we still have to use an outhouse. Of course, it *is* a two-holer. I guess you could say that's a **smidgeon** fancy, eh? No waiting, ladies and gents; two seats; a luxury accommodation! Which reminds me..." he stood up and headed for the back door.

On Sunday morning, after a family devotional, Alice and the girls finished unpacking and storing things away, as Frank took Carsie and Tucker outside.

"You wanted to help build the house, boys? Well, here's your chance. In about a month it's going to get hot here. The summers are really something. So I thought we could build your mama a summer kitchen and wash house. We can connect it to the house with a roofed passageway that the east coast folks call a dog trot."

Frank had staked the outlines of the added building. "See, the dog trot will be open on both sides, to trap the summer winds and lead them into the back door. In winter, the wind will mostly hit the back side of the wash house and help keep drafts out of the house."

"Where are the logs for the wash house, Papa?" Carsie looked around. "Do we have to cut the trees down, too?"

"No, green logs aren't good for building. They warp and shrink up causing gaps in the walls, then the chinking falls out. The logs are stacked for drying on the other side of the house. They've been there since last fall when I cut the house timbers."

During Sunday's supper, Frank told them about building the house. "Some of the Indians who work around the mill came up and taught me how to cut and place the timbers. They're experts; you ought to see them. They whack away with hatchets and wind up with surfaces as flat as if they'd been planed."

"What are the Indians like?" Grace wanted to know.

"I like them," her father said, "I take a lot of kidding about it. Some of the men are still saying, 'The only good Injun is a dead Injun. If I ever hear any of you scalawags talking like that, you won't be able to sit down for a week!"

"I'll add to that," Alice said. "You have to remember that you and I have some Indian blood, too. That's where Tuck and little Frank and I get our dark coloring and sister gets her dark brown eyes."

"You've never told us that, Mama." Carsie said. "Tell us more about it."

"It's really your grandma's story. She said they might come to visit us this summer. You can ask her then."

"Why are there Indians here, Papa? Ilda asked, "Is there an Indian village nearby?"

Frank looked around at his family, and his eyebrow twitched, "You mean I didn't *tell* you? How could I have been so careless, tch, tch. We'll have to remedy that immediately!"

His manner brought smiles of anticipation as the children gathered around him.

"Well now, the most important thing is that we are guests of the Indians."

"What do you mean, Papa?" The little faces in a half circle around their father were wide-eyed. "This is **our** house; how come we're **their** guests?"

"We are just about **smack dab** in the middle of the Umatilla Indian Reservation! How does that strike you?"

At this announcement, Alice came to join the group while she nursed the baby. "You didn't tell me that. How did the timber company get permission to log off and build the town? I thought Indians didn't allow white men to live and work on their land."

"The company has to hire a certain number of Indians, and they pay rent on the land the town is built on," Frank explained. "So do we; for this land our house is built on."

"How about the timber that's coming from the Indians' mountains? Doesn't that belong to the tribe?"

"Absolutely, but I suppose they have an arrangement of some sort with the company."

"What **are** the Indians like, Pa?" Carsie wanted to know.

"Do they wear feathers and war paint like the pictures in our books?" Ilda asked, wide-eyed. "Can we see some one day?"

"You'll see them alright; you never know where they'll turn up. Unless you go to the Indian village when they're celebrating, you won't see feathers and such, though. The men wear their hair long, in a braid down their backs, just like the women. Most of the women wear calico dresses that are loose, and they all wear moccasins instead of shoes. Some of them are pretty, too, like the ones I brought you in Bridal Veil. Do you remember, Sister?"

"Yes, and Grace wore them out after I outgrew them. Tell us more about them, Papa."

Frank kept them entertained until bedtime. Carsie hung back when the others went upstairs. "Pa, is there work for me here? Mr. Swenson gave me a letter of reference that says I'm a good worker. I'd really like to get a job here, too."

"I thought you'd be glad for a vacation from the mill and maybe work on the summer kitchen for a while when you feel like it."

"I'll dig up Mama's garden and work on the building, too, when you're here to show me. But I can do that on weekends, Pa, like you do, and work, too."

"Let's see what's available, Son. I'm going back up to the camp tomorrow morning. It's not far, so I can come in every weekend. You'll have at least one week to do what you want, anyway."

"Pa, would it be alright if I went into town, to the mill, to see about work?"

"Not this week, Son. I'll ask around first. Now off to bed with you!" The pride on Frank's face was obvious as he watched Carsie climb the ladder.

The next Sunday evening, Frank told Carsie to pack a kit. "You've got a job at the camp with me, Son. We'll leave early in the morning, if it's alright with your mother. If she objects, we'll go down to the office in town, to see if the mill has any work for you."

"If you're going to be at the mill all winter, Frank, it'll be a treat for Carsie to learn some woods lore at the camp this summer. He'll have to come back down early to start school, though," said Alice, hoping he would.

"Thanks, Ma, I'd really like to work at the camp instead of at the mill. Are you sure you won't need me?"

"It's alright, Son; Sister is getting big enough now to take over your chores, and Grace is old enough to help with the baby. We'll make out fine."

Frank cleared his throat. "There's one other thing I forgot to tell you. There isn't a school started yet. Some of the folks send their children into Weston and board them out."

"No school?!" Alice's face became still but her eyes smoldered. "How could you not tell us? The children need schooling. We can't afford to send them all into town!" She turned to her work to compose her thoughts and gain control of her temper.

"You said your folks were coming over this summer. I thought maybe you could write to your father. I would think he'd be willing to bring some books and lessons for them. That way they can keep up by studying at home." Frank came to stand behind her and put his arms around her waist. "It'll work out, you'll see. Maybe by next year there **will** be a school. We can work with our friends to see if we can get something started."

Alice struggled free of Frank's grasp and went to sit at the table. She sat with her forehead resting on her hands for a minute. Finally, she looked up with a sigh. "I'll get a letter off to Papa tomorrow. It looks like we're going to have our own private school."

The other children were listening from the stairs and voiced their approval. "Have you been listening all this time? Off to bed now, you scalawags!" Frank scolded, with a twitch of his eyebrow.

Carsie was put to work stoking. It was a hard, hot job keeping the fires of the steam donkey engine at full heat. In the pauses between carrying the three-foot lengths of firewood, he watched, fascinated, as huge logs went sailing across the sky on heavy cables. The tall, bare spar trees, their pulley wheels spinning, bent with the weight of their burdens. Sometimes, as the logs dipped far down in the middle of their journey, he feared for the safety of the men who worked beneath their path. What if a cable should snap or a spar tree split? He kept his worries to himself until evening, when he could talk to his father about them, alone.

"It's alright, Son. I'm glad you have the foresight to realize that it could happen. It shows you have a brain under that sandy mop of yours. I've never seen a cable snap, but I've heard of it happening. It doesn't happen often enough to worry about. The sound of the cable snapping would be like a very loud shot, and those men would scatter like rabbits."

On another day, the donkey engine's boiler split a seam. The boiling water fanned out rapidly. The engineer grabbed Carsie and yanked him out of the way, barely in time to escape being sprayed with the live steam. Carsie had nightmares for weeks that a trail of steam was chasing him, no matter where he ran to escape it. Any hissing noise caused him to jump and look wildly about, poised to run.

In four weekends, Frank and Carsie, with Tucker "unhelping," as Frank told Alice in confidence, had the summer kitchen with its stone chimney and fire box finished. Frank found a sheet of iron to set across the top for a cooking surface. After that, the house stove stood idle. Alice started the outside fire in the morning for breakfast and cooked food to serve cold for lunch and dinner.

Open windows and doors set up enough cross-draft to keep the house almost bearably cooler. It filtered through wet sheets that Alice had hung over the openings.

"It is *such* a blessing not to have to heat up the house with cooking. I never realized what a difference it would make." Alice said, as she and Frank sat talking together in the house one evening, reveling in the cool air blowing through.

"Ma, can we bring our quilts and come down there to sleep?" Carsie, as usual, the spokesman for the other three, stood on the stairway. "It's so hot up here under the roof that we can't sleep."

"Why not?" Frank answered. "We can make it an adventure!"

"It might be cooler for summer and warmer in winter if we had pads of dry moss between the rafters." Alice suggested. "Suppose on our walks during the week we homebodies gather the moss while we look for herbs and berries?"

"That's a fine idea!" Frank agreed. "There's so little rain in the summer here that the moss will dry out in the yard. I'll get slats from the mill to hold the moss in place."

Moss gathering picnics became the routine of the day during the week. In the afternoons, it was cooler in the woods. Alice taught the children to walk quietly so they wouldn't disturb the animals as they studied the plant life and replenished her supply of herbs for cooking and medicine.

Chapter Twenty Eight

QUARANTINE

Alice's friends living in town soon passed the word that she was a nurse/midwife. Patients and their families began arriving at her door seeking help, since there was no doctor closer than Weston. She took baby Frank along when she went on calls and tried to avoid leaving Ilda, Grace and Tucker home alone except for brief periods. It was a big relief to her when her parents arrived in mid-July.

When Alice and the children met them at the stage stop in Milton Freewater, Alice was shocked. "Papa, what happened to you? Why didn't you let me know, Mama?"

Ernest got down from the stage so slowly and feebly, that Alice and Ercyline had to help him to a bench nearby.

"He had pneumonia again just after you left us," her mother said. "Dr. Williams said it wasn't a bad case, but it seemed to drain all his strength.

"The doctor thinks he may have some sort of lung damage. The weather has been cold and miserable, and you know how your father is. He just had to go to work and school board meetings no matter how bad he felt."

"Did Dr. Williams give you permission to make this trip, as weak as you are, Papa?"

"He insisted," Earnest replied, "He said getting up to this high, dry climate was the best thing for me. So I guess you'll be burdened with us for the rest of the summer."

"Hurray!" yelled Tucker, surprising everyone.

"The whole summer, Grandpa? I'm so glad!" Ilda hugged him.

"Me, too!" Grace joined in on the hug.

"Well, you just rest right here while I go find a buggy to get us home. It's much too far for you to walk in your condition, Papa."

Alice soon returned from the livery stable with a flatbed wagon pulled by a swaybacked nag. "This is all that was available," she apologized.

Using a valise as a pillow, Ernest stretched out, happily surrounded by his grandchildren.

Ercyline sat beside Alice holding baby Frank. "Are you sure this pitiful old horse can get us up this hill?" Ercyline said, with mock concern in her voice.

"Well, if he can't, you'll all just have to get out and push," Alice teased. "I'll have to use the brake coming back down. I doubt the poor thing will have the strength to hold back even this light rig."

As soon as they rounded the bend and Ercyline saw the house, she exclaimed, "Oh, my, it's so lovely!"

Ernest remarked, "I had no idea Frank was such a good carpenter."

"Frank put up a bed for us in the summer kitchen. You'll sleep in our bedroom," Alice explained, as she and her mother helped Ernest into the house.

"No, Alice," he protested, "Dr. Williams said to get as much fresh air as possible. I'm sure the outbuilding is more open than any room in the house. Let us stay out here, please. That way we'll all have more privacy, also."

"Dr. Williams said he should sleep as much as possible, so maybe that would be best," Ercyline added, "It'll be quieter out there, and the children can be as noisy as they want without disturbing him."

"You're right, Papa, as usual. Let's get you settled in. I'm sure you're ready for a long rest after your trip." The two women helped him to the bed in the summer kitchen shed, while Grace and Tucker brought in the luggage and Ilda took Ernest a cool drink of water. Alice and Ercyline sat in the dog-trot for a talk, while they had a drink.

"It's so nice to be here in the shade of the passageway," Ercyline remarked. She leaned back to rest her head against the log wall. "It must get very hot here later in the summer. It'll be good for your father, though. He's been doing so well since we came to Bridal Veil, until recently. He's nearly sixty now and has a harder time getting over such a serious illness."

"I was so shocked at how old he looked when he got off the stage, Mama. He seems to have aged twenty years in the six weeks since we moved. Now that he's here, we'll see that he gets good care. We'll soon have him back to his old self.

"While we're talking, Mama, I have a favor to ask you. I've nearly weaned little Frank because I'm getting so many patients of late. Would you mind keeping an eye on the children when I'm away? Sister has been awfully good, but I've hated putting the whole responsibility on her."

"Of course I don't mind. It would be my pleasure. Papa and I have to earn our keep while we're here."

She took a long drink and motioned toward the garden. "I've been eyeing your garden and itching to get my hands in the dirt again. There's so little space at home for anything but a few flowers. I have to intersperse them with lettuce and carrots."

Through the weeks following, Ernest basked in the heat and lost some of his pallor. By the first week in September, he was feeling back to normal. "I'm going to miss this place," he told Frank. "The dry air sure does agree with me."

"Maybe so," Frank replied, "but in a few weeks, you'd be begging to get back to the valley. You've been lucky. The local folks say we have two seasons here; winter and August. The hot weather has lasted longer than usual, I understand."

A heavy frost heralded Ernest and Ercyline's departure. Alice and the children missed them, but kept busy harvesting the vegetables from their garden and storing them in the root cellar that Frank had dug. The lessons and books Ernest had brought with them had been unpacked. Regular study hours became the order of the day, with Carsie putting in his study time after work and on weekends.

Winter set in quickly. "The wind howls around the house like a demon possessed with the idea of blowing it down!" Alice commented to Frank one evening. "It reminds me of the widow-maker winds on the gorge."

By November first, the danger of wind-felled trees closed the camp, so Frank and Carsie went to work in the mill. "I feel sad that he's missing so much schooling," Alice said, "but I haven't the heart to ask him to do more, when he's so tired at night."

"It's alright," Frank told her. "Our children are getting more lessons than the other children in town. Carsie is a good worker and he's filled out as he's grown these last months. By spring he'll be as tall as you."

It was good that they had lots of food stored up, as they were snowed in for weeks at a time that winter.

By mid-spring, 1899, when the camps opened again, Carsie, at thirteen, had grown to within an inch of Alice's five feet, eight inches. "I'll pass you up this summer, Mama. I may catch up with Papa by next year at the rate I'm growing!" he predicted as he and his father packed their gear for camp.

"Don't hurry it, Son," his mother told him. "If you grow up too quickly, you'll likely not grow strong enough in bone and muscle to make up for it. Be careful to eat well and get lots of rest while you're gone."

Alice was six months into another pregnancy when the hot winds of early June began to blow. She wrote to her parents that she'd have to cut back as much as possible on nursing cases that summer. The heat drained her energy. It was hard to say "no" when folks needed her, but she had the baby to think of, as well as her own health.

The Beebes arrived at the end of June to spend the summer. "I'm staying over until the baby comes," Ercyline informed Alice in a determined voice. "Your Papa can go back when he's needed at school, but I'm going to be here when this baby comes! Five times I've felt guilty about not being with you when your time came."

That July was one of the hottest on record in Eastern Oregon. Alice was kept busier than she wanted to be, caring for sunstroke and heat prostration cases. At times, she was too tired, so far into her pregnancy, to respond to pleas, and had to send instructions for care with those who came asking for help.

At midday, just after the first of August, when Alice was home alone and the rest were off in the woods, the sound of horse and wagon, at breakneck speed, roused her from a catnap. The rig stopped just outside the back door and Frank came into the house holding a limp Carsie in his arms.

"The boy collapsed from the heat. We moved him into the shade and sloshed cold water over him, but when he didn't come to, I brought him to you."

Carsie was pale. His skin was hot and paper-dry.

"What he needs is to be cooled off all over, and in a hurry! Carry him out to the dog-trot. I'll get the bathtub from the shed."

Frank laid Carsie on a canvas cot and began to fill a pail with water, while Alice undressed the boy.

"Lift him into the tub now and fill it. Keep the water running over him all the time, up and down his body," she told Frank. "We've got to break through the dry heat and get his blood flowing."

"Dear God," she prayed, "let me save my son. He's worked too hard for one so young. Are we to blame for letting him go to work at such a tender age?"

Ernest, Ercyline, the girls and Tucker came laughing and frolicking through the trees behind the house, just as Carsie began to stir.

Ercyline hesitated at the edge of the trees when she saw them, then began to run toward the house. "Something's wrong, what is it!" she asked. "I could tell by the way you both seemed so intent." She stopped and looked with concern at Carsie's still form.

"What happened to him?" Ilda said, as she caught up with her grandmother.

"Heat stroke," Alice replied. "He's coming to, praise God! Mama, will you bring me that tray from the kitchen shelf? We need something to fan him with. We haven't had time to go inside.

"Sister, get some sheets from the cupboard, please."

When Ilda came back out, Alice plunged a sheet into the tub, then spread it on the cot. "He's coming out of it. The cold water will be too much now. Frank, take him out of the tub so I can wrap him."

Swaddled in the wet sheets and fanned continually, Carsie gradually woke up. He looked around groggily and struggled to sit up. "Gotta get back to work; broiler fire needs wood," he mumbled.

The wet sheets, wrapped tightly around him, restrained him until he was fully alert. He looked around him. "Mama, what are you doing here? Gramma, you, too?"

"It's alright, Son, you're home. Rest now." Alice stroked his forehead.

"How did I get here? I was working and got kind of 'woofly, like Tucker says. Did I faint?"

"You sure did, boy!" Frank moved to where Carsie could see him. "You did one fancy fall, just like a stage actor. Everyone thought you'd been practicing; you went down so slow and easy-like. I brought you home as fast as I could."

Carsie started to sit up. "I've got to get back to work, Pa. There's no one to stoke the boiler."

"Whoa, boy, lie still! You're not going anywhere for a while." Frank held him down.

"You need some rest and lots of cool things to drink. You haven't been getting enough water to make up for what you've been sweating out. That's why you fainted." Alice's gentle tone calmed him.

"Sister, will you please get some of that fruit juice from the cooler for Carsie? I think he's able to handle it now.

"We need a little more water over him. Frank, the sheet is drying out."

On a diet of fruit juices, salty broths and milk, Carsie got stronger over the next two days.

In the middle of the third night, the household was awakened by a sharp cry, "The fire's going out; gotta get more wood!" Carsie jumped up from his cot in the big room and started for the door. His eyes were wide open as he crossed the room. Frank caught him just as he reached the edge of the front stoop. "Gotta get back to work! Let me go!"

Alice helped Frank get Carsie back inside. She felt his forehead and exclaimed, "He has a high fever. I was afraid of this. It's probably what Mam Ginny called brain fever; meningitis."

She glanced around when she heard the other children on the stairs. "Go back upstairs, now! Stay there until I call you. Carsie's very sick and I don't need to have the rest of you down with it."

"What do we do now, Alice?" Frank's face was a mask of concern as he held Carsie down. Is it *that* contagious?"

"Good Lord, yes, **horribly**. We'll have to isolate him in the summer kitchen and move Mama and Papa in here."

"What do we do first?" Frank asked.

"Take the canvas cot from the shed and put it up outside, away from the house for now. It's warm enough that he won't get chilled. Would you carry him out there and get the fire started? Then you'll have to take your night shirt off outside and take a shower.

"I'll tie him down so he won't get up again and then start working to break his fever."

Alice got to the doorway of the summer kitchen just as her parents were coming out. "What's all the racket? Is Carsie sick again?" Ernest was startled, as Alice backed away from him.

"Wait, don't get near me! I was just coming to get you. Yes, it's Carsie; meningitis, I think. I'll need to stay out here with him. There's a lot to be done."

We'll get dressed and come right out," Ercyline offered, "then you can tell us what you need us to do."

"Mama, when you come out, bring the lye soap. Papa, bring the wash tub and stand. Put them up in the yard so we can get a fire going under them."

When Frank was dressed in clean clothes, everything that had been within five feet of Carsie's cot was scrubbed with lye soap. The Beebe's possessions were moved into the house, along with all the cooking utensils that were used during the summer. Carsie's cot was moved into the shed and he was placed on it.

Finally, Alice was able to take a break. "Mama, will you please get me some clothes now? I've just about sweated this nightgown through. I'll use the water in the pan from the dog-trot to sponge myself."

The rest of the family was kept busy fetching, carrying and cleaning for the next two weeks. Everything that left the sick room had to be boiled before it could be touched by any of them.

Word got out to the town, and many prayers went up for Carsie and the whole family.

Carsie's fever dropped and rose, again and again. Each time it dropped, Alice prayed that this was the one that would mean the crisis was over. Then, relentlessly, the fever returned, each time worse than before. On the tenth day, as Alice sat by his bed fighting to cool the burning demon that possessed her son, he began to sweat heavily, as his tense body relaxed.

"Oh, please, Lord, let this be the last. He can't stand much more," Alice prayed again.

Hour by hour, Alice changed the bedding as it became sodden with Carsie's sweat. He was only semiconscious, but enough so that she persuaded him to swallow, first by teaspoonfuls, then increasingly more; nourishing liquids to replace what he lost through his skin.

Alice finally left Carsie's bedside when the fever had been gone, without returning, for over three hours. She tapped on the kitchen door lightly. It was half past midnight. Her mother opened the door and stepped back, as she had been taught.

"Mama, the crisis is past. He's sleeping quietly," Alice told her. "If everyone were not asleep, I'd shout it so loud, they'd hear me in Weston. Our boy's going to be well again!"

Carsie's already spare frame had become almost emaciated during his illness. He couldn't walk without help for almost two weeks after his fever passed. He began to complain that he ought to be back at work.

"Alright," his mother told him, "when you can walk to town and back, you can go back to work."

"I'll show you!" he answered and got up off his cot. His legs were still a bit wobbly.

"First, I want to see you go up the ladder to your room," Alice directed.

Two steps up, he stopped and rested his head against the stair. "I guess you're right. Please help me lie down again, Ma."

"Let's try just a few more steps each day for a while, alright, Son?"

On September eighth, as Ercyline and Grace were struggling up the hill from a shopping trip into town, the wind came up and blew them back one step for every two steps forward. They were not far from the house but upwind, so that Alice's voice was powerless against it when she called to them.

Carsie had gone to meet them, Little Frank was napping and Ilda and Tucker were gathering wood. She set out the necessary equipment and barely had time to prepare the bed before her eleven pound fourth son, pink and nearly hairless, made the usual, sudden appearance.

"Honestly, Alice, if I didn't know better, I'd say you did this on purpose just to prove your independence!" Ercyline stood in the doorway of the bedroom and shook her head. "Almost thirty-four years old and still shucking babies out like peas from a pod."

"I inherited the talent from you, Mama, remember?" Alice grinned sheepishly. "I'm just thankful that I didn't have to go through another delivery like Tucker's."

"I'm so glad I could be there to help you out during that time in your life. I'm so sorry that I wasn't much of a mother when you were growing up."

"I understand, Mama. You weren't much more than a baby yourself and didn't have an ideal childhood experience to draw upon, either."

They embraced each other for a long time, until Ilda and Tucker came in from their wood gathering foray.

Ilda was excited and pleased at the surprise arrival, but Tucker, in his usual stoicism, said, Oh, good, a boy. I'm hungry. I hope supper isn't going to be late."

The others all looked at each other and shrugged their shoulders. Then they all laughed as they split up to attend to their various duties.

With Alice's permission, Frank named their newest son Ernest. "I think it's time we named one of our sons after your father," he said when he came home, "and if you don't mind, for his middle name; Lafayette. It's sort of a tradition in my family. Somewhere back among the Francis Marions and such, one of the many boys was the godson of De La Fayette." With American pronunciation, his nickname became "Lafe".

Carsie continued to regain his strength and was back to work at the mill within two months, with strict orders from his mother to drink a quart of water every hour. Frank was charged to make sure he carried it out.

That autumn a school was opened in a back room of the store. It was built on for that purpose by the loggers that couldn't afford to send their children to Weston. One of the wives had some experience as a school teacher.

The room was also used for other community functions and for a church meeting place whenever there was a circuit preacher passing through.

Chapter Twenty Nine

MOONSHINE

The summer of 1901 was not as hot as the two previous years, but there had been only a trace of rain and very little snow that whole time.

Frank came home from work the day the Beebes arrived, just in time for the Fourth of July celebration, saying, "The timber is dry enough that there are traces of brown heat-burn on the evergreens clear up to the tree line in the hills. "We're moving the whole camp down to the more open forest next week. We'll be only half a mile from here, so Carsie and I can come home every night all summer."

"We can have more time for all of us to visit in the evenings, too. Not that I mind having our ladies mostly to myself," Ernest said with a wink at Alice, "but sometimes I'd like a little more man talk."

"I'm glad to hear that." Ercyline chimed in. Then, as she watched her daughter waddle across the room, "Alice is so big with this pregnancy, I *do* hope it's not twins. They have such a large brood already."

It was early September and the time for Ernest to go back to Bridal Veil came too fast. "I'm going to stay until this baby comes, too, Alice," Ercyline announced. "You're moving with a lot of difficulty. I wish you'd slow down. I thought you'd taught the folks around here enough about heat and sun stroke the last two summers that they could take care of themselves by now."

"I *am* quitting, Mama, as of today. Riding in the backboard the other day was so painful. I plan to sit down after supper and write out copies of instructions to hand out. I have some things to make for the baby yet, and there's not been enough time to finish them."

"Good. It's about time you had a thought for your own welfare for a change. Since you were small, you've always thought of others first."

Grace and Tucker, now twelve and ten years old, respectively, walked their grandfather to the stage stop the day he left. Afterward, they stopped at the store to get the things on the list that their mother had given them. They each carried a canvas tote sack that Alice had made for such occasions.

"I hate to go by this new saloon on the way home," Grace told Tucker. "There's some pretty rough looking men hanging around here. You'd think the marshal would be watching out for them."

"He does. Haven't you noticed how he's around this end of town so much?" Tucker asked. "He must keep track of what's going on."

"Look out!" Grace pulled her brother to the other side of the street. A big man came staggering through the door, stumbled on the top step and came catapulting toward them.

The children ran a short way then looked back. "That's the Marshal!" Tucker exclaimed.

"And he's drunk, too. Look at him trying to get up. Someone's going to have to help him," Grace remarked.

"Not us." Tucker pulled at her arm. "Let's get out of here!"

They started walking on the river road that ran around the edge of town.

"Come on, Mama will tan our hides if we're late for supper," Grace urged.

"I gotta rest a minute. This bag is heavy and I'm hot." Tucker put down his burden and stepped into the reeds a few feet away. "Come on over here in the shade; it's cooler here." He dipped his bandana in the water and offered it to Grace. "Here, wipe off your face and arms, it'll make you feel better."

She left the road, put down her bag and took the bandana from her brother. "Whew! You're right; it is cooler here. Thanks for the water idea; it's nice, but we'd better get home now."

"Wait a minute, I hear somebody coming. Let's wait and see who it is," he whispered.

They ducked down out of sight just in time to hear the reeds nearby rustling and a few splashing steps into the water. Both children peered between the reeds and saw a man putting two jugs into a tow sack. He put the sack into the water and tied the neck of the sack around a stake driven into the mud. Then he went back to the road and toward town.

"Did you see who that was?" Tucker asked.

"Sure; it was the man who owns the saloon," Grace replied.

"What do you suppose is in the jugs?" Tucker was curious.

"I'm not interested, Tucker. We've got to get along home. Come on or I'm going to tell Mama!"

"Go ahead, I'm going to see."

"Oh... all right! I'll be in trouble if I go home without you anyway!"

They slipped through the reeds and Tucker untied the sack. "Hey, look, it's whiskey! Wonder what he put it here for?"

"I don't want to know. We need to go on home, and right now!"

Grace retreated to where they'd left their tote bags. Tucker followed reluctantly. Just as they were ready to leave the reeds, they heard the sound of pony's hooves.

"Come back here, Tucker," Grace whispered. "We might be in trouble if someone knows what we saw. Get down!"

They squatted low just as an Indian brave got off his pony. He walked into the reeds and picked up the tow sack. In a moment, he remounted and rode off the way he had come.

Waiting until the man was out of sight, the two children scampered back onto the road and set off at a trot for home.

Their family was at the supper table when Tucker and Grace came in the door. "Sorry we're late, Mama. The side of the road gave way and I fell in the ditch, didn't I Tucker?"

"She really did, Mama. C'mon let's get washed up." They put down their tote bags and hurried outside the door to the wash pan.

"Sit down, you two. Everyone else is almost done." Alice told them when they returned.

Ilda had gathered up all the dishes and was cleaning up the table as Grace and Tucker got up. "Grace, how'd you get your skirt all muddy? There's no water in the ditch this time of year."

"It was there where the river reeds come down by the road. Do you want me to wash dishes while you dry?"

"Now I know something's wrong. You never offer to wash," Ilda said in a low voice. "What've you two been up to?"

"I'll tell you later, after we go upstairs."

"Do you have any idea what it was all about?" Grace asked when she'd told her sister the story.

"Sure, they'd have to sneak it somehow. It's against the law to sell liquor to Indians."

"It is? Should I tell Mama and Papa about it?"

"Better not," Ilda said. Mama's not feeling well and it'll upset her. Besides, everyone knows the Marshal's in cahoots with that gang that hangs around the saloon. If he's one of them, then he probably knows about it, so what good would it do to tell anybody? Just stay away from that place from now on."

The next morning, Ercyline doled out collapsible canvas buckets to the girls and Tucker as they left for school. "All of you go down to the river bank and fill the buckets with water on your way back home tonight. The creek that pipes into the house is dry. When we turned on the tap last night, nothing came through."

"In that case, set out the two big metal pails," Frank said. "Carsie and I will make a couple of trips to the river after work. It's down to the river for baths Saturday night." his left eyebrow quirked as he looked at the children.

Ilda made a face at him. Oh, Papa! You know the river's too cold, even for swimming!"

"I guess that means we'll have to all use the same bath water like poor folks do." Carsie's eyebrow twitched a little.

"Go on, get off to work! If you think I'm going to bathe in the same water you stinky ol' boys have used, you've got another think coming!" Ilda answered.

"Scoot, all of you!" Ercyline scolded. "You're disturbing your mother. She needs her rest."

A few days later, Tucker and Grace stopped by the store again. Ilda had hurried ahead to help Ercyline with supper.

Again they stopped just beyond the bend when they heard a horse coming along the road behind them. It was the man from the saloon again.

"He's carrying a tow sack again, Grace. I bet he's going to leave the whiskey for the Indian again."

"So what? It doesn't concern us, Tuck."

"Yes it does; Papa says the Indians aren't supposed to have it. I'll fix em! Go on ahead; I'll meet you at the place we get water."

"Don't do it Tucker! You're asking for trouble!"

"I'll be careful. Besides, Mama and Papa said we shouldn't let bad things go on if we can do something about it."

"Don't tell me." Grace put her hands up, as if in surrender, "I don't want to know. You just go ahead and get yourself a whipping!" Then she stomped on down the road.

Tucker backtracked until he saw the saloon owner going back toward town. When the man was out of sight, Tucker went into the reeds.

"Sure enough, here they are," he said to himself. He felt around in the water until he found a fist-sized stone and smashed the jugs.

Just in time, he heard the Indian's pony and slipped through the reeds into the hiding place from which he had first seen the whole thing.

The Indian dismounted and stepped into the reeds. When he picked up the sack, Tucker heard the pieces of the jugs clinking together.

The Indian grunted in anger. He loosed a string of cuss words and looked around him. Tucker ducked down out of sight. The Indian turned around and tromped determinedly back to his horse, the tow sack in his hand. This time he rode toward town.

Tucker ran to the road and took off like a scalded cat. He caught up with Grace, panting and grinning.

"What did you do?" she asked.

"A good deed, I hope," came his reply. "Lucky you took off your shoes," she said. "Your pants cuffs are wet, though. Maybe Mama and Grandma won't notice, or else you can tell them you went into the water to fill our buckets."

"Sure was one noisy goings-on in town tonight," Frank told them at dinner. "The marshal was up by the saloon and had an Indian in tow with his hands tied behind him. The Indian was screeching and cussing something awful. With that rough bunch around, we didn't stop to see what it was all about. Oh well, we'll probably find out tomorrow."

Tucker and Grace carefully feigned ignorance and avoided looking at one another.

Saturday afternoon, Carsie and Frank came home from town with a story. "The superintendent's house was robbed while he and his family were in Weston," Frank told them. "There have been a lot of robberies and hold-ups lately. The gossip is that that bunch that hangs around the new saloon are responsible."

"Why doesn't the Marshal arrest them?" Alice asked.

"Some folks say he's in with them or else they've got something on him and he doesn't dare do anything."

"Frank, it's not like you to pass on gossip," Alice said. "Is there anything to substantiate such talk?"

"Well, no, only that the marshal hangs around the saloon with the roughnecks. He drinks pretty heavily, too.

"One of the men at the mill wanted a sewing machine for his wife. He says he talked to one of those men and a few days later a couple of fellas turned up with one to sell him; almost new, he says."

"That doesn't prove anything," Alice commented, "Although it does sound suspicious, doesn't it?"

Mid-week, when Frank and Carsie came home after work, Frank took Alice aside. "Did anyone call on you from the mill today?" he asked.

"No, why do you ask? You look worried."

"The supply wagon driver came into camp today and said that Jim Lindall got hurt bad today. His boy, Tom, took the foreman's horse and rode off through town to come get you to take care of him. Folks said the marshal hollered at him to slow down because he was riding too fast in town. When the boy kept on going, the marshal shot him dead. Jim was dead before anyone thought to get word back to the mill.

"Folks are getting pretty disgusted with the marshal. The grocer said he was drunk, as usual. They're getting a committee together to go fire him and run him out of town."

"I hate to think of the children knowing about such things," Alice said. "They'll get the idea that outlaws can run a town."

"It looks like they're doing just that," Frank answered. "Maybe the committee had better go to the County Council or the Tribal Chiefs."

A committee from the town and the mill was formed. When they made a visit to the marshal's office, he was not in. The deputy volunteered to find the marshal and set off toward the saloon. The two lawmen returned within half an hour; the Deputy supporting his boss to keep him upright.

"Waddaya want?" The Marshal's voice was thick and his eyes unfocused.

"We've come to demand that you turn over your badge to us and get out of town. You've been a disgrace to your office and nothing's been done to round up that gang of thieves!"

The marshal straightened up, nearly toppling over, until he steadied himself against his desk. "I'll show you who's the law here! Get out!" He reached for his gun, but fortunately for the committeemen rushing for the door, he fumbled with the flap on his holster and fell down before he could free it.

In the following week, the homes of several of the committeemen were burned in the night, with the loss of several lives.

"Everyone is too terrified to gather in any groups, for fear the outlaws will suspect more plotting," Frank told Alice and her mother. "I think it would be better if our children came up the back path toward home and avoided the road past the saloon altogether. We'll all go down to the river together about dark to get water."

"But Papa," Sister protested, "that's a steep path up behind town. Then we have to go down again across our lower creek bed and back up the hill to get home again. It takes a lot longer to go that way."

"You heard me, all three of you! No more going on the south road; that's an order!" Frank's ordinarily gentle voice was firm. The expression on his face told them that he really meant it.

"Darn!" said Tucker, struggling up the hill with a tote bag a few days later. "It's sure a lot harder getting home carrying stuff up this hill!" He stopped at the top to get his breath. "Next time, I'm going to sneak around behind the buildings across the street from the saloon, then through the bushes 'till I get past it."

"You'd better not! You'll get a whipping if Papa finds out!" Grace warned him.

"He doesn't need to know. The back path comes out around the bend from home, so no one'll see us."

"See you, you mean! I'm not going to try it and get in trouble, too!" She picked up her tote and started home, leaving Tucker to catch up.

The next time they were to stop at the store, Tucker had to stay after school to finish a lesson. "You go on ahead, Grace. You can leave the list with Mr. Lang at the store. Divide the stuff up between the two totes and I'll pick mine up when I'm done."

"All right, but be sure you take the back way home, like Papa said."

Tucker was tired when he stopped at the store. He took one look at the hill path and turned along the alley behind the buildings. Coming out of the bushes beyond the saloon, he passed the saloon keeper on his way back into town.

I'll bet he put whiskey in the reeds for the Indian again, Tucker thought. The closer he got to the river, the more he thought about it. He decided to hide his books and tote in the ditch on the other side of the road and smash up the jugs again.

It was cool in the reeds. Tucker dipped his bandana in the water and cooled his face with it. Then he thought, whiskey must taste good. The men in town sure like it, and I'm thirsty. He untied the sack and took out one of the jugs. The cork was loose and pulled out easily. He sniffed it. It didn't smell very good but maybe it tastes better, he thought.

"Ugh!" he spluttered; he'd tipped the jug too fast. The whiskey gushed out, filling his throat and splashing all over his shirt. He wondered how anybody could stand to drink the stuff. Then he grabbed up a rock and smashed both jugs just in time to slither into his hiding place before the Indian came along.

The Indian found the broken jugs and started to look around angrily for the culprit. Just then the sound of a wagon came from the road heading toward town. The Indian quickly remounted and rode off.

Tucker began to feel a little light-headed by the time he got back on the road and picked up his things. A short way down the road, the wagon came back from town and its driver stopped the horses.

"What's the matter, boy, not feelin' good?" the driver asked. "You need a ride on down to the fork? Hop in the back!"

"Yessir, thanks. I'm awful tired," Tucker said as he put his gear on the wagon and climbed up. "I'll just jump off at the fork, if you'll slow down a bit."

At the fork in the road, Tucker picked up his books in one hand and the tote in the other as the wagon slowed. "Thanks a lot," he said as he pushed off. The driver called to his horses and drove on, whistling to himself, not knowing that Tucker hung from a loose nail caught in the seat of his pants.

By this time, Tucker had dropped his books and tote onto the road and was too dizzy and confused to call out for help. A mile further, his pants finally gave way and he dropped onto the middle of the road.

Tucker had not reached home yet when Carsie and Frank came home to find Alice and Ercyline walking the floor with worry.

Frank confronted Grace. "Did Tucker say anything about stopping off anywhere?"

"No, Papa, but he *hated* that hill climb. He's been threatening to go to the edge of town, by the lane, and then cross back over to the road."

"C'mon, Carsie; let's go and see if we can find your brother." Frank picked up his hat and the two left.

Grace took her books and went to her room. She knew her mother's piercing look would soon have her telling the whole story if she stayed downstairs.

Just as Frank and Carsie got to the main road, a small wagon pulled up. "Hey, Fat, did you lose a boy?"

"Sure seems so. Have you seen him?"

The man started to chuckle and then laughed aloud. "I found him in the middle of the road about a mile back. He was crawling on all fours and mumbling about losing something."

"Where is he now?" Frank asked.

"In the back, split britches, bundle, books and all," he grinned. He's dead drunk and passed out. He smells like a moonshine still. I thought you folks were tea-totalers, Fat. Seems like you've got a black sheep in the family!"

"Thanks, Ben, we'll take it from here. He'll have some explaining to do after he sobers up and I tan his hide!"

Frank handed Tucker's tote bag and books to Carsie, slung Tucker over his shoulder, then waved the driver on.

"Oh, Lord, is he sick or hurt?!" Alice asked, as Frank carried Tucker into the house. "Sister, get the cot from the shed! Grace!" Alice called up the stair, "Bring down Tucker's quilt, please!"

"I guess you could say he's sick," Frank answered as he put Tucker on the cot.

Alice wrinkled her nose. "Whew! Smells like he threw up, too. I wonder where he got the liquor. Help me undress him so I can look him over for any injuries."

Tucker slept off his stupor while the family ate supper. "Best thing for him, but he's going to school tomorrow no matter how bad he may feel," Frank said, "And that's an order, Alice. He got into this by himself and he'll have to learn the hard way what the consequences are."

Tucker had a painful time sitting down for a day or so after Frank and Alice got the whole story about the whiskey jugs out of him and Grace. He was willing to climb the hill coming home from then on.

Chapter Thirty

THE END OF EDEN

At noon on Wednesday, September twenty fifth, 1901, Carsie was in town on an errand, the girls and Tucker at school. Ercyline, four year old Frank and two year old Lafe were at the far end of the garden. Alice was in the kitchen putting lunch on the table.

Uh, oh, here I go again, she thought. I'm glad Mama's here this time. She stepped to the door and called, "Mama, it's time; better come in a hurry. Leave the boys there; it won't be long."

Alice heard Ercyline say to little Frank, "You be a good boy now and watch out for Lafe. Your mama wants me for a bit. I'll be right back."

Alice saw her mother get up from her knees, brush the soil from her skirt and take two quick steps toward the house. She twisted her ankle and fell sideways.

"Are you alright, Mama?" Alice called.

"Yes, I'll be right there. Go ahead and start getting things ready." Alice went back into the house and did not see her mother stand.

Ercyline's left foot collapsed under her and she fell again, with a muffled scream. After Alice prepared her bed, she looked through the window. Her mother was lying motionless on the ground. Just then, a strong contraction gripped her body. She thought, I've no choice now. If I go to Mama, my baby may be born before I can do anything for her.

"Frank," she called through the open window, "come and get a cup of water from the pail. Get your handkerchief wet and wipe it on Grandma's face."

She watched and listened as he filled the cup, then she pulled up her skirt and fell on the bed just in time to prevent the screaming baby from catapulting onto the floor. After a moment to recover from the horrendous birth contraction, she wrapped the baby girl, afterbirth and all, in Frank's pillowcase and went to get the twine and scissors from the cupboard across the room.

She returned to the baby. "Come on, now, let's get your cord cut. Well, here you are my little Dolores. Go ahead and yell. You *are* a big one! We'll take care of you and then I'll go see to your grandma."

After she had done only what was absolutely necessary for the baby, Alice tucked her into the cradle, picked up a sheet from the shelf and dragged a chair behind her out to the garden. "Mama, are you alright?"

The wet handkerchief had revived Ercyline somewhat. "Ooh! I don't think I can walk. I think I broke my ankle or something. Give me a minute and I'll crawl into the house, if need be, to help you."

"No, don't get up yet. I'm going to put this sheet over the chair to shade you until you can move."

Alice started chuckling while she was arranging the sheet.

"What's so funny? You get back in the house, girl, before you drop that baby!"

"Too late, Mama, the baby's here; a *whopping* big girl. Don't you hear her bawling in the house?"

"Oh, my God, What are you doing out here then?!" Ercyline snapped. "Get back to your baby! You've no business out here!"

Alice collapsed onto the chair, laughing. "Poor Mama, cheated again! The baby's fine and so am I. Ilda and Grace will have to stay home a few days and take care of all three of us and the boys, too."

Ercyline sat up quickly, too quickly, and fell back, nearly fainting again.

"It's alright, Mama. I'll tear the hem off this sheet to tie up your foot. Then you just rest a while. Little Frank can get you a drink of water."

While he did so, she bound her mother's ankle firmly. "When you feel stronger, you can use this chair as support to get into the house. I've got to get back and get the baby cleaned up and properly wrapped."

Alice got up and walked slowly toward the house, realizing she hadn't padded herself and she was a mess. "Whooee, I'm a bit woofly, too! Better take it easy."

Alice held onto the doorways and walls until she reached the bedside. "Oh my, I'll never be able to clean the baby. There, there, little one." Alice unbuttoned her bodice and lay down again. "Here's the nipple to quiet you." Dolores suckled greedily while her mother fell asleep.

On Saturday, ten days later, the family took baby Dolores to the store and had her weighed.

"Twelve pounds and eight ounces! Mrs. Walden, you've sure perfected the art of producing half grown young 'uns!" The storekeeper's wife cooed over the baby, who's arms and legs were a series of fat little rings.

Frank and Alice beamed with pride, as did the children. "We've got to do our shopping and get home. My mother's there alone," Alice said.

"Yes, I heard she fell. Did she break her leg?"

"No, it's just a bad sprain. She's been pretty uncomfortable, but she's getting around pretty good now. Frank made her a crutch. I'm going to keep her here until she can walk without pain. We're sending the girls back to school on Monday."

"I'm glad I don't have to go home just yet," Ercyline told them all at supper. "It's so hot, I think I'd *die* on the train! The cars just *bake* in the sun!

"Papa's letter says he's getting pretty good food at the boarding house. I hate to think how thick the dust will be when I get back."

October passed and the drought continued. The grasses and bushes were dead and brown. The temperature dropped to freezing at night and soared into the nineties in the afternoons. The weather became the most common topic of conversation in town, as well as on the reservation. On November fifth, towering thunderclouds gathered in the east and sent winds rising to gale force ahead of them.

Rumors flew that lightning had started fires on the east slopes of the Blue Mountains and on the plains near the Idaho border.

On the morning of November sixth, lightning flashed and thunder rolled as the charcoal gray clouds darkened the sky over Milton Freewater.

"Mama, come here a minute!" Alice called. She was standing in the yard looking up at the hills half a mile away, where Frank and Carsie were working. "What does that look like to you?"

"It looks like a fire reflecting off the clouds. Let's hope it's not near where our men are working." Ercyline's brows furrowed.

Alice and Ercyline took turns watching the fire's glow become brighter and brighter. They were washing up after lunch when they heard little Frank's voice. "Papa? Papa! Papa's coming!"

"The boys are in the back yard. How could they see Frank coming up the road?" Alice said aloud. She stepped out the back door to see Frank racing out of the trees into the clearing. She could see terror on his face and ran to meet him.

A doe and her fawn burst out of the woods, raced past him, veered around the house and bounded down the hill. Behind them followed a few smaller animals, some with patches of burning fur on their backs.

Frank didn't stop, but grabbed her arm as he passed and pulled her toward the house. "Come on, we've only a few minutes! Lightning hit the stack of the donkey engine and exploded the boiler; killed the engineer. Luckily, Carsie'd stepped away a minute before. He got a ride on the road into town to get the others from school."

"Is the fire heading our way?" Alice asked anxiously as they went in the house.

"The fire's crowned out. It's spreading across the tree-tops. **Damn** the East wind! I came straight down the hill, only a few minutes ahead of it." He gulped some water and caught his breath. "Bundle up the baby and get the others running downhill toward the river. We won't have time to follow the road."

"Help me get some things together!" Alice's voice had picked up his panic.

"There's no time! Get the boys and your mother on their way! You take the baby and I'll get the wool blankets from our bed to protect us. Git, Woman!

"Ma!" Frank roared at Ercyline, who stood at the window, frozen with fear. He walked to her and slapped her face sharply. "Get out of here, to the river!"

She turned and walked slowly, as if in a trance. Frank ran to the bedroom, picked up two wool blankets and, returning, put his arm around Ercyline's waist and followed Alice and the boys out the door, across the yard and down the hill.

Alice stumbled and Frank caught her arm to steady her, letting go of Ercyline to do so. "Ma, run!" he yelled and pulled sharply at her arm.

Alice looked back. "It's got the trees behind the house, and the wind's blowing firebrands onto the roof! All our books and treasures will be burned!"

"Don't look back! Run, or we won't make it!" They caught up with the boys. Frank gave Ercyline a push to keep her going. Her face was frozen and her eyes glassy. "I can't watch you and take the boys, too! Get on ahead and keep running, Ma!" He picked up one of his sons under each arm, almost dropping the blankets as he did so.

The smoke was getting thick and the air around them was full of flying, burning twigs as they reached the shallow river. "Get in, in the middle, down in the water!" Frank yelled above the roar of the fire. He threw the blankets in the water, then, spreading them out, covered everyone with the wet heaviness.

Lafe began to echo the baby's cries, "I'm coad and scawed, Papa. Weah's Mama and Gamma?" he sobbed.

"They're right here. I'll stay with you all. I know you're afraid, boys. I am, too. Come on; let's keep splashing water onto the blanket. As long as it's wet, it won't burn." Frank groped for the edge of the other blanket and lifted it a bit. "Alice, are you three all right?"

"Yes, dear. Mama's literally scared stiff. She keeps calling for Annabelle. I think this has taken her mind back to the plantation fire. I keep splashing water on the blanket over her head, but she doesn't respond."

"Maybe it's just as well. It's better than having her in screaming hysteria," he answered.

"Papa, the water's getting warmer," little Frank said. It won't get hot and hurt us, will it?"

"No, I don't think it will. This water was pretty cold to start with." He lifted an edge of the blanket and peered out. "I think the fire's gone by, but the smoke is pretty thick, yet. We'd better stay put for a while. The water won't get much warmer now."

"Alice spoke up next, "Frank, I think it's getting quieter. Let's all pray together for the safety of the other children, the townspeople and the Indians."

After they'd both said a prayer, Frank peeked out again and lifted the blankets. "It's all clear now, Alice. We'd better wade on down the shallows toward town and find the others. The ground will be too hot to walk on for a while."

"Look, there are still glowing embers on the bank there," Alice observed. "Frank, I'll go on ahead. You can watch Mama.

"Bubba, you hold onto Papa's belt so you won't fall in if you lose your footing."

Frank had already hefted Lafe onto his shoulder. "We'll look for the girls and Carsie. You'll probably have patients to take care of when you get there."

The wanderings of the river made the wading into town a difficult journey for all of them, except Lafe, who fell asleep on his father's shoulder within a few minutes.

"You doing fine, Bubba? His father asked.

"Yup!" Little Frank was an easy going, happy child. He seldom got as excited as the others. "This'll be a story to tell, Papa, won't it?"

"For a long time, buddy boy, for a long time. Someday, you'll be telling your grandchildren about this day."

Alice gasped as they came around the last sweeping bend above town. "Looks like everyone in town is still in the river."

"Look at the mill! It'll probably be burning for hours yet. The sawdust piles will probably smolder for weeks." Frank commented.

People and animals sat or stood in the shallow water. The animals suffered burns, as did people who had not thought to bring cover to the river.

Ercyline was still quiet and stunned, but more responsive than she was earlier.

"Mama, take the baby," Alice said. "I'd better see if I can help some of these folks.

"Keep your burns under water, if you can. That's the best thing for them," Alice said as she waded among the crowd. "There's nothing else we can do for you otherwise, without medicine." She recruited petticoats and asked men to tear them into strips for bandages for the worst burns.

Downriver there arose a shout, as wagons came up the road from Weston. The roads and clear spaces had cooled enough to walk on and people began to wade ashore.

"Mrs. Walden?! Where's the nurse? Mrs. Walden?!" The doctor from Weston was standing in his wagon. "There you are! I was hoping you'd be here! There's a lot to do: Food, clothes, and blankets are coming along soon. The railroad ties are burned out halfway to Weston, which was spared, thankfully."

Alice came to the wagon and replied, "Folks who got to the river quickly are mostly all right, but we'll be needing some laudanum for some of them who are badly burned. I hope you brought a good supply."

More wagons came into town and tents began to spring up. Tables of saw horses and planks were loaded with food and drinks. Cots were brought into the tents, while blankets, quilts and warm clothes were handed out.

"You Weston folks got going in a hurry," Alice remarked to a man who came up in the doctor's wagon.

"A couple of your men rode down to tell us the whole town was in the path of the fire. People came to City Hall within half an hour and started loading wagons. It was unbelievable how fast the news traveled."

A well-dressed man climbed up on a wagon and began to shout for attention. "Folks, if you'll get your families together, we'll start you out for Weston! The City Hall, churches and schools are getting ready for you! Some of you will have to stay here overnight until there's wagon room for you! As soon as all your family is together, send one person over here!"

His words brought Alice up short, "My family; are they all safe?!" She spotted Frank's head over the crowd and waved to him, a questioning look on her face. He waved back, nodded and mouthed, "All right here." Alice sighed and went back to helping the doctor.

By evening, as the air began to cool, wagons were already on the road with blanket-clad families huddled on them.

With but a few people left in the line by the doctor's wagon, Alice asked, "Will you be able to handle the rest, doctor? I need to see to my own family."

"Surely, Ma'am; you've been a blessing. I may need you tonight, though, for the folks who are pretty bad off."

"I'll be back as soon as I nurse my baby and see that they're all well." She left, stopping to ask the whereabouts of her family. She found them in a tent in the middle of what had been the main road through town.

"Where's the baby?" She looked about, frantically. "She must be starved by now. My breasts are about to burst!"

The older children gathered around her, all chattering at once about the day's adventures.

"Hold it, you scalawags!" Frank ordered, "Your ma's tired! Here, sit down, Alice." He pushed her onto a cot.

"Where's the baby?!" she demanded.

"She's a couple of tents down and fine. Mrs. Dougherty, whose baby you delivered last month, has her. She says she has milk enough for two. As soon as the baby began to nuzzle and fuss, your ma went to pieces. Thank God, she calmed down and went to sleep a while ago."

"Carsie, did you find the girls and Tucker right away?" Alice took the boy's hand in hers.

"Yes, Mama. The teacher had them all headed for the river when I got to the school. I caught up and went with them."

"How did you manage not to get burned, with nothing to protect you from the fire?"

The children looked at each other and grinned. Then Ilda spoke up. "Grace and I took off our skirts and used them for cover. Carsie was with me, and Grace with Tucker. There were a few tiny holes burned in them, on the top layer, and we got some smoke, but it worked. Some of the other girls saw us, and pretty soon all the women were doing it, too."

"We can be pretty proud of our offspring, Alice; a bunch of *cool* heads there!" Frank said, beaming.

"I am so proud of all of you. Come here and let me hug you!"

The children gathered around her quickly.

"Sister, would you please go get Dolores? I'll finish nursing her while I rest. I could use something to eat, too. Whew, I'm more tired than I thought." She lay back on the cot and was instantly asleep.

Ilda looked questioningly at her father. "Yes," he whispered, "get the baby; Mama needs to relieve her breast pressure."

Ilda nodded and left. When she returned, Frank unbuttoned Alice's bodice, turned her to her side and put the baby to her breast. Alice didn't stir but slept on, unaware that her need and the child's were both being met.

Frank knew that Alice's father would be worried about them as soon as he heard about the fire, so he sent a message to him via a returning wagoner.

By Saturday, all but a few families had left for Weston. A dozen men stayed behind to clean up the mill site and watch for more flying bits of sawdust as the huge piles smoldered and fell in on themselves. They also dug through burnt buildings, looking for bodies in the wreckage.

Frank made a trip to the log cabin alone. "As I figured," he reported with a sigh, "there's nothing left but embers, twisted metal and the chimney,"

Alice and the children all gathered around him and comforted each other.

The ever-cheerful Carsie reminded them that they still had each other and the ability to start over again. "Think of it as an adventure!"

Frank tussled his hair and said, "That's my boy!"

At last, there were no more patients in need of Alice's nursing. She changed the last bandages and rounded up her family. They held an impromptu prayer meeting, thanking God for sparing their lives. "Nothing left for us here; everything and everyone are gone." she said sadly as she and the children clambered aboard a wagon for Weston.

"I'll see you in Bridal Veil when I'm through here," Frank said as he kissed them all goodbye.

And so, a new chapter began in the life of Mary Alice Beebe Walden, as she and her children rode to Bridal Veil singing hymns and praising God.

THE END

I hope you enjoyed reading this enough to recommend it to your friends and family and write a review of it on Amazon and/or my webpage: maryalicegypsynurse.com. You can contact the co-author via: cleeowen@comcast.net or <Facebook.com/Cora Brantner> for speaking engagement information or to order signed copies of either book.

Watch for the sequel, MARY ALICE Gypsy no more, due out in the summer of 2016.